T'

The Secrets of Mary Bowser

Lois Leveen

HARPER LUXE

An Imprint of HarperCollins*Publishers*

THE SECRETS OF MARY BOWSER. Copyright © 2012 by Lois Leveen. All rights reserved. Printed in the United States of America. No part of this book may be used or reproduced in any manner whatsoever without written permission except in the case of brief quotations embodied in critical articles and reviews. For information address HarperCollins Publishers, 10 East 53rd Street, New York, NY 10022.

HarperCollins books may be purchased for educational, business, or sales promotional use. For information please write: Special Markets Department, HarperCollins Publishers, 10 East 53rd Street, New York, NY 10022.

FIRST HARPERLUXE EDITION

HarperLuxe™ is a trademark of HarperCollins Publishers

Library of Congress Cataloging-in-Publication Data is available upon request.

ISBN: 978-0-06-210702-2

12 13 14 ID/RRD 10 9 8 7 6 5 4 3 2 1

If the whole of history is in one man, it is all to be explained from individual experience. . . . Each new fact in his private experience flashes a light on what great bodies of men have done, and the crises of his life refer to national crises.

—RALPH WALDO EMERSON, "HISTORY," 1841

Who shall go forward, and take off the reproach that is cast upon the people of color? Shall it be a woman?

—MARIA STEWART, "LECTURE DELIVERED AT THE FRANKLIN HALL, BOSTON," 1832

Author's Note

This novel tells the story of a real person, Mary Bowser. Born a slave in Richmond, Virginia, Mary was freed and educated in the North but returned to the South and became a Union spy during the Civil War. Like many ordinary people who choose what is right rather than what is easy, she did extraordinary things.

Few details about Mary Bowser are known today. In the nineteenth century, little effort was made to record the daily lives of most slaves, free blacks, or women of any race. The scant facts about Mary Bowser that survive cannot tell us what we most want to know: What experiences in freedom would make her risk her life in a war she couldn't be sure would bring emancipation? How did this educated African American woman feel, subjecting herself to people who regarded her as ignorant and even unhuman? How did living amid the death and destruction of America's bloodiest war affect her?

The Secrets of Mary Bowser interweaves historical figures, factual events, even actual correspondence and newspaper clippings, with fictional scenes, imagined characters, and invented dialogue, to answer these questions. Like Ralph Waldo Emerson, who lived at the same time as Mary Bowser (and who, in the style of the period, often said *man* when today we would say *person*), I believe that the crises of an individual life can shed light on national crises. The novel tells the story of one woman's life—but it also tells the story of a nation torn apart by slavery, and brought back together by the daily bravery of countless people like Mary Bowser.

The Secrets of
Mary Bowser

Prologue

Mama was always so busy. Busy tending to Old Master Van Lew and Mistress Van Lew, Young Master John, Miss Bet. But she was never too busy to riddle me. She said it was the first kind of learning she could give me, and the most important, too. Be alert, Mama meant. See the world around you. Find what you seek, because it's already there.

"I spy with my little eye, where the bird goes when he doesn't fly," Mama said one mid-day, her words floating on the Richmond heat as we carried empty cookpots through the yard to the kitchen.

I sing-songed the riddle to myself, eyes half closed against the bright Virginia sun. What could she mean, with no birds in sight? Then I spotted it, set in the crook of the big dogwood.

"Oh, Mama, a bird's nest!"

But Mama frowned. "I made a rhyme to riddle you, Mary El. You're old enough to rhyme me back your answer."

Whenever Mama said *you're old enough,* it meant something new was coming. Something hard I had to do, no matter what—cleaning all those fireplaces, polishing the silver, helping her serve and clear the Van Lews' meals. Old enough was never good news yet. And now old enough was ruining our favorite game.

I pouted for a bit, until Mama said, "No new riddle, until you answer that one proper."

I wanted the next riddle so bad, the words burst out of me. "Up in the tree, that little nest, is where birdie goes when he wants a rest."

Mama smiled her biggest smile. "A child of five, rhyming so well." She set her armload of iron pots down, scooped me up, and looked to the sky. "Jesus, I know my child ain't meant for slavery. She should be doing Your work, not Marse V's or Mistress V's."

She kissed me, set me back on the ground, and picked up the cookpots again. "But meanwhile, I got to do their work for sure."

Mama's gone now. Though she worked as a slave all her life, she saw me free. She even put me onto the train to Philadelphia so I could go to school.

But a decade up North taught me about being bound in a different way than all my years in slavery ever did. Living free confounded me more than any of Mama's riddles, until I puzzled out the fact that I could never truly savor my liberty unless I turned it into something more than just my own.

Once I realized that, I knew I had to come back to Virginia. Knew I was ready to take up the mantle of bondage I was supposed to have left behind. Except instead of some slave-owning master or mistress, it's Mr. Lincoln I'm working for now.

Mama, your little girl is all grown up, and still playing our best game. I am a spy.

BOOK ONE

Richmond
1844–1851

One

Mama and I woke early, put on our Sunday dresses, and stole down all three sets of stairs from the garret to the cellar, slipping out the servants' entrance before the Van Lews were even out of bed. We walked west down Grace Street, turning south past the tobacco factories to head toward Shockoe Bottom. The Bottom was nothing like Church Hill, where the Van Lew mansion sat above the city. Buildings in the Bottom were small and weather-worn, the lots crowded with all manner of manufactories and businesses. I held tight to Mama's hand as we ducked into a narrow passageway between two storefronts along Main Street.

Papa stood tall on the other side of the passage, same as every Sunday, waiting for us in his scraggly patch of yard. As soon as he caught sight of me and Mama, a smile broke across his face like sunshine streaming through the clouds. He hugged and kissed us and then hugged us some more, looking me over like I'd changed so much since the week before that he feared he might not recognize me.

I may have changed, but he never did. My papa was so lean and strong, his muscles showed even through his Sunday shirt. His rich skin shone with the color and sheen of the South American coffee beans that made Richmond importers wealthy. Large brown eyes dominated his narrow face, the same eyes I found staring back at me whenever I passed the looking glass in Mistress Van Lew's dressing room. What a strange and wonderful thing, to see a bit of Papa in my own reflection. All the more delightful when I pestered Mama with some peevish five-year-old's demand and she chided, "Don't look at me with your papa's eyes." Mama's complaint told me that I was his child as much as hers, even during the six days a week we spent apart from him.

Standing beside Papa, Mama seemed small in a way she never did when she bustled about the Van Lew mansion. Although she was not a heavy woman, she was fleshy in a way Papa was not. Her skin was even darker than his, so deep and rich and matte that whenever I saw flour, I wondered that it could be so light in color yet as sheenless as Mama's skin. Her brow and eyes curved down at the outside edges, making her seem determined and deliberate, whether her mouth was set straight across, lifted in one of her warm smiles, or, as was often the case, open in speech.

But for once, Papa was talking before Mama. "About time you ladies arrived. We got plenty to get done this fine morning." Papa spoke with the soft cadence of a Tidewater negro, though he hadn't seen the plantation where he was born since he was just a boy, when his first owner apprenticed him to Master Mahon, a Richmond blacksmith.

Mama's voice sounded different from Papa's, as sharp as though she and Old Master Van Lew had come from New York only the day before. "What can we have to do at this hour on a Sunday?"

"High time we return all that hospitality we been enjoying at the Bankses. I stopped over there on my way home last evening, invited them to come back here with us after prayer meeting."

"That whole brood, over here?" Mama eyed Papa's cabin. The four-room building had two entrances, Papa's on the left, and the one for Mr. and Mrs. Wallace, the elderly free couple who were his landlords, on the right. Even put together, Papa's two rooms were smaller than the attic quarters where Mama and I slept in the Van Lew mansion or the summer kitchen where the cook prepared the Van Lews' meals. One room had but a fireplace, Papa's meager supply of foodstuffs, and a small wooden table with three unmatched chairs. The other room held his sleeping pallet, a wash-basin set on an old crate, and a row of nails where he hung his clothes. The walls were unpainted, outside and in, the rough plank floors bare even in winter. The only adornments were the bright tattersall pattern of the osnaburg curtains Mama had sewn for the window and the metal cross Papa had crafted at Mahon's smithy.

The way Mama frowned, I could tell what she was thinking. Broad and tall, Henry Banks was a large presence all by himself, a free colored man who risked enslavement to minister to the slaves and free negroes who gathered each week in the cellar of his house. A two-story house big enough to accommodate him, his wife, and their six children. On those Sundays when Mama, Papa, and I were invited to stay after prayer meeting for dinner with their family, I savored the chance to amuse myself among all those children. So though Mama frowned at Papa, I was delighted to hear that the whole pack of youngsters was coming over today.

Besides, Papa was already soothing Mama. "It's warm enough to do our entertaining outside. All we got to do is borrow some chairs and plates and whatnot from the neighborhood, so it'll all be ready when we get back here." He smiled. "Honestly, folks'd think you married a fool, the way you carry on, Minerva."

To everyone else in Richmond, colored or white, Mama was Aunt Minnie. But Papa always called her Minerva. Whenever he said the name, she made a grand show of rolling her eyes or clucking her tongue. So I figured Mama wasn't nearly so put-upon as she pretended to be, planting her hands on her hips and shaking her head. "Don't you start with me at this hour, Lewis, don't you even start."

Papa winked at me. "Don't you dare stop, she means. And I ain't one to disobey her." With that he hustled me and Mama about, gathering up what we needed to serve our guests before he hurried us off to prayer meeting.

All through the morning's preaching and praising, my head buzzed in anticipation of hosting company. Each week, when Mama, Papa, and I walked back from meeting, I took care to lag a few paces behind, then come barreling up between them, my arms flailing in the air. Mama and Papa would each grab one of my hands and swing me forward, calling out, "Caught." Once caught, I walked the rest of the way between them, my hands in theirs, my face beaming. But this

Sunday I was so excited to be with the other children I forgot all about getting caught until Papa turned around, his big eyes searching for me. I wrinkled my nose at him and went back to chattering with Elly, the oldest and prettiest of the Banks girls. When I looked ahead again, Papa was no longer watching me.

Once we reached the cabin, Papa hauled a bucket of water from the well, and Mama called me from my playmates to help serve our guests. When I carried the first pair of filled cups to where Reverend and Mrs. Banks sat with Papa, I marked how Mrs. Banks was shifting in the straightbacked chair, trying to catch a hint of shade from the lone box elder tree in the tiny yard.

"I'm sorry there's no ice for your drinks," I said as I served. "Papa don't have an ice room, but if you come visit my house, we can give you lots of ice and cushions for your chairs, too."

In a flash, Papa yanked me to him. He turned me over his knee and swatted me hard.

"That big house ain't yours, Mary El, it's the Van Lews'. And you don't mean no more to them than the cushions or the chairs or any other thing they got for their comfort. Understand?"

He kept his tight hold on me until I murmured, "Yes, Papa." As soon as he let go, I ran into the cabin. My Sunday joy curdled to shame at being treated so in front of Elly and the other children, and I sobbed myself to sleep on Papa's cornhusk pallet.

I woke hours later, to the sound of low, angry voices in the next room.

"The child need to know her place is with me, with us, and not with them Van Lews," Papa said.

"Well, you're not gonna teach her that with a spank," Mama replied. "Slaveholders can't get enough of beating on negroes, you need to do it, too? To our own child?"

"What should I done? Smile and pat her on the head? Mary El can't be acting like she better than other folks just cause a rich family own her. This is our home, whether them Van Lews let you here one day a week or one day a year."

"Lewis, you think I like it any better than you? Wake to them, work for them, doze off at night to them, every moment aching for you. But what are we supposed to do?"

"For one, you can stop carrying on about *we in the house* this and *we in the house* that. You in the house like them pretty horses in the barn. There to do the Van Lews' work till you no use to them anymore, and then—"

Mama caught sight of me, and sucking her teeth hard to cut him off, she nodded toward where I stood in the doorway.

"What's the matter, Papa?" I asked. "What'd Mama and me do wrong?"

He rose and walked toward me. I shrank back, afraid he might hit me again. My terror drew a look of bitter contrition I'd never seen before across Papa's face. He knelt and reached out both hands, palms up to me.

"Mary El, you more precious to me than a ice room or fancy cushions or anything in that big house. Am I more precious to you than them things?"

I wanted to please Papa, to set everything right between him and me and Mama. Slipping my small hands into his large, strong ones, I nodded, my own shame at being spanked fading next to all the fear and humiliation in Papa's question.

Old Master Van Lew was always a shadowy figure in my childhood, already suffering from the breathing troubles that everyone whispered would kill him. In the fall of '44, not long after we'd exchanged the canvas floor coverings for wool carpets and taken the mosquito netting off the beds and paintings, he finally passed.

As Mama and I dressed the drawing room in black crepe, preparing for mourners who would call from as far away as Pennsylvania and New York, all she said was, "We in the house have plenty to do, good days or bad, happy times or sad."

We in the house meant the seven Van Lew slaves. Me and Mama. The butler, Old Sam, who toiled beside us in the mansion and slept across from us in its garret. Zinnie, the cook, and the coachman Josiah and their daughters, Lilly and Daisy, who were quartered together above the summer kitchen at the side of the lot. We knew things people outside the Van Lew family couldn't have guessed, things the Van Lews themselves wouldn't care to admit. We listened close when Young Master John stumbled in after an evening at Hobzinger's saloon, reeking of whiskey and raving about being made to stay in Richmond to tend the family business, when at the same age his sister, Miss Bet, was fanfared off to a fancy school in Philadelphia. We discovered the embroidered pink bonnet that the widowed brother of Mrs. Catlin, a neighbor woman, sent spinsterish Miss Bet, cut to pieces and stashed inside her chamber pot. Mama taught me how we were to mark such things and, with a few spare words or a gesture, share them among ourselves whenever the Van Lews' backs were turned.

We in the house were always decently dressed, while some Richmond slaves didn't even have shoes to wear on the city's unpaved streets. Though Old Master Van

Lew's family held slaves, including Mama and Old Sam, when he lived in New York, neither Old Master Van Lew nor his Philadelphia-born bride could quite abide the way human chattel were treated in Virginia. We were Van Lew property. To Old Master and Mistress Van Lew, keeping us suitably clothed and fed was a measure of both their financial and their moral accomplishments.

The Van Lews were Northerners enough that when their housekeeper set her eyes on a handsome young blacksmith twenty-five years earlier, they understood she meant to be a proper wife to him. Though they made it clear they would neither sell her nor purchase him, they consented to the match. But no law tied my mama to my papa, or either parent to me.

Much as we slaves studied the Van Lews, still we didn't know whether they had more capital or creditors. Which meant we didn't know what might happen to us when the time came for the settling of Old Master Van Lew's estate. The morning that George Griswold, the Van Lews' family attorney, called on our widowed mistress, we lurked outside the drawing room, knowing we had as much interest in the terms of the will as the Van Lews themselves.

We heard how the mansion and all its contents—that meant Mama and me and our fellow slaves, along with the inanimate possessions—were held with a handsome annual income for Mistress Van Lew, until her death or remarriage, at which point they would pass to Young Master John. He was sole heir to his father's businesses, hardware stores in Richmond and Petersburg, which Griswold reported had substantial assets and little debt. Miss Bet would receive a ten-thousand-dollar inheritance, a share of the annual yield from a small market farm the family kept southeast of Richmond, and residence in the mansion until her death or marriage.

That last stipulation had Zinnie snorting to Mama, "Guess we'll be waiting on Miss Bet till the Good Lord take her home."

In the months and years after Old Master Van Lew's death, it seemed this prediction would surely come to pass. Miss Bet was headstrong just for the sake of being headstrong, constantly railing against show and ought, her favorite expression for anything expected of her that rubbed her as too constricting. Balls were frivolous, beaux were overbearing, ladies' parlor conversations only dulled an educated mind—she so seldom accepted a social invitation, she hardly seemed to notice when they no longer arrived. She preferred to pore over the daily news-sheets until her fingertips were stained inky black, lecturing her mother and brother about what she read, and clipping out articles to stick in her scrapbook the way other belles might preserve pressed nosegays.

Miss Bet was so contrary she even declared she couldn't abide slavery, claiming she came to understand its horrors when she was away at school up North. But such proclamations didn't make her much of a favorite among her servants. "She needs her chamber pot emptied just as often as the rest of them," Mama would mutter, to which Zinnie would reply, "She's got to, 'cause she takes her meals just as often as they do." Miss Bet's anti-slavery sentiments seemed to owe more to her family's and her neighbors' embrace of the peculiar institution than to any true understanding of the feelings of us slaves. Especially when all her abolitionist speechifying only seemed to tat out trouble for us.

Papa, like many of the slaves who worked as skilled laborers in Richmond, received a small sum from his master each month to cover the costs of his room and board, as well as his clothing. He stretched this allotment as best he could, always saving enough to donate to some worthy cause or other at prayer meeting. And from time to time Papa laid by a few cents to purchase a trinket for me.

I knew come Christmas or my birthday I'd get such gifts, but the ones I enjoyed most came without my expecting them, what Papa called the *just-because.*

"Just because you my treasure." "Just because you helped Mrs. Wallace tote water from the well without being asked." "Just because spring come at last." Any old just-because was special coming from Papa. When we arrived at his cabin one Sunday morning late in 1846, he presented me with a length of bright orange ribbon, "just because the color almost as pretty as our Mary El." He dangled the satin strand high in the air above me, demanding all manner of hugs and kisses before lowering it into my greedy hands.

The hue was rich and beautiful, and I sat on the cabin floor, winding the ribbon back and forth between my fingers. As I watched the ends flutter against my Sunday skirt, I thought of Elly Banks, with her bright dresses always so nicely trimmed. "Mama, will you sew my ribbon onto my sleeves?"

She frowned at the question, but it was Papa who answered. "It's the Lord's day, Mary El. No laboring today."

"But we go to meeting today. And I want to wear my ribbon to meeting."

"Meeting is for praying, not for showing off your new things." Mama flashed a look at Papa. "See how such trifles fill her head, Lewis."

"Pride ain't vanity, Minerva. Time enough we teach the child the difference." He nodded to me. "Mary El, leave your ribbon home today and give thanks for it at meeting. Be good this week, and your Mama gonna teach you how to fix the ribbon to your sleeves yourself before next Sunday."

Though Mondays were always tiring for me and Mama as we made up the chores from our one day off, that Monday night I begged Mama to stay up and show me how to sew.

"Sewing is work, not play," she said. "You sure you got the patience for it now?"

I nodded, and she went to our trunk and drew out the sewing kit she used to mend our clothing and Papa's. She carefully chose a needle and measured out some thread.

"You're not about to take any fancy stitches, so for now, hardest part will be just getting your needle threaded." Quick as you please, she drew the thin strand through the eye of the needle. Then she drew it out again and handed me the needle and thread.

I squinted in the dim candlelight, imitating the way she licked the end of the thread. But even after several passes, I couldn't loop the strand through the impossible hole.

"Mama, can't you do it for me?"

"If you're old enough to sew yourself some trim, then you're old enough to thread a needle." She laid one of her hands on each of mine. "Just tell yourself you can do it, like it's a riddle you set yourself to solve."

With her hands on mine, I held steady and drew the strand through. "I spy, with my little eye, a girl who's got her thread through her own needle's eye," Mama said, her laughter more splendid than a whole spool of orange rickrack. Then she grew serious. "Mary El, that's a hard task, and you should be proud you did it. You know the difference between pride and vanity?"

Remembering Papa's words, I wanted to say yes. But fact was I didn't know the difference, though I sure did know Mama would catch me if I lied. "No, Mama."

"When you work hard at something, or do right by a person, it's proper to be proud. The day Mr. Wallace took so sick, and your papa walked through that blizzard to fetch Aunt Binah to doctor to him, I was real proud. Taking all that risk to be out in such weather, just to help his friend." She smiled, more to herself than to me. "Years ago, just about the time Miss Bet got born, Old Marse V went to Marse Mahon's smithy and ordered up three fireplace sets. Your papa made those sets, and when he delivered them was the first day I ever seen him. The look of pride on his face as Mistress V admired what he'd made, well, he caught my eye right then."

"Why didn't Papa make enough sets for all the fireplaces?"

"Back then, three was all the fireplaces the Van Lews had. We were in a smaller house, farther down the slope of Church Hill. When Old Marse V moved the family here, he went back to Marse Mahon to have Papa make up five more sets, all to match the ones he made ten years earlier. You ever notice a difference in them?"

I shook my head. If you laid the andiron from one set beside the ash shovel from another, I couldn't have said which rooms they came from, though I tended the fires often enough.

Mama's smile broadened. "That's a sign your papa knows smithing well, which is something to be proud of."

"Is pride like money?"

"Just the opposite, nearly. What put that idea into your head?"

"When customers go to Marse Mahon's smithy, they give him money for the work he does. And when Mrs. Wallace hires Ben Little"—Mama nodded at my mention of the free colored boy, a few years older than myself, who lived near Papa and his landlords—"to run an errand, she pays him money. So I thought pride is what slaves get instead of money, when they do something for somebody."

"You can be proud of something you get money for, like Old Marse V was proud when his business grew so big he could buy this house. Sometimes, when your papa does a job that's extra hard or gets it done extra quick, Marse Mahon even gives him a bit of money more than his usual board and keep. And Papa, he usually turns around and spends that money on a just-because for you or me, 'cause he's proud he can. But slaves got a right to be proud of all the work we do, even when nobody pays us for it."

"Like Zinnie's proud of being the best cook in Richmond?"

"Well, that brings us round to vanity. Zinnie declares she's the best cook in Richmond to put herself over Ida Tucker, whose marse said she was such a good cook he set her free. One time, when Ida's marse was to dinner here, he said Zinnie's harrico mutton was the most delicious thing he ever ate. I told Zinnie, and she's bragged on it ever since." Mama gave her teeth the slightest little suck, just enough for me to make out her gum squeal of disapproval. "Zinnie feels bad that Ida got free for being a good cook and she didn't, so she likes to say she's a better cook than Ida. Which maybe she is and maybe she ain't, as I never tasted a thing Ida cooked and neither to my mind has Zinnie. We know Zinnie is a fine cook from eating her food every day, and she got a right to be proud. But if she thinks it and says it just to feel better than someone else, that's vanity. Same as if someone wants to wear a new just-because to prayer meeting to show it off and make other girls jealous, that's vanity, too."

Catching Mama's hint, I tried to direct her attention away from me and my ribbon, which it seemed we weren't going to get around to sewing any time soon anyway. "When Miss Bet brags on her fine Philadelphia education, or Mistress Van Lew brags on how many books they got in Old Marse's library, is all that pride or vanity?"

Mama got real quiet. She wasn't one to talk up her masters' saintliness, but she didn't like to say too much flat out critical about them, either. Once Young Master John bought himself a riding horse that was real wild, and Josiah said the only way to break that stallion was to refuse to let it know how ornery it was. Just bridle and saddle it and hang on as best you could, trying not to let on how scared you were it might rear up and throw you. That's how Mama was with the Van Lews, struggling to keep control over a beast bigger and more powerful than herself.

"White people live by different rules than us, Mary El. The rules I'm telling you about, pride versus vanity, those are Jesus's rules. We got to try to live by His rules and by the ones whites make for us, both at once. That's hard enough without worrying ourselves up all night about whether or not white people are holding themselves to Jesus's rules, too." She coaxed the threaded needle from my hand. "Why don't we lay this by for now and get some sleep. Tomorrow I'll show you how to make a nice stitch, and you'll have that ribbon on your Sunday dress in no time."

By the next night, Mama was done teaching on pride versus vanity and settled right in to teaching me chain-stitch, which she made me practice over and over on scrap until I could sew nice and straight. Once she was satisfied I could make strong, even stitches, she gave her nod. Sewing the ribbon to the fabric while taking care not to sew the sleeve closed took more concentration, and my head ached by the time both elbows of my Sunday dress were festooned. But when I held my handiwork before me, I shone bright as my ribbon with delight.

"Now you can be proud of having trimmed that up yourself," Mama said, "because you worked hard to do it."

Though I smiled up at her, I was still all vanity on the inside, impatient as ever to show off the ribbon.

The next afternoon, when the Van Lews were out and Mama was scrubbing the hall floor and I was supposed to be making up the bedchambers, I snuck up to our quarters, threw off my everyday frock, and put on the Sunday dress. With my sleeve ribbons tied into the biggest bows I could manage, I stole back down to Mistress Van Lew's dressing room and twirled before the looking glass, losing myself in scenes I played out in my head, in which Elly Banks begged to know where I got such a fine gown.

Mama must have been calling me a good long time, because her voice was hot with anger when I finally noticed it. "Run get the floor cloth quick, Mary El. Miss Bet's waiting outside to come in." I fetched the cloth to the front hall and stretched it open along the floor, so Miss Bet could walk across without slipping or dampening her shoes. I forgot all about my Sunday dress, until I looked up and saw Mama's face.

Before she could reprimand me, Miss Bet came inside. "How charming you look, Mary. Is that a new frock?"

Mama answered for me. "It's her Sunday dress, Miss Bet. She must've just slipped into it while my back was turned. Child knows better than to wear a Sunday dress when we're working hard, don't you, Mary El?"

I nodded, but Miss Bet shook her head like she was trying to loose herself from her own yellow curls. "It's an offense the child should have to work at all. Mary, don't you wish you could wear such outfits every day, like white girls do?"

I didn't need to see how fiercely Mama was squinting and frowning to know the danger in answering that question. "I only wanted to see how my new ribbons look. Papa bought them for me just-because. And I sewed them on myself."

The last part was drowned out by the sound of the Van Lew carriage arriving outside. "Mary El, you get upstairs this minute and change, 'fore Mistress V comes through that door." Mama clipped her words so quick, I didn't dare dawdle. "Miss Bet, please don't say anything about this. The child's young, but she works hard, even when Mistress is out of the house."

"Nonsense, Aunt Minnie. Mary, come right back here. I want Mother to see how nice you look."

Much as I wanted to hide myself away from Mistress Van Lew, there was no ignoring Miss Bet's command. Already partway up the staircase, I turned back just as the front door opened to Mistress Van Lew and Young Master John. Mama, Miss Bet, and I must have made quite a tableau, because they looked at us like we were three foxes in a henhouse.

"Mother, you know I have asked your leave to pay our servants some small remuneration for their labors," Miss Bet said.

"And you know Mother has denied that request," Young Master John answered. "There is no need to antagonize her, or to disgruntle the servants." In the two years since his father's passing, Young Master John had grown important in his role as man of the house. He reprimanded his older sister the way Zinnie slaughtered a recalcitrant sow, sighing aloud over the duty, though we all knew he took pleasure in performing it.

But Miss Bet wouldn't be scotched so easily. "The servants are hardly disgruntled. Look how happy Mary is, wearing a ribbon her father bought her." By then I felt about as happy as a housefly caught in a barn spider's web. But Miss Bet wasn't paying me much mind. "Surely, if a man of Timothy Mahon's standing can give his slaves wages, so can we."

Mistress Van Lew's face flushed fever red, and she turned to Mama. "Aunt Minnie, am I a good mistress?"

There's only one way for a slave to answer when her owner asks that question. "Yes, ma'am," Mama said.

"Have you or your child ever gone hungry in my house?"

"No, ma'am, never."

"Do you go about without proper attire, summer or winter?"

"No, ma'am."

Mistress Van Lew turned back to Miss Bet. "I provide for my servants far more than law or custom require. I will not have anyone make a mockery of my generosity." She looked up at me. "Mary, come here."

Dread thudded low with each slow step I took. As soon as I got near, Mistress Van Lew reached out and snatched the bows from one elbow, then the other. My stitches broke easily under her firm tugs. Holding the bits of ribbon out to me, she nodded toward the drawing room. "Put these on the fire."

Miss Bet hurried up beside me, protesting, "Mother, I cannot agree—"

Young Master John cut her off. "This is a matter between Mother and her servants. It is none of your concern."

I walked across the drawing room and stood before the fireplace, squeezing my clenched hand so the smooth silk of the ribbon rubbed across my palm. I thought of how Elly would never see my just-because. How nobody could ever treat her and her brothers and sisters the way Mistress Van Lew treated me. How it wasn't fair that after I worked so hard to sew on the ribbon, now I wouldn't have it at all.

Only when the heat began to singe my wrist did I open my hand and let the pieces fall. As I watched, the flames licked up, consuming the orange ribbon till the colors of the fire and the colors of my lost just-because blurred inseparably. I still couldn't tell pride from vanity, but I sure could tell slave from free.

When early spring warmed the Virginia morning, Mistress Van Lew and Miss Bet took their breakfast on the back veranda. The garden just past the house, the fruit arbor that sloped to the edge of the property, and the view of Richmond and the James River beyond were all so pretty that looking out at them seemed like a hazy slumber dream, until a dull ache in my overworked arms roused me from my reverie. As I fanned the first flies of the season from the Van Lews, they buzzed around my head instead. I didn't dare swat them away. I'd been told enough times not to wriggle or shift during these meals, to stand perfectly still except for the movement of my arms. No motion allowed except what served the Van Lews.

To distract myself, I listened as Miss Bet read to her mother from the Richmond *Whig*. Most days she chose dull stories about the Virginia legislature or President Polk. But this morning she read the report of a dashing swindler who posed as a gentleman to rob travelers on the train between Richmond and Washington.

Such a story set my eight-year-old self wide-eyed with wonder, and I hung on every word. More than that, I remembered every word.

This was my solitary amusement, listening as grown-ups spoke and repeating their conversations to myself while I was working. Rehearsing the tale of the train robber in my head made the rest of the Van Lews' breakfast hour pass quickly, and before I knew it, Mistress Van Lew announced she was ready to take her morning stroll about the arbor. As Miss Bet led her mother down the steps to the garden, Mama gathered the breakfast things onto the silver serving tray. I hung the fan in its place behind one of the white columns that rose two stories to the veranda roof. Clearing the news-sheet from the table, I began to recite the wonderful story out loud.

The crash of china startled me. Mama was not a clumsy woman. Never one to drop a cup and saucer. Perhaps it was a trick of the heat, but as I turned to look her way, it seemed the whole world stood still, except for me and the buzzing flies.

And then all at once, Mistress Van Lew stormed back up the steps. "Aunt Minnie, we are not in New York. You know the laws of Virginia, and we have made our wishes very clear on this matter. You were not to teach the child to read."

Mama fell to her knees. "Ma'am, I never taught her to read. I swear to Jesus, I didn't."

Mistress Van Lew knew Mama wasn't one to swear to Jesus falsely. Our irate mistress turned to her daughter.

"Bet, this abolitionist nonsense of yours has gone too far. How you have managed it, I do not know, but now at least you see your faith in the servants is poorly placed. The girl may know how to read, but she does not know enough to keep your secrets." Her eyes went narrow. "Perhaps sending Mary to Lumpkin's Alley will teach you both a lesson."

Fear cramped my stomach, catching its echo in Mama's low moan. White Richmond called the public whipping post Lumpkin's Alley, after the slave-auction house next door. But to colored folks it was Devil's Half-Acre, the most dreaded spot in the whole city.

Miss Bet jutted out her chin. "I am not sorry to see a slave learn, it is true, but this is as strange to me as it is to you. If you have the child flogged to punish me for something I haven't done, you will only prove that slavery is every bit as evil as I believe it to be."

Mistress Van Lew whirled at me, cracking a hard slap against my cheek. I felt the sudden sting and knew it was a pale promise of the beating I'd get at the whipping post. "Who taught you to read, child? I will stand no lies."

"No one, ma'am. I don't know how to read." Mama was so near, yet I sensed she didn't dare reach out to comfort me, that I needed to say more to make Mistress Van Lew leave us be. "Miss Bet read the story to you. I only remembered what she said."

Mistress Van Lew snatched the news-sheet from my hand and passed it to her daughter. "Tell us now, without the paper, what Miss Bet read."

And so I repeated the story, as Miss Bet followed along in the news-sheet. After only a few sentences, she burst out, "Mother, it is remarkable. The child recites the article word for word." Miss Bet beamed at my accomplishment. "She wasn't reading at all. Stranger than that, she can recall exactly what she hears."

Mistress Van Lew spent a long moment considering what this meant. Finally, she looked from me, to Mama, to Miss Bet. "No one is to know of this, do I make myself clear to all of you? This is a dangerous thing. Do not speak of it again." Her daily promenade in the garden forgotten, she went into the mansion, leaving each of us to make our own sense of what I'd done.

Mama took the revelation of my talent as a sign from on high. For as long as I could remember, I'd heard her recount every tale in the Bible about a barren woman, remembering how she spent the first twenty years of her marriage childless. "I prayed every day, thinking of Sarah and Rebecca and Rachel. Wasn't a one of them bore a child right off. That poor wife of Manoah, not even a name for her, who had Samson. Elizabeth, who carried John the Baptist. Those women were blessed with a child to raise up to serve the Lord, and year after year I begged Jesus to do the same for me. Then at last you come along."

Mama's vow to dedicate me to Jesus's service always gave her reason to cajole and connive Him and me both. "You know this child is meant for Your work, Jesus"—thus would begin anything from a reprimand of my ill behavior to as outlandish a demand as nagging Jesus to set me free. If Mama suspected either Jesus or me of slacking in fulfilling the plan she envisioned, she was sure to let us know. And whatever she felt I did right became certain proof to her that this plan was already writ in stone.

So despite the law and Mistress Van Lew's prohibition, after that morning on the veranda Mama set time aside every Sunday for my lessons. She'd trace out a few words in the ashes of Papa's fireplace. Keeping her voice low, she always began, "This being Virginia, I sure can't teach a slave that this writing means . . ."

and finished by saying what she'd written. It didn't take any more instruction than that for me to learn to read and write.

Miss Bet, ever fain to flout her mother, took her own interest in me. As I grew older, she pressed books from her father's library on Mama, nodding my way. Now and again, she even sat me down for an arithmetic lesson while the rest of her family was out. But my memory for Mistress Van Lew's anger was just as keen as my memory for what I heard and read. I hated her for it, until I was grown enough to realize the lesson she taught me was as valuable as any of Mama's: A slave best keep her talents hidden, feigned ignorance being the greatest intelligence in the topsy-turvy house of bondage.

Two

Colored Richmond didn't suffer the isolation that benighted plantation slaves. Between the news-sheets surreptitiously gathered by those who could read, and the white people's conversations carefully monitored by slaves and free negroes in the businesses, streets, and homes of the city, we followed the political goings-on in Washington more easily than many whites in the far-off Western states and territories did. And we understood that we had as much of a stake as them in the outcome. At prayer meetings and market days, negroes who knew more stole time to inform those who knew less. Come 1850, this talk centered on a harsh new law to force the free states to return runaway slaves to their Southern owners, passed by the federal Congress in exchange for California's entrance into the Union as a free state.

Hearing about the new Fugitive Slave Act, we all shivered vulnerable. Every colored person in Richmond knew folks who'd already disappeared North to take their freedom, as well as some still in the city who, though they didn't advertise the fact, were planning to do the same real soon. Richmond was the north of the South, close enough to the Free States we nearly breathed their air, or so we liked to believe. The Fugitive Slave Act turned that free air to slavery's stink, right in our mouths and noses.

Virginia's slaveholders wanted California and the rest of the Western territories open to slavery. They railed when Congress passed the Compromise, cussing Federal this, proclaiming States' Rights that. So white Richmond was vindicated and colored Richmond was scared come autumn, when a special state convention began its own series of debates, which seemed calculated to show they could outdo the national politicians in boxing in slaves and free negroes alike. But worrisome as the convention was, I found myself grateful for what it offered me in the way of political education.

Miss Bet's thirty-second birthday coincided with the start of the convention, and she celebrated with a birthday dinner after her own fashion, attended by a dozen guests she deemed adequately aligned to her principles.

A dinner party of this size—even one filled with anti-slavery talk—required a week of redoubled efforts for us slaves. Lilly and Daisy, who normally did the laundry, attended Mistress Van Lew, and helped with the housecleaning, were temporarily recruited to assist Zinnie with procuring ingredients and preparing the meal. The house, which wasn't ever dirty by any stretch, needed to be immaculate, and so Old Sam and even Josiah joined Mama and me as we set to work sweeping, dusting, and polishing everything in sight.

At age eleven, I well understood that the arrival of any visitor was an opportunity to enlarge our holding of that most valuable commodity: information. My keen memory proved especially useful on such occasions, so as soon as I was old enough to be put to tasks before company, Mama encouraged the Van Lews to do so. I didn't much mind helping serve and clear rather than laboring elsewhere in the house, with all the Van Lews' guests gave me to listen to. In the days following such events, I recounted what I'd heard, so that no morsel was lost. I didn't necessarily understand everything I repeated, until Mama and the other grown-ups chewed it out among themselves, with me listening as carefully to them as I did to the white people. But that night I made out enough to wonder what the debate among Miss Bet's guests might signify for her, and for me.

"Such fuss at the train station," complained a plump redhead whose well-powdered face I didn't recognize. "And all those hacks clogging the streets."

"And for what? To hash out another of these infernal compromises." Frederick Walker was Miss Bet's age, and every bit as brash. I relished his visits, which nearly always riled Young Master John into dudgeon and Mistress Van Lew into a conniption fit. "Better to settle the matter once and for all."

"Settle?" a gray-haired man seated beside Mistress Van Lew repeated. "Impossible. Do you suppose our dear Virginia will ever rid herself of slavery?"

"Even where slavery is steadfastly entrenched," replied Franklin Stearns, another of Miss Bet's favorites, "it is hardly universally embraced."

This last sentence stuck with us for months to come, repeated whenever we in the house faced a particularly distasteful chore, or when one of the Van Lews grew especially cross. "Not hardly universally embraced," Daisy would mutter, scraping manure from Young Master John's riding boots. "No time for universal embracing," Mama would warn, shooing me to work in the cellar until one of Miss Bet's sour moods passed. We knew that as long as there were slaves in slavery, the institution was hardly universally embraced. But Miss Bet's anti-slavery set didn't think to count the lowly bondsmen's opinion on such matters. And so we continued our rounds about the room, serving and clearing in silence as they kept up their debate.

"Virginians who hold no slaves are tired of seeing their interests subsumed to those of the planters," said Walker. "Slavery benefits them not a whit, so why should they support it?"

"We are not planters," Mistress Van Lew reminded him. "Yet how would we manage without our few slaves? Do you suggest we let the poor mountain folk from the western part of the state dictate how we live?"

I wasn't quite sure what mountain folk were, though I liked the notion of anyone who might dictate to my mistress. I quickened my pace as I circled the table with the cabbage pudding, to be nearer to Walker as he made his reply.

"Madam, with all due respect, I must disagree that the planters' interests are your own. Your husband was a mercantile man. Such men build fortunes in the North, employing only free workers. Surely the same can be true here."

I thought *mercantile* was some sort of insult, from the frowning way Mistress Van Lew signaled Old Sam to bring her more claret.

Young Master John, who showed little sympathy and less patience for his sister's guests, leaned forward to challenge Walker. "Your nephew has gone to Charlottesville to study law. Do you think we should have so grand a university there without slavery? Buildings like those all over the eastern half of the state were built with hardware we sold, hardware bought with the proceeds of slaveholding."

"A sensible businessman looks to the future, not to the past," said Stearns. He always insisted on whiskey instead of wine, and when he drew so long a sip, Mama gave a little nod to make sure I marked whatever he said next. "Virginia's soil has grown so poor, the Tidewater plantations produce more slaves than crops—and the profit from the latter does not cover the costs of feeding and clothing the former. Why not wean ourselves from slavery altogether, as the Northern states did a generation ago?"

Young Master John relished the chance to disagree. "Those excess slaves are one of our greatest resources. They can be leased or sold off, within the state and throughout the South—and West, if new territories are settled to our interest." He directed Mama to ladle gravy onto his plate until it covered the rabbit and pooled around the pudding. "My dry-goods suppliers in Boston and Philadelphia complain they are increasingly subject to the interests of a few financial houses in New York, which control more and more of the Northern economy. If Richmond is to prosper, we should model ourselves on Charleston and New Orleans, not on cities in the North. Our future rests in distinguishing ourselves from those New York dominates."

William Carrington, a reserved physician who lived in the row of Carrington family residences on Broad Street, attempted to cool the heated exchange. "John, do you believe the state convention will bring customers into your stores?"

Though the question didn't much interest me, I marked how Young Master John puffed up with pride when he answered. "I hope it will. There are men attending with whom I usually do business only by post. And others with whom I've never had dealings but who will take the opportunity to see what wares we sell that they can't easily obtain in their own parts of the state."

"Well then, observe those western Virginians closely," Dr. Carrington said. "They have ingenuity, even if they lack the capital to establish plantations. They no longer consent to having only the wealthiest among us electing our leaders, and I venture they won't leave Richmond until they obtain suffrage for all white men in Virginia."

Walker didn't hold back his enthusiasm at this prediction, lifting his glass as he replied. "Once they secure a voice in the legislature, things will change in their favor, however gradually. We will be wise to align our interests with theirs."

I wasn't sure what those western Virginians' interests might mean for negroes. Before I could puzzle it out, Miss Bet jumped in, avid as ever for the last word. "Whatever new laws they make for male suffrage won't give me the right to vote. But I come into the final portion of my inheritance today, and I mean to use as much of it as I can for the cause of abolition."

She rang the hostess bell. As her guests began the next course, Mama, Old Sam, and I stepped back from the table, little imagining how her vow would change all our lives forever.

For slaves from the countryside who were rented out to Richmond's factories and mills, the period between Christmas and New Year's was a holiday. Most returned to their plantations to spend the week with family, reappearing on the first of January to throng the streets in a frenzy of hiring negotiations, which would set the place and terms of their labor for the coming year. Richmond seemed empty during their absence, our prayer meeting especially so. But it was gay times, too, for those who remained.

No week off for the house slaves, of course. Slaveholders could hardly go a whole week without a cooked meal or a cleaned dish. We were given the day after Christmas off, our celebration delayed so that we might tend the white people at their holiday dinners. The Van Lews fancied themselves especially benevolent, so I was excused from chores through to New Year's, and Mama was given leave to spend every night of the week with Papa—so long as she was back on Church Hill before the Van Lews were awake, laboring there as always until after they were gone to bed. The blacksmith shop was closed, and with the week away from his labors, Papa doted on me. All year, I looked forward to spending those short, magical days promenading through Richmond's streets with him.

But the weeks leading up to Christmastide were filled with extra labors. Only a few years earlier, a German minister arrived to serve at St. Paul's, the new church across from Capitol Square. By 1850, all the prominent white families were joining in the queer yule-tide custom he practiced. It was no playful riddle, just plain old riled, that had Mama muttering, "What do we in the house need with a tree in the house?" as we arranged the drawing room furniture to accommodate the evergreen arrival. Mistress Van Lew got it into her head to decorate the tree with homemade candy, which she would distribute at the Richmond orphanage on Christmas Night. She was awfully thoughtful of all those poor white children, though less thoughtful of Zinnie, who had to cook up confections enough to cover the tree from highest to lowest bough.

For weeks beforehand, I was set to cutting and tying ribbons for the branches. Every now and again, Zinnie slipped me a bit of candy from what she was preparing, and as I sucked on the sweet, I thought over our familiar Christmas Day routine. In the morning, the Van Lews would cross Grace Street, walking a block north to Broad Street to attend morning service at St. John's Church. They would come home to a large holiday dinner, joined by at least half a dozen guests. By five in the afternoon, the meal over and the visitors departed, the slaves would be called into the living room and given our Christmas gifts. We happily received these little adornments chosen by Mistress Van Lew, raised our voices in a requisite hymn or two, and then even more happily dispersed. Papa always waited for Mama and me outside the Twenty-fourth Street entrance to the Van Lew property, as excited as I was for the week ahead.

But this year Miss Bet was behaving even more bizarrely than usual. By early December, her anti-slavery tirades racketed to such a tense crescendo it seemed she might spoil our whole holiday. Even when she finally gave off haranguing her mother, Mistress

Van Lew fell to such sighing and shaking of her head, she seemed certain Miss Bet couldn't allow anyone so much as a momentary peace. But what really set me worrying was when Miss Bet told Mama, "Please have Lewis here when we return from church on Christmas. We will need him during dinner."

In all my memory, Papa never set foot in the Van Lew mansion. Even Papa's owner, Timothy Mahon, an Irishman with a steady blacksmithing business, would hardly be expected through the servants' entrances of the grand houses atop Church Hill. I understood that Papa must obey Master Mahon just as Mama and I must obey the Van Lews, and I knew instinctively the deference with which any colored person, free or slave, acted around whites. But to have Miss Bet assuming Papa was at her beck and call—it was so astonishing even Mama hardly knew how to respond.

"Miss Bet, Lewis isn't trained to house service. He'd be clumsy in front of your guests. I'm sure that Old Sam and I can manage without him."

"Aunt Minnie, I don't need anyone to tell me my own mind. If I say we must have Lewis, then I expect you to see that he will come."

Trammeled by Miss Bet's insistence, Mama play-acted meek. "I'll let him know you want him, ma'am, when next I see him."

That was Saturday, and by the time we entered Papa's cabin the next morning, Mama was anything but meek. "That woman confounds me more each day. One minute she's barking about the sins of slaveholding, the next she's ordering around every negro in Richmond. I'll tell her you're busy for Marse Mahon. Maybe that will remind her that you aren't her slave, too."

"What use do Mahon have for his smiths on Christmas Day?" Papa cocked his head toward me and shirked his shoulders, a signal he gave Mama whenever he had something to say he didn't want me to hear.

I turned my back to my parents and pretended to fiddle with the buttons on my cloak, listening hard for the near-whisper that followed. "That woman got presumption enough for ten white men, it's true. But you know well as she do, I don't got a thing to do Christmas Day, 'cept wait for you and Mary El. So don't go giving off a lie so big you get caught for sure, and who know what she do then. What I gonna do with my whole week's holiday, unless my daughter get her holiday, too?"

Papa came around to me, tipping my head up and smiling, trying to appeal to Mama through me. "Look like I'm gonna enter Fortress Van Lew at last. Scale them walls and race Mary El all through the house. Once we get done poking about, I got to 'prentice myself to Old Sam, who gonna teach me to walk and talk just so among them strange pale creatures. Quite a time we gonna have." The way he winked at me, I wanted to believe we'd really caper and play, without a care for Miss Bet or any of her family. "And the ending gonna be best of all, when I walk my beautiful wife and daughter out that fortress and bring them home with me."

Christmas morning, I woke before Mama, feeling the cold floor right through our cornhusk sleeping pallet. The garret quarters, stifling in summer, were always freezing in winter. When we went to sleep our room was warmed a bit by the heat from the fireplaces in the Van Lew family's bedchambers below. But by daybreak their fires were long out, only to be rekindled once Mama and I set to work downstairs. The bricks we'd heated, wrapped in rags, and carried into our pallet the night before were stone cold to the touch by dawn, and the water in the chipped porcelain pitcher on the wooden table just inside our doorway was long gone frigid. We usually washed and dressed in near silence on winter days, our movements quick and deliberate against the bitter air.

But not this morning. I kissed Mama and wished her good morning, my voice loud against the sloping ceiling of our room. She smiled at me out of her sleep as I scrambled up to the washstand. "We go to Papa's tonight," I said, as if she could have forgotten such a thing. "We have to be ready."

"Mary El, that's not for hours yet. There's work enough for us to do before then. And don't you think we might take time for a prayer, today of all days?"

In my excitement over my imminent departure for Shockoe Bottom, I'd forgotten all about the baby Jesus's long ago arrival in Bethlehem. That was just how the morning went, me trying to pull time itself ahead, only to have Mama or Zinnie or Old Sam remind me of some task or other I needed to do. The very minute the Van Lews left for church, I began peering out the window for Papa, not wanting to miss a moment of fun showing him about.

But Papa kept his eyes low and his thoughts to himself once he arrived. I led him from the cellar door through the warren of basement service rooms, then up the servants' stair to the china closet. As we moved from the back of the first floor to the front, he didn't care to leave the wide, long hall to romp through the dining room and library on the east side of the house, or the drawing room and sitting room on the west. Though he followed me up the main staircase, he barely nodded as I pointed to Mistress Van Lew's bedroom and dressing room, and Young Master John's and Miss Bet's chambers across the hall.

Only when we climbed the narrow back stair to the third floor did his interest pique. Open doorways led to Old Sam's room on one side, and the room Mama and I shared on the other. Papa had to stoop beneath the sloping roof to enter our garret quarter. Turning a complete circle to take in the space where his family slept, he came to a stop facing me. "You like this room?"

I thought for a moment, wanting to please him. "I like being here with Mama, when we don't have to take care of the Van Lews. And I know some slaves live worse places than this, places I'm glad I don't have to live. But I get so excited about spending a whole week at your cabin, I guess I like that better."

He hugged me to him and whispered, "Merry Christmas, Mary El." We walked hand in hand back down to where the rest of the slaves were gathered on the ground floor, waiting for the Van Lews.

When our owners returned from St. John's, Old Sam was in the front hall to help them off with their hats and cloaks and boots. We'd laid the table for eleven, as Miss Bet had instructed early that morning. But after only a few minutes before the drawing room fire, Miss Bet rang for Mama and told her to begin serving the meal, although no guests had yet arrived.

Mama shook her head as she repeated the order to all of us downstairs in the warming kitchen.

"Putting fine food out to get cold at empty places." Zinnie banged her pot lids as she laid the meal onto serving platters. "Miss Bet gone batty at last."

Miss Bet stood sentinel in the dining room to oversee Lilly, Daisy, Old Sam, Mama, and me in our serving. Once the fine china plates and crystal goblets were filled, she sent Old Sam to the parlor to summon her mother and brother and told Mama to fetch Zinnie, Josiah, and Papa. When the Van Lews had taken their places at the table, Miss Bet wished us each Merry Christmas. Then she said, "Sit down and join us for dinner."

None of us moved. She might have been speaking to eight specters only she could see, so unfathomable was the idea of slaves sitting beside their owners in a dining room on Church Hill.

Young Master John broke the silence. "You cannot expect the servants to—"

Miss Bet cut him off. "There is no need to lecture me on show and ought. Much that I could not expect has already come to pass." She smiled and gave her mother a proper little nod. "For who would have imagined I should enjoy Christmas dinner as an owner of slaves in my own right?"

My breath caught at the idea. Miss Bet, with her own slaves? Who was she bringing into the household, to upset the routine we knew so well? How could she so capriciously reverse her feelings about slavery?

Miss Bet looked hard at us. "Why are you still standing there? Haven't I told you to sit?"

We spent several awkward moments shuffling into the empty chairs, Old Sam hardly knowing how to get himself seated once he had adjusted everyone else to their places. Miss Bet turned to her brother. "Do you care to lead us in grace? Or shall I do it myself?"

Young Master John didn't seem eager to grant his sister opportunity for any more of her odd declarations. As we bowed our heads, he gave thanks for such obedient servants, and asked God to preserve his delicate mother's health and to give his sister and himself the wisdom needed for sound domestic management. We all muttered amens enough to show we understood the meaning he put into those words. All except Miss Bet, who was as determined as ever to have everything her own way, no matter what her brother or anyone else thought.

She took up her fork and began eating, glancing about insistently to make sure we did the same. I might have marveled at how different Zinnie's cooking tasted, served hot in the dining room instead of snatched down cold afterward in the kitchen. But the heavy silver I'd spent my childhood washing and polishing felt so cumbersome here, compared to the wooden spoons and forks with which I normally ate. Mama, Old Sam, Lilly, and Daisy seemed to share my sudden trepidity over the china and crystal we handled so deftly when serving and clearing the Van Lew meals. Papa, Josiah, and Zinnie were rendered even more inept than those of us who'd long observed white people's dining habits while waiting table. And Mistress Van Lew and Young Master John seemed just as uncomfortable as we were to have negroes dine beside them.

Miss Bet surveyed the table. "Yes, this year I celebrate Christmas as an owner of slaves in my own right." She caught the eyes of Old Sam and Josiah, Zinnie and Lilly and Daisy, Mama and even Papa, and finally me, all in turn. "For my mother has consented to sell me her slaves, so that I may set them free."

Bet's outlandish pronouncements usually elicited a knowing cough or skirt rustle from the Van Lew slaves. But this time we were stunned still.

The news tied even Young Master John's tongue. He stared speechless at his mother, who kept her own eyes low while Miss Bet pecked out her plan for us. She would write out our free papers come the New Year. We would be at liberty to leave the house and even the city then, although she suggested we remain in her employ for a few months, to earn enough to support our removal to a free state. For, she informed us, unlike the free blacks we knew—her words made me think of pretty Elly Banks and elderly Mr. and Mrs. Wallace—whose forebears were manumitted over fifty years before, newly freed negroes could remain in Virginia for no more than one year, or they would be seized by the authorities and resold as slaves.

The mouthful of Christmas goose I'd been savoring stuck in my throat.

"Ma'am? What about Lewis, ma'am?" Mama asked.

Miss Bet set down her cutlery before answering. "Aunt Minnie, I'm terribly sorry. I told Timothy Mahon I would pay whatever he thought was a fair price, but he will not entertain an offer of any size. He says as a blacksmith Lewis would be difficult enough to replace, but his work as foreman of the shop and supervisor of the apprentices is indispensable. He deems Lewis 'invaluable property,' and he will not sell under any circumstances."

And so the finest meal we had ever eaten, the greatest present we could ever receive, were spoiled by the news that Mama and I would have to choose between Papa and our freedom.

Three

O nce Miss Bet said her piece, we ate wordlessly. The noise of silverware scraping against china set me on edge as I sensed Zinnie and Josiah's joy on one side of me, and Mama and Papa's worry on the other.

It wasn't much relief when at last we left the table and crossed the broad hall to the sitting room. Young Master John read Luke 2:1–20 from the family Bible, just as he and his father had during all the Christmases anyone could remember. Then Miss Bet took her place at the piano to play "Amazing Grace." But even Josiah's strong baritone could not bear the emotions loosed by Miss Bet. The strain of uncertainty hung in every note, sounding a choir of sentiment all its own.

As soon as we in the house said our farewells to the Van Lews and retreated back to the dining room, Zinnie nodded at Mama. "The girls can clear and wash, you go on with Lewis now." Mama murmured her thanks, and as quickly as we could bundle up against the cold, Papa shepherded us out of the mansion.

Snow was falling, but I was too distracted to care for the wet, white flakes whirling around me. We set off in silence, me in the middle gripping tight to my parents' hands. I wasn't sure what it meant to be caught between them, now that I might really be free.

When we reached the end of the Van Lews' lot, Papa let out a long, low whistle. "Sure are some memorable dinner parties them white folks of yours put on, Minerva."

His teasing stopped Mama in her tracks. "What are we gonna do, Lewis? What are we gonna do?"

It scared me to see Mama so uncertain. Papa scooped me up, shifting the weight of my body onto his left arm, holding me in a way I thought I'd long outgrown. Then he wrapped his right hand around Mama's waist and gathered us against each other, forming our family into a tight little circle at the edge of the street. "We gonna be thankful our daughter will grow up free. We gonna figure out a way to be together. And some of us gonna have to admit all your talk about Jesus has a plan for this child may not be so crazy after all."

We stood there a long, long while. I felt the snow collecting on us, as it did on the trees and the buildings and the big yards of Church Hill. I wanted to stop time, to make Mama's and my one year of allowed freedom in Virginia last forever. Finally, Papa kissed Mama and then me, set me back on the ground, and began to hum "We Will March through the Valley." He remained between us, taking our hands as we started walking again. I felt not quite so scared and confused as before, but not like I really believed everything was going to be all right either.

I spent a good part of Christmas week pretending I'd dozed off early in the evening or hadn't yet awoken in the morning, or feigning absorption with some solitary game, all the while listening close to every word my parents said to each other.

"And if we go North, where we gonna go?" Mama wondered that very first night.

"You got people in New York."

"You my people now. Nobody in New York even recognize me, my mother dead and my sisters and brother scattered who knows where. They take the Van Lew name when they freed? Or our daddy's? Maybe my sisters married, or they and my brother made up their own names when their freedom time came."

"You ain't gonna find them if you don't try. Maybe Miss Bet help, least write her father's family and see what they know."

"I don't expect a family knows much that gives out other people's children as going-away presents." That was how Mama had come to Richmond, gifted to her owner's younger son when he moved South. But she was more than just angry at the memory of losing her family—she was frightened of going through that loss all over again with Papa. "No, Lewis. No New York for us without you."

"You heard Miss Bet," Papa said. "Mahon won't sell. What you want me to do, if I can't go legal?" We'd heard plenty of stories about bounty hunters finding runaways, especially since the new law said there was no safe harbor even up North. "I ain't gonna be tracked like no animal, tore away from my wife and child. Maybe made to watch while some slave-catcher hauls you into court, claiming you is runaways, too. And after that, slavery ain't come-and-go-as-you-please Richmond. Mahon'll sell a captured runaway to the Deep South, same as any slaveholder."

I didn't know whether to be grateful or hateful to Miss Bet, for vexing Mama and Papa, and even me, so. From where I lay on my pallet, I could make out Mama sitting at the table in the next room, the tallow candle throwing her hunched shadow against the wall. "We married with a promise to stay together no matter what. All these years we managed it. How can freedom, the one best thing that's ever happened to me, pull us apart? What's freedom without my family together?"

Papa leaned forward and kissed her. "You and Mary El got something I may never get. You freedom bound. I can't ask you to give that up."

And so the week went. Papa attempted to distract me during the day, leading me on adventures throughout the city. But for once his winking humor felt forced. I cursed Virginia's law expelling newly freed negroes just as surely as I ever cursed slavery. I hated how our news could change so much so fast, even change my smiling Papa and his easy way with me.

Mama's nightly reports from Church Hill reminded me that after my holiday ended, I wouldn't be returning to the life I'd always known. The snatches I strained to overhear were as strange to me as the Van Lews' conversations, and every bit as troubling. "Zinnie and Josiah gonna stay for six months, earn what they can, and then try for Ohio. They're worried about Lilly, though. The girl has her eye on some sweetheart works at one of the tobacco factories and don't seem too happy to be leaving him. Lilly don't know but Josiah means to talk to the boy, tell him she has her freedom coming and soon enough headed off. If the boy is decent, he won't want to break up the family or make her do anything crazy, and Josiah says maybe if they court serious through the spring, Lilly can work once they get West, help buy him out."

Strange as it was to think of the house without Zinnie and Josiah and the girls, at least their departure was a long way off. Not so with Old Sam. "He says he ain't got time to wait around earning a piddle bit here or there. He's asked Miss Bet's leave to write his brother's children in New York, see if they have room to take him in right off. Miss Bet says if they do, she'll pay his fare to travel North. How he can imagine going back at his age, I don't know. Can't even think of it at mine." Mama got quiet for a long minute, and when she spoke again her voice was low and tight. "Left three children of his own when we were brought away from New York. Girl baby always was a bit sickly, nobody expected her to live. But those two strong boys, running and climbing everywhere. Heard way back his wife's owners took them all and moved somewhere far off. Far off in time and place from Old Sam's freedom, that's for sure."

Mama's revelation astounded me. I understood that she and Papa had people they'd been sold or sent away from, their memories of those families so tender they kept them wrapped tight inside, the way I wrapped Mistress Van Lew's tortoise-shell hand mirror in her silk handkerchiefs when she went for a week's holiday at White Sulphur Springs. But Old Sam, with a wife and children? I could no more conceive of it than I could fathom which tree our plank table was hewn from, or what chicken our egg supper might have hatched up to be.

I barely had time to dwell on Old Sam's mysterious past before he was departing for an equally mysterious future. He was the first of us to hold free papers in his hand, and we shared his pride in touching those pages, at once so fragile and so weighty. On a windless and chill Thursday afternoon not long after New Year's, Mama, Josiah, Zinnie, Lilly, Daisy, and I walked down with him to Rocketts Landing to await his boat. It was the first time we'd all been together off the Van Lews' lot. And the last.

Old Sam and Mama held to each other in long recollection of all they'd shared, and most especially of how being brought to Virginia robbed them of the freedom promised to slaves in New York State. At last Mama said, "When we stood together on that Long Island dock, you told me you'd make it back. Looks like you knew this day would come."

Old Sam shook his head. "Good thing I didn't know. Couldn't have imagined it taking this long. Maybe wouldn't have wanted to know what there'd be left to go back to now."

A stout white man approached, rubbing his hands against the cold that had already reddened the half cheeks above his blond beard. He was the ship's captain, well aware of Old Sam's presence. Fear of slaves' escape meant that any boat taking a negro out of Richmond's river port required extra scrutiny, so Miss Bet made Old Sam's arrangements with care. The captain nodded at us, indicating it was time to board. We hugged once more all around, Zinnie presenting Old Sam with a basket of what she declared was "the last decent food you'll get till who knows when"—she'd been born in Virginia and sincerely doubted anyone, colored or white, could cook an edible meal way up in New York. Then Old Sam followed the captain up the gangway, away from Richmond forever.

Life without Old Sam made each of us feel even more keenly the varied emotions surrounding our own freedom, the way your gum aches more just after a sore tooth is pulled than it did before. This ache was one of pain but also pleasure. Missing Old Sam, anxious about my family's future, I rolled the word *free* around my mouth, wondering how it would apply to me.

Hard as I listened all Christmas week and every Sunday thereafter, Mama and Papa still must have managed a few private conversations when they sent me out on some errand to a neighbor or the store. Because by the time I heard about Philadelphia, it was clear they'd been talking on it for quite a while. And talking wasn't celebrating, that's for sure. It was one thing for Jesus to have a plan for me. Mama put all her prayers and hopes and demands into that. But for Miss Bet to have a plan for me, well, that was something else again.

Miss Bet was eager to secure my education, which she believed would prove the folly of the peculiar institution—and confirm the virtue of her own benevolence. Slave or free, there was no opportunity for a negro to acquire formal schooling in Richmond. Virginia had no public schools, even for whites, and the spare handful of private girls' academies would no more enroll me than they would a barnyard turkey. Besides, these institutions designed their courses of study to narrow, not broaden, young ladies' minds. Even Mistress Van Lew acknowledged as much when she sent Miss Bet to school in Pennsylvania twenty years earlier. And so Miss Bet insisted that Philadelphia was the best place in the country for any child to get an education.

But Philadelphia was two hundred miles from Richmond, as the crow flies. And I was no crow. It would be days by train or boat to get from home to this city neither I nor my parents had ever seen. More than that, it might be a one-way journey, for Miss Bet grudgingly admitted that any negro who left Virginia to receive an education was barred by law from ever returning.

The blows against my family were coming so fast and furious, I felt tender and bruised, like I wasn't my solid self any longer. Mama and I couldn't stay in Richmond and keep our freedom. Papa couldn't leave. Mama wouldn't go without him. Miss Bet wanted to send me far off to be educated. Everything stood at an impasse, until the matrons of Church Hill came to call.

Like any Southern gentlewoman, Mistress Van Lew practiced fine needlework, whiling away many an afternoon at her embroidery, joined by neighbor ladies. "Needlework indeed," Mama would say. "Needling each other is more like it, with all their gossip and bragging, whose child this and whose house that."

One afternoon late in January, Mistress Van Lew called Mama to tend the drawing room fire and serve tea to her stitching visitors, tasks that Old Sam previously performed. I was across the hall waxing the furnishings in the library, for now that Miss Bet was my owner, she insisted I tend this room. She meant the assignment as a way to give me leave to read, not understanding how little time I had for such pursuits—especially since Old Sam's departure, which made the rest of our workloads that much heavier.

Miss Bet hadn't made a public show of her plan to free all the family's slaves just yet, because so much with me and Mama was undecided. But it was generally known that Old Sam had been given his liberty, and Mama's presence in the drawing room reminded the guests of this unusual development.

"Why, it must be right much of a loss to you, Old Sam leaving after so many years." Mrs. Randolph's high, haughty voice condescended clear across the hall. "He came to Richmond way back with your husband, didn't he?"

Before Mistress Van Lew could respond, Mrs. Whitlock said, "Your Bet and her odd ways, sending the man off to some distant relations at his age. But then, I suppose that's a product of her Yankee education."

"I myself had a Philadelphia education." Mistress Van Lew made the name of her native city sound especially mellifluous against the hard syllables of the word *Yankee*. "And an excellent one it was. Young ladies were schooled at fine academies there even in the last century. It is a tradition of which we are proud."

"Proud, yes, of course," Mrs. Whitlock said. "But your education did not keep you from marrying and raising a family, rather than taking up such fool-nonsense as abolition. Some of your daughter's peculiar leanings must try a mother's pride, and her patience, too."

Whatever puncheons and barrels of consternation Bet provoked in her mother, Mistress Van Lew wasn't about to admit a drop of it to the neighborhood gossipry. I was so curious to hear how she might answer without fibbing outright, I stepped into the archway between the library and the hall. I set my dust-cloth to the mahogany and brass-wire birdcage with such feigned diligence that the goldfinch twittered in dismay. When Mistress Van Lew looked over to see what disturbed her beloved Farinelli, she held her eyes on me for a long moment. But instead of reprimanding me, she turned to reprove her guest.

"A child is not a thistle-bird to be kept in a cage, happy only to peck at her seed. My late husband and I educated our daughter that she might know her mind and act on it. Her independence and her interest in causes of freedom are nothing less than the legacy of Pennsylvania's Revolutionary fervor, in which my own father was very much involved, you know."

The First Families of Virginia always carried on as though their forebears had invented the American

Revolution single-handed. Mistress Van Lew tended more to amity than antagonism with her neighbors, so on the rare occasion when she reminded the Richmond FFVs of Philadelphia's role in the birth of the Republic, everyone knew she was upset.

The visitors must have been relieved when she shifted her attention to Mama, who was tending the blaze in the large marble hearth. "There is no need to brood about. You have built a strong enough foundation, and you can trust your handiwork not to smolder out, even when you are not present." Her voice softened a bit. "Mind what I'm telling you, Aunt Minnie, mind what I'm telling you."

"Yes, ma'am, I'll mind you of course," Mama replied, curtsying her way out of the room.

She barreled down the broad hall without so much as glancing my way, then disappeared through the china closet to the servants' stair. I heard the rear door to the cellar open and close, and from the back window I watched her scurrying toward the privy, cleaning supplies in hand. This was Mama's especial task, the thing she set herself to whenever she wanted an excuse for serious contemplation. "Time to set the privy to right," she'd declare, disappearing for half an hour or so before returning quiet and determined. It was our most distasteful chore, and Mama put herself to it only at moments when she needed to think on some important matter without being disturbed.

As I watched her cross the yard, marching hard against the winter wind, I already knew what she would resolve while she scrubbed and limed and whitewashed. And so I returned to my own labors, humming to myself as I began to imagine what my life would be like in Philadelphia.

Mama didn't say a word about the matter for the next few days. But I anticipated the coming Sunday would bring much important discussion between her and Papa. Supposing Mama was already concocting excuses to get me out of Papa's cabin so they could speak freely, I began contriving excuses to stay. I meticulously collected everything we needed before leaving the Van Lews', so there would be no reason to send me back to fetch a forgotten article. I let out a careful sneeze or two, so that I might claim a cold if they instructed me to go on an errand. Then I thought perhaps a cold would give them an excuse to leave me inside while they went out together, so I ceased sneezing immediately. The conniving weighed on me all week. But it turned out all my scheming was for naught.

As soon as we arrived at Papa's cabin, Mama set all of us down for a talk. When Papa started to send me off to check on his elderly neighbors, Mama stopped him. "What I have to say concerns Mary El, she needs to hear it for herself." She turned to me. "You're old enough now to keep the family confidences, aren't you?"

When she said *you're old enough,* I thought of all the times that phrase meant some new, unwished for responsibility, and how it always struck a pang of resentment in my heart. But now I wanted things to be different. I wanted to feel intrepid rather than timorous or obstinate about what my old-enough self would be expected to do. "Yes, Mama," I said. "I'm old enough."

And so I sat beside Papa at his little table and listened to her plan. Freedom meant little without opportunity. Wasn't that precisely what Virginia's restrictions on free negroes and freed slaves proved? Education would increase my opportunity, and so an education I would have. And since a Philadelphia education was the only one good enough for Miss Bet, it surely was the only one good enough for me. My parents would miss me, but Old Master Van Lew and Mistress Van Lew must have missed Miss Bet, and anything they could bear my parents could certainly bear, too. It was a good thing, not a bad thing, after all, to be living apart from a daughter who was getting such a fine Philadelphia education, better than any white family's daughters got here in Richmond.

Right about there, Papa cut in. "Minerva, no need for you to be talking yourself through missing Mary El when you gonna be right there with her. Gonna get that Philadelphia opportunity yourself."

"No, Lewis, I'm not." Mama didn't seem sad exactly, though her voice held a dim sort of sorry over not even quite knowing what she was giving up. "I remember how lonely it was when I first came to Richmond. I'm not ready to be that lonely in Philadelphia now. Or to leave you to it here. Child grows up, leaves her parents, that's natural. Wife leaves her husband, though, that's something else."

"You know the law," Papa said. "Only got one year, and then you be sold off to the highest bidder, who know where you end up. I won't allow it."

"We have one year, but not one year from now. One year from the day the state of Virginia knows I'm free. What if nobody knows, nobody that doesn't have to?"

And so Mama outlined the rest of the plan. She'd remain in Richmond, working for the Van Lews, earning wages just as Josiah and Zinnie and their girls were doing. But she'd stay as long as need be, until Mahon agreed to sell Papa to Miss Bet or free Papa himself. Miss Bet would write out free papers for Mama, but she wouldn't file them with the state, nor would Mama register as a free negro. She would be free, but no one in

Richmond besides her, Papa, and the Van Lews would know it. She wouldn't have to worry about leaving the state or facing re-enslavement so long as Miss Bet remained alive and well. Every month Miss Bet would make the free papers over again with the new date, destroying the old ones, so if something happened to her, Mama would still have a year, more or less, before she'd have to leave Virginia.

"I don't like my wife posing as a slave, that's for sure," Papa said. "But I never been wild about my wife being a slave, neither." It was the first joke I'd heard him make in weeks. He turned serious again before he continued. "Minerva, I been searching for the strength to let you go, but I ain't found it yet. If you sure you want to stay this way, I ain't about to stop you."

"I'm sure," Mama said. "If I go North now, I'm gonna work hard for some white family or other, who knows how they treat me or pay me, where I'm gonna live, or any of it. I stay in Richmond, I stay with you. I'll make Miss Bet give me leave to spend nights here, instead of the Van Lew house." Mama's mouth tugged down with the weight of all she was considering. "I'm hard-pressed to trust any white person, but she's trying to do right by my daughter, I think she'll pay me fair, and I'll have my freedom papers the whole time. I been a slave wishing for freedom my whole life. Being a free woman play-acting at slavery can't be harder than that."

I was so used to pretending I wasn't listening to such conversations that I forgot Mama'd given me leave to participate. When I remembered, I spoke up. "If I go to Philadelphia for school, I can't come back to Virginia." The excitement I'd stoked all week long was instantly tempered as I thought on everything I stood to lose. "I'll never see you and Papa again."

Mama squeezed my hand so I felt all the love and fear and hope passing between us. "No one besides Miss Bet needs to know where you've gone to, and if they don't know, they can't keep you from coming back." Her voice caught. "Listen enough to white people talk, seems like none of them agree about slavery at all. I hear Miss Bet read to Mistress V from those abolitionist papers how whites and negroes up North even work together to end it. Smart girl like you, living free in Philadelphia, maybe you be the one who figures out how to get rid of slavery once and for all."

That day Mama taught me that what other people see you as doesn't determine who you really are. She could let people think she was a slave, if that meant she could be free and live with Papa. We could let them think I'd been sent to work the Van Lews' market farm or rented out to a family friend in Petersburg, if that meant I could go to Philadelphia without imperiling any chance of coming back to Richmond. And who knows what I might do—not just for myself but maybe, like Mama said, for all the slaves—if I could have my education and still pass between North and South. Miss Bet always howled and raved against show and ought. But for colored folks in Virginia, survival meant biting our tongues and biding our time, while scheming like Mama did all the while.

As soon as Mama gave her the nod, Miss Bet began sending letters off to Philadelphia to secure a place for me. Miss Bet wouldn't think of sending me to the city's lone colored public school, in which two hundred students met with a single teacher in a broken-down building over a mere dozen books. But it was no easy matter for her to find a private school that would enroll me. A few Quaker-sponsored institutions existed to educate negro boys, but they were just as closed to me as the white academies. Yet Miss Bet kept at it, the way she always did when something fueled her ire. As weeks passed, then months, she tried to distract us from the delay by tutoring me herself, insisting it was preparation for my formal schooling.

It was nearly Easter when word arrived of Sarah Mapps Doug-lass, a colored woman who kept a small academy in her home. When Miss Bet annouced that Miss Douglass had agreed to accept me, Mama negotiated for me to stay in Richmond a bit longer, to spend my birthday with her and Papa. It was always a sore point with Mama that neither she nor my father knew their own dates of birth—Papa wasn't even sure what year he was born, separated as he was from his family so early on—so Mama was mighty careful to remember the day I came into the world, May 17, 1839. With my twelfth birthday approaching, Papa determined to outfit me for my new life any way he could.

Miss Bet, eager to ensure the success of her personal experiment in negro improvement, provided me with the basics of a new wardrobe—two summer day dresses, both fine enough even for Sundays, and one evening dress, plus a night-shirt with matching sleeping cap, new shoes, hose, and my first real set of lady's undergarments. To Papa were left the purchase of items "necessar-y to a free young la-dy," as he called out in sing-song. Unlike the whimsical just-becauses of my childhood, these gifts came deliberately chosen, talismans of all Papa wanted me to be and do, once I was far from him. A toilet set and matching combs, my own Bible, even a bonnet as fashionable as any white girl my age wore—each gift appeared to his merry rhyme. My favorite of all was a sewing kit. Not any old rusty needle and scrap of thread but a proper tortoise-shell box containing a whole case full of new needles of every size, along with a plump satin pincushion, a worked-metal thimble and matching scissors, and a rainbow's array of spooled threads. All of it meant not just for mending but for the kind of fancy needlework I didn't yet know how to do.

Richmond's slave markets supplied human goods to much of the upper South, and I was old enough to understand the horror of families ripped asunder, with no idea where a child or parent auctioned in the city would eventually be taken. As foreign as Philadelphia was to us, we knew it wasn't slavery and it wasn't the South. Knowing I was freedom bound, we savored that time when the future was a promise that had not yet come to pass.

As I blinked my eyes open my last morning in Richmond, I made out the iron cross hanging on the wall of Papa's cabin. Most Sundays of my childhood, I spent half an hour or more tracing over its whorls and flourishes, fascinated that my papa had created such a beautiful thing. But this morning I was ticking too full of emotion to lay gazing at his cross.

In just a few hours, Miss Bet and I were to take the train North to Washington, where we would transfer to the rail line to Philadelphia. Miss Bet had fussed about how cramped boat passage was, but Mama harrumphed at her protestations, informing me in private that Miss Bet just had a tendency for seasickness. Though I had never been on either a boat or a train, the latter seemed more modern and formal to me, with all the noise and smoke, so I felt glad for Miss Bet's infirmity.

I thought my excitement would have me up earliest of my family, but Papa and Mama were already dressed in their workday clothes and seated at the table, a small pot of coffee between them. I quickly rose and readied myself, splashing water on my face and rinsing my mouth. Undoing the plaits I normally wore, I swept my hair back from my face, securing it with my new combs. Stepping back from the doorway to preserve my privacy, I reached for my pile of new clothing.

I slipped into the knee-length chemise that would protect my undergarments, then struggled into my new corset. As I labored to lace myself in, the stiff fabric pulled my shoulders down and back, causing my rib cage to poke out and constraining me so, I could barely bend and wriggle my way into my new petticoat and corset cover, and then my crinolines, followed by another petticoat. At last I pulled on my dress, a green-and-yellow-striped silk. Unlike the loose frocks I'd always worn, this dress had a lady's fitted bodice.

The double-row of covered buttons down the front followed the lines of the corset, and the elegantly formed sleeves began inches below my shoulders, tapering down to my narrow wrists. The collar, trimmed with green lace, was fashioned broad and low in anticipation of the summer heat, leaving a scoop of skin below my collar-bones exposed for all the world to see.

Mama and Zinnie always wore unadorned blouses and skirts, no sewn trim, with underblouses and under-skirts only when needed to guard against cold weather. The lively patterns of the gingham from which their garments were cut quickly grew dull with wear and washing. As I slipped on my hose and then my new ankle boots, I ruminated on how the shaped undergar-ments and the tight cut of my dress created the effect of a figure I hadn't yet developed. Though I could barely move for the weight of all those layers, I tried to carry myself as I believed Mistress Van Lew or Miss Bet or any real lady would, as I stepped into the next room.

Papa stood, his large eyes blinking at me. "Philadelphia lucky to have such a fine young lady, pretty as she is smart."

Most days I would have beamed with pride at such a compliment, but the thought of leaving him caught my mouth closed. I crossed the small room and held him tight, surprised at how tall my new shoes made me against his large frame. He kissed the top of my head, as he often did, but he no longer had to stoop to do so.

"I hope you saved room in that satchel for one final gift, necessar-y to an-y free la-dy." He gestured to the table, where two wrapped packages sat. "One for each of my free ladies," he said, handing one to Mama and the other to me. We opened them in unison, to find identical stacks of cream-colored writing paper, each with a set of a dozen steel pen nibs on top. "My ladies be writing each other furious often I bet, and be through these piles in no time. Why, if Minerva gonna write down all she got to say, I best be saving for the next pile of paper already."

Mama scowled in mock disapproval of Papa's joke. I was ready to tease him back, asking where his stack was. But just before speaking I caught myself. Papa had no use for letter paper. He wasn't literate.

Six days out of seven during my childhood, Mama enjoyed a connection to me that slavery denied my father. Now that I was going North to freedom, he couldn't even share the solace of writing to me and reading my responses.

We left the cabin and made our way up Church Hill, arriving just as Josiah pulled the larger of the Van Lew carriages, drawn by four of the family's six white horses, to the front of the mansion. As Papa helped him load the trunks, Zinnie came out to bid me farewell, flanked by Lilly and Daisy. The sight of their family together brought a tremble to Mama's lips, and after speaking only a few low words wishing me well, Zinnie hustled her daughters back into the house.

Papa marked how high the sun was in the sky, and we both knew his good-bye couldn't be put off any longer. "We always knowed you was special, Mary El. Now you got to prove it to the world. Mind how your mama and I raised you. And remember, some folks mighta been born to more than you, but none been born better than you." Comforting as those words would be in the months and years ahead, I was startled by what came next. "And don't let none of them Northern colored gentlemen run off with you, without asking your papa's leave first." Before I could object that no gentleman would be interested in me, he added, grinning as best he could, "Since you Minerva's daughter, only fair I warn any suitor what he be up against. Now go along and make us proud."

"I will, Papa," I promised. He kissed me and Mama and then turned back toward Shockoe Bottom, hurrying to his day's labor at the smithy.

I couldn't bear to watch Papa disappear down Grace Street, so I turned to the mansion. Josiah was holding the door as Miss Bet emerged to stride down the curving stairway. She wore her slate gray traveling suit, and the gray hat sitting atop her golden ringlets brought out the icy blue of her eyes.

"Hardly appropriate garments for a servant traveling two days by train," she said when she saw me. "But I suppose there is nothing to be done for it now." The feather in her hat wagged as she spoke, reminding me of how Mama shook her finger at me whenever I did wrong. We took our places inside the Van Lew carriage, Mama and me riding backward as we faced our former owner. I spent all of my first-ever carriage ride fretting about how I'd fare traveling alone with Miss Bet.

Once we arrived at the train depot, Josiah handed us down from the carriage, directed a porter to unload the trunks, and secured our tickets. Miss Bet nodded to Mama. "Mary will be fine with me, Aunt Minnie. Don't worry about a thing, and do look after Mother while I'm away." She turned to me. "Shall we go?"

Mama answered before I could. "Please, Miss Bet, can Mary El and I have a minute to ourselves?"

Her subdued tone seemed to catch Miss Bet off guard. "Yes, of course. I shall wait on the train. But mind the time. You've got only a few moments."

As Miss Bet walked off, Mama took me in her arms, holding me so close our hearts pounded one against the other. "I've been hoping and praying for this day all your life, longer even. Was enough to imagine you free some day, but off to get some fancy private academy education? Your life gonna be different, special, not just from mine but from most colored folks'. You got to learn enough up there for all of us, hear?"

The truth of leaving home caught me quick, rendering me as immobile as one of Papa's wrought iron creations. "Mama, I can't leave you and Papa. Don't make me go."

"Make you go? What are you talking like that for? This is a dream coming true for you, not some punishment. If you ain't smart enough to see that, well, that's just one more thing they're gonna have to teach you in that Northern school." She softened a bit and pulled back from me. "Let me take one last look at you, my beautiful girl."

But the train whistle blew, so loud my head echoed with the vibration. "All aboard," called the conductor.

"I love you, Mama," I said as I turned away. "I love you, too," I heard from behind me as I rushed to the car Miss Bet had entered.

Just as I got there, a sallow-looking white man stepped in front of the entry. "Where you think you're going, gal?"

I fumbled for my ticket. "Here you are sir, I'm going to Washington."

"Not in this car, you ain't." He nodded toward the fore part of the train. "Niggers ride in the baggage car, just behind the locomotive. You best run down there quick, train's about to start moving."

"But, sir, I'm supposed to—"

Before I could finish, Miss Bet appeared behind him. "Surely my servant can ride here, to attend me."

He turned and took in the quality of her suit, lifting his cap to her. "Pardon me, ma'am. She never said nothing about attending a lady. Thought she was one of them free niggers, putting on airs."

He stepped aside, and Miss Bet yanked me up, deriding me loudly enough for half the compartment to hear. "You impudent pup, what did I tell you about minding the time? Need I remind you it is your duty to obey me? Come along."

"Yes, ma'am," I muttered, trying to keep steady as the train bucked forward beneath my feet. I knew Miss Bet was playing a necessary part in front of our fellow passengers, that she was reminding me of the need for me to play my part as well. But her words stung me hard. As we took our seats, my head hung heavy with loneliness.

By the time I remembered to look out the train window for Mama, the station had already slipped past.

BOOK TWO
Philadelphia
1851–1859

Four

All my childhood, Richmond always seemed the most important place in the world. Factories and mills and mines. Grand houses on the Hill and hidden homes in the Bottom. The massive Tredegar Iron Works, one of the largest metal manufactories in the nation. Yet staring out the carriage window as we were jostled along Philadelphia's streets that first afternoon, the difference astounded me. The noisy bustle of the crowds, cityscapes hued only in russets and grays with no greens, the rush and push that charged the air, all stood in contrast to home. Even the streets themselves, not dirt like Richmond's—dirt that turned to mud and muck so much of the year, dirt we were endlessly cleaning off the Van Lews' stoop and shoes and clothes and floors—but paved with cobblestones, row after row for miles. And everything so tight and narrow. These Philadelphia thoroughfares squeezed themselves between the packed brick row houses, just as the row houses squeezed themselves between one another, all jammed in quick as could be.

Each year during Christmastide, Papa and I played a game in which he led me about the city with my eyes closed, and I had to guess where we were by what I smelled. That was Richmond. Your nose could tell you as much as your eyes, if you knew the difference between the sweet aroma of tobacco factories and the stink of Butchertown, the enticing scent of a bakery or the heavy odor of the docks. I feared that in Philadelphia I'd be lost even with my eyes open, no sight, sound, or smell familiar to me. The brick facades of the buildings seemed indistinguishable, and who could remember so many new streets? I leaned back against the carriage seat, wondering if this city set everyone's head spinning the way it did mine.

Miss Bet had arranged for me to board with a negro family, a widow and her twenty-year-old daughter. Now she began to talk of my good fortune at having such a fine home.

Papa hadn't even wanted me to think of the Van Lew house as home. It hardly seemed right to imagine any place I might live in this alien city becoming home to me. But I reminded myself that Papa and Mama wanted me to come here. They would wish me to act warm and not standoffish toward my hosts. I fiddled the edges of my cuffs over it, until at last the hack pulled to a halt.

"Here we are, ma'am, 168 Gaskill Street," the driver announced as he swung open the carriage door. Emerging from the cab after Miss Bet, I looked up at the narrowest building on the block. No more than twelve feet wide and crammed so tight between its neighbors, it put me in mind of how Mama struggled each morning to fasten Mistress Van Lew and Miss Bet into their corsets. The first floor had only one window, while each of the three stories above it had just two, covered by a series of mismatched shutters. The shutters and the front door badly needed fresh paint.

Miss Bet surveyed the dilapidated exterior. "What do you think, Mary?"

I looked the building up and down, trying to summon some enthusiasm. Or at least to hide my surprise over how run-down the home of a free family of color was. "Four whole floors, Miss Bet. How very luxurious."

"No, Mary, it's not . . . that is to say . . . this is an apartment building. The family with whom you will be living occupies only one of the floors."

Plenty of the slaves in Richmond were housed over some work space or other, the way Zinnie and Josiah and the girls were quartered above the summer kitchen. But I'd never heard of a building four stories high, divided up floor by floor like that. Free Northerners living as crowded together as the hens in the Van Lew chickenhouse.

Miss Bet fished a calling card out of her reticule and handed it to the driver. "Please bring this up to Mrs. Octavia Upshaw."

A smirk danced across the cabman's wind-chapped face, but he took the card and disappeared inside the door. Within minutes a window on the third floor flew open, and a woman's voice chirped down to us.

"Why, Miss Van Lew, I'm a-waiting you up here. Don't be shy none, come on up." The gray-haired head slipped back inside, and the window slammed shut.

When the driver reappeared, Miss Bet instructed him about which baggage to bring upstairs. Then she led me inside, tilting her broad skirts this way and that to fit through the door and down the short hallway to the stairwell at the middle of the building. I'd spent countless hours up and down the servants' stairs of the Van Lew house, which were every bit as narrow and dark as these tight steps. But Miss Bet was unused to such confined spaces. She kept reaching her hand to the wall to right herself as we climbed.

"Come on dears, you almost here," Mrs. Upshaw called as we turned onto the final half-flight of steps. As we reached the landing, she held open the apartment door with one hand and urged us inside with a grand sweep of the other, nodding like a poppet-doll and chittering "Hello" and "Howdy do" all the while.

The tiny parlor was crowded with shabby furnishings playing at respectability. The upholstered chair and sofa were threadbare. Faded rag rugs of assorted sizes and shapes lined the floor. A motley collection of gaudy trinkets, many of which showed chips or cracks, cluttered the end table. On the mantel of the fireplace sat an ornate clock, its hands immobile at five minutes past twelve. In a corner by the window stood a ladies' worktable stacked high with a pile of folded fabrics and topped with needle case, scissor case, and pincushion—the sewing work Miss Bet had told me my landlady took in. Along the other side of the room, a small bed was made up for day use. And in the midst of it all was Mrs. Upshaw, proudly submitting to our inspection as she gushed her stream of welcome.

A small woman about Mistress Van Lew's age, she chatted constantly, never pausing for a response, until at last she disappeared to make us some tea. Once

Mrs. Upshaw was gone, Miss Bet wagged her fan back and forth so furiously, she seemed to be trying to flap her way right out of the wearisome room.

Miss Bet might be imperious, but at least she was familiar. Sitting in my stiff new clothes and listening to the thuds of the cabman hoisting my trunk up the stairway, the clop of footsteps in the apartment overhead, and the muffled noises Mrs. Upshaw was making at the back of the house, I missed my own world so. Part of me wanted to throw my arms around Miss Bet and beg her not to leave me.

But the idea of clinging to Miss Bet, of all people, was ridiculous. I held myself still until Mrs. Upshaw returned, then kept my eyes low as we drank down the weak tea.

"My cousins must be quite anxious for my arrival," Miss Bet said, the very moment the driver brought in my things. "Mary, I shall call for you in the morning to take you to Miss Douglass's school. I'm sure you and Mrs. Upshaw will have a nice time getting acquainted in the meanwhile." She nodded stiffly and followed the cabman out.

With Miss Bet gone, Mrs. Upshaw chattered more than ever. She wanted to put me at ease, I guess, but her prattling set me on edge. "Anything the matter, dear?" she asked finally.

Everything was the matter. But I forced myself to shake my head. "I'm just tired from the journey. May I see the rest of your lovely home?"

"Our lovely home. You gonna have a fine time living here." She gestured to the next room. "Here's where you sleep. The bed's real feather, you know."

I'd never slept on anything but a husk pallet. My heart leapt at the thought of having my own feather-bed. But it fell again when I entered the narrow, windowless room and saw the scuffed wood frame slung with a thin, lumpy mattress.

"Ain't that something?" Mrs. Upshaw spoke as though she were showing off the Queen of Sheba's own boudoir. "Have a try, dear. No being shy round here."

The mattress sagged badly on the bed ropes, making it difficult to sit upright. Perched on the edge of the bed frame, I could smell how musty the feathers were.

"Quite a luxury," my landlady said. "You believe I had that bed since I first married up with the late Mr. Upshaw?"

"Yes," I answered without thinking. "I mean, no." Not wanting to seem rude, I searched about for a distraction. A wardrobe occupied the narrow space between the bed and the side wall. Its doors had been removed from their hinges, because there was no room for them to swing open. Two worn dresses hung inside. "What are those?"

"Why, those is my Dulcey's things. Won't it be cozy for you girls, sharing this nice room? You never gonna get lonely with us."

Sharing a fusty bed with a stranger wasn't my idea of company, or comfort. I followed as Mrs. Upshaw led the way out of my new quarters into the third and final room of the apartment, an awkward space in which an ancient cookstove, a wobbly table ringed by an assortment of chairs, and a dented wash-basin made up the makeshift kitchen cum dining room. "My Dulcey be along soon. She works for a nice family up on Prune Street—that's over to Society Hill, you know. Why don't you refreshen yourself while I get up supper?"

She handed me the wash-basin and waved me through a low doorway to a rickety wooden stair on the back of the building. At the bottom of the steps I found a hydrant pump, from which I filled the basin. I splashed my face as best I could, nearly gagging at the stink from the rotting garbage piled around the tiny yard.

As I carried the emptied basin back up the stairs, I could hear Mrs. Upshaw's gibble-gabble overhead. Why, the woman don't stop talking even when she's alone, I thought. But then I made out another voice, low and bitter, answering her.

"I'm sorry you couldn't seen Miss Van Lew. She was some dignified."

"I see white people all day long. Nothing dignified about any of them when you got to wash their drawers. Or mend them, as you should know."

"No need to be nasty, Dulcey dear, we all wear drawers. Shouldn't be jealous of wealthy people, just 'cause they don't have to wash and mend their own things."

"Shouldn't worship them 'cause they don't, either."

"Why, I never said to worship anyone but the Good Lord. I'm just saying Miss Van Lew is very proper, and so is Mary. I'm sure we gonna benefit from sociating with her."

"Only benefit is the dollar a week the white lady paying you, which will go right to the butcher for ground meat that's all gristle, the grocer for bread that's already gone moldy, and the landlord for this rat-trap apartment, where I can't even get a moment's peace after working all day."

Mrs. Upshaw sighed. "We got to make a virtue out of necessity. We got the privilege to know a genuine schoolgirl, and her so far from home, only right to make her welcome."

"Don't worry, I'll make our Virginia pickaninny feel right at home."

Pickaninny. That was a word not even the Van Lews used. To hear the term called out by a negro and applied to me, that was past bearing. I was ready to turn round and run back down the stairs. But to where?

As I looked down at the walled-in yard, I could hear Papa's voice calling out, *My free young la-dy.* I was a free lady, no Mama and Papa to protect me. I told myself I had to show this Dulcey I was no pickaninny. I marched myself back inside, trying not to wonder whether my hands were shaking with rage or with fear.

Dulcey was civil, though barely so, to my face. All through supper and after, Mrs. Upshaw's prating kept either of us from needing to make much effort to speak. Dulcey muttered something about how tired she was and slunk off to the bedroom good and early. I retired an hour later, only to find her propped up in bed, arms crossed against her chest, glaring as I turned my back to her to remove my clothing and put on my nightdress. Only after I slipped under the covers did she speak.

"What that white lady want with you, bringing you up here? Trying to hide the family shame, no doubt."

"What family shame?"

"Her father's, maybe her brother's. Though dark as you are, seems like it'd be hard for anyone to tell. Still, if she needs to scurry you away, must be some family likeness."

Anger flushed warm across my face. "There is a likeness, to my papa. A colored man, married to my mama."

"Sure, honey, you go on insisting. But remember, no shame in it. Slavewomen got no choice about such things, and sometimes makes it easier for themselves, they pretend they want it, too."

I saw enough in Richmond to know how some white men molested slavewomen. I knew such women—girls even, some of them no older than I was already—were not to be blamed when white men took up with them. But still, I didn't want this Dulcey Upshaw, or anyone, thinking that of Mama. I didn't even want to think it of Old Master Van Lew or Young Master John.

"Miss Bet thinks slavery's wrong. She freed all her slaves. She wants me to have an education, so she brought me here."

"Freed all her slaves? Then where's your mama?"

I bit my lip. It was tempting to blurt out the whole story, but Mama and Papa had drilled me over and over about the need to keep our family's secret. "Mama agreed to stay with Miss Bet, in exchange for her taking me North and putting me through school. Later, I'll work up here so I can pay Miss Bet back, and then Mama can come North, too."

Dulcey snorted. "So she's holding your mama captive till then? What you need to pay her back for, anyway? And why you still calling her 'Miss Bet' like you down South?"

I opened my mouth but closed it again when I found nothing to say.

All my childhood, we in the house were allied in constant conspiracy against Miss Bet. I learned from watching Mama and the rest to smile and nod at her, but then roll eyes and mimic her words once her back was turned. Even after she announced our manumission, Miss Bet remained a force to be reckoned with, someone around whom Mama schemed and maneuvered. Now here I was in the North, and about the first thing I had to do was defend her, and to a colored woman.

I lay awake much of the night, listening to Dulcey's snores.

Come morning, I was so anxious to escape the Upshaws' apartment, I stood waiting at the curb long before Miss Bet appeared. No, not Miss Bet, just plain Bet, or so I willed myself to think of her, although I didn't dare say it to her face.

She arrived in her cousin's carriage. When the liveried driver stepped down to open the door for me,

I smiled at him, but he avoided meeting my eye. Stung at being snubbed by the first colored man I'd seen in the city, I reminded myself it was just his training, the same servants' deference I'd learned as a child. But glad as I was to be done with waiting on the Van Lews, still I didn't feel as though I'd crossed over and become the sort of person who got waited on instead.

As the carriage began to roll, Bet said, "Miss Douglass keeps school at her home on Arch Street, some blocks from here. I remember when it was called Mulberry Street, and I cannot understand why ever it was changed, as that is surely the nicer name."

Arch was at least easier to distinguish from the other streets we crossed. Pine. Spruce. Walnut. Chestnut. Whoever named these thoroughfares must have had quite a sense of humor, as I didn't see a tree on any of them. Just more rows of those indistinguishable brick facades, lining most every block. "How many people there must be in all these apartments."

Bet was quick to correct me. "They're not all apartments. This street is full of stores, and the next contains large homes. Still, there are a great many people here, three times as many as Richmond."

I tried to picture three of each of the Richmonders I knew—three Bets, three Mistress Van Lews, three Mamas, three Papas. As I wondered whether the tripling of people I liked would outweigh the tripling of those I didn't, the carriage stopped.

The Douglass house was a three-story brick building, not so grand as some, but decently kept up. When our driver rapped the heavy brass knocker, the broad door swung open to reveal a neatly dressed woman. Some twenty years older than Bet, she was tall and thin, her hair pulled back in a prim bun and spectacles on her nose. Her dark blue dress was unadorned by jewelry or fancy trim. She stood ramrod straight, her face so serious it seemed stern.

"You must be Miss Van Lew, and Mary," she said. "Right on time, I am glad to see. I am Sarah Mapps Douglass. Please come in."

She led us into a large room that took up most of the ground floor. Rows of small desks faced a low platform dominated by a larger desk. Along the walls were glass cabinets filled with books, globes, and mannikins of all manner of birds and animals.

Miss Douglass took her place behind the large desk and directed us to sit at the center of the front row. "The accommodations are somewhat limited, I realize. I hope you are not too uncomfortable, Miss Van Lew."

"Not at all." Bet squeezed herself into a student desk, her head tilted back to look up at Miss Douglass.

No colored woman I'd ever known could put a white woman into such a pose.

Miss Douglass peered at me through her glasses. "Our girls generally start at a much younger age, so you must expect to work very diligently to make up for lost time." I nodded solemnly. "Miss Van Lew has spoken highly of your abilities. What have you studied?"

"I can write and do figures, ma'am, and most anything I read or even hear I can remember word for word."

Instead of shining with encouragement, Miss Douglass's bespectacled eyes bore down harder. "The ability to read is only so valuable as the quality of what you read. And while the predisposition of a good memory will help you when it is time to recite your lessons, memorizing is not the same as true comprehension. Indeed, it may do you more harm than good if you are not trained to use it properly."

Now it was Bet's turn to nod. Miss Douglass promised to be a demanding teacher, and Bet was all for discipline, as long as she wasn't the one being subject to it. I began to wonder at my fortune of trading one such mistress for another, when a loud knock at the door announced the arrival of the other pupils.

Bet extricated herself from the desk. "Where shall I sit to observe the class?"

"I'm afraid that won't be possible. Some of the girls' families would object to a white person monitoring their children, however well intentioned."

In Richmond, there was no space to which a colored person, free or slave, could deny a white person entry, and no negro could lawfully refuse a white person's observation. Though she'd never admit to it, it was clear Bet hadn't considered that it might be otherwise in Philadelphia. As Miss Douglass extended her hand to bid Bet farewell, I ran my fingers along the edge of the wooden desktop, wondering if Bet would let me stay, now that she herself had been dismissed.

My former mistress took the colored woman's hand in her own. "I suppose you know best about such things. At what time shall I call for Mary?"

"It will not be necessary for you to call. Some of the other girls can walk Mary home. Good day."

Miss Douglass swung open the door. As Bet passed the cluster of girls waiting outside, they stared at her and then me, curiosity all over their faces.

Miss Douglass waited for the rest of the class to arrive and remove their bonnets, which they all did promptly—clearly, our schoolmistress brooked no dawdling—before introducing me. "As you see, we have a new student. She has just arrived in Philadelphia, and I expect you will all make her feel welcome. I present Miss Mary Van Lew."

All my life, I'd been Aunt Minnie's Mary or Lewis's Mary. I'd never had call for a last name, and I certainly wouldn't have taken Van Lew if I did. But Bet hadn't consulted me or Mama about such matters, hadn't imagined my wanting a name that tied me to my own family rather than to hers. And so I was Mary Van Lew to Miss Douglass, and now to all the girls around me.

I barely had time to swallow down my pinpricks of disappointment as Miss Douglass informed me that the students were seated according to their success with their lessons, with the first row reserved for the girls with the highest marks. "However, as I will need to monitor your work closely, you may remain in the front for this week." She turned to the lightest of her pupils, a strikingly pretty girl whose azure silk dress was adorned with gold buttons that matched the color of her fine, straight hair. "If everyone in Phillipa's column will move back one row, we can begin."

Phillipa swept forward to clear her things from the desk I was to occupy, and Miss Douglass rapped three times on her massive desktop and began calling on students to recite their Latin lessons.

I listened in amazement as one girl after another rose to speak. The youngest recited from their primers.

Older pupils recalled whole passages from memory. And the most advanced students presented their own translations from British literature into Latin. Once Miss Douglass corrected everyone to her satisfaction, she announced a new set of assignments.

As the rest of the girls began their work, she summoned me to her desk and handed me a primer, nodding toward the youngest girls in the room. "For now, you will recite with the beginner group. Only after you master the grammar will you advance with the girls your own age." She reviewed the first conjugation and sent me back to my desk to copy out my lesson.

I took my seat, my head swimming with the thought that I was truly in school. My excitement turned to consternation when I realized I'd left the supply of nibs Papa gave me at the Upshaws'. I looked up uncertainly and caught Miss Douglass's eye.

"Is something the matter, Mary?"

"I forgot my pens at home, Miss Douglass."

She pursed her lips and squinted in disapprobation. "Who can lend Mary a pen this morning?" I heard a rustle behind me. "Very well, Phillipa, thank you."

I swung round in my seat to take the pen, which Phillipa offered with a broad smile. "Just be careful with it. The nib may be a bit dull, so press down very firmly as you write."

I thanked her and turned back to my primer. I read over the words, hearing them as Miss Douglass had pronounced them. Closing my eyes to concentrate, I arranged letters in my mind, then opened my eyes and took up the pen. I dipped it into the inkwell affixed to the corner of the desk, and brought it down hard on the page. With the first stroke, the nib snapped off, ricocheting up from the page and landing in my lap. An inkstain a half-inch wide spread across my new skirt.

"A pen is a tool, not a toy," Miss Douglass said. She didn't offer a whiff of sympathy as she directed me to the washroom under the stairs. When I returned, she announced that henceforth I would have to use chalk and slate, as it appeared I hadn't mastered writing well enough to handle a nib.

I felt all the other girls' eyes on me as I took my seat. Remembering it was Phillipa's pen that I'd broken, I whispered, "I'm sorry, Phillipa. I'll give you another pen tomorrow."

"Oh, don't be sorry about that old thing." She smiled. "It was my pleasure to lend it."

I barely finished filling the slate with my assignment before Miss Douglass announced that it was time for the next subject. And so the class moved from language to literature to history. I was awestruck at all the other girls knew, all that I would have to make up. By the time my various classmates were reciting the various names of the various kings and queens of the various European nations, I'd given up trying to follow along. At last Miss Douglass announced it was time to recess for dinner. As the students stepped into the cloak-room to fetch their bonnets, she added, "I expect some of you girls to please walk Mary to her lodgings."

Outside, a small knot of girls surrounded me. "Where do you live?" one asked.

"On Gaskill Street."

"On Gaskill Street?" Phillipa repeated. "Don't you mean off Gaskill Street?" The girls about us giggled.

I wasn't sure what the difference was. "On, I guess. When we arrived yesterday, the hack driver announced 168 Gaskill Street."

Phillipa smoothed the ribbon of her bonnet against her golden hair. "The hack driver? Good thing your family hasn't a carriage, or you shouldn't know where you live at all." My classmates laughed even more loudly.

"Do colored families in Philadelphia keep carriages?" I asked.

"The better sort do, and the lesser sort is kept on them." Phillipa pointed to a rather elegant clarence passing by, with a negro driver seated at the front and a young negro boy, in brown and gray livery that matched the colors of the coach, standing upon a box at the back. "Now I wonder, which sort are you?"

A girl who had been standing outside the little group broke in. "That's enough, Phillipa. You go running home to your mama now. I'll show Mary her way."

This other girl was a year or two older than us, and the way she stood with her hands on her hips made her seem older still. One of her eyebrows arched higher than the other, making her appear serious, perhaps even a bit angry with whatever she regarded.

"But we're having such fun trying to make out Mary's queer little accent, aren't we? Besides, it will be so lovely to stroll down Gaskill Street, I haven't had reason to go there in ages."

Another round of titters broke out. But the older girl wasn't laughing. "I was just worried for your pale little nose," she said. "Your bonnet don't quite cover it, and the sun is rather strong today. I should think you wouldn't want to walk even a block farther than you need to, lest you darken up."

As Phillipa glanced up at the edge of her bonnet, the other girl leaned forward. "I know you played that pen trick on purpose, and if you don't let Mary be right now, I'll march back inside and tell Miss Douglass so."

"Hattie Jones, you are a prig, and always will be. Take her, then, and won't she be sorry never to have any fun, just like you."

Hattie watched to make sure Phillipa and the rest of the girls cleared the block before she turned to me. Then she smiled and stuck out her hand. "Mary Van Lew of Gaskill Street, I presume?"

"Hattie Jones, prig, I presume?" I took her hand in mine and grinned back at her.

"Don't pay Phillipa any mind. She gets positively feline, mousing after any new girl in class." She told me how she'd been the new girl, too, when her family moved from Baltimore years earlier.

I admitted that I didn't understand half of what Phillipa said, or at least not why the other girls thought it was funny. Hattie explained that though Gaskill Street was not so impressive as some of Philadelphia's grander thoroughfares, it was the alleys and the courts off streets like Gaskill where the poorest of the poor lived, a dozen people huddled into a one-room shack tacked up out of boards filched from warehouses along the waterfront. "Phillipa lives on Lombard Street, which her mama tells anyone who will listen is the very best row in all the city. Which does make a person wonder why most of the white families who lived there are moving all the way west to Rittenhouse Square, where they won't risk meeting up with Mrs. Thayer or her darling daughter any time soon."

Hattie squinted at a clocktower on the next block. "It's getting awfully late—are you expected at Gaskill Street for dinner?"

"I don't know," I said, thinking of Mrs. Upshaw hovering over me in her cramped apartment, "but I don't mind if I don't go."

"Good. My daddy's gone to Chambersburg on business, so I won't be missed at home. Miss Douglass told us to make you welcome in Philadelphia, which means I must introduce you to pepper pot."

She grabbed my hand and dragged me to a bustling market she called Head House Square. From over half a block away, we heard an old colored woman shouting, "Pepper pot! Smoking hot!" Hattie led me into an arcade filled with stalls, elbowing her way through the crowd surrounding the woman.

"How many?" was all the greeting the woman offered.

"Two, please." Hattie fished a few pennies from a purse tucked inside her skirt.

The woman dipped a jar into a large wooden tub of stew, from which a wonderfully scented steam was rising. She poured the contents of the jar into a bowl, plunked in a spoon, and passed it to me. After she did the same for Hattie, we retreated to a bench set against a nearby storefront.

I rushed to take my first mouthful of the Philadelphia delicacy—and nearly choked on it. "What's in here?" I sputtered.

"It varies day by day, but usually it's pepper, and tripe, and pepper, and ox feet, and pepper, and—"

"I've never had so much spice in all my life. Did Phillipa put you up to this?"

Hattie laughed. "Don't worry, you'll get used to the spice. My daddy always says pepper pot alone is reason enough to come to Philadelphia, though I suppose Phillipa would about croak if the thought of pepper pot so much as entered her head."

"How come she's so stuck up?"

"That's the way of the colored people here, at least those with the means to send their daughters to Miss Douglass's school."

I took a cautious spoonful of stew. "You aren't like that."

"You forget, I'm from Baltimore. Thanks to Maryland's preservation of the peculiar institution, colored folks there know how to look out for each other." Hattie had more piquancy than the pepper pot as she railed about how standoffish the dozen families who proclaimed themselves Philadelphia's better sort of colored people could be. "Even the ones who talk anti-slavery and equal rights for all negroes, why, they want you to know just the same they're not like all negroes themselves."

She lowered her voice to a conspiratorial whisper. "Even our dear teacher carries on that way, always saying her name as 'Sarah Mapps Douglass,' so you know who her uncle was, as well as her father. Her cousin does the same, 'David Bustill Bowser,' holding connection to the Bustill family, even though his mother married a man without a nickel to his name or an ounce of standing in colored Philadelphia society. My daddy always says, nothing's more trouble than a three-name negro—except any two-name white man."

Hattie carped on about the elaborate family trees of colored Philadelphia, Bustills and Douglasses, Fortens and Purvises. The revelation that there were negro families who could trace their genealogies to way back before the War of Independence, just like the FFVs, flabbergasted me.

"Are all the girls in Phillipa's set descended from Revolutionary War heroes?" I asked.

"Heroes, hunh. Profiteers and toadies more like—Cyrus Bustill made his coin selling bread to

Washington's troops, and James Forten was a powder boy for a privateer during the War, earned his money later by shimmying up ship masts to repair the sails. Phillipa's own grandpappy wasn't any more than a waiter in a rooming house, till the cook took sick one day and he stepped up to the stove. Now her father proclaims he's got the oldest catering house in the city, bragging how white people throw money at him to make their parties go just so."

I could tell from Hattie's tone she didn't mean for me to be impressed by those families, but I couldn't help myself. "To think colored folks can be so rich."

"Rich isn't always the case—most of those families don't have a tenth of the wealth they pretend they've got. You think Miss Douglass teaches school out of the goodness of her heart?" She kicked a cigar stub someone had tossed on the sidewalk, sending it tumbling into the street. "How are you enjoying our colored girls' academy?"

"Seems like Latin and all that will be fun, like knowing a secret cipher. But history was awful dull. I never thought about any of that stuff, and I don't know why I should start now."

"History's not so bad, once you get past who's who and start learning what they did to each other. Those whites can be as nasty to one another as they are to us, if they're kings and queens and whatnot." She paused to spoon up the last of her stew. "Maybe you'll like the afternoon lessons better—though mathematics and the sciences make my head ache. We best hurry, or Miss Douglass will have our hides." Leaving our empty bowls in the pepper pot vendor's pile, we headed back to Arch Street.

Five

My dearest Mama & Papa

I am fairly bursting with news I almost cannot write fast enough to tell it. After we recited our lessons today Miss Douglass assigned us new places. Guess what? I moved up two whole rows! Miss Bet got herself so pleased when I told her she even gave me extra toward my pin money as a model of the rewards for hard work. I did not contradict her of course but studying my lessons is not nearly so much hard work as waiting on her & her family & cleaning their things.

The truly hard part is finding a place to study. Mrs Upshaw does like to chat at a person & Mama you understand that a person cannot read very well

*if someone is chatting at her the whole time. Also if
I leave my books out Dulcey or Ducky as I think of
her the way she quacks & quacks at me she scatters
them every which way around the apartment &
I have to hunt them up. Sometimes she tries to hide
that she has gone through my things but she leaves
my written pages in all the wrong order so I must
lock everything in my trunk the very moment I am
done with my studies.*

*Another thing I am studying in my own way is
Philadelphia. Where do they keep the negroes
I wonder every time I am out. So few colored faces
compared to Richmond. Hattie has been living
here so long she must have forgot the South because
all she can say is Philadelphia has more colored
people than any other city in the North. Maybe so
but more is not near enough by my count.*

You are ever loved & missed by
Your devoted daughter
Mary El

Writing home was all the comfort I had, yet never
comfort enough for all the ways I missed my parents. Even the things that nettled me all through my
childhood—how Mama's muttering in her sleep would

wake me some nights or the way Papa's Sunday shirt itched me when he hugged me tight each week—now were things I longed for. Whether I scribbled my missives out fast or took my time crafting every curve of every letter of every word, still they couldn't seem to say near what I would share with Mama if I could talk to her first thing when I woke up and last when I went to bed, like I always had. Looking down at those pages before I sealed them and sent them made me all the sadder, realizing how impossible it was to lay out in writing everything I was doing and thinking and feeling, when Mama and Papa never had the chance to do or think or maybe even feel anything quite like it themselves.

When it was originally decided I'd go North to be educated, everyone talked about the fine opportunity I'd have. But I was more fretful than grateful those first weeks of my formal schooling. Reciting was hard for me. I couldn't forget that long ago morning on the Van Lews' veranda, how my gut wrenched up over Mistress Van Lew's threat to send me to the whipping post. Nobody could try that now that I was free, but standing up before the whole class, I stumbled over more than a few things I could say perfectly well when no one was around to hear. Phillipa caught me one afternoon on the way out of class, saying how she hoped I liked the view from the back row, seeing as it seemed I'd be there permanently. That set me seething and simmering. The next time I stood to recite, I said each word perfectly just to show her I could. After I finished, Miss Douglass beamed and Phillipa scowled. The smile and the frown, they urged me on, and I made sure to recite loud, clear, and steady after that.

Once I got over my nervousness, I discovered what a joy it was to be in school, even if I lagged behind in most subjects. Like when you think you're not all that hungry but you sit down to a real fine meal and suddenly you realize you were ravenous after all. Though Phillipa called me Polly, saying I was no more than a poll-parrot repeating back what I read or heard, I was too eager to pay her much mind. I asked Miss Douglass for extra assignments to take home so I could catch up with the girls my age, and our teacher nodded her prim approval. That was as much fanfare as she ever seemed to offer, and I relished it.

Even more than that, I relished Hattie's friendship. Right from my first week in Philadelphia, Bet set up an allowance for me on account with her cousin's husband, who was an attorney. She made it clear he was to give me pin money aplenty, even after she finished visiting with her relations and returned to Richmond. It was generous of her, I suppose, but it was Hattie who gave what to me was real riches: companionship. Hattie walked me home from school each day and was waiting at the curb to accompany me back the next morning. Later, when Miss Douglass taught us about Lewis and Clark and how Sacajawea—a colored woman, she reminded us proudly, though not African—had guided them and interpreted for them, it made me think back to those first few months when Hattie was the Sacajawea of my Philadelphia life.

We'd promenade through the city, and she'd point out this or I'd ask after that, the two of us making up all manner of stories for what we saw and laughing over any nonsense that came into our heads.

"Miss Hattie Jones, prig, whatever is a humidor?" I'd ask, pointing at the sign on a tobacconist's shop.

"Well, Miss Mary Van Lew of Gaskill Street, the better sort of colored Philadelphia worry that this heat will frizz their hair and make them look quite negro. This good gentleman secures them in his humidor until such time as the weather cools."

"Why, I believe I see Phillipa's parasol in his umbrella stand."

It sure was humid. Summertime in Richmond, Lilly was out at dawn on laundry days, stirring the Van Lews' clothes and linens in vats of boiling water before the day grew to its hottest. In Philadelphia, the air felt just as steamy as if you were standing over a row of laundry pots at mid-day. Heat radiated off the brick buildings and cobblestone streets, which stayed warm to the touch even after sundown.

"Hattie, I don't think I can make it so far as Head House Square today," I said during one sweltering recess. "It's too hot for pepper pot anyway."

She smiled slyly. "Then let's get some ice cream instead."

The only ice cream I ever had was what Zinnie snuck off from what she made up for the Van Lews. And given how wild her Daisy was for ice cream, there was never much left to slip to me. I fairly skipped as Hattie steered me down Arch Street.

We stopped before a low building midway along the third block. It was built right up against the stores on either side, no way to get around to the back. "Where's our door?" I asked.

"That's it, silly. Right in front of your nose."

"We go in that way?"

"We go in, we sit down, we eat our ice cream. Ain't they got ice cream in Virginia? What's all that Dolley Madisoning about down there, and no ice cream parlors?"

I explained that in Richmond, negroes calling at the confectioner went round to the rear of the building, where they'd buy a dish to carry away. Papa had never even tasted ice cream, because he refused to be served so.

"Now you're in Philadelphia, you can come right on in the front door." Hattie led me inside, looking as proud as if she'd invented ice cream parlors herself.

She ordered vanilla, though I couldn't imagine why she overlooked strawberry. Bland as Mrs. Upshaw's cooking was, I couldn't order something as plain as vanilla once that man told us they had strawberry, too.

"This ice cream has positively restored my delicate constitution," I announced as my spoon hit the bottom of the parfait glass.

"Pleased to be of service," Hattie answered. "My daddy always says I'm practically made of ice cream, I eat so much of it all summer."

By now, I'd heard *my daddy says* so many times from Hattie, it seemed I practically knew the man myself. Which always made me wonder why I never heard about her mother. "And what does your mama say?" I asked.

Her faced turned to stone. "Nothing. She's dead."

Dead—that's just the way she said it, not *passed on* or *gone to Glory* like most folks did. The hardness of the word sank right down past all that ice cream to the pit of my stomach, the way a rock tossed off the wharf would sink deep into the James River. Not the James, I reminded myself, you're not in Richmond anymore. Ought to say the Delaware instead.

"I'm sorry, Hattie, I didn't realize."

"Well, now you know." She pushed her empty dish to the center of our table and stared at the wall above my shoulder.

Death was something I hadn't thought much about. Folks we knew from prayer meeting passed away from time to time, but I'd never condoled the mourners much, child that I was. Now I wasn't supposed to be a child anymore, and I struggled for something to say.

I remembered how after Old Master Van Lew died, Bet wove locks of his hair into a braid and wore it as a mourning bracelet. "Did you keep anything of your mama's, after she passed?"

Hattie nodded. Reaching into her purse pocket, she pulled out a worn patch of pale green poplin, patterned with forest green flowers. The middle of the swatch was just about worn away from where her fingers had rubbed at it.

"It was my favorite of all her dresses. When Daddy told us each to pick something of hers, this was all I wanted, a piece I could carry with me wherever I go. Charlotte, my oldest sister, had a fit. She wanted the whole dress for wearing herself, but Daddy said no,

I was youngest and got to pick first. He cut the piece right then, handed it to me with a kiss." She blinked her eyes and frowned. "I can remember the cut of the dress, the way it swished around when she moved, like I saw her in it an hour ago. But I can't remember a thing about my mother besides that. Try to call up her face, I just get the daguerreotype they took after she died, which everyone says doesn't resemble her at all."

My mind struggled for images of Mama and Papa, Josiah and Zinnie and the girls, Old Sam, too. I didn't want to believe you could lose people like that, right out of your memory.

Hattie ran her thumb over the scrap of cloth. "The thing I most wish I remembered was her voice. She had a song she used to sing to me and my sisters, 'Walk Together Children.' Daddy sings it sometimes now, but it's not the same."

"What does your daddy say she sounded like?" I asked.

"Like me."

I ventured out my hand to pat hers, even offered a half smile, the kind you can pull back down in case it isn't met warmly. I saw her chest rise up and fall, one deep breath, and got the same half smile back from her.

As we strolled back toward school, arms linked liked always, I confided, "When Old Master Van Lew died, we were all supposed to go in and pay our respects, but I hid out in the smokehouse I was so scared."

"My daddy always says we can do more harm to the dead than they can do to us."

I looked at her sideways. "He some kind of Voudoun master?"

"No, silly, he's an undertaker. I was thinking of inviting you over for dinner this Sunday, but if you're so frightened of dead folks . . ."

The idea of visiting the undertaker's ran chills up and down my spine, even in the mid-day heat. But I said, "Of course I'm not."

"Good. Come by about one o'clock. My sisters will all be there with their husbands, and a load of nieces and nephews. We'll outnumber the spirits for sure, just in case you take fright."

The shoes Bet outfitted me with before I left Virginia weren't at all the fashion in Philadelphia. I noticed it myself, but when Phillipa made a comment about "certain people who drag their skirts through the streets, one can only presume to hide their most unfortunate footgear," I counted over the coins I'd carefully accumulated from my allowance, eagerly anticipating the purchase of a fine new pair to wear to meet Hattie's family.

A small wooden sign proclaiming MUELLER AND SONS, SHOEMAKERS hung from the second floor of a building on the Upshaws' block of Gaskill Street. Though Mama and Old Sam often sent me to the cobbler in Shockoe Bottom on errands for the Van Lews, I was befuddled by what I found when I pushed open the Muellers' door that Saturday. It took a few moments for my eyes to adjust to the dim interior, and when they did, I saw about the oddest sight I'd ever seen.

There sat an older man and woman, four younger men, and two girls. They were all sewing shoes, even the females. Stranger still, they were sewing eight identical shoes. And only sewing the leather tops of the shoes together. In the corner of the room rose a high pile of these bottomless wonders, not a sole on any of them.

The older man nodded toward me and spoke to one of the girls in a guttural language. She set down her work and asked, "Have you business here?"

"Yes," I said. "I need new shoes."

"We do not take one order." She seemed to grope for words. "No order from just one person."

"But I am only one person, and I want to buy one pair of shoes."

She looked at me as if I'd asked for a pound of butter or a carriage wheel. "We do not sell. The jobber brings pieces, and we sew." She gestured at the pile in the corner. "Then he brings to the Schmidts to put on soles. Then takes to the stores on Chestnut Street. You go there to buy."

"How does the store know which kind I want, and what size I need?"

She shrugged. "They have every kind. Pick what you like."

Her father called to her in their strange language, motioning her to return to work. I thanked the girl and left.

As I walked toward Chestnut Street, I thought about how Bet always insisted the North was more advanced than the South. I couldn't fathom what was so superior about having someone called a jobber drag pairs of half-finished shoes all over town, with no idea whether anybody even wanted to buy that size or style.

When I reached Chestnut, I walked up and down several blocks, eyeing the elegantly dressed white ladies who disappeared into the various storefronts. A five-story building, bigger than any I'd ever seen in Richmond and proclaiming itself BARNES AND CHARLES, PURVEYORS OF LADIES' AND GENTLEMEN'S WARDROBE, BOOTS TO BONNETS seemed especially popular.

Stepping through the grand doorway, I found myself in a large salon, some forty feet across. Behind long counters on either side, clerks were selling a variety of wares for ladies. Rich carpet covered the floor, and way above my head protruded galleries of counters filled with gentlemen's goods. In the middle of the salon stood a waist-high mahogany stall, topped with marble. When I told the woman inside the stall that I was in need of new shoes, she directed me to the far end of the room.

Mama always lowered her eyes and waited for all the white people to be served before she stepped up to the counter in a Richmond store. Even little children or people who came in long after her would push right by without a thought on their part or a complaint on hers. But when I stood before the counter that day, marveling at the rows and rows of shoes along the wall, the clerk smiled right at me in turn and asked what I would like.

I had just the shoes I wanted in mind, a half boot in light beige kid, something I could wear right through autumn. But before my mouth could explain all that to the clerk, my hand was pointing to a pair of silk slippers. They were pale yellow, with deep blue rosettes on the toes and a trail of glass beads around the tops.

I knew such shoes were not made for traipsing all over Philadelphia with Hattie. But I also knew they were the most beautiful shoes I'd ever seen, prettier than any Bet or her mother ever wore. Just looking at those slippers, I forgot all about kid and boot and sturdy walking heels.

When the clerk laid a pair in my size on the counter, I understood for the very first time how Papa must have felt when he bought a just-because. The things Bet gave me were nice enough, and it seemed like I had a rich wardrobe compared to Ducky and Mrs. Upshaw. But these shoes were more than rich and pretty. They were the very first things I ever bought myself, picked out just because they pleased me and paid from my own purse, albeit with funds Bet had pressed on me.

I decided to celebrate my purchase by riding the omnibus down Chestnut Street. These large, horse-drawn contraptions filled with rows of seats fascinated me. I supposed them terribly expensive, as Hattie never suggested we take them, even when I hinted about the dreadful heat on our long walks home from school. But emboldened by my successful shopping adventure, I was all too eager to spend a bit more of Bet's money, for the fun of such a ride.

I walked two full blocks in the opposite direction to ensure I'd have a goodly length omnibus trip back to Fourth Street. A stout white man paced back and forth along the corner, pausing every few minutes to pull out his watch, mutter to himself, and shake his head. When the omnibus arrived, he waved it to a stop, stepped on, and paid his fare. Smiling, I stepped up behind him and offered the collector my money.

"Step down, please," the collector said.

"But I have the fare." I jingled the coins in my hand.

"You cannot ride this conveyance. Please step down."

As I glanced about the half-full car, the man who had just boarded caught sight of me. He turned red as a beet and shouted at the conductor, "Some of us are in a great hurry. If you won't throw the nigger off, my Jesus, I will."

The fare collector moved toward me. As I backed away, my heel snagged on the step. The driver whipped the horses forward, sending me stumbling to the ground. Passengers looked out through the windows as the omnibus pulled past, some glaring and some pitying. People walking by stopped to point and whisper.

I ducked into a narrow passageway between two buildings. Shame shook my legs so, I had to lean against one of the walls, the heat from the bricks seeping through my dress.

The stout man's words echoed in my head, *nigger* and *Jesus* both falling from his mouth. *Nigger* made me think of Virginia. I wondered how a place so different as brotherly love Philadelphia could make me feel the same—worse even—than that Old Dominion of slave-holding. And *Jesus* made me think of Mama. I missed her so. Missed her when Philadelphia was a source of wonder and delight, but especially when it caught me in its strangeness, its loneliness, or its downright meanness. Mama would know how to turn from that man to the Jesus whose name he took in vain.

"Do You really have a plan for me?" I spoke aloud, in a low voice, talking to Jesus just like Mama would. "Walking on cobbled streets while whites ride in an omnibus, buying shoes at a clothier's store rather than from a shoemaker—what's all that got to do with my being special, like Mama and Papa and even Bet say I am?"

Back when Mistress Van Lew got it into her head to have the whole household vaccinated against small-pox, Mama asked Jesus whether she and I should take the shots. The very next day, a whole brood of shad making their way down the James River ended up in the Westham canal just above Richmond. No one could guess how the fish got there, and they died by the hundreds, trapped in the basin. Mama took this as a certain answer that we should receive the vaccination. When I asked how she knew that was what those belly-up shad were supposed to mean, she told me it was between her and Jesus, and people too young to read His signs shouldn't be bothering grown-ups with so many pesky questions.

Now I searched for some sign I could read myself. To my left, people and carriages hurried purposeful as ever along Chestnut Street. To my right, the passageway was darker. I walked in that direction until it widened into an alley ten feet across.

Though bright sunshine lit the boulevard, the alley lay in shadow. A dozen or so shacks hewn of shabby wooden boards crowded together, doors open to the stink from the lone outhouse that served the mass of inhabitants. Two goats and a handful of chickens added to the noise and mess. A mob of children—mostly white, though I made out a few mulatto and black faces among them—played in the muck between their makeshift homes.

One tow-headed child scrambled over and pulled on my skirts. Its face was so dirty and its clothing so tattered I couldn't tell if it was a girl or a boy, even as it asked, "Spare something?"

I still held the unused omnibus fare. The coins seemed to burn with all my mortification at being cast from the public conveyance, and I gladly dropped them into the grimy hand.

The creature let out a whoop. Instantly, the other children swarmed around me. They tugged and yanked and pleaded so, I fished the rest of the coins from my purse and pitched them as far back in the alley as I could. While the ragamuffins scrambled after the money, I fled back the way I came.

I emerged into the bright light and bustle of Chestnut Street and began the hot walk back to Gaskill, the smells of the alley still clinging to my mangled skirts.

When I found my way to Hattie's father's lot on Sixth Street the next morning, I was reassured to see that the undertaking business was in a separate building, set between a small stable and the brick residence. The house hummed with voices. Hattie had five sisters, every sister had a husband, and most had children as well. "Daddy always says, easiest to meet everyone in order," she said as she led me upstairs to introduce me to her father. "Start at the oldest and work on down."

Alexander Jones rose from the horsehair armchair in the front parlor, where he was debating with his many sons-in-law, to extend his hand in greeting. Hattie took after her father so strongly, I felt like his face was already familiar. The air of scrutiny suggested by Hattie's raised eyebrow seemed even more forceful when coupled with his gray hair and deep voice. I would have thought he doubted my very being, save for the warm words with which he welcomed me.

Hattie's sisters were scattered about, preparing the meal and tending their various broods, so there was much tramping through the house to find them in order, with Hattie returning me to the parlor to introduce each husband just after I met his wife. That did help me keep everyone's names in order. Charlotte, Diana, Emily, Fanny, and Gertie all looked alike, none of them resembling Hattie or their father a whit. They were all quite beautiful—I felt like I was a traitor to Hattie to notice that—and their husbands were all fine-looking gentlemen. This was a source of especial pride to Gertie, whose husband was the handsomest of the lot.

"Mary Van Lew, the youngest of my elder sisters, Gertie Overton." Hattie's introduction made her sister frown.

"Mrs. John Overton," she corrected. "My baby sister ought to know the proper way to introduce a married lady."

I always thought my older friend so world-wise. Hearing her own sister call her a baby, I couldn't imagine what Gertie might make of me. Diana laughed and said, "Please excuse Mrs. John Overton. She's only been married three months and remains quite taken with her newly elevated station."

"And quite convinced it's suddenly made her much more mature than a certain person who used to be her playmate not so long ago," Hattie said.

"Hattie, a child in your state simply cannot understand how matrimony transforms a lady. And Diana, well, you've been married for ages, and have forgotten it all, I am sure." Gertie turned back to chopping parsnips with such a pout that Hattie consoled her by suggesting she come up to the parlor to introduce me to the handsome Mr. John Overton herself.

Once all the introductions were done, I had a proper tour of the house, nine whole rooms in all. The bottom floor contained the dining room, the kitchen, and a washroom complete with a running-water bath tub. Not even the Van Lews had such a thing. "We got the yellow fever to thank for that," Charlotte explained. "Hit Philadelphia so hard, the civic high-a-mucks put in a city-wide water system back when other places didn't even imagine it could be done." The middle story contained the front and back parlors, and a door Hattie didn't open for me, which led to her father's bedroom. And the top floor was all Hattie's.

I was amazed. "I've never so much as had my own room, and you've got three."

"These three held six of us, once. Then five, then four, then three—that's when we each had our own room for the first time. Then for the longest while there were still two of us, till Gertie abandoned me for Mr. John Overton."

Small wooden boxes, all different sizes but none bigger than nine inches per side, were placed all over Hattie's rooms. I picked one up from the dressing table. "What are these?"

"My daddy's scraps."

"Scraps?"

"From the coffins." I hastily put the box back down. Hattie smiled. "Don't worry, I don't keep any teeny-tiny dead folks stored away. Go on, open it."

I drew off the lid. Inside was a small scene, constructed out of moss and seashells and dried flower petals. I lifted the cover from another box, and another. One scene was made up of pebbles and pinecones, another of honeycombs and robin's eggs. Each was beautiful.

"Where do these come from? I've never seen anything like them."

"I made them."

"All of them?"

"Oh yes. Daddy always says every young lady needs a talent. Charlotte is the best voice in our church. Diana is brilliant on the pianoforte. Emily draws, Fanny paints, Gertie crochets. There wasn't hardly anything left by the time I came along, so I sort of made this up myself. Gathering materials gave me my first excuse to explore the city."

I'd hardly looked into a quarter of the pine boxes before a bell rang, calling us to dinner. The meal was worth coming for, too. Whoever said too many cooks spoil the soup ought to sample a meal prepared by a kitchenful of Hattie's sisters. And the conversation across the dinner table was even more savorous. Whenever I sat through Mrs. Upshaw's mealtime prattle, accompanied by Ducky's grunts of discontent, I longed to eat in silence. But really I missed the mealtime gossiping of the Van Lew slaves, or the teasing and conferring when Mama and Papa took meals together. At Hattie's, the conversation was more serious, but every bit as enthralling. The menfolk chewed over every political issue of the day, and the sisters chimed in just as adamantly, when they weren't called from the table to tend the howls of the children, who'd already been fed their porridges.

I didn't follow much of what was said, the names of white politicians and colored ministers all running together in my mind, until Mr. Jones turned his attention to me. "Tell us, what do you miss about Virginia?"

Gertie cut in before I could respond. "What's there to miss about slavery?"

"I do believe I asked about Virginia, and not about slavery. And I believe I asked Mary, and not anyone else." Mr. Jones kept his eyes on me.

I set my fork and knife down, to show I was giving his question my full consideration. "I miss my mama and my papa, very much. Lots of other people, too. And the food." I blushed a moment, looking at Hattie's sisters. "Not that this meal isn't delicious, but in Richmond, every meal I ate was this good, even if the food wasn't so fancy. I miss living on the Hill, smelling the flowers and fruit in the garden and looking out to see the James and all the trees across the other side of the river. I miss walking right on the earth instead of pavement, and having space between the buildings. I miss the soft way people speak."

I hadn't even thought some of those things to myself, and here I was saying them out loud to folks I just met. "I miss an awful lot, I guess."

Gertie sniffed. "I don't hear anyone saying they miss slavery."

"Who could miss slavery? Only, at least in Richmond slavery's the reason for why we're treated so bad. What's the reason here? Just pure hate is all I can figure. And in Richmond, I knew all the rules. But here, each time I want to try something new, I don't know whether I'll be allowed."

Mr. Jones's imperious eyebrow shot up a little farther, and he nodded at me to say more.

I hadn't meant to tell them what happened with the omnibus, but the next thing I knew, the story was spilling out of me.

"Some of the conductors will wink and let you stay," Charlotte said quietly. "But those aren't the kind of men you want to be beholden to, if you know what I mean." Her husband swallowed hard at the thought.

"Sometimes when an omnibus passes by, I imagine the horses rearing up and tossing the car over, smashing everyone on board," Hattie said.

Emily, the most delicate of the sisters, frowned. "Hattie, don't talk so."

"Might as well talk that way, if I think that way."

"Better not to do either," Mr. Jones said. "If we wallow around hating, we're not going to end up any better off. I always say, if negroes mean to be treated differently, we must organize and act rather than just fume and hate."

I expected Hattie to resent the reprimand, but instead she beamed at her daddy as he launched into more talk about which politicians opposed the Fugitive Slave Act, and which were for returning the franchise to colored men. I hadn't realized negroes could ever cast a ballot, until he explained how they lost their voting rights in Pennsylvania only a decade before.

Above Mr. Jones hung a painting of an eagle, its wings outstretched and its talons clutching a stars-and-stripes emblazoned shield. He nearly resembled that proud bird, he seemed so serious, even formidable. Not a bit like Papa, who teased and funned us through our hardships. Mr. Jones gave the impression he didn't have time for joviality, he was so busy planning for the rights of the colored people. Papa couldn't do any more than joke, when all his planning hit up against the brick-and-mortar fact that he was the property of another man. I wondered what Papa would be like, Mama, too, if they'd grown up free like Hattie's daddy.

But free didn't mean all we'd imagined back in Virginia. That was clear from how my story about the omnibus started everyone commenting on the various injustices colored people faced in Philadelphia. Higher rents, fewer jobs, being turned out of a store or chased down an alley. Mobs gathering from time to time, to harass negroes right out of their own homes.

The way Hattie's family talked, I could tell they'd learned to live with these things, just the way my family lived with the Van Lews and Master Mahon, avoiding what they could, comforting each other over what they couldn't. It was better than slavery, I could see that from looking around a home crowded with a whole big family gathered together. But still it wasn't what freedom ought to be.

As soon as the dinner things were cleared, Mr. Jones eased himself from the table and consulted his pocket watch. "I must go to the shop. I am expecting a delivery from Chambersburg, which I must take to Bucks County."

Hattie's arched eyebrow curled down in disappointment. "But, Daddy," she said. "It's Sunday. And I—we—have a guest."

"And this body has a family, waiting for it to arrive." He smiled at me. "This business isn't like the Philadelphia and Columbia Railroad, where they schedule regular arrivals and departures. I always say—"

Diana finished for him, "when the wind blows from the South, nothing you say or do can stop it."

"And if you face it and spit," Fanny added, "you're just gonna end up covered with your own slobber."

We all laughed at that, even Hattie. I thought it a grand joke, though it'd be years before I understood what they were saying.

Bet remained in Philadelphia for a month and a half, visiting with relatives. Before returning to Richmond, she took care to entrust her cousin-in-law attorney with a copy of my free papers, the originals of which I carried with me at all times. Though Bet wouldn't say it herself, we both knew that if I were accosted by someone claiming me as an escaped slave, my own testimony and papers held in my possession would mean nothing in a courtroom without a white person's word of guarantee. Every so often during my time in Philadelphia, there'd be a big ruckus about some free negro seized by slave-catchers. I always wondered how many were taken quietly, folks who were free but had no white person to raise a fuss for them.

As Bet and I rode home from meeting with the attorney, she told me about the farewell supper her great-aunt was hosting for her the next evening.

"I have spoken so highly of your promise as a scholar, I am sure they are all eager to meet you. The gathering will be a very intimate affair, only family and a few close friends, so it will give everyone a great chance to know you."

Though I couldn't refuse the invitation, I didn't relish the idea of being the only colored person among a crowd of whites. Or not the only colored person, I corrected myself, the only colored person besides the servants—even worse. I dawdled all the way home from school the following afternoon, and when I arrived at the Upshaws', the carriage was already at the curb. Bet was pacing the walk, red-faced.

"I apologize for keeping you waiting, Miss Bet. I didn't expect you for half an hour yet."

She waved away my words. "It is I who must apologize to you. There has been a great misunderstanding. No, not a misunderstanding, a mistake. You see, I was mistaken to assume, to believe, that you, or rather I should say that I, or that Great-aunt Priscilla—"

"She won't have me in her home."

I think I was as surprised as Bet at the way I broke in on her. Such outspokenness would have earned me a reprimand or worse, back in Virginia. But now it brought some relief to Bet's agitated face.

"I'm so sorry, Mary. It never occurred to me that my family here would harbor such race prejudice, as bad as our neighbors on Church Hill. When Great-aunt Priscilla declared that she would cancel the supper before she would invite a negro into her home, I told her to do just that. I could not be guest of honor at such a gathering."

We in the house always fixed Bet as fractious, a spoiled child who'd grown into a woman without the respect or decorum to obey either her mother or social conventions. Part of me wanted to think only of how thoughtless she was to invite me before consulting her great-aunt, how inconsiderate she was to detail the old woman's antipathy toward me.

But another part of me made out a side of Bet I never much thought about until then. She seemed truly chagrined by her relation's actions, genuinely hurt that anyone she cared about could treat me so. Without the commiserating roll of Mama's eyes or cluck of Zinnie's tongue, I found myself on a new footing with my former mistress.

"You're upset just now because race prejudice has inconvenienced you. But it's worse than an inconvenience to us negroes, every single day." Making Bet understand me seemed important in a way it never did before. "I appreciate you saying how wrong it is for even your own family to carry on so. You see what other whites won't, that we're just as good as anybody, if white people will let us be."

She looked hard at me. "Why, Mary, that is quite a little speech. Six weeks in a free state has already turned your head." I feared I'd been too bold until she added, "If you continue at this rate, before the year is out you will be even more outspoken than I."

It was Mama's outspokenness, not Bet's, that inspired me. But there was no need to tell her that.

She reached into the carriage, extracted a small package wrapped in brightly colored paper, and handed it to me. I pulled at the cord and the paper fell away, revealing a small book.

"Benjamin Franklin's *Memoirs*," she said. "Mother gave this very copy to Father for their first wedding anniversary, and Father gave it to me when I left Richmond to come here for school. Franklin was a remarkable man, a great model of what you can achieve through diligence and intelligence."

I'd dusted the Van Lew library often enough to know the book occupied a place of prominence there. Mistress Van Lew would be sore as could be when she learned how Bet disposed of it. That alone made me treasure the gift.

"Thank you, Miss Bet." I fingered the well-handled leather. "Please tell Mama that I miss her and Papa, but I'm pleased and grateful for all you've done for me."

"You're quite welcome. I shall let Aunt Minnie know that you are well established, and that we should all expect the very finest accomplishments from you."

My dearest Mama & Papa

My highest mark today was in Latin which is a foreign language just like French which Miss Bet speaks. Only it is different than French because they speak French in France every day & Latin was from a long time ago in Rome which was one little city that took over lots & lots of other countries. As though Richmond took over the whole United States & Mexico & Cuba too. Those Romans did lots that was admirable building fine roads & temples which is what they called churches & writing long long histories of themselves & whatnot but I cannot admire them too much on account of they had slaves. Miss Douglass gets a sour face if anyone mentions that in class. But still I like learning Latin because it is fun to be able to say the same sentence in a whole new way & know some folks cannot understand. Sometimes Hattie & I speak Latin when we walk around town just to keep secrets. I wish we in the house had all known some other language so we could have said what we thought without the Van Lews knowing.

Hattie sends her regards as always. Her family is very kind to me. Her daddy always says that with six daughters of his own one more young lady in the house cannot amount to too much more trouble. Of course I try not to be trouble at all! They have me over every Sunday for dinner sometimes I go to Church with them first. The Church is a special kind called African Methodist Episcopal that colored folks came up with just for themselves.

That name sure is a mouthful so most folks here just call it Mother Bethel. Everyone there is real nice but it is so big! Even Hattie does not know everyone there are so many. Some weeks the thought of going to that huge building filled with strangers makes me miss our little prayer meeting so much I just rather walk down to look at the Delaware by myself. I imagine how its water might maybe flow out to the Ocean & meet up with water from the James.

Just like that water flows so flows my love to you both. Does that sound poetic? We are reading some poems by Mr. Edmund Spenser & Mr. John Donne in school & it makes a person think of all sorts of extremely poetical ways to say things. But when you get right down to it all I really need to say is I love & miss you both.

I hope you are proud of
Your devoted daughter
Mary El

Post-script. I am enclosing my marks from Miss Douglass. As you see she writes in a very very proper hand. Some of the girls say she is so methodical she hates the waste of having to raise her pen to dot an i or cross a t. That sounds disrespectful maybe but really we all respect her plenty I assure you.

My dear Mary El

Your letter arrived Today making us very prowd indeed. I showed Miss Bet your Marks & she wanted to ~~payspaste~~ the sheet into her Scrapbook. You know how she is with her Scrapbook she aint happy till she has the World closed up in there. I pretended I hadnt showed the Marks to your Papa yet just to get them away from her. Course I showed them to him befor her & he had his hart set on tacking them up rite on the wall of our Cabin wich is what he did. Not so fancy as all the ~~pictyers~~paintings the Van Lews have on there walls but it means more to Us then every oil painting in Richmond. Your Papa will show that paper to all the World if I dont remind him we need to keep this bisness Private.

Zinnie & Josiah & the girls are abowt ready to leave us. Miss Bet convinced Mistress V to sell the ~~Baroosh~~Barouche & buy a Gig & Josiah is teaching Miss Bet to drive it Herself. If she dont put Mistress V into the Grave with that the woman should live to be a Hundred. Miss Bet hired Terry Farr a Free Colored woman as the new cook. If she is any good I cant say because Zinnie wont let her within Fifty feet of the Kichen. I suppose Zinnie will be half-way to Ohio before Terry even sets foot in the Yard. Miss Bet was Hell-bent on not hiring any slaves at all. Couldnt bear the thot of paying money to a Slave-owner never mind her Father was one his hole life. But finaly I convinced her to take on Mrs. Wallace's Two nieces Joesy & Nell to help me with the House Work. They buy there Time from there Marse & hope to save enuff to buy Themselves free & clear. Joesy got Herself engaged to John Atkins but they wont Marry till she is free. Miss Bet will send all the laundrie out so I suppose three Grown women can manage the house just as well as Sam & I ever did with you Girls.

Your Papa planted me a vejtabel garden outside the Cabin. Hard to spare any Yard at all but he does like to go on abowt my poor Cooking till finaly I told him a woman needs what to cook with. Next thing I turn around & he got everything from Turnips to Mustard Greens in the grownd. Every meal we eat now I got to hear how his fine grown vejtabels make all the Flavor but that is your Papa if he isnt looking at me with those eyes & saying who knows What to teaze me I dont think I should know him at all.

Off to the Van Lews now. Young Marse John is having his bisness assoshiates to Supper tonite. Driving me dis-tracted all Week inspecting my cleaning as tho I didnt clean his behind the Day he popped into this World.

All your Papas love & mine
Mama

I beamed with pride to think of my marks tacked up on the cabin wall—you can bet I sent home every set I got after that. But all our correspondence made me ache. It was hard to picture strangers in the house, working beside Mama. I didn't miss the labor, but it didn't sit quite right knowing someone else could take my place so easily. And Papa seemed more and more distant with each letter. No matter what Mama wrote he said or did, it wasn't the same as having him say it or write it himself. Besides, I didn't always tell Mama and Papa everything in my letters, either.

My dearest Mama & Papa

Today was the most wonderful day I have had in Philadelphia yet. No I did not eat ice cream or read

*a new book. I went to a parade instead. Maybe you
are thinking it is the first August & not Independence Day or Militia Day so what parade is there
today? It is the most wonderful parade of all. A
parade held entirely by the colored people of Philadelphia in honor of the anniversary of British Emancipation. That is a fancy way to say it is the day when
slaves in the West Indies got their freedom. Colored
folks here do not soon forget a thing like that!*

*Mr. Frederick Douglass a former slave who
wrote his own book & newspaper says the fourth
July means nothing to negroes only a show of how
wrong slavery is. Even Mr. Ralph Waldo Emerson
who went to Harvard University & is a white minister says the first August is a great day in history
because so many colored folks got freed. Every year
in Philadelphia all the churches & benevolent soci-
eties & whatnot all the colored ones I mean sponsor
a big parade. Negroes march through the streets
singing & praying & praising. Also some white
people called Quakers though they dress & talk so
strangely Hattie & I call them Strangers but still
they march along right with the rest though without a hint of any singing or praising like our folks
do. After all the parading there are speeches &
pledges to get freedom for all the slaves here, too, if
Britain can do it why not America?*

Hattie's daddy marched with his lodge the Grand United Order of Odd Fellows which is a funny name isnt it? They have such uniforms they wear I cannot even describe but it made me proud to see our men dress up so & march about. Hattie & I cheered the most for her daddy's lodge but lots for everyone. Now my throat is a little sore & my feet a lot tired but it was worth it. Afterward we went to her sister Charlotte's house for punch & cake.

It is very late. I must get to bed but had to tell you before I could sleep.

Your loving daughter
Mary El

I was happy and tired when I wrote that letter, trying to put all the wonders of the day down for them to share. Even so, there was a fly or two in the cream I neglected to mention. What I didn't write was, some white boys came out and threw bottles at the marchers, calling them all sorts of names. I didn't write that while I waited for Hattie, I heard one of the fire companies, which were really nothing but gangs of thugs more intent on fighting each other than fighting any conflagrations, saying this was the best day of the year to get some niggers because you always knew where to find lots. I didn't write that Hattie and I saw a white man whose accent sounded real South spit and say, "Better celebrate what them darkies got in the West Indies, they'll never get the same in Alabama."

Hattie and I just looked at each other when we heard that, neither of us said a thing. Then we turned back to the parade and squeezed each other's hands real tight as the choir from Zoar United Methodist Church marched by, singing to glorify God and Emancipation.

Six

During my first months in Philadelphia, the eleven trees Hattie and I passed along the mile we walked to Miss Douglass's school each day came to seem like familiar friends. But come autumn, when those trees began to lose their leaves and their bare branches jabbed into the chill air, they suddenly appeared awkward and ugly. Especially against my remembrance of the countless trees that lined Richmond's roads and filled the yards of Church Hill. Seeing those piddling few Philadelphia trees stripped of their foliage was like looking at my own loneliness.

As the weeks seeped on toward winter, I couldn't help but think of Christmastides past, Mama and Zinnie singing hymns across the Van Lew property like two birds calling to each other on a spring morning.

And the sweet anticipation of my time with Papa, seven precious days that were always even lovelier than I'd imagined, once they finally arrived. What I wouldn't give for even an hour with Papa now.

I caught myself quick when such thoughts entered my head. Not freedom. I wouldn't, couldn't, give up freedom, even for that. Still, knowing I was free didn't feel like happiness, with my parents so far away and Papa not yet freedom bound himself.

Miss Douglass must have noted the shift in my mood, for she kept me after class one late November day. "Do you know what the Philadelphia Female Anti-Slavery Society is?" she asked.

I shook my head.

"We are a group of women who work together to end slavery. We have a gift fair every Christmas, selling goods we've made. During the year, we spend the money to support abolitionist speaking tours and publications."

I remembered the articles Bet read her mother from her abolitionist newsletters, describing all sorts of nasty attacks from pro-slavery groups, buildings burned and people beaten, even killed. "Is it dangerous?"

"Not the fair, no. Nor the preparing of goods to be sold, as you shall see tonight, if you are willing to join us. Our sewing circle is meeting at the Forten home on Lombard Street."

I'd marked the Fortens' house already. It was one of the grandest I'd seen in Philadelphia, as fine as the homes that sat atop Church Hill. I couldn't quite believe a colored family owned it, knowing most Philadelphia negroes were kept so poor they could barely feed and clothe their children. I thanked my teacher and fairly galloped to the Upshaws' to collect my things. When I bolted through the apartment door, I startled Mrs. Upshaw so, she pricked her finger with her needle.

"Mary dear, what's got you in such a state?" she asked.

"I'm sorry, Mrs. Upshaw. I'm just in a rush."

"What for? You're not the least bit late. My Dulcey ain't even home from Prune Street yet."

I didn't bother answering as I made for the bedroom to retrieve my sewing kit.

When I returned to the front room and Mrs. Upshaw caught sight of the tortoise-shell box, she beamed. "You set right to your mending, while I get supper ready."

"Oh, I'm late as it is. And I'll be having supper out."

"But there ain't no need for that." She scooped up the latest pile of piecework she'd collected from her customers, to make room on the daybed. "You can sit right here, by me. Won't it be lovely for us to sew together?"

I was so eager to get to the Fortens', I blurted out, "That's not the sort of needlework I'm doing."

Her face fell. " 'Course it ain't. I'm sure a schoolgirl like you don't ever do the kind of sewing I do."

Sewing for pay, she meant. The truth of her statement hung in the air between us. "I won't keep you no longer," she said. "You got important places to go."

I felt as stuck as her broken mantelpiece clock. I knew I ought to stay and apologize, but I couldn't bear any delay, lest Miss Douglass and the members of her sewing circle think me rude for being tardy. "I'm sorry," I said, passing as quick as I could to the apartment door. "I may be home rather late. Good night."

For once, Mrs. Upshaw made no answer.

I hurried down to the sidewalk, striding along Gaskill to Fourth and then crossing up to Lombard. Only four long blocks separated the Upshaws' from the Fortens', but they might as well have been an ocean apart, for all the buildings said about the fortunes of their respective residents. The Forten house sat squat and certain, three stories tall and even broader than it was high, with a low brick wall along one side enclosing a private garden. The marble stairs leading up to the double front door were nearly as wide as the Upshaws' whole building. Pulling myself tall, I gathered my skirts and trotted up the steps.

Before I even rang, an elderly butler opened the doors. "The ladies are in the sitting room," he said. He hung my cloak and bonnet among the others on the ornately carved hallstand, then led me along an elegantly carpeted hall. Though I longed to peer in as we passed the drawing room and dining room, I held myself to curious glances at the gilt-framed mirrors and marble-topped mahogany chests lining the hall. The furnishings were prim and old-fashioned, as though everything, even the servant, was preserved from the earliest era of the family's wealth.

The butler paused before the third doorway and whispered, "Your name, miss?"

My heart thrilled. I'd never been announced in company before, and certainly not to a room full of society ladies. "Mary. Mary Van Lew."

But when he proclaimed, "Miss Van Lew," to the two dozen or so women gathered inside the large parlor, all I could think was, that ain't me. It's Bet.

I blinked in the harsh glare of the gas lamps, which glowed brightly all through the lavish room. Even the Van Lews didn't have gas lighting inside the house. Nobody in Richmond did.

One of the ladies stood and walked toward me. She moved with the same confident manner as Phillipa Thayer, her dark skin nearly glowing against her emerald muslinet gown. "I'm Margaretta Forten. I'm so glad you could join us, Miss Van Lew."

Seeing how all those ladies sitting in intimate clusters of twos and threes stopped their chatting and sewing to turn their inquisitive faces toward me, it put me in mind of Bet's abolitionist friends. Quick to condemn slavery but slow to recognize the colored people they relied on every day. I didn't want to be such a person. Didn't even want to spend an evening with them. I just wanted to skulk back to the Upshaws'. But then I remembered I didn't fit in any too well there either.

One of the white ladies rose and crossed the parlor. She was younger than the rest, though older than me, a grown-up lady for sure. Dressed in a plain gray frock with the broadest collar I'd ever seen, white without a stitch of lace on it, and a sheer cap over her hair. She had lovely gray eyes, sweet without pretension.

"Mary, isn't it? My name is Cynthia Moore, but everyone calls me Zinnie." Her eyes twinkled. "As I like to say, to take the *sin* right out of *Cynthia*."

You could have bowled me over with a feather at the thought of this thin, tall, pale lady sharing anything with the Zinnie that I lived with my whole girlhood. Zinnie who was dark, and short, and about as broad as a woman could be, every piece on her—mouth and nose and bosom, cheeks so round you could barely find her eyes above them.

Not at all like this Miss Moore. It made me truly understand the expression rail-thin just to look at this woman, who had scarcely more to her than there was to a narrow wooden post. Lips so light and small they hardly seemed to be there at all, no bosom to give even the slightest rise to that white collar, and barely enough nose to get the business of breathing done. Then again, all that plainness gave those kind eyes all the more room to stand out.

And they did, still warm as she said, "Miss Douglass has told us all about thee. If thou will sit by me, I'll show thee what we have made, so thou may choose a project."

With the strangeness of it all, me a colored Miss Van Lew and her a white Zinnie and her bizarre Quaker way of speaking to boot, I couldn't bring myself to answer.

Miss Douglass shifted ever so slightly on the settee. "Perhaps you would be more comfortable here by me?"

Zinnie Moore's face flushed, and I realized that she thought I was spurning her. I didn't want my teacher to think I was scared of this white woman, or any white person—I didn't want to think it myself. And I didn't want to be intimidated by Margaretta Forten's fancified house, any more than by Phillipa's snooty airs.

Searching out the room, my eye caught on an oil painting hanging on the wall, larger even than the one in Mr. Jones's dining room but bearing the same proud eagle. I breathed in so deep, I might have been readying myself to loose one of that great bird's chirring caws. "So long as there's no sin in it," I said, "I'd be happy to sit beside Zinnie Moore."

She smiled and led me across the length of the parlor to a small worktable displaying a number of pincushions, aprons, bookmarks, and other finished wares. Much of the needlework—beaded purses, muslin caps, crocheted collars—was more advanced than I could manage. While the other women around the room returned to their sewing and conversing, I searched through the pattern case until I found a punched-paper pattern for a wall motto with the passage REMEMBER THEM THAT ARE IN BONDS, AS BOUND WITH THEM. HEBREWS 13:3. Nothing could be easier for me than that, the remembering and the stitching both, so I laid the pattern onto the worktable and drew a needle from my sewing box.

Zinnie nodded at my choice. "Thou hast picked wisely. The labor goes quickly that speaks to the heart."

As I selected colors from the store of Berlin wools, vanity got the better of me. Keeping my voice low so that none of the other groups of ladies might hear me, I asked, "What did Miss Douglass tell you about me?"

"That thou hast come from slavery only this year, and hast already made great progress in school. She is very proud of thee, for proving that neither blackness nor slavery is an impediment to intellect." Miss Douglass wasn't one to flatter, so hearing her praise secondhand made me shine. "She tells us that thy parents are still in Richmond, in the condition thou lately left. I pray this may be the last Christmas thy family spends apart, and that when thy mother joins our sewing circle, we may sew only for our pleasure, because our struggle will be won."

The thought of Mama sitting quietly among the ladies in the group amused me quite a bit. But I let Zinnie Moore think my smile was agreement with her sentiment, as we settled into our needlework.

I stitched a good half hour before summoning the courage to ask Zinnie Moore the question that was gnawing at me, as I considered how primly my teacher sat among the ladies on the far side of the grand parlor. "Miss Douglass dresses simply, but she doesn't speak like you do. Is she also Quaker?"

"Grace Douglass, her mother, attended Arch Street Meeting every week, though she never applied to join the Society of Friends. Sarah often came with her, but I do not believe she attends anymore." I wondered that Zinnie blushed as she added, "Most of the Friends in our sewing circle attend Green Street Meeting." Before she could say more, the butler brought supper in.

I was disappointed that he set only a plate of buckwheat cakes, fruits, and cheeses on our worktable. Zinnie peeked out mischievously from beneath her funny cap. "Margaretta will fret that thou may think her miserly for providing such simple fare. She does it out of respect for the Friends, who keep to modesty in all things, even eat and drink."

"Zinnie Moore, are you gossiping?" I only meant to tease, the way Hattie and I always did, but as soon as the words came out, I feared they might offend this strange lady.

She pursed her lips a moment but then grinned back at me. "'Tis not gossip to compliment a lady's good nature. Nor sinful if I preserve thy high opinion of my generous friend."

Friend. I'd never head a white lady address a negro so. This Zinnie Moore was something. A pale, slender, Quaker something.

I was up into the wee hours that night writing Mama and Papa, and I slept mighty late the next morning. When I rushed downstairs, Hattie was stamping her feet against the cold. "At long last. I was beginning to wonder whether Mrs. Upshaw had fussed you to death once and for all."

"Sorry to keep you here freezing." We began walking, arms linked, toward Arch Street. "I forgot you'd be waiting."

"Forgot? Aren't I here every morning?"

"I stayed up so late last night, I don't think I'm quite awake this morning."

That caught her concern. "How come Miss Douglass kept you after session? I wanted to wait, but I had to get to Emily's right away." Hattie's sister was just about on her third confinement, and Hattie was fairly living at her house, helping look after Emily's two boys. "What has our schoolmarm ordered you to?"

"Not ordered, invited. To—let me see if I can get the name right—the Philadelphia Anti-Female Slavery, I mean Female Anti-Slavery, Society."

"You went to a Society meeting?"

"Oh no, just the sewing circle. They have a gift fair every year and—"

"Yes, I know it. Everyone knows it. Funny, I didn't think Miss Douglass invited girls your age to her sewing circle."

Hattie didn't usually make much of the age difference between us—two years that, like the difference between Baltimore and Richmond, between born free and born slave, didn't seem to add up to much, given how close we felt to each other. I looked over at her, but she held her gaze straight ahead.

We were about to cross Market Street, and suddenly I remembered my letter. "I need to stop at the post office."

"We can't stop. We'll be nearly late as it is."

For weeks I'd been too glum to eke out a word to Mama and Papa. Now that I had a proper letter, I didn't want to delay posting it. "You go on, I'll be there right off."

Hattie withdrew her arm from mine. "Just remember, even Phillipa Thayer doesn't dare come tardy to the schoolroom." Her voice was as frosty as the morning air. "I'd hate to see you lose your new favor in Miss Douglass's eyes." With that, she walked off.

I hurried to the post and then up to school, barely slipping into my seat before Miss Douglass called the class to order. Hattie wouldn't even wink or nod to me. Though I couldn't understand what had her so ornery, I figured we'd make up as we walked home for dinner recess. But mid-morning, a knock came to the classroom door. It was Susan, the Jones's housekeeper, with a note for Miss Douglass. When our schoolmarm read it, she instructed Hattie to gather up her things. Emily's confinement had come, and Hattie was needed to help with the children.

The sewing circle didn't meet but twice a week, so I sewed at the Upshaws', too, starting that very night. As soon as we finished supper, I pulled my sewing case out and, knowing there weren't but three rooms to the whole apartment, headed to the parlor.

Ducky eyed the case. "What's the matter, that white lady cut off your allowance?"

Ignoring her, I smiled my contrition at Mrs. Upshaw. "Since sewing is such a fine ladies' pastime, I've joined a sewing circle. I need to finish some pieces, so they can be sold at our charity fair."

Mrs. Upshaw lit all over the idea. "A charity fair, dear, ain't that something. Perhaps Dulcey and me can help some, too."

Ducky squawked. "We start trying to give charity, we're gonna end up needing to take charity."

For once, I saw the truth in what she said. Mrs. Upshaw could outsew just about every lady I'd met at the Fortens'. But taking even a half hour a day away from her paid work would be more than she could afford.

"Mrs. Upshaw, you're very kind to offer, and we'd do well to have such fine things as you can make. But none of these ladies sew nearly as well as you, and I think it might shame them a bit to have their work laid up next to yours." I could tell by the way she nodded my tack was working. "You know how some people just aren't happy if they don't feel superior."

Ducky snorted.

Over the next fortnight, I grew so lonely for Hattie, I bundled up against the bitter cold come Saturday and walked all the way down Shippen Street past Eleventh, to the little cottage that Emily's husband rented for his family.

I knocked and waited, then waited some more, until Hattie finally swung open the door. She was wearing a worn dress topped with an old apron, her hair covered by a head-wrap. "What are you doing here?" she asked.

"Aren't you even going to invite me in? I'm a regular icicle out in this cold."

"You've got to mind the floors if you come tramping in here. I've only just washed them."

I applied myself carefully to the boot scraper and lifted my damp skirts high before stepping inside. "I've missed you so, I can't wait to tell you all that's been happening at my sewing circle. And of course I want to hear what you've been up to."

"What I've been up to is drudgery and nothing but. Cinderella to my sisters, who order me here and there like I'm a servant with five mistresses. And two demonic little masters." She crossed her arms in that tired-of-being-tired way that Mama got whenever one of the Van Lews took sick so quick they didn't have time to ring for a slop bucket or haul themselves to a chamber pot. "My nephews will be up from their nap any minute, ready to tear the house apart, so I've got no time for your silly little stories."

Hattie was never so cross with me. "I know you're working hard, but so am I. Zinnie Moore says my sewing has already improved a bundle. I've finished two wall mottoes, and I've even started to embroider a tea cozy."

"That is cozy, for you, playing at being a snob like Phillipa."

"What's Phillipa got to do with it?"

She rolled her eyes, like I was some kind of fool. "All this time you act like you're making fun of the better sort of colored Philadelphia, then first chance you get you run off and join them and their white ladies. You may be falling all over impressed by yourself, but I'm too busy to sit about sipping tea and listening to your nonsense."

"It isn't nonsense at all. The fair raises loads of money for abolition. You have to understand why that's important to me. My father is a slave, my mother is—"

Before I could continue with the usual half-truth, she cut me off. "And my mother isn't. Isn't alive. And my father is always shooing me away every time the wind blows, so he can go off to Chambersburg on business. My sisters are all huddled upstairs with Emily, carrying on as if it's some secret society and I can't be a member because it's only for married ladies." She turned away, speaking more to herself than to me. "And now you go leaving me, too."

I caught her arm. "Don't be jealous. You're still my best friend. Just not my only friend. After Emily is recovered, you can come to the sewing circle, meet the Quaker ladies, and be friends with them like I am."

"If you're such good friends, why don't you go over to the Quaker Meeting sometime, instead of tagging along with my family to Mother Bethel? See how you feel about Quakers then." A toddler's cry sounded from upstairs. "I've got to go. Please be so good as to see yourself out."

She was up the staircase before I could say another thing.

Her words stuck with me as I walked back toward Gaskill Street. I spent plenty of Sundays at Mother Bethel, for the pleasure of being with Hattie and her family. But services there always made me miss our Richmond prayer meeting. Like trading warm woolen mittens for a pair of leather gloves all decorated with fancywork, only to realize the gloves were too thin and too tight to be any comfort against the cold. So maybe I wouldn't bother tagging along, as Hattie put it. At least not till she was done fuming at me.

I wasn't about to join up with the Friends, of course, but I was curious about them. Before I met Zinnie, I thought the stiff and somber Friends as ill-named as Spruce and Pine and Chestnut, Philadelphia's nearly treeless streets. But Zinnie proved me wrong, she was so friendly. Still, I wasn't sure I dared to walk into her prayer meeting.

Then I remembered that Zinnie said most of the women from the sewing circle attended the Green Street Meeting House. If I went to the Meeting House on Arch Street, I wouldn't be likely to see anyone I knew. If I liked it there, then I could go to Green Street, too, sometime. Hadn't Zinnie told me Miss Douglass's mother went to meeting for years, without becoming a regular member?

The idea was still catching in my head as I crossed beneath the sign for GRIFFITH BROS. SHIRTS, COLLARS, GLOVES, & HOSIERY. Looking up at the store, I thought of the Quaker women in the sewing circle, with their nearly identical clothing. Even when I passed a stranger on the street, it was easy enough to tell if she was a Quaker by her clothes. I couldn't go to one of their Meetings wearing something that might seem extravagant. I had one dress, a navy blue bombazine, that might do.

I stepped into Griffith Bros. and bought a plain white collar and shawl, along with a five-pleated gray bonnet, the kind Quaker ladies wore over their sheer caps when they went out in public. The collar would cover the bright buttons on my bodice, and the shawl would hide the full sleeves. I spent the afternoon back at the Upshaws', taking out the stitches on my lace cuffs and skirt trim.

The two-story Arch Street Meeting House stretched the better part of a block, and Sunday morning it loomed no more welcoming than Mother Bethel. I paced the walk outside for a quarter hour, nerving myself to follow the steady trickle of people going through the plain, heavy doors. Inside, rows of wooden benches rippled forward from all four of the unadorned white walls, befuddling me. There wasn't so much as a pulpit, and not a single cross to be seen. The wide planks of the wood floor weren't even varnished. Broad square columns along three sides of the room supported a balcony where children milled about.

All around me, people were taking their seats. Slipping into an empty pew, I kept my head down, occupying myself with straightening my gloves.

I hardly even knew when the worshipping started. No preacher spoke. People just stood one at a time, here and there, saying whatever seemed to come to their mind. They didn't shout to glory or recite a hymn or any such thing. Ladies stood and spoke just as often as men. Sometimes it was quiet for a minute or two before someone rose. I couldn't even be sure they were prayerful, until one young man thanked God for blessing him and his wife with a healthy new son.

As I looked over to where he was standing, a pinched-looking white woman in the pew in front of me caught my eye. She breathed in sharply, her mouth tight and her nostrils flared, and pointed to a bench in the back row, behind one of the squat pillars.

Ashamed to be found out of place, I gathered myself up and moved. As I came around the side of the pillar, I saw that the only other occupant of the bench was an elderly negro, stooped with age.

"You new here, too?" I whispered as I slid in beside him.

He shook his head. "I was coming here long before thou was born. Nearly sixty years, since I first worked for a Quaker family."

"So why are you on the newcomers' bench?"

"Newcomers' bench? The Friends have no such thing."

I nodded toward where I'd been sitting. "But a lady over there directed me to move back here."

"We must sit here, on the bench for negroes."

The man's words stung me like a slap.

It was insult enough to be kept out of the academy Bet attended, and degradation aplenty to be thrown off an omnibus. But the way Zinnie Moore sat beside me at the sewing circle, even sharing supper, I never thought Quakers could be so cruel. Despite all the seeming sweet and humble, this prayer meeting was no different from St. John's, the Van Lews' church, where slaves were sent to the balcony while their masters worshipped below. Mama was fit to be tied the one time Bet brought us there. Without a word, I rose and left the Meeting House.

I walked bent and bowed against the hard rush of chill December air, as I hurried away from Arch Street. I was angry at that weasel-faced woman for sending me back to that bench, angry at the Quakers for having such a bench at all, angry at the elderly colored man for sitting on that bench for five decades or more. Angry at Zinnie for pretending Quakers were different from other whites. But I was most angry at myself, for forgetting what Mama and Papa taught me, the thing that guided every moment of my life in Richmond. I could hear Papa saying that the best way with white folks is out of their way, could picture Mama maneuvering about the Van Lew house or the city's shops, ever vigilant for any harm that might be directed her way, or mine. Missing my parents so, I berated myself for not remembering their most important lesson. And I vowed to hold myself more cautious when it came to Zinnie Moore, the same way Mama did with Bet.

It was the very first Christmastide I even had so much as a purse to jingle coins in, and you can bet I set myself to thinking what to buy Mama and Papa.

I considered every practical thing you could imagine, clothing and kitchenware and whatnot, and rejected them all. Papa's just-becauses had always thrilled me, and now that it was my turn to purchase, I couldn't choose a necessity over an indulgence. As December wore on, I sewed and thought, thought and sewed. What I really wanted was for us all to be together. Though I couldn't manage that, at last I puzzled out a way to send something that was as close as I could get to going home myself.

My dearest Mama & Papa

Merry Christmas! My gift to you as you can see is a daguerreotype of me. I know it may seem extravagant as colored folks in Richmond never have such things. *Negroes can get daguerreotypes made here easy enough though not the poorest ones which I guess is most negroes but those who can afford it do not have to worry because there is a colored man to make them for us.*

It is Miss Douglass's own cousin David Bustill Bowser. He is a painter but also a daguerreotypist & a sign-maker & sometime barber. It is too bad that he cannot earn enough just as an artist as his paintings are very fine & Hattie's father & all the best colored families have one for their house but lucky for me he makes daguerreotypes too. I saw him last summer marching in the parade leading the Loyal Order of Odd Fellows. I did not know he was my teacher's cousin till Hattie told me so. Only close up did I see he has the same serious eyes & purposeful manner as Miss Douglass though with stocky build & neatly trimmed goatee.

His studio is something to see! It is over on Chestnut Street between Seventh & Eighth on the very top floor so his customers all colored folks of course have the longest climb but he says it is for the best as he gets the most light which makes the best pictures of anyone in the building. The studio has three sets of windows running floor to ceiling that swing full open. It was hardly like being inside

a building with all that outside coming right in.
I do wonder how a building stands with so much
window & so little wall.

I sure miss you both. Papa who will walk all
over Richmond with you Christmas week? Mama
if I were there I would sweep up all the pine needles
in the Van Lews' drawing room I know how they
drive you mad when they fall. Most of all if I were
there I would kiss you both.

> *Merry Christmas from*
> *your devoted daughter*
> *Mary El*

Once I posted the packet, I turned my thoughts to the Upshaws. Thanks to Bet's largesse, I could buy my landlady something she couldn't get herself. I worried over what that thing should be, until I realized I'd had the answer months before.

Way back in August, Mrs. Upshaw had brought home an issue of *Godey's Lady's Book* rescued from one of her customers' dustbins, which she showed off as proudly as though she were Mr. Louis A. Godey himself. "Just see how pretty these pictures is. To think someone was gonna put it out with the rubbish. Why, I got a mind to hang such pictures on the wall." She passed the magazine to me, open to one of the color plates. "Look at that bird, drawn all lovely and lifelike. I wonder what kind it is."

"It's a black-throated warbler," I said. "They tell all about it on the facing page. There's even a little poem about its song."

Mrs. Upshaw took back the magazine. "'Course there is, yes, of course," she said, as she rushed to flip the page.

That's how I realized the Upshaws couldn't read.

When Mrs. Upshaw first cooed, "Why, Dulcey and I so admire all your learning," I thought, Ducky don't admire me, she hates me. It maddened me when she went through my things, upsetting books or scattering sheaves of lessons. But that day with the *Godey's*, I understood that she didn't hate me, she resented me. Mr. Upshaw worked his whole life as a stevedore, loading and unloading ships along the Delaware wharves, his salary so meager his wife had to take in sewing to help pay the family's bills. He passed on when Dulcey was quite young, though like many a poor child she was old enough to be put to work. At twenty, she was probably at service longer than I'd been a slave, without any chance for schooling. Here I was, fresh out of Virginia bondage, with opportunities she, born free in Pennsylvania, would never have.

I recalled all of this when I saw that one of the white ladies in the Philadelphia Female Anti-Slavery Society had made up a batch of reading primers to sell at the Fair. She'd decorated them by hand, leaving the usual places to practice writing out the letters. On the cover was just such a bird as Mrs. Upshaw had showed me from *Godey's*. So it seemed like I was meant to purchase two of those primers and instruct her and Ducky myself. We wouldn't even have to sneak around to do it, like Mama did when she taught me.

The evening I brought the gift home, I made sure to fill Mrs. Upshaw with lots of praise for her supper. "After a meal that fine, you should just set and rest a piece in the parlor. I'll get to the dishes," I said.

Mrs. Upshaw let me push her toward the sofa. "Come along, Dulcey dear, let Mary be, she so good to lend a hand."

But Ducky crossed her arms and stayed at the table. "I sit where I please in my own home. Quite a show in here, watching Miss School Girl play the little char-maid."

I turned to scrubbing the supper things in the big pot of water Mrs. Upshaw had heated on the stove, feeling Ducky's eyes on my back the whole while. When I finished, she followed me to the bedroom, pushing wordlessly past as I unlocked my trunk to extract the present.

Mrs. Upshaw was hard at her sewing when I entered the parlor. "I thought you'd be relaxing a bit, not working already."

"Lots to do, 'fore the holiday. My ladies must get their things all fixed up on time."

"Well, I hope you can spare a moment, because I have something to give you. You and Dulcey both."

Ducky harrumphed, but Mrs. Upshaw chatted on like she hadn't heard. "For us? Ain't you sweet to think of it. Only I'm afraid we don't got anything for you."

"I don't need a thing, unless maybe you'd care to show me how to do some of that fancy crochet you're so good at." I held out the magazine. "I thought you'd like your very own subscription to *Godey's Lady's Book*. Now it will come for you every month, you just stop at the post office to pick it up." Her eyes lit up. "And I got you each a primer, too, so I can help you learn to read."

Doubt tugged her smile into a defeated frown. "You sweet to offer, but I'm too old for all that. Looking at them lovely pictures is enough for me. Dulcey can learn for both of us."

"No thank you," Ducky cut in. "All the hours a day I work, I got better things to do with my little spare time than stare cross-eyed at some stupid book the way a certain pickaninny do."

That word snipped the very last strand of my forbearance. "Don't you want to make something of yourself?"

Ducky waddled at me. "What am I going to make of myself? You think I learn to read and write, I can make myself mayor? Maybe make a passel of white men cook and clean for me, 'stead of the other way round? You believe that, you even dumber than I thought."

I didn't know what to say, so I kept my mouth pressed shut. Which didn't stop Ducky.

"Maybe you ought to start worrying about your own self stead of telling me what I should do. What you think is going to happen to you and Hattie and the rest once you grow up, Miss School Girl? Marry if you're lucky, and still you'll likely end up sewing or cooking or cleaning for white people. Only things a colored woman can do, since our men can't get decent jobs. All that schooling, and you're still too ignorant even to know that much."

Sour though Ducky could be, I could see the truth of what she said. Even Bet, white and well off, didn't try to make her way alone in Philadelphia. I had no fine family mansion to return to, and I couldn't imagine where I might end up instead.

I wasn't about to let on how Ducky's words nipped and gnawed at me, no more than I let on that I marked the way those primers had disappeared by morning, the ash-heap in the fireplace grown that much larger overnight.

I tried to distract myself from my failure with the Upshaws by concentrating on all I had to do at the fair. The Philadelphia Female Anti-Slavery Society rented a large hall on Walnut Street just past Washington Square, which we hung with evergreens and lined with booths to sell what we'd made. Not just our sewing circle, either. Ladies far outside Philadelphia sent along all manner of goods. I volunteered to make up a table out of some of those things, since I hadn't sewn enough myself to fill a booth.

I chose a spot at the rear of the hall, happy to tuck myself out of sight from Zinnie Moore and the rest. I had my back to the room, arranging my table, when a voice called, "Miss Mary Van Lew of Gaskill Street, I've found you at last. What are you doing way back here?"

I turned and shrugged at Hattie, not wanting to admit that she'd been right about the Quakers. "School's been mighty lonely without you. You coming back after Christmas?"

"Yes. Emily's little girl is pulling through all right, so she's ready to send me packing." She glanced around, taking in the bustle all over the hall. "Daddy always says, the harder it is to admit you were wrong, the more you need to do it. So I guess I must really need to say I missed you lots. Not just when I was keeping house at Emily's, but when my family went to Mother Bethel without you, too. That's why I thought I'd better hunt you up, bring you these." She held out a large basket in which a dozen of her homemade landscapes were nestled side by side.

"Oh, Hattie, I'll treasure them forever. I'll find someplace special to tuck them away, so Ducky can't get at em."

"I hope you won't. They're not for you at all. They're for the fair. Don't you see, they'll go so nicely with the things on your table." She raised her eyebrow. "Of course, with so much more to sell you might need twice as many clerks at this booth. So I'd like to apply to be your aide for the duration of the fair."

"I suppose I do have a bare spot or two your treasures can fill. And I will be very happy for your assistance, if you can drive a hard bargain for our cause." We laughed and hugged, glad to lay aside whatever hard feelings had passed between us.

For the next two weeks, Hattie and I had plenty to keep us busy. Shoppers by the hundreds swarmed the hall, nearly all of them white. Maybe before my trip to the Arch Street Meeting I would have told myself all sorts of tales about how nice it was to see so many of them caring about abolition. But now I wondered what brought them to us, what it meant that we worked so hard to fashion the needlework collars and painted china pieces that would be their presents come Christmas morning.

I couldn't help but notice that none of my Gaskill Street neighbors, white or negro, could afford to shop at the fancy stores on Chestnut Street, nor at the fair. Most of colored Philadelphia had no more money than the Upshaws, and while plenty of white people didn't either, lots of whites had more. It was their money we were taking, their money we would use to try to set the slaves, set my own papa, free. I didn't know what to make of all that, even as the pile of goods at our booth dwindled and our receipt-box filled.

Hattie's landscapes were bought up right away, and my wall mottoes and tea cozies didn't last much longer. By the twenty-fourth, even the hanging plants and such were finally sold off to the stragglers who picked their way through the hall.

I was packing up the table decorations when Zinnie Moore came by. "May I speak with thee a moment?" she asked.

I nodded.

"The Friends do not celebrate Christmas, for we do not believe any single day is holier than another. There is even criticism of those of us who participate in the fair, which some say encourages worldly indulgences. The Friends in our group feel our work is Christly, so we continue in it, though we do not engage in gift-giving ourselves." She glanced about, making sure no one was observing us. "But when I think of thy parents, so far from thee, I hope that these might be a comfort to them."

She withdrew two small packages from her apron pocket. One contained a pair of men's slippers, the other a needle case. Both were worked with the message BY THEIR FRUITS YE SHALL KNOW THEM. I stared at the carefully turned stitches, unsure what to say.

My silence forged a furrow along Zinnie's broad, high brow. "Thou does not care for these things?"

"I only wonder why you made them, why the Quakers work so hard to free slaves, when you believe us all inferior."

Surprise flashed in those gray eyes. "I believe no such thing, and thou must surely know it. Did I not say our work is Christly? Have I not spent many hours toiling beside thee, and Margaretta Forten and Sarah Douglass and the rest?" She reached out to touch my face. Her hand was rough from work, not soft like Mistress Van Lew's. "What has made thee so hard with me these last weeks?"

"I went to the Arch Street Meeting. I know your church keeps a separate bench, a nigger bench. Just like the slave-owners do."

My words might have been red hot coals, she drew back her hand so quick. "I told thee I do not worship there. Most in our Anti-Slavery Society are Hicksite Quakers, different from those among whom thou went. Had thou come to our Meeting, thou would have been welcome to sit beside me."

"Would I have been welcome to sit beside any of the white people there?"

Those gray eyes kept steady on me, firm but not hard. "The Hicksite Friends are many, and I cannot speak for all of them. No more than thou may speak for all negroes."

I thought of Phillipa, Ducky, too, when she said that. I dropped my eyes from hers, but she held the gifts out to me. "Thy parents have much reason to be proud of thee, and I hope thou will accept these, for their sake."

I thanked her and took the presents, though I wasn't sure whose sake I had in mind when I sent them along to Richmond.

My Dearest Mama & Papa

Merry Christmas Eve to you & I hope you like the Christmas package I sent last week. Here are two more gifts for you made by one of the ladies from my sewing circle. I suppose you can tell the needle case is for you Mama & the slippers for Papa & the inscription means people here can see you did a fine job raising me.

Please do not think it odd to receive presents from a stranger as she & I have grown close in the past weeks. I think you should like her very much if you could meet her.

I felt a pang as I wrote that sentence, knowing Zinnie Moore would want me to write *you will like her very much when you meet her.* But I was less sanguine than Zinnie about that happening.

Glad as I was to help the Anti-Slavery Society raise funds, if I thought on it too long, it all seemed hopeless. I knew too well the tenacity that led Mahon to refuse an offer of any size in exchange for a single slave. I doubted that a hundred such fairs, or even a thousand, could raise money enough to persuade all slaveholders to part with their valuable possessions. And what other inducement could there be for them to free their human chattel?

"Slavery doesn't take holidays, so neither can abolition." That's what Margaretta Forten said when she called our sewing circle to order a fortnight after the fair. Meaning, proud as we were for making so much money—over eight hundred dollars after the expense of the hall was paid—there would be no resting on our laurels. That very January evening we were stitching again, laying in wares for the next year's fair before the Anti-Slavery Society would spend even two of our hard-earned dollars on its annual subscription to *Frederick Douglass' Paper*.

Whenever someone said something like "slavery doesn't take holidays," or any kind of slavery is and slavery does sort of thing, I could feel all the women's attention shift my way. No heads turned or eyes slid to where I sat, everyone was too polite for that. But still, the fact hung in the air around us—I had been in slavery, they had not. Not even the colored ladies.

That struck me as strange at first, when Philadelphia was full enough with former slaves. Of course anyone who ran off from bondage had to keep quiet about it, but there were still quite a few in the city who had bought themselves out or been manumitted. I wondered that none of them turned up at the Anti-Slavery Society, until I thought of Mrs. Upshaw. If just getting by was so hard for her, it must be harder still for women who came out of slavery, needing to put together a home and a life out of the nothing they were able to call their own in the South.

Curious as the other ladies were, I held my tongue whenever any slavery is–slavery does comments were made. It seemed like there were about a million kinds of slavery. I'd never so much as laid eyes on a plantation, couldn't imagine the horror of slave-breeding farms, the humiliation of the fancy trade, or any of that. Such things were as distant from the life I lived in Virginia as—well, as my life in Richmond had been from Miss Douglass's life, or Zinnie Moore's. Or what mine was now.

Colored and white, the abolitionists who gave speeches against the peculiar institution cited its most extreme manifestations. But the slavery I was born into, though every bit as unjust, felt very different indeed. Theirs, the sharp sting of the whip, the family wrenched apart by sale, the years spent without proper food or clothing, in excruciating labor. Mine, the dull ache of exhaustion from long hours of work, the longing for grandparents, aunts, uncles, and cousins I never met and never would. The never time enough with Mama and Papa and me all together. I didn't know how I could make the ladies in the sewing circle understand all that, without making it sound as though I were saying some slavery wasn't so bad just because it wasn't as terrible as slavery got.

I hadn't wanted to admit it at first, proud and excited as I was when Miss Douglass invited me to join them, but deep down it hurt to realize what all the anti-slavery people thought of slaves. Just about everywhere I'd turned my head at the fair, I saw things—note paper, embroidered pot holders, even broadsides to hang on the wall—decorated with pictures of slaves, always drawn up the same. Male or female, wearing nothing but a loin-cloth, shackled hand and foot, the slave knelt, hands clasped not like prayer but like begging. The abolitionists loved all the degradation and desperation in that image.

Something sour prickled my skin whenever I saw those figures. Was that how people in the North pictured Papa and Mama? Did they think I'd been half-naked and chained up like that, till Bet rode in on a white horse to liberate me? I don't know why the other colored ladies in our group didn't feel the same way I did, even if they'd never been slaves. We were making money for the anti-slavery cause, I guess, and it was easy enough to see what sold.

Come that spring, another white image of slavery appeared, and pro-slavery or anti-slavery, plenty of people found it just as troubling. Bet sent a missive railing about how they didn't dare sell *Uncle Tom's Cabin* in Richmond. She instructed me to purchase the novel and send it to her at once. She even insisted I buy a second copy for myself.

Although all the attention Mrs. Harriet Beecher Stowe was getting piqued my curiosity, it was two months before my name made it to the top of the list at the bookseller's. The clerk apologized profusely for the delay, explaining that the publishers' presses were running around the clock, people were buying the novel in such droves.

After I posted Bet's copy, I settled down to read my own, running my hand along the scene of the slave cabin embossed in gold on the brown leather cover. I admit, I dropped a tear here or there among the pages, the stories of enslaved families forced apart too dolorous not to move me. But there was much that didn't sit well with me, especially the way the slaves doted on that Eva. Even if a slave was inclined to treat a white child so—and that was a stretch of my imagination right there—it wasn't as though slaves had time to carry on singing and chatting and reading with their owners. How did Mrs. Stowe think anything got cooked, cleaned, made, or done in the South if slaves weren't working day and night to do it? Perhaps she meant well, but she didn't know the first thing about what bondage was really like.

With all the fanfare abolitionists gave the novel, I wondered whether anyone else reacted to it as I had. So I was glad when Hattie invited me to go with her and her father to the Gilbert Lyceum to hear a program on the book. The Lyceum was colored Philadelphia's very own lecture hall, where all manner of speakers came to address matters of interest.

Large as the auditorium was, it was near full by the time we arrived. As we found places in the back of the room, I nodded toward a figure with neatly trimmed mutton-chops sitting in the front row. "Who's that white man?"

Hattie laughed. "Robert Purvis? White as he seems, his grandmother was a Moor and a slave, so by good old American alchemy, he's as negro as you or I. He wouldn't think of passing for white, and he even married a woman several shades darker than himself—though just as rich, of course."

Before she had a chance to pass along any other gossip, James Bustill, the Lyceum president, banged on the podium and called the room to order.

"As you know, Mrs. Stowe's novel has proven quite popular, stirring up as much response from Southerners who haven't read it as from Northerners who have."

Scattered chuckles greeted this remark. "Given its momentous import to our people, the Lyceum board has decided on an open meeting this evening. We hope that as many of you will join the debate as time allows. Our recording secretary, Mr. Augustus Baggott, has the honor of beginning discussion. I now grant him the floor."

Mr. Baggott rose. "We must commend Mrs. Stowe for bringing the plight of our enslaved brethren before white audiences. However many of us may read Mr. Frederick Douglass or hear Miss Frances Watkins lecture, surely we must acknowledge that more whites will pick up this novel."

"That's reason to condemn the book, not commend it," said David Bustill Bowser, the burly daguerreo-typer who was my teacher's cousin. "Stowe's novel is sprinkled with images plucked from the coon shows."

Mr. Baggott wouldn't yield. "Some characters are unfortunately drawn, I grant you, but others show negroes displaying the finer sentiments. Think of the maternal devotion that leads the slave mother Eliza to flee with her child rather than have him traded away from her. And the powerful manhood of her husband, George, willing to take up pistols and fight to protect his family."

"And to what end?" asked a woman on the far side of the hall, her voice ringing with a coloratura of determi-nation. "So they may go to Canada, and then to Africa.

Stowe can no more tolerate free negroes in America than the slaveholders can. We cannot celebrate a story that suggests we have no place in our own nation."

Well, that did it right there. Escaped slaves stole their way to Canada fairly often, especially since the Fugitive Slave Law left them in jeopardy anywhere in the United States. And plenty of free negroes, weary of the daily discrimination and fearful of the sporadic race riots, made their way there, too. Now those who had friends or family north of the North launched into a heated debate on the merits of emigrating.

At last, a dapper man in the second row pounded his walking stick against the floor. "But to return to Mrs. Stowe's novel. What disturbs me most is the character of Uncle Tom. He's the very opposite of George, sacrificing ties to his family in a rush to do as his supposed Master bids him. If I met anyone like him, I'd denounce him to his face." Murmurs of approval sounded through the hall. "Any creature who would choose to remain enslaved rather than take his freedom does not deserve the title of man."

"That's not fair." My words flew out before I realized it. Hundreds of faces turned toward me in surprise. "Plenty of those who don't come North are truer men, or finer women, than many of the self-proclaimed better sort of colored Philadelphia."

I wasn't about to abide some Pennsylvania dandy condemning my papa for not running off from Master Mahon. To be sure, some slaves managed to steal their freedom and build lives in the North, despite the way negroes were kept out of most jobs, most residences, too. But those fugitives lived with the knowledge that what they worked so hard to build could topple in an instant if the slave-catcher came to call. I refused to think of Papa's remaining in Richmond, and Mama's staying with him, as a less worthy choice than theirs.

The debate continued after my outburst, but I paid little attention. Everyone else was trying to decide whether Mrs. Stowe should be sainted or damned. But I was fuming as much at them as at her. What a white lady writes in her book, what she makes her characters say or do, that was one thing, but what about all those fellow negroes all around me, acting as narrow-minded as could be?

Between the white abolitionists and the free negroes of Philadelphia, I wasn't sure who'd ever understand my mama and papa, all they did for each other and for me. I might have cracked the fine leather binding on that novel right to the stitches, and still I couldn't figure how to keep my parents, and my past, bound to who I might grow to be, now that I was living free.

Seven

I n the fall of 1852, after nearly twenty years of fits and starts, a private high school for negro boys opened in Philadelphia. Not just another Mr. So-and-So's school, set up in the front parlor of someone's house, but the Institute for Colored Youth, in its own brand-new building constructed just for the purpose. Lots of girls from Miss Douglass's school walked the extra blocks to Lombard and Seventh before class each day to giggle and gape at the matriculants. Hattie and I were known to pass the lot more than once, hoping to see a young George Patterson, on whom she'd set her eye.

Luckily for us, it didn't take another twenty years for girls to be admitted to the Institute, too. That winter, Grace Mapps was hired to teach high school classes for young ladies, and Miss Douglass moved her school into the building as the "girls' preparatory department."

I hadn't even been in school two full years then, so I didn't expect to be promoted to Miss Mapps's class right off, like Hattie was. At least we were still in the same building, and she was the one suffering Phillipa. Besides, the best thing about the Institute wasn't in any classroom. It was the library.

Before the school even opened, the trustees purchased five hundred dollars' worth of new books, as much as Old Master Van Lew had spent on his collection in an entire decade. That library became my greatest respite from the Upshaws' cramped apartment, especially once Hattie and George started courting.

Big as the room was, still I had it to myself most of the time. I always sat in the same leather and mahogany elbow chair and went right to my lessons for the day. Then I gathered up whatever suited my latest fancy—Mr. Geoffrey Chaucer or Miss Phillis Wheatley, Mr. Pliny the Elder or Mr. Olaudah Equiano. I'd pull down whole piles of books and luxuriate in the hours that spread before me. It didn't matter if it took me days, even weeks, to make my way through some of those tomes. I had time and quiet and lots to read, and that contented me.

Come spring, Miss Douglass had our class memorize Mr. Henry Wadsworth Longfellow's "The Village Blacksmith." *The smith, a mighty man is he, / With large and sinewy hands; / And the muscles of his brawny arms / Are strong as iron bands.* I fell in love with every syllable of those lines, how they venerated a man so much like Papa. That very afternoon, I searched the library to find what else Mr. Longfellow had written. From the very first stanza of *Evangeline,* I was as good as transported to the forest primeval. But when I reached the last canto of the first section, my breath caught. It wasn't Longfellow's verses that stunned me. It was the engraving of the Acadians being forced into exile by the British—row after row of white men, bound in chains.

I'd learned by then that Hattie was right, history was full of whites who were as nasty to each other as they were to us. But this story took place only a hundred years before, in Canada—the very place where so many fugitive slaves were now seeking freedom from their own chains. I stared at the picture for nearly a quarter hour, until the resident custodian came to lock the library for the evening.

I was distracted all through the next day's lessons, anxious to learn what happened to Evangeline and her betrothed. When I got to the library, I rushed to the shelf where I found the poem the day before. But it wasn't there. Only when I turned to see if I'd left the book on the table did I realize I wasn't alone. Seated in an armchair in the corner was one of the high school students, so deep in his own reading he didn't seem to have noticed me.

I cleared my throat. "Pardon me, do you have Mr. Longfellow's *Evangeline*?"

He looked up in surprise. "Yes, I do. Do you need it?"

"I began it yesterday, but I hadn't time to finish."

"Well then, you take it. I can wait until you're done." He held the book out to me.

"No, I couldn't. You were here first." Not that I wanted to wait, but I thought I ought to be polite.

"Perhaps we can read it together," he said.

"But you've only just started, and I'm halfway through already."

He shrugged. "I've read the poem before. I just want to look it over again, I've forgotten so much of it. Isn't it maddening when that happens?"

I knew better than to tell him it didn't happen to me. My skill for recalling anything I read or heard had gotten me teased enough among Miss Douglass's students. I wasn't about to mention it to this handsome young man.

For he was handsome, and more a young man than most of the boys I saw around the Institute. I was never overfond of pale skin, but his was so smooth, his coloring warm and not wan, set off by the waves of his light brown hair. His eyes were a pretty greenish-brown, looking out from lashes as long and lovely as a girl's. He had what Mama always called "an easy smile," and when he smiled it at me, I quickly agreed to read with him.

He held out his hand. "I'm Theodore Hinton, by the way."

"And I'm Mary Van Lew." I settled into an armchair near his, and we began taking turns reading aloud.

If I knew all that happened in the second half of that poem—Evangeline and Gabriel searching for each other all those years, then finding one another just in time to die in each other's arms—and how it would have me dabbing my handkerchief at my eyes, I suppose I never would have consented to read it in front of Theodore Handsome Hinton. He was all gallantry, even insisting on escorting me home when we were through reading. As we strolled toward Gaskill Street, he went on about Longfellow and the American Romantics until I couldn't tell whether he was making me out to be a great literary scholar or just mocking my sentimentality.

When Hattie and I turned onto Lombard Street the next morning, we nearly collided into Theodore Hinton, who made a grand gesture of doffing his hat and bowing to us. He was barely out of earshot before Hattie said, "Why Mary Van Lew, I do believe you're keeping company with that young man."

Of course Hattie, who turned giddy every time she brushed past George in the Institute's hallways, would draw such conclusions. I explained that he and I had only been thrown together by the necessity of sharing a library book.

She looked at me as though she was trying to be sure she recognized me. "That's about the silliest thing I ever heard. There isn't a book in that library the Hintons don't own."

"How can you be so sure what books they've got?"

"Don't you know? Mrs. Hinton is Phillipa's aunt. When she married, her husband took her rather handsome dowry and used it to purchase lots all over Philadelphia. Edward Hinton owns more real estate than any other colored man in the city. More than all but a half dozen white men, even. Anything the dear scion wants, they can buy."

I frowned in confusion while Hattie grinned and patted my arm. "You poor lamb, did that ole wolf guile you into thinking he was only hanging round to share a pile of dusty library books?"

"Some way for a prig to talk, Hattie," I said, before escaping into Miss Douglass's classroom.

When we walked home for mid-day recess, Hattie kept up all manner of bleating and howling and sheep-and-wolf conversation. I giggled and told her she was giving me a headache, wondering to myself if Handsome Hinton could truly be as taken with me as she claimed.

As soon as we turned onto my block, Mrs. Upshaw called down from her window. "A letter come for you, Mary dear. On very fancy paper, brung direct by a servant."

Hattie raced to the apartment house and up the stairway, with me trailing behind. Between her and Mrs. Upshaw, I was nearly smothered before I could break the seal on the letter.

"*Mrs. William T. Catto*," I read, recognizing the name of one of the colored ladies from the Anti-Slavery Society, "*would be pleased to have Miss Mary Van Lew at a ball at her home, on the twenty-third.*" Chap-fallen, I said, "It hasn't anything to do with Mr. Wolf."

"Oh, see if it doesn't," Hattie said. "I'll wager the whole flock that Mr. Wolf is in attendance."

"What are you girls on about? Who is Mr. Wolf?" asked Mrs. Upshaw.

I shot Hattie a look that said, don't you dare or I'll never hear the end of it. "He's a cousin of Hattie's,"

I fibbed, "though I've never met him myself. But Hattie's expected home to dinner right away, perhaps she'll see him there." With that, I pushed my friend toward the door.

"Is it here?" I asked, the moment Hattie swung open her front door on the afternoon of the twenty-third.

"Hello to you, too," she said, leading me inside. "Haven't I told you that you could have your pick of any of my sisters' gowns? Mrs. John Overton has the loveliest brocade barege, the color of fresh-churned butter."

"Indeed I do," her sister Gertie broke in. "Dairy pure. Perfect for an unmarried young lady. And there's not a hint of wind today, so we can install ourselves next door, turn Daddy's shop into a seamstress' paradise, and have you fitted up in no time. What do you say?"

The sisters winked and whistled, because they already knew my answer. Just the thought of being in the undertaker's shop sent a gale of shivers up and down my spine, much to the amusement of the Jones family. Besides, I knew with all a schoolgirl's certainty that I wasn't about to wear one of Gertie's, or anybody's, old dresses for my very first ball. Not after spending so many hours hunting out every dressmaker on Chestnut Street, until I settled on one to make my first proper evening gown. A burgundy silk moiré so stiff it weighed as much as any three of the other dresses I tried, and as intoxicating to me as a half-dozen bottles of the wine whose color it shared.

At my final fitting two evenings before, as I instructed the dressmaker's clerks to send the bill to Bet's attorney, I also directed them to send the finished gown to Hattie's house. I felt lucky to have my pick of such fine things. I didn't care to lord my good fortune over Ducky. Nor to let her quacking about Bet spoil an iota of the pleasure I took in such a purchase. But now Hattie wouldn't let me so much as see my dress.

"No point you oohing and cooing over what you're going to wear," she said, "until you've mastered what you've got to do." And so she led me through the dozens of steps of the dozen dances she insisted I'd need to know at the Cattos' ball.

Lucky for me, she'd already attended a few such events, and had watched her sisters ready themselves for many more. "George Patterson shall take my hand like this," she said, "and lay his hand like that." I giggled as she whirled me and twirled me until we were both dizzy, neither of us bothering to mention to whom I hoped to offer my hand.

"I never knew a dancing master could be such a despot," I said when at long last she deemed me schooled enough in the Redowa and the waltz cotillion to bathe and then don my gown.

"You think I've worried you, wait until my sisters get a hold of that hair." She laughed and turned me over to the sororal jurisdiction of Emily, Fanny, and Gertie, who primped and prodded me until I thought I'd never get to the festivities. Finally they led me with my eyes closed to the rosewood-edged mirror that hung in Mr. Jones's front hall. When they declared I could open my eyes, I nearly didn't recognize my own reflection.

"Miss Mary Van Lew of Paris, France, you might as well be," Hattie said, giving a little clap of joy at my transformation.

I thanked Hattie, and each of her sisters, and Hattie again. I studied every inch of myself, from the curls Emily had set in my hair to the dancing slippers Fanny had set on my feet. I made sure to memorize each detail, so I could write it all out for Mama and Papa, even as I fretted to myself over whether I'd know just how to carry it all off when we finally arrived at the ball.

Hattie and I hardly had time enough to set our wraps in the Cattos' cloak-room, before George Patterson whisked her off to dance. I was watching them glide among the other couples when Theodore Hinton appeared at my elbow.

"Miss Van Lew, I'm so glad to see you. I've something of yours I've been meaning to return." He reached into his pocket and drew out one of my handkerchiefs. "I must have taken it up by accident when we were reading together."

I felt my cheeks warm. "What a coincidence that we arrived at the library to read Mr. Longfellow on the same day. Especially since you must have your own copy of *Evangeline* at home."

"Miss Van Lew, are you accusing me of bribing the custodian to reveal your reading habits, just so I could have a chance to meet you?" Those long lashes came together and then apart, as though pleading his eyes' hazel innocence. "Next you'll say that isn't your handkerchief at all, that I merely noted the style and monogram on the one you held that day and had a matching one made up, so that I would have an excuse to speak to you at this dreadfully dull party to which I somehow contrived to have us both invited."

"Why me? I mean, why go to all that trouble, when you don't know me, Mr. Hinton?"

"I will tell you, on two conditions." He paused long enough for me to nod. "The first, that we do away with Mr. Hinton and Miss Van Lew, and try Theodore and Mary instead. Mr. Hinton is my father, not me."

"And Miss Van Lew is my former owner, even worse. Very well, Theodore." I took more than a little pleasure in pronouncing those three syllables. "What's the second condition?"

"That you won't denounce me at the next Lyceum meeting, now that you know what a duplicitous scoundrel I can be."

All at once, the same dizzying fury I'd felt at the debate about Mrs. Stowe's novel set upon me. I wasn't about to abide anyone ridiculing me for defending Papa and Mama. "I'm trying to avoid any such public proclamations in the future, lest I offend the better sort of colored Philadelphia." I turned and headed down the hall.

"Mary, wait." Theodore strode to catch up. "Your audacity that evening was quite impressive. I was longing to say something to that lot of pompous fops myself. When I saw you around the Institute this term, I vowed to find a way to meet you." He smiled that easy smile. "I would even be willing to subject myself to your outspokenness, for the honor of dancing with you."

He wasn't mocking my outburst at the Lyceum, he was praising it. And I had practiced dancing for the longest time, hoping I might be asked. Hoping Theodore Handsome Hinton would be the one asking. I held my gloved hand out to him, matching his smile with one of my own.

Though I'd tripped in nervous confusion when Hattie and I rehearsed the various steps, with Theodore leading me I executed the quadrilles and germans and all quite well, until at last he steered me toward the edge of the room. "I've shown off my good fortune to the other dancers long enough. Now I'd like to parade my lovely partner before the wall-flowers, if you will do me the honor."

I slipped my hand through the arm he offered. Show me off, Handsome Hinton? More the other way around. "Everyone here seems to know you," I said as various clusters of guests nodded at us.

"It's my family they know. There's not a dollar spent in colored Philadelphia without my father's knowledge, nor a bouquet given, a gown worn, or a baby born without my mother's."

"I hadn't realized I was under surveillance by the entire Hinton clan."

"Oh, I think I'm the only one who's observed you yet. But I suppose we must rectify that by introducing you to Mother."

He led me toward an elegant side table where two ladies sat surveying the party. Between them, they wore more jewels than Bet and her mother owned altogether. They both beamed so brightly at Theodore, I could hardly tell which was his mother, until he faced the broader of the two.

"Miss Mary Van Lew, my mother, Mrs. Edward Hinton." He turned to the thinner lady. "And my aunt, Mrs. Phillip Thayer. I trust you will enjoy getting acquainted, while I fetch Miss Van Lew some punch."

As soon as Theodore left us, Mrs. Hinton narrowed her eyes at me. "Van Lew—I don't believe I recognize the name. Where are your people from?"

"I was born in Richmond, although we're not from there, exactly. Old Master Van Lew brought Mama with him when he came from New York, way back in '16. And Papa, he was born on a plantation in the Tidewater. I'm not sure which one, as he doesn't like to talk about it. But they're in Richmond now, at least until Master Mahon—"

"Yes, well." She turned to Mrs. Thayer. "How is Phillipa coming on at school? I understand she is now Grace Mapps's star pupil."

I listened silently to Mrs. Thayer's recounting of Phillipa's triumphs, until Theodore returned and steered me off to see the conservatory that Mrs. Catto had fashioned out of a sunporch at the back of the house. As we stood among the flowers crowding the candlelit room, he insisted on knowing why I was suddenly so glum. Fiddling with the crystal punch cup, I told him what had happened.

"Oh, you mustn't mind Mother and Aunt Gwen. They've been plotting my betrothal to Cousin Phillipa since before either of us could walk or talk."

I nearly sputtered out my punch. "Your betrothal?"

"You needn't be so worried. I have no interest in becoming a stepping stool for my stuck-up cousin's rise to the zenith of colored Philadelphia. Not when there are girls as sweet and lovely as you about." His wooing warmed me faster than the brandy-punch, until I heard what he said next. "Only, you oughtn't go on about your parents being slaves. People might hold it against you."

"Hold it against me? Whatever for?" I looked past the conservatory to the sitting room, full of colored people of every complexion, dressed in as much finery as their varying financial means allowed. "Surely everyone here is descended from slaves."

"Indeed, and they hardly wish to be reminded of their own proximity to the 'unfortunate condition.' When it comes to Mother, I suggest you accommodate that wish. After all, you wouldn't want to abandon me to Cousin Phillipa, would you?"

I couldn't help but grin. "I suppose not."

"Good. Then may I have the honor of the next dance?" He bowed with mock formality.

"Of course you may." I returned his bow with as deep a curtsy as I could manage in my moiré and crinolines. The pianist played the first delicate minor notes of a mazurka. As we took our places among the dancers, I soon forgot all about his family, and my own.

"I never expected your head to be turned by light skin and a large fortune," Hattie teased once Theodore and I began courting.

"I didn't seek him out," I reminded her. "And I didn't know he was rich till you told me."

Even among all Miss Douglass's and Miss Mapps's students, Phillipa was the only one who was truly rich, and her carrying on didn't make the small group of wealthy colored families seem any too admirable. And whatever complaints Papa had about Mama raising me dicty, she never fell in for the worship of light complexions, not as dark as she and Papa both were. So though I shivered with pleasure over Theodore's good looks, I assured myself that it wasn't his coloring or his money but his confidence, his charm, and that easy smile that attracted me. I half hoped some of his aplomb might rub off on me, if I spent enough time with him.

Theodore had his own little phaeton, maroon with gold wheels, his initials embroidered in gold all over the maroon leather seat and inside the hood. "I see

Mr. Hinton has sent his most gracious driver to collect me," I joked the first time he handed me up and then settled in beside me.

"My mother has a driver." He flicked the reins, and the white Arabian pranced off. "I can't bear him. A man should handle his own horses."

I recalled Mama's reports of Bet's antics with her gig. *Folks on Church Hill finaly found a way to keep there Chickens from wandering in to the Road. Just let Miss Bet come careening arownd a turn & Feathers are flying every wich way till them Birds are out of site. Course she dont know Herself what a Terror she is. She even offers to drive Me on my errands! No Mam I say finding every Excuse I can why I need to walk down to First Market insted of ride. She drove Terry Farr out to the farm one day to see what Produce to ecspect in to the house all Season & by the time they got home Terry was Whiter then Mistress V from frite over how Miss Bet ran that gig all over the Streets.*

"And what about a lady?" I asked, wondering what Theodore would make of Bet.

"Why don't we see about that for ourselves?" He held the gold-studded reins out to me.

I was about to laugh and push his hands away when he added, "I thought you were the type who'd take on a whole team of wild horses. Perhaps I was wrong."

I snatched the reins right then. I wasn't the type to take on a whole team of wild horses, or at least I didn't think I was. But if Theodore wanted to believe that of me, I was willing to try.

It felt good to hold the weight of the leather straps in my hands, Theodore leaning against my arm as he instructed me on how to guide the Arabian. That easy smile was all over his face, and I met it with one of my own as I led us along Washington Square. "You're not worried it will damage your reputation, to be driven by a female?"

"I can only be the envy of anyone who sees me, to have such a lovely and skillful companion. My sole concern is that some rival will try to steal you away. To drive his coach, I mean." But from the pleased look on his face, I knew he wasn't worried one whit. And from the thrill of pleasure I felt riding with him, I knew he had no reason to be.

Though Hattie and George happily kept company the way all of her sisters and their beaux had, visiting at each other's houses in the evening, the same couldn't be said for me and Theodore. I couldn't bear the idea of submitting him to the Upshaws, but I didn't much care for calling at his home or his aunt's, either. Those mansions made me long for the tiny houses where free negroes or boarding-out slaves lived in Richmond. At least there, everyone was together, making their own good time laughing and talking and singing. But the two families that declared themselves the very best of colored Philadelphia naturally had better ways to do things, or so they thought. Which meant that after the guests endured a solemn six-course supper beneath the marble-eyed hunting trophies that lined the dark-paneled dining room, the men disappeared into a separate parlor to smoke and play cards. Theodore couldn't possibly join the ladies, he explained, it just wasn't done. So I was left with the womenfolk, who only addressed me when they thought I needed to be put in my place.

After effusing praise for a tune Phillipa played on the pianoforte, or complimenting another young lady's performance on the Spanish guitar, Mrs. Thayer would turn to me. "But we mustn't be rude to our new guest. Do play something for us, Miss Van Lew."

"You've forgotten, dear sister," Mrs. Hinton would say, "Miss Van Lew can't play."

"How unfortunate," Mrs. Thayer would reply, "I am so sorry to hear of it."

But she wasn't really sorry to hear of it, nor to remind me of it, because she brought it up on just about every visit I paid. The years her pretty, pale daughter studied music, I spent waiting on a white family, and she wasn't about to let anyone in the ladies' parlor forget it.

Though the ladies lavished admiration on each other's fancywork, only one other guest ever asked after what I sewed. When I proudly held up the glengarry cap I was trimming and explained it was to be sold months later at the fair, her curiosity withered away.

"A seamstress for customers, how . . . interesting," she said, turning back to her own needlework.

Mrs. Thayer, Mrs. Hinton, and their guests didn't bother with any charity fairs. They sewed only gifts for new brides or new mothers. And sometimes it seemed they only did that to make me feel more unwelcome.

"What a fine match Mrs. Dunbar's son has made. Precisely the daughter-in-law she always knew was right for her boy," Mrs. Hinton said as she embroidered a pillow for the young couple.

"The Dorsey baby is lovely," Mrs. Thayer assured everyone while she sewed lace onto her newest godchild's christening gown. "And so promising, descended on both sides from the oldest and best families in Philadelphia."

Colored families, she meant. Because though the Hintons and the Thayers seemed to want more than anything else to be white, they acted as if white people didn't exist, and especially as though negroes, at least the few negroes they deemed worthy of inclusion in their social set, never faced such a thing as race prejudice. Even Theodore carried on that way, and I couldn't possibly explain to him why I felt less at ease sitting with the ladies of his family than working beside Zinnie Moore and the other women in my sewing circle, or listening to the impassioned lectures at the Lyceum.

Though it had taken all Hattie's persuading to convince me to return to the Lyceum after the Stowe debate, when I did, I found the speeches of visiting abolitionists like Mr. Frederick Douglass, Mr. William Wells Brown, and Miss Frances Watkins—a woman who spoke with such eloquence and fervor even the menfolk leapt to their feet to applaud her—enthralling. But Theodore refused to accompany me, complaining, "They're as predictable as parrots, repeating the same dull phrases over and over."

There were other Lyceums and Atheneums and all manner of theaters in Philadelphia, of course, with operas and concerts and so forth. But we weren't welcome there. So though my beau owned genuine mother-of-pearl opera glasses made in Paris, there wasn't a venue in all of Pennsylvania where he might use them. Theodore and I never spoke of it, him too proud and me too incensed to dwell on the places from which we were excluded. Perhaps he was right about the predictability of the discussions at the Gilbert Lyceum, but I preferred that to the unpredictability that race prejudice brought to the rest of colored life in Philadelphia.

One hot Saturday afternoon, Theodore drove us all the way past Rittenhouse Square. When I mentioned how my throat parched from all the dust the horse kicked up along the ride, he suggested we stop for a dish of ice cream. I felt as elegant as could be when Theodore pulled the phaeton up beside a confectionery, tied the reins to a waiting-post, and promenaded me inside.

A wooden counter ran along one wall of the store, and a ring of tables was set before a dark curtain that hung across the entryway to the kitchen. A white girl, no more than three years old, stood before the counter in a dirt-streaked pinafore, sobbing. Wondering that any child who lived in a confectionery could have a thing in the world to cry about, I knelt beside her, murmuring a stranger's words of comfort.

The girl held out a doll, its arm dangling loose. As I reached for the broken toy, the curtain rustled behind me and a man asked Theodore, "What can I get you, sir?"

Watching me struggle to push the doll's porcelain limb back into its socket, the girl let out such a howl, one might have thought it was her own arm that was dislocated. "Maggie, leave the customers be," the man said.

I turned to tell him it was all right. But before I could speak, he caught sight of my face. His features hardened, and he barked his words at Theodore. "What do you mean, bringing one of them in here? Get your darky concubine away from my child."

I thought by then I'd heard every aspersion some hateful white person might fling. But nothing prepared me for the shock of that shopkeeper mistaking my light-skinned beau for a white man and presuming I was his harlot, calling me so right to our faces.

Hearing me harassed, Theodore straightened to his full height, holding his eyes on the confectioner and carefully fastening the pearl button that had come undone on his gray kid riding glove. He arced his hand along the countertop, sending platter after platter of daintily arranged meringues crashing to the floor, before turning and offering me his arm.

Much as I wanted to match his gallantry, still I trembled with mortification as I held the broken doll out to the little girl. When she shrank away, whimpering, I laid the pieces on the nearest table and slipped my arm through Theodore's.

Once we were outside, I was grateful for how quickly he unhitched the phaeton. We rode across Philadelphia without a word passing between us, his silence the only solace he could offer for the insult I'd suffered.

The next time I saw Theodore, we were both careful to avoid any conversation that might recall that afternoon. Much as I longed to forget the indignity done to me by that white man, I should have known Theodore was too chivalrous to let it go unanswered. A few weeks later, as we took our Saturday ride, he seemed especially purposeful about our route. That same igneous shame blazed over me as I realized we were headed back to Rittenhouse Square.

"George took Hattie to Lemon Hill last week," I said. "She told me the gardens look beautiful this time of year. Let's go right now and see them."

But Theodore was determined. He wouldn't even speak until he guided the phaeton to the spot where we'd stopped before.

"See what I've done." He nodded triumphant at the building.

The storefront was empty, every sign of the confectionery gone.

"It seems my father had the opportunity to acquire some realty in this neighborhood not long ago. And, as the proprietor of a certain establishment could not bear to serve a negress, I certainly didn't want to do him the indignity of paying rent to a negro, either. So I had him evicted." He smiled. "You see why I've no patience for all the talk at your Lyceum of petitioning the legislature and organizing for our rights. What is the point of all that rigmarole, when a man who is shrewd with the dollars in his pocket can get his way well enough?"

As he flicked the reins, directing the horse toward Lemon Hill, I thought of the sobbing girl and her broken doll. She'd have no new toy now—likely no dinner to eat or place to sleep, even. Her suffering lent little balm for my own, though I knew I couldn't make Theodore see that, proud as he was for all he'd done to defend my honor.

Theodore's phaeton seemed like an enchanted chariot, the night we rode all the way to Byberry for the grand ball the Purvises held at their home. I'd never been so far outside the city, and as we drove along I basked in the warm colors of the sun setting over the fields. Theodore and I had been keeping company for over two years by then, the giddy I first felt at being courted grown into a deeper gladsome at the ways he doted on me. Theodore was born to charm, and he always made it easy for me to adore the way he adored me.

The Purvis house was in a style Theodore called Italianate Villa, and my breath caught at the sight of it. I felt like I was in a fairy tale as we stepped beneath the archway to the carved front door. But I was brought back to reality once we were inside.

"Why, here comes Miss Van Lew, in her rose silk." Phillipa spoke just loud enough for me to hear but low enough to make me feel like I was eavesdropping. "Just see the way it brings out the pink in her cheeks. No wonder she wears it every chance she gets."

The flush I felt on my face deepened. Whenever I went to Bet's attorney for money, he gave me all I asked for and ten dollars more. But still, I only purchased one evening gown each season. I couldn't countenance spending sixty dollars or more on a new dress every time I was invited to a dance. Not when I thought of how Papa and Mama were living. Not when I hung my fine things next to Dulcey's same few dresses, which grew more patched and faded every year. Besides, most of the ladies at the Purvises' had only one or two fancy dresses anyway.

"Thank you for the compliment, Phillipa. I'm relieved to hear you value having color in one's face. Especially since some unkind people say just the opposite of you." Before she could respond, I turned to Theodore. "Would you be so good as to escort me to the garden?"

As soon as we reached the courtyard, its air heavy with the scent of wisteria, he chuckled. "That should keep the hounds at bay."

I didn't much care for being taken for hound bait. "Theodore, sometimes I think you only court me because I'm not Phillipa."

"Don't be absurd." He plucked a cluster of the delicate purple buds, offering them up as an addition to the bouquet pinned at my waist. "I care for you very much."

"In direct proportion to the amount that your cousin doesn't care for me?"

"I see Aunt Gwen is incorrect. The Institute's algebra lessons do have practical applications for young ladies." Realizing I was in no mood for such teasing, he grew serious. "I care for you because you are as fresh and unspoiled as the first breeze of spring coming through the window of a house that's been shut up all winter. You're the antidote to the insufferable society Mother keeps."

Though such compliments captivated me more than a whole hothouse full of flowers, a part of me still wondered why he always seemed to take such pleasure at how Phillipa and I hissed at each other like alley cats—and why I relished the way Phillipa glared whenever Theodore chatted warmly with me in some secluded corner.

Eight

All through Hattie's courtship with George, and mine with Theodore, she still met me outside the Upshaws' every morning so we could stroll to the Institute together. We needed a chance to gossip and giggle about those boys, after all. So I was mighty surprised to arrive downstairs one bright autumn day in '55 and find no Hattie.

She was never even two minutes tardy, and that day of all days, I figured she would be punctual. Miss Mapps had arranged for Miss Elizabeth Greenfield, who sang at Buckingham Palace before Queen Victoria only a year earlier, to visit our class. Hattie was already lording it over her sister Charlotte that she was to meet the famed Black Swan. Yet here she was, or rather here she wasn't, about to make us both late.

Hattie was always up long before school, taking breakfast with her father before he crossed the property to tend North Star, the chestnut mare with a bright blaze that he kept to pull his glass-paneled hearse. But as I hurried up Sixth Street to their lot, I saw the stable doors were locked, the shutters still closed on the undertaker's shop. I made my way to the house, worry catching my breath. When Hattie answered my knock, I saw her hair wasn't pulled back, and her bonnet sat crooked on her head.

"What's the matter?" I asked as she jammed her hands into a pair of mismatched gloves.

"Daddy's been burning up with fever all night. I've got to fetch the doctor." A floorboard creaked above us, and she frowned. "Susan took the week off to visit her mother out to Bridgeport, and I'm afraid to leave him. He keeps muttering about going next door, saying how the shop can't be left untended."

Her distress must have rubbed off on me, because before I realized it, I was offering to stay at the undertaker's shop while she was gone.

I hadn't ever warmed to the idea of setting foot inside a building where corpses came and went. Usually Hattie teased me about my fear, but now she forgot it entirely as she hugged me her thanks and pressed the key her father kept at his watch chain into my hand.

"Don't worry about North Star, I'll tend to her later," she said. "Just mind the shop, and I'll be back as soon as I've found Doc Weatherston."

I felt all the cold of that metal key as it turned in the lock of the undertaker's shop, revealing a small, square parlor where Mr. Jones received his customers. The walls, painted a condolent yellow, were decorated with embroidered mottoes. A mahogany étagère in the corner held a display of Hattie's landscapes. Though the pall of death was too close for my comfort, I took my place on one of the figured damask settees set around a low rosewood table. I drew out my *Metamorphoses*, meaning to distract myself by reading ahead in my lessons. Captivated by Mr. Ovid's tales, I started when the front door swung open some half an hour later.

"Hattie, you gave me such a fright." I laughed as I looked up from my book.

But what I saw stopped up my laughter. The person standing across from me wasn't Hattie. It was a short white man, his face doughy beneath a shock of orange hair.

"What do you want, sir?"

I hadn't called a white man sir since leaving Richmond, but the appellation slipped out without me even realizing it. A white man has no business at a colored undertaker's. And a colored female has no business being alone with a strange white man.

"I'm wanting Joons." His accent was rough and heavy. The sound of trouble.

"He's not here."

"What I hae for him will not wait. Fetch him, or we will all be sorry."

"Mr. Jones is too sick to come to the shop."

"Is he abed next door?" His cold eyes shifted in the direction of the house.

I thought of Mr. Jones alone in his sickbed. "The doctor is there with him, tending his fever." I ventured the lie as boldly as I could. "He was raving earlier, so the physician won't have him left alone."

"Raving?" The man pulled out a handkerchief and mopped at his brow. "What has he said?"

"I don't know. I haven't been to the sickroom myself."

Without so much as a good-day, he turned and went out the door. I watched through the window as he climbed onto the driver's bench of a high-sided buckboard and charged away.

I was still worrying the lace on my sleeve when the buckboard reappeared a half hour later, with a colored man sitting beside the orange-haired one. The white man remained on the driver's bench while his companion jumped down. When he swung open the door of the shop, I saw it was Miss Douglass's cousin, David Bustill Bowser.

"Miss Van Lew, what are you doing here?"

"Looking after things while Hattie runs an errand." I dropped my voice, though I knew the stranger outside couldn't hear. "You know that man?"

Mr. Bowser tugged at his goatee. "He's a friend of ours. He came by earlier to make a delivery. On behalf of the Odd Fellows."

I'd seen Mr. Bowser and the other members of the Odd Fellows burial society marching behind Mr. Jones's hearse as it wound through Philadelphia's streets to the Lebanon burial ground. But the idea of a white man doing odd jobs for a negro fraternal order didn't make any sense to me. "He didn't leave anything when he was here. Just said he had to speak to Mr. Jones and then stormed out."

"I hope McNiven didn't frighten you. He's a Scot, he forgets about custom in this country. I don't imagine he can understand how a young colored lady feels to find herself alone with a white man." He motioned to the back room. "If you unlatch the rear entry, we'll bring our cart around and unload the delivery."

Mr. Bowser went out to lead the cart horses along the narrow passageway to the rear of the shop, leaving me to open the communicating door between the parlor and Mr. Jones's work room.

Stacks of planked wood lined the walls, carpenter's tools neatly arranged on an adjoining bench. Smelling cut pine standing ready to be assembled into coffins made the hair on the back of my neck rise up. I couldn't bring myself to more than glance over to the embalming table, with its assorted tubes and funnels.

Not caring to see that white man, nor the corpse he meant to deliver, I unlatched the service entry as quickly as I could, then hurried back to the parlor. I closed the communicating door tight, trying to ignore the sound of the broad back doors being swung open and Mr. Bowser and his peculiar companion carrying their delivery inside.

A few minutes later, Mr. Bowser came through the communicating door.

"I've latched the back entry. Be sure to keep it so, and don't let anyone through this way, except for Mr. Jones, or one of his girls."

He passed outside and headed off on foot, the Scotsman and his cart already gone.

I tried hard to calm myself after that. But whenever I started into a passage of Mr. Ovid's poetry I'd see a metamorphosis right before my eyes, devil's horns sprouting from the stranger's orange hair.

I longed for the distraction of my workbox. Zinnie Moore was teaching me how to work a lace collar, which was quite a joke between us, since my Quaker friend would never wear any lace herself. But Zinnie was a keen businesswoman, and she knew lace sold well at the fair. I closed my eyes and was concentrating hard on the steps she'd shown me, when I heard the knock.

Not a knock. More of a thump, really. From the back room.

I told myself it was only my imagination, when— thump—it came again. I crept to the communicating door and leaned an ear against it.

No thump now. Even worse—a low moan. Half-human, it went through my bones like a wet wind on a dark night.

I was so scared I was beyond scared. Whoever or whatever that white man was, he'd brought some restless spirit into the shop.

I tore my way out of the parlor, clapping the lock on the front door. My fist was still clamped tight on the key when, wide-eyed and dry-mouthed, I spied Hattie coming down the street with her sister Diana and a tall white man in a dark suit. Diana led the man up to the house, while Hattie continued over to me.

"Mary, what's the matter?"

"Some strange white man came here. Appeared out of thin air, I didn't even hear his cart. McEvil or McDemon or something. Worried me half to death, then he was gone as quick as he came. Only to come back later, with David Bustill Bowser of all people. And they brought a"— my voice dropped to a whisper as I glanced at the shop door—"a body. Only that body isn't resting peaceful. It's tossing and turning, thumping and groaning."

Hattie stifled a little laugh, but then her mouth drew back down into a determined line across her face. She pried opened my fingers, took the key, and unlocked the door. "Come inside."

"I'm not going back in there."

"I'm sorry you had such a fright. But you've got to listen now. I'll explain it all once we're inside."

Shaking head to toe, I followed her into the parlor. But I kept a yell ready at the back of my throat, just in case that restive spirit came to get us.

"I've got to tell you something, only I'm not supposed to," Hattie said. "Not supposed to tell anyone, ever. So you can't ever tell anyone either. Not Theodore, not your parents, nobody. Promise?"

I wasn't about to set that yell aside just yet, so I nodded.

"You know my daddy's an undertaker. Only, some of his undertakings, they aren't exactly what you might expect."

I remembered how I joked years back about her father being a Voudon master. Now I wondered if he might really be a spirit doctor after all.

Hattie shifted nervously. "Daddy always says he'll skin us alive if we talk about this outside the family. But you've been in slavery, your parents are still there." She drew in a deep breath. "You ever heard of the Underground Railroad?"

I managed to murmur a small "mmm-hmm."

"Well, this is a stopping place. Sometimes Daddy collects baggage from down in Chambersburg. Sometimes he forwards it up to Bucks County himself. Sometimes another conductor transports the baggage instead." She gave me a moment to take in what she was saying. "That white man, Mr. McNiven, he's one of the best. Rides right into Delaware, Maryland, even Virginia and brings his cargo all the way here."

"That's a slave back there, closed up in that coffin?"

She nodded. "If I realized the wind was blowing from the South today, I would have sent you on to Diana's and waited here myself."

"What's the wind got to do with it?"

"That's what we say to mean baggage is headed this way. And baggage is what we say to mean—" She gestured toward the other room. "Daddy always says we owe it to them to mind how we speak, even among ourselves."

I thought of all the times I heard Mr. Jones or one of his daughters or sons-in-laws talk about the wind. I wondered what else they'd said in front of me that I hadn't understood.

Hattie practically bent over apologizing, she felt so bad about deceiving me. "Are you sore I never told you before?"

"Of course not."

"Well, Daddy can do what he wants when he finds out, but I'm glad you know. I hated having any secrets between us, and now we don't."

When she said that, I knew I couldn't hold quiet. "We've still got a secret. And if I tell you, you've got to promise me you'll never tell anyone either. Okay?"

"Miss Mary Van Lew of Gaskill Street, to think you've been holding out on me all these years," she teased. But when she realized I wasn't yet ready for joking, she turned serious again. "I swear, I'll keep your secret."

"My mama, she isn't really a slave." Hattie's eyebrow nearly raised right off her head as I told her about Mama's subterfuge.

She might have been trying to undo the tautest sailor's knot, the way she mulled over all it meant. "Mr. McNiven's brought baggage from Richmond a bunch of times. I always think of your folks when I hear he's headed that way. Maybe he could help your papa escape from Mahon."

I shook my head, worrying whether I could make Hattie understand. Scared that if I didn't, it meant we could never be truly best of friends.

"Papa thought about running, when Bet first freed Mama and me. But he won't." I glanced toward the back room. "You see the baggage headed North, all hope and daring because they're freedom bound. In Richmond, we see the fugitives who've been caught. Whipped, branded, sometimes even maimed to keep them from running again. Then sold South, into a slavery that's ten thousand times worse than the slavery we knew in Richmond. Which is plenty bad enough." I ran a hand along the seam of my skirt, trying not to think too hard on just how bad life as Mahon's slave might be. "In Richmond, Mama and Papa can be together, and they know I'm safe here, getting an education. If Papa runs, there's no guarantee we'll end up someplace where they can earn enough to live on and I can go to school. Papa won't put me and Mama in jeopardy like that. He's too good a man."

Hattie gave me just the answer I needed to hear. "Of course he is."

A thump from the back room made us both jerk.

"I better get some water and food back there," Hattie said. "Why don't you go along to the Institute now?"

I gathered up my books, promising to come by after school and sit with her while she tended her father.

Mr. Jones was well again before the week was out. Curious as I was about the Railroad, I never said a word on it, knowing I'd keep Hattie's confidence, just as surely as she'd keep mine.

Nine

It was a day too cold even for February, when the letter arrived. Ducky was at work, and Mrs. Upshaw had braved the icy winds to collect a new round of piecework from her customers. Alone in the apartment, I pulled the parlor chair close to the fire and tore at Bet's seal.

My dearest daughter

You see this letter in young Miss Van Lew hand maybe you guess the sad news I got to tell. This very day your dear Mama my beloved Minerva passed. She took ill quick just as quick was gone from us. Shocked as we is to lose her so fast it seems somehow right she was not one to waste away slow.

Strong near till the end lovely as ever when her eyes closed finally.

Her last words was Jesus got a plan for you make her proud and she loves you. Then some thoughts for me Im gonna keep private. We bury her at the colored cemetery out by Shockoe Creek tomorrow. I expect a large turnout you know the people love Aunt Minnie.

Jesus comfort us

X

The bile of grief flooded my mouth, choking me. My biggest fear when I left Richmond was that I'd never see my parents again. Now that fear had come part true.

Days of my childhood, it seemed anyone I might ask would know Aunt Minnie, and it made me feel special just to tell people I was her daughter. Whatever Theodore and Hattie and Zinnie Moore meant to me, to them I was Mary Van Lew, not Mama and Papa's Mary El or Aunt Minnie's Mary, as I'd always been at home. It tore at me to think there wasn't a soul I could talk to in Philadelphia who knew my mama. The near five years I'd lived in the North stretched behind me, seeming like too many to bear. Fingering Papa's shaky cross mark on that letter, thinking of him as alone in his grief as I was in mine, I wondered if maybe it was time to go home.

The idea caught me tender at first. I wanted to believe being with Papa might stop up the agony I felt, knowing Mama was gone. Wanted to believe I might assuage the same agony he must be feeling, too. But as the wind cracked at the thin panes, it blew doubt in along with the cold.

Ceding my life here would be like contemning Mama's insistence that Jesus had a plan for me. I'd never quite believed in it until that day Bet sat us down in her dining room, and even after that it seemed more a product of Mama's willful invention than any true calling. Yet to deny it now would mean betraying Mama's memory, something I wasn't about to do.

Besides, Mahon still wouldn't sell. Bet had renewed her offer more than once without getting so much as a maybe from the smith. My being there couldn't do any more to win Papa's freedom than a pile of her money had. And to return to a Richmond in which there was no Mama—how could I have stayed away so long, and go back only when I knew she was gone?

All I remember about the next months is that I walked through them in a haze. I barely noticed the murmurs that followed me through the Institute halls, students and instructors alike wondering at my mourning attire. I had trouble concentrating on my studies, though I tried very hard, knowing how Mama wanted me to succeed at school. Theodore kept his kindest words and his finest handkerchiefs at the ready during our Saturday drives, never complaining when I begged off invitations for anything more than our solitary rides. Hattie coaxed me to her house at least once a week for a cup of tea, listening close while I told and retold stories about home. Grief like mine was something she knew from way back. She understood that for a while I needed to keep my thoughts more with the dead than the living.

I worried Papa didn't have anyone to do for him what Theodore or Hattie did for me. It was hard to send much comfort to him care of Bet. I knew she meant to do right by my family, but she never was one for regarding people's feelings. Still, I didn't have any other way to get word to him, so I kept sending letters to Grace Street, then waiting and waiting for a reply. Not from Bet, she scratched out her missives right away, but Papa—even when Bet said she'd read him my letters, she didn't always have a response from him to send. Reticent as he was around white people, I suppose he didn't take too well to having her scribe for him.

Sometimes a sentence or two would turn up in a different hand, when Papa enlisted some literate negro or other to take down a few words for him. These epistles seemed too stilted to come from my sure and easy-going Papa, all the blank space on the page saying more than the spare bit of writing. While it might be easier for him to share his private thoughts with a colored person than with Bet, easier wasn't necessarily easy, not with him grieving his beloved Minerva. It was like losing both my parents at once: Mama gone, and with her the only real connection I had to Papa.

All the time I lived in Philadelphia, I always looked forward to the first signs of spring, when the ice on the rivers broke up and birds twittered out their songs again. That year, the only notice I took of the seasons was when the weather grew so warm I had to go to Besson & Son's store to replace my winter mourning outfit with something suited for summer. I stood tall in that dress to cheer Hattie on as she graduated, but I slumped back into grief just as quick as she doffed her mortar-board and gown. With school out of session, I channeled my sorrow into churning out tea cozies and seat cushions, coaxing all manner of potted plants to maturity, even sketching a few scenes of Richmond, all for sale at the fair. Miss Douglass and Miss Forten nodded with approval, and Zinnie said how Christly work was always a comfort. Though it didn't begin to fill the hole that Mama's death rent in my heart, I kept at it, even in the new school year, which was to be my last.

The previous December, we doubled the entrance fee for the fair and still drew huge crowds. Rumors circulated that this year we might even have to turn visitors away. I hoped the busy hours running my booth would leave me little time to dwell on facing Christmas without so much as a note from Mama.

The doors had just opened, customers streaming into the hall, when I caught sight of Theodore.

It gladdened me to see his face among the crowd of strangers. "How sweet of you to come." Usually he couldn't be dragged within a half mile of the fair.

"I had to come," he said. "It's the only way I can see you."

"I'm sorry I've been so busy. After the fair, I'll have more time for you, I promise."

He smiled. "Good. Then I shall expect you to accompany me to the Purvises' New Year's ball."

I gestured toward my dress. "You know I can't. I'm in mourning."

"A daughter's mourning need only be worn for six months, and you've kept yours nearly a year." He might have been reciting from Lea & Blanchard's *Etiquette Handbook*.

Before I could answer, a plump white lady standing at the side of the booth picked up one of my embroidered bookmarks. "I should like to take this, please," she said, handing me several coins.

I accepted the payment and thanked her for supporting our cause, waiting until she departed to turn back to Theodore. "This isn't the time or place for discussing personal matters. I have to tend my customers now."

"I'll buy everything you have." He pulled two fifty-dollar notes from his wallet and tossed them onto my table. "You can keep the change for your Society. Just promise you'll come to the ball. Make it your Christmas gift to me."

I looked at those bills, cast down as if he were playing a game of jack-straws. "I work very hard to make this fair a success. Please don't mock my efforts."

My plaintful tone melted any mockery away. "I'm sorry, Mary. I didn't come here to upset you. I only came because I miss you, and I wish to see your beautiful smile again. You can't hide yourself away forever. Please, let us start the New Year together, happy."

The way he pleaded at me with those hazel eyes, I wanted to wrap his words around me, a goosedown comforter against the lonely chill that had settled on me all year. "I don't mean to hide myself away. It's only, I feel so alone. More alone when I'm in the midst of other people."

"You don't have to be alone." He stepped around the table and took my hand. "I wanted to wait until New Year's, to take you to a moonlit corner of the Purvises' garden, before I spoke. But I've started now and I might as well finish."

He pulled an embroidered stool from among my goods, guided me to sit, and knelt beside me. "Missing you all these months has made me care for you more than ever. I hope you will do me the honor of being my wife."

I didn't know what to say. The last thing I expected that day was a marriage proposal.

Theodore didn't wait for me to find my voice. "You must know I care for you," he said. "And I believe you care for me. Don't you?"

I thought of how he doted on me, even in the face of his family's disapproval. How his calling me pretty made me see a different person in the looking glass than the Mary I otherwise found there. Theodore always made me feel bold and special, things I wanted very much to be but mostly didn't believe I was. Hattie already wore George Patterson's betrothal ring, and she teased me enough through all the years Theodore and I courted that I might have known his proposal would

238 · LOIS LEVEEN

come sooner or later. I even thrilled with the hope of
it, before Mama died. Now, worn from my year of
mourning, I longed for the happy future he promised.

Then I remembered Papa's words to me the day
I left Virginia. "I care very much for you. Only, I can't
accept, until you ask Papa's consent. You'll have to
write Bet, have her read him your letter and send you
his response."

Triumph rang out on Theodore's face. "Hang Bet!
I'll buy your papa and ask him myself. Surely that will
be a grander purchase than all your anti-slavery gew-
gaws put together."

I thought of the half-naked, kneeling slave figure
that decorated goods at fair booths all around us, and
of my father, standing proudly beside me as we said
our farewells that May morning so many years before.
I hated that Papa was a thing Mahon could sell or not
sell, as he chose. And suddenly I hated Theodore for
talking about him that way, too.

In a moment, I was on my feet. The stool toppled
over, its clatter turning heads throughout the hall. But
I didn't care. "How can you speak of my papa so?"

"Because I adore you. Once we're married, you can
have everything you ever want. A whole wing of our
house to keep old Papa in magnificent style. A new dress
every day of the year. Opportunities to reciprocate all

the invitations you've ever received a thousand-fold."
He beamed at the idea, not bothering to consider what
I might make of all the grand intentions he had for me.
"You won't need to worry about earning a penny here
and a penny there for the Anti-Slavery Society. We will
make them over a great check every year, so you can
spend all your time just being my darling wife."

Something in his words put me in mind of the ant-
lers mounted in his parents' dining room. My stomach
always turned at the sight of them, as I imagined how
each elk or deer felt at the moment it was shot. Wasn't
that what I'd become if Theodore had his way? Another
animal caught and displayed, tribute to the wealth and
power of the Hinton clan.

"My dresses may not be so numerous and ostentatious as your cousin Phillipa's, but they suit me fine.
My work is important to me. If you really loved me, it
would be important to you as well." I nodded toward
the people staring at us. "You've embarrassed me in
front of many friends and still more strangers. I will
thank you to go. Good day, and good-bye."

I strode out from behind the booth, making my way
toward the small corner table where Zinnie was selling
holly wreaths. Evergreen reminders of His everlast-
ing love, she called them. Her hands grew scratched
and red as she fashioned dozens of wreaths in the days

before the fair, though they sold more slowly than nearly anything else we offered.

My heart, grown so heavy since Mama's death, seemed to splinter into a million piercing shards whenever I thought over that conversation with Theodore. He must have been as sore with me as I was with him, because for once he relented without getting his way. And so what I broke off that day stayed severed.

But as the busy weeks of the fair blurred into a cold Christmas and then my solitary New Year's, I realized I was more sad than sorry over what had passed. Much as I cared for Theodore, I knew there were things for which I cared more deeply, even if he never seemed to set much stock by my political causes.

Hurt as I was by much of what he said that day, still I could see he was right about one thing. I'd let myself sink too deeply into mourning, refusing to feel anything but grief about Mama. And I was grateful that Theodore made me realize it, made me ask myself why I was doing as I did.

What is wearing all those dark mourning clothes but white people's custom? No colored person I grew up with ever did anything like that, not even free negroes. Colored folks in Virginia generally wore white for mourning, though not like whites wore black. Usually white was only a ribbon or gloves, not so showy as all-over mourning clothes but something respectful none-theless. In Philadelphia things were different, but then in Philadelphia being the better sort of colored had an awful lot to do with mimicking whites. Now that I thought on it, I knew I needed to figure my own way to honor my mama, without losing myself in grieving forever.

Once I set my mind to that, what I heard wasn't the sorrow thoughts that had been in my head all year. It was Mama's voice.

Mary El, I'm sorry I died without a chance to say good-bye proper to you. But we all got to die. What matters is what comes first. Don't be so sad I died that you forget to live. That's what a child's for, living long after her mama and papa are gone. And if you don't start living again, how you gonna do Jesus's work?

It didn't come all at once necessarily, but bits and pieces here and there, adding up to that. And when it did, suddenly everything felt easier to bear.

The one thing no one could do the whole year past was console me like Mama would. Now she seemed ready to comfort and love and badger me even from Heaven above. I smiled to think of it, imagining her wheedling and conniving to get the archangels them-selves falling into line.

Finding Mama again was like having a veil of sorrow lifted from before my eyes. After that, it was easy enough for me to lift the real veil myself, fold it up and tuck it away with the rest of the mourning attire. I couldn't figure what to wear instead, until I went to Barnes and Charles on Chestnut Street and found the most beautiful lavender poplin day dress, not too showy but still a color you could swim in, it was so pretty and true.

Mama used to bathe in lavender every spring. "Time to wash away winter's gloom, know I'm carrying spring around with me," she'd say as soon as the ground began to warm and the green shoots to bud. January in Philadelphia wasn't April in Richmond, but somehow it seemed right, washing away my year of mourning with that color.

If wearing lavender was one tribute to my mama, the other was finishing up at the Institute with the highest marks in the whole girls' school. But still I feared that once I graduated, all Ducky's quacking about domestic service being the only work allowed a colored woman would prove true. I was plenty vexed over it, until Miss Douglass summoned me to her classroom, making me feel like the same nervous twelve-year-old who first appeared before her a half dozen years earlier.

"Miss Mapps and I think you should attend college," she said.

College? For a colored lady? "I'm pleased you both think so highly of me, but I don't know any colleges that might take me."

"Oberlin, in Ohio, has been educating females of both races for some time."

I shook my head, knowing I was far enough from Papa as it was. "I've made such good friends in Philadelphia, and I like working for the Anti-Slavery Society. I don't think I could bear leaving."

Miss Douglass frowned but didn't press the point. "Very well then, there are some schools in the area to which you might appeal. Perhaps Haverford, the Quaker college—"

My visit to the Arch Street Meetinghouse flashed in my mind. "I'm not too eager to be in a college that I'd have to fight just to let me enroll."

"If our people only stay where we are wanted, our lives will be very circumscribed indeed."

It was almost funny to hear someone as stiff and formal as Miss Douglass telling me not to accept being circumscribed. But imagining life as the only negro tossing in a sea of white students wasn't so amusing. "I know that, ma'am. But I also know I can't learn from someone I don't respect, someone who doesn't want to educate me."

She looked at me, weighing whether to take umbrage at my pertinacity or to be flattered at how I set her teaching above that of white college professors. "If that is your choice, Miss Mapps has offered another suggestion. She requires an assistant for the secondary school class starting this fall, and she is willing to take you on."

My heart soared at the idea. I felt more at home in the classrooms of the Institute than anywhere else in Philadelphia, and now I wouldn't have to give them up. Quite a compliment, too, being told I was good enough to turn around come the new term and teach high school. I didn't bother to weigh the offer, as though I might choose to clean house or take in sewing instead. I thanked Miss Douglass and accepted on the spot.

"You should have heard the way Mrs. Upshaw carried on when I gave my month's notice," I said to Hattie as we took afternoon tea at Bishop & Hawes a few weeks before I was to start my new job. We were sampling every bakery in Cedar Ward, trying to decide which would have the honor of making Hattie's lemon chiffon wedding cake.

Hattie carefully inspected her plate, scrutinizing the exact hue of yellow in the curd separating the layers of cake, before asking, "What did she say?"

"What didn't she say. *Why would anyone ever leave our cozy home, dear? I'm sure you won't find no real featherbed anywheres else, dear. How can anyone survive the dreadful anonymosity of some boardinghouse, dear?* You would have thought I was threatening to throw myself off the Arch Street wharf, the way she went on about it."

Hattie laughed and gave a nod to signal it was time to taste the confection. As I sunk the tines of my fork down, scooping up frosting, curd, and cake all at once, she said, "Mrs. Upshaw's right, you know."

"Right about what?"

"Spending a fortune just for some tiny hole in a boardinghouse."

The limitation of my imminent salary was a sore point with me. Now that I'd be managing on a schoolmarm's pay of just one hundred and seventy-five dollars per annum, I realized it wasn't merely affection for the Hicksite Quakers that kept Miss Douglass wearing those same simple dresses year in and year out, without so much as a turned muslin collar to fancify her outfit.

"I've got to live somewhere. I would at least like it to be a place I choose, not the one Bet chose for me."

"You wave your fork at me like that, I'm liable to bite that taste right off for myself," she said. "Why not live where you can have three rooms to yourself, plus all your meals cooked for you? Better than Mrs.

Upshaw or any boardinghouse keeper ever made.
Heaven knows better than you can make yourself."

"Where do you propose I can live like that?"

"My house. Which won't be my house much longer,
which is exactly when you should move in."

"Your daddy hasn't stopped celebrating the idea of
finally marrying off daughter number six, and now
you're suggesting he take me in?"

She raised her linen napkin and daintily wiped a
crumb from her mouth before jotting a note on her list
of bakeries. "Daddy always says the first word a man
learns when he has a daughter is no, and when he's got
six daughters it's about the only word he needs. So don't
you worry about him. It was his idea. Or at least he
proposed it to me. It was Mr. Bowser's idea originally."

"Mr. Bowser? What's he got to do with it?"

Hattie dropped her voice, so none of the ladies seated
at the nearby tables might hear. "Daddy's been fretting over what might happen if someone brought baggage by when he was called away on business. There's
always been one of us girls around the house, until now.
He mentioned it to Mr. Bowser, who put the notion of
you staying at our house into Daddy's head."

Until that moment, I wasn't sure Hattie ever even
let slip to her father that I knew about the Railroad
business. Mr. Jones never so much as looked at me

sideways, let alone mentioned it to me. But now he and Mr. Bowser meant to trust me to help in it.

I told Hattie I thought she ought to choose Bishop & Hawes bakery for sure. There was something more than the usual rich and sweet to their lemon chiffon. A zest and tang, the kind of taste your mouth can call up for ages to come.

Ten

"**B**aggage will need tending today."

That was all Mr. Jones ever said to me about the Railroad work. He'd pass the message while we sat at breakfast. It meant I was to stop by during dinner recess and again once afternoon classes were over, to bring food and drink next door.

When he said that single line, he always looked me straight in the eye, calm as could be. I'd expected he'd drop his gaze to his plate while he uttered so great and dangerous a secret. But Mr. Jones spoke like he acted, with neither self-importance nor worry. Just matter-of-fact purpose.

He only spoke so on days when he had to be away, dressing a corpse at someone's house or leading a funeral to Lebanon burying ground. It wasn't ever more than twice a week, sometimes no more than once a month, that he required my assistance. The first few times my stomach lurched, but I returned his look as steadily as I could and said, "I can see to it." After a while, I heard the phrase with no more of a reaction than if he had asked me to stop at Head House Square and purchase a bucket of oysters for the housekeeper to serve for supper.

Hattie taught me what to do when baggage needed tending. I'd gather a jug of milk, a loaf of bread, and some cold meats from the kitchen, and carry them across the property. I was long past my days of fetch-and-tote for the Van Lews, and whenever I hoisted that load, I smiled to think the only fetching and toting I'd ever have to do was against slavery, not in it.

Letting myself into the back room of the shop, I'd set the food and the jug out on the woodworking bench. Then I knocked on the cover of each of the long pine boxes—some days there was only one, sometimes as many as three—and slipped back to the front room. "Daddy always says it's best for the baggage the fewest number of people who see them," Hattie explained. "This way you can pass someone in the street tomorrow and not even know he's the person you helped out of slavery today."

I knew she was right, but standing in the front room of the shop, I wondered about who was on the other side of the communicating door. I listened close to hear the heavy thud of the box tops laid off, the movement of bodies trying to make no sound at all. Sometimes the murmur of low speech on days when there were two or three boxes, or quiet sobs on the days when there was only one. I'd lean against my side of the door, my throat aching with sadness. Nobody left slavery without leaving somebody behind, I knew that well enough myself.

And nobody came out of slavery all at once, neither bought nor manumitted nor escaped. Being freedom bound wasn't like putting on a new overcoat. More like shaking off a long illness. Only over time did freedom truly take hold.

Not slave but not yet free, cargo and still not human, that's what they were when they came to us. I knew Mr. Jones meant me to be dignified and purposeful about it, like he was. But I never came back from the shop without feeling as though my heart had taken on the weight that had been lifted from the food pail. I'd sit down to my dinner or to planning the next day's lessons, and an hour later I'd find my meal or my books untouched. Find myself pondering on who I'd fed, where they had been, and where they might go. What made them board the freedom train just then.

What little I heard from Papa only made him seem farther away. One time it was *Mahon dont no more know how to work a slave than to work a piece of metal. Either one gonna snap if you let it go too cold beat it too hard.* My heart stopped at the word *beat.* I'd never known Mahon to beat Papa. Would Papa and Mama have kept that from me? Or was it something that came on lately, some new horror of Papa's life he wouldn't say much about?

Then a month or so later came *Man can only take so much. Mahon act like he dont know whatall he gonna make me do the way he keep at me. Some days seem like I dont know neither but know it aint gonna be good.* That scared me, Papa saying something so vague and threatening about a white man, letting another negro set such words down on the page. Papa had never been one to sing the glory of his owner, especially not after Mahon refused Bet's offer, but the way he was giving himself over to bitterness frightened me. And then I felt all the worse for judging him. As though from freedom's side I could possibly understand what his life in Richmond, in slavery, had become.

Bet kept up her correspondence, too, though it hardly felt like news of home to read about the Richmond she described.

Dear Mary

I have only a moment to dash out a few words before sending this to the post—Mother must have me with her to Mrs. Catlins for tea and needlework. A fine round of show and ought that will be—sewing banners for the Union Guard. The militia is mere sport I think—husbands and sons playing at soldiering. Which to them is all drinking and parading. And the ladies imagining themselves heroines from Sir Walter Scott are just as ready to play along.

Mother is disappointed John does not join the militia. He is too busy with the stores—at least that is all he says when she speaks of the Union Guard. I believe my brother has got sense enough at last to see the folly of such things. But the sewing means much to Mother—so I shall go along at least for a few hours.

I would prefer to be sewing for your Abolitionist Fair instead. I suppose it is just as well for me to send funds as goods to the fair—I do not fancy myself much with a needle. Do promise to tell me if you need anything for yourself. I do not imagine the Institute can pay you much and to live in comfort in Philadelphia is I realize quite dear. If you want for anything I am glad to supply it from

Richmond—or pay for it at least if you must obtain it in Philadelphia.

Yours
Bet Van Lew

Bet didn't loose a single word about directing her letters to a new address, though I supposed she wondered why I left the Upshaws, always hinting that maybe I needed her support after all. And she did like to carry on about the fair. Sometimes I wished I hadn't told her about it at all. Maybe it was wrong, wanting to keep such things private from her when she'd done so much for me, and she did always send along a nice little sum to add to the Society's proceeds. But all her offers to do for me only made it worse that Papa couldn't offer as much himself.

Neither Papa nor Bet knew about my work with the baggage. I wouldn't have dared hint it, it would put so many at risk. I didn't need to brag on it, I was doing such a small part, but it felt strange to keep such a secret from Papa. Strange, too, to hear Bet going on about abolition without her imagining how deeply involved in it I was.

From time to time, I passed that orange-haired McNiven as I walked up Sixth Street. He always looked straight past me as he rode by. Something about him gave me the shivers, and I was relieved he didn't mark my crossing paths with him. Only, I was wrong about that. He remembered me, and he was making plans for me already.

"Thomas McNiven wants your assistance," Mr. Jones said one evening. We were sitting down to supper, Hattie and George joining us to celebrate the end of my first term as an instructor.

"How could I be of assistance to Mr. McNiven?" I glanced over Hattie's way. She kept right on eating, as though her father hadn't said anything unusual. I began to suspect she knew the answer already, that she was there to persuade me to agree to whatever he was about to propose.

"We have a shipment that must go through to New York immediately," Mr. Jones said. "McNiven is willing to take the baggage, but he thinks it best to bring someone along."

I'd never even been north of Germantown. "What good could I be to him?"

"It's not to him, it's to the baggage." Mr. Jones gathered himself to the task of breaking his own rule of not revealing anything about the fugitives. "A girl no more than fourteen, she was attacked by a white man and is in some kind of waking stupor, no reaction to anything around her. McNiven worries that if she comes to her senses while traveling alone with him, she might not trust that he is there to help her."

"I don't know why I can't be the one to go," Hattie said. George looked as if she proposed walking straight into a herd of stampeding buffalo.

Mr. Jones didn't take his eyes off me. "McNiven has asked for Mary."

"Why me?"

"The girl is from Richmond. I suppose that's why McNiven thought of you. Will you go, for her sake? It will be a journey of two days each way."

I'd been so curious for so long about the baggage, and now at last I might meet some of it. Someone of it, I reminded myself, a real person. Someone who needed my help. My skin tingled and my heart sped loud as I consented.

Later I'd have time to puzzle over how McNiven knew I was from Richmond, when and why he learned so much about me. But now there was barely chance enough to finish up supper and gather together quilts, warm clothes, and food for the trip. Usually Mr. Jones never moved a body except in broad daylight. "No need to raise suspicion by sneaking about, when I have legitimate business reasons to travel by day," he always said. But this baggage was different, and I hurried to be ready.

After Hattie and George hugged me good-bye and departed down Sixth Street, Mr. Jones and I waited in silence until McNiven appeared, guiding his buckboard wagon into the narrow alleyway behind the shop. He didn't offer any greeting to me, not so much as a kindly look, before he and Mr. Jones lifted the closed coffin into the wagon bed, spreading quilts along the top. Then McNiven took his place on the driver's bench, and Mr. Jones returned to where I stood.

He laid his hand on my shoulder, warming me like a benediction. "You're doing right, my girl. When the wind blows from the South, we must help it along as best we can." He lifted me onto the back of the conveyance.

"Lay her doun." The Scotsman's command was thick and throaty.

Though I chafed at being ordered so, I burrowed between the high wall of the wagon bed and the pile of blankets that covered the coffin. Mr. Jones raised the tailboard, and McNiven urged his team forward, slowly turning the wagon and pulling back into the street.

As I listened to the creaking rhythm of the carriage wheels, it seemed to me there was something thicker than pine boards separating me from the girl who lay beside me. I looked up, hoping to trace out the constellations Miss Mapps taught us to find in the winter sky. But the clouds hung low and wide, hiding every star.

I woke with a start. Frigid night stung my face. Damp air penetrated my bones. I made out the walls of the buckboard and realized the wagon wasn't moving.

I couldn't tell how many hours had passed or where we might be, as I heard footsteps on frosty ground. The tailboard slammed down, and McNiven climbed toward me.

"Awake are you, lass?" He pulled himself into the wagon bed. "That's good. I'm wanting you."

Fear warmed me against the icy night.

I searched about for something I might use as a weapon. Why hadn't I worn a hairpin instead of combs?

I yanked my reticule off my wrist and threw it as hard as I could at him. But it drew little more than a startled glance.

"I mean to do what I'm about, and you canna stop me," he said. He pulled the quilts back and reached for the coffin lid.

Scrambling to a crouch, I hissed, "You leave her be, or I'll tell Mr. Jones."

"Joons be a good man, but he thinks like an undertaker, every body in a box. This lass has been through enough without waking in a coffin, thinking she's aweady dead and gone."

I didn't have time to wonder at his consideration for the girl, before he slid back the pine lid. In the darkness, all I could make out of the interior of the box were the whites of the girl's eyes, wide with fright though she lay unaware of her surroundings. I shuddered. Seeing her alive yet motionless, witless even, terrified me more than any corpse ever could.

"Cover her, quick," McNiven said. "They catch a death o' cold easy when they hae taken a shock like that."

I wrapped each of her stiff, unmoving limbs and lay a quilt across her chest. "Best cover her face along with the rest," he directed, "in case we hae oorselves an encounter." Her shallow breath didn't alter and her wild eyes didn't blink, as I laid a shawl across her face. I wasn't sorry to hide those eyes from my own.

McNiven lowered himself from the wagon bed and closed us back in. I heard his footsteps alongside the cart, then the creak of the buckboard as he pulled himself up onto the seat. One of the horses snorted as the reins fell on its back, and we were moving again.

I stared at the pile heaped next to me, contemplating such horrors as could leave a girl dead to the world around her, even though she lived.

McNiven drove through the night and all the next day. By the time darkness fell again, the horses' gait had slackened and McNiven's shoulders sank with exhaustion. At last he pulled the cart amid a cluster of trees, too weary to continue.

I thought of how urgent it was to get the girl to safety. "Perhaps I can drive a bit, while you rest."

"Has the lass driven a wagon team?"

"I've driven a one-horse phaeton."

"Through rutted country roads, or only upon cobblestone streets? On a night with neither stars to guide you nor moon to light the way, or only by broad daylight?"

I'd felt so grand sitting beside Theodore, leading his fancy gig. But now I saw how trifling my achievement was. "At least take my place here," I said. "I can keep watch while you lie down."

McNiven agreed, crossing to the back of the wagon and extending a hand to help me down. The cold of his touch sent shivers along my spine. "Indulge me no more than an hour or two. We maun be under way afore dawn." He pulled himself up, and I secured the tailboard behind him.

I paced the hard ground beside the wagon for a good long while, relieved to stretch my limbs and hoping to warm myself. But eventually I grew lonely. Longing to see the girl, or rather the pile under which she lay, I hoisted myself onto the driver's bench. One of the rough planks snagged my skirt, and I let loose a star-tled stream of hard words.

My cussing split the night right open.

"I heard a wench. Don't tell me otherwise." The voice was low and menacing, a human growl.

"It's the drink you heard," answered another voice, shrill and tinny, like a knife being sharpened. "And it'll be ringing in your head some fierce tomorrow."

These were white men's voices, coming toward me from deep in the woods.

"Go back to Higley's cabin like a babe to its mam-my's tit, if you like," the growler said. "More fun for me if I find the gal alone."

Even in the light of day and best of circumstances, a man like that wouldn't take too courteously to seeing a colored lady sitting on the driver's seat of a wagon.

I launched myself into the wagon bed, landing hard beside where the girl lay. McNiven jerked awake, and I cupped my hand over his mouth, pointing in the direction of the men's footsteps.

"What have we here?" the shrill voice called out. "Someone's left us a wagon, seem like."

"Wasn't a wagon I heard, was a wench. You can have the goddamn wagon as long as I get her."

McNiven clambered to a stand. "Ho, there! Canna a fellow take his hour's rest?"

"It's not a fellow's voice called us from the woods," the first man shouted. "Where is the gal?"

I rose up from the wagon bed, and the man whistled as he squinted in the dim before-dawn. "Not just any wench. A darky."

His companion rubbed his hands together. "An escaped slave, I bet. Likely with a bounty on her head."

The men started closer toward the wagon. McNiven drew a revolver from his coat, the metal glinting. "The lass is free, and with me. If you be kind enough to take your leave, I'd much appreciate it."

They looked from the firearm to me and back again. "Queer business, a white man raising a gun to protect some nigger gal."

My worry for the fugitive brought the lie on quick, pouring from my mouth like water from the faucet in the Joneses' soak-tub. "Please, sirs, I's just the house-maid. If his wife find out, I lose my place for sure. My pappy's all laid up, I supports us both. Only come here so us can get some privacy."

McNiven took up the tale as quickly as I laid it down. "Hush, Sally. Your mistress is not going to find us out, I hae told you that a hundred times these past three months." He grinned at the men. "Man's got to take his pleasure sometime. Surely you fellows understand."

"Mighty cold night you've chosen for it," the shrill-voiced man said.

His companion leered. "Darky wench can keep a man as warm as all the devils in hell. Though I might treat you better, gal, than to make you cry out like he did." He lumbered toward me.

McNiven fired, sending a deathly warning right between the men's heads. The shot set the horses whinnying, and the girl beneath the quilt pile moaning. As the cart bucked forward, I dropped down beside her, covering her moan with one of my own.

"Come on, Bart," the second man said. "Might as well let him to his dark-meat feast."

As their footsteps fell away, his companion called back, "Better keep an eye out, once you're back atop her. Wouldn't want to catch you with your britches down."

I barely pulled myself up the wall of the wagon before I began retching. In the pale orange light of daybreak, I watched what little I'd eaten in the past day dribble down the outside of the wooden panel. "I'm sorry."

McNiven waved my words away. "Twas nothing to be sorry about. Quick on your feet and clever like that, who ken what you may do for us."

The first time I ever saw McNiven, I'd feared what threat he might be, to Mr. Jones and to me. Now because of him, I'd been in the greatest true peril I ever knew—but he'd had as much to do with getting me out of it as with putting me into it. It proved he was no more like the two men who'd threatened us than Zinnie Moore was like a slave mistress, white though they all were. The Scotsman shared something of the Quakers' values, though without their renouncement of violence—and for that I was indebted. As my stomach twisted up again, I leaned back over the wagon's edge, wondering what else he might mean to ask me to do.

McNiven didn't say another word on what had passed, just settled onto the driver's bench and started the team back toward the road. As the cart wheels turned, I knelt and lifted the shawl from the girl's face. Her eyes focused on me, and she whimpered her despair. She was back among us, but maybe not for long. Not if she got another fright.

"You're all right now," I whispered. "Not in Virginia anymore. You're free." I hoped that last part proved true. Fugitive and free weren't exactly the same thing.

She struggled to form words. "How I get here?"

I stroked her forehead, meaning my touch to reassure her. "We've got people all over, South and North, helping slaves get to freedom. Even have some whites working with us, bringing our folks out." Though I figured that would make things easier when she saw

McNiven, still I worried the mention of white people might yet stop her up with fear.

But there wasn't room for any more fear in her face, and she didn't struggle out another word.

I asked if she wanted something to eat. She nodded, and when I brought a spoonful of cold broth to her mouth, she drank the liquid greedily. She must have been three-quarters starved by then, and I fed her all the broth I had.

Let that sit for a while, Mary El, I heard Mama's voice saying, *give her stomach a chance to get used to food again.*

I tucked the quilts around her. "We still have a ways to ride. Why don't you rest a bit? I'll be right by you, watching and listening. If you need anything, just let me know." Her lips trembled a bit, not exactly into a smile, but at least away from the purse of fear they'd been in. She blinked her agreement and closed her eyes.

The girl woke from time to time, and I gave her a bit of bread or water, said what I could to soothe her. When I ran out of palliative words, I recited one of Miss Frances Watkins's poems, or one of Miss Phillis Wheatley's. I realized the girl couldn't know they were colored ladies, one an abolitionist and the other a slave herself, who wrote such fine verse. Just the rhythm of the lines calmed her, though, and she eased back into sleep.

She never asked where we were going, didn't seem curious about who was driving the team. I suppose curiosity was far past her in that condition, and in a way I was glad. I wasn't much over being scared of McNiven myself. I could only imagine how he might seem to someone in her state.

He was careful to stop to tend the horses only when she was asleep, I noticed that. It was at just such a stop, late on our second full day of travel, that he told me we'd soon reach our destination.

"New York?" I wondered where in that vast state we might be.

"Not quite. Yet in New Jersey, a settlement what delivers baggage for our fowk."

Somehow I'd gotten it into my head that we were taking the girl all the way to New York. I told myself it didn't make much difference. But now that she'd come out of her stupor right to me, it seemed wrong to leave her.

When she woke next, I explained that we'd soon leave off traveling for a while. "We'll get you inside to a proper meal, then I have to go back home. Folks where we're stopping will carry you on to where you need to go."

She didn't say anything, but she squeezed my hand hard. We sat like that, wordless but holding tight, for an hour or more, until McNiven eased the wagon onto a narrow lane off the main roadway. When he reined the team to a halt, I drew my hand from the girl's and stood. Over the high sides of the conveyance, I saw a small farmhouse, surrounded by a cluster of outbuildings and acres of snow-covered fields.

The noise of the horses brought an elderly couple from the house. The dark hue of their coats turned their pale skin ghostly against the white landscape.

"Isn't there a colored person, can come for her?" I asked McNiven.

He narrowed his eyes at me. "Be sure you tell Joons I was right about the lassie wanting a companion she could trust."

"Send Chloe round first, will you?" McNiven called out. The woman turned back to fetch their servant from the house while her husband stood to the side, waiting.

"You have no reason to be fretting." McNiven broke the silence as we started home the next day, me lonely in the wagon bed while he drove. "She'll be fine afore long. A fighter for sure, that one is."

"A fighter? She's barely eating, barely breathing, said no more than four words in two days."

" 'Tis not these two days past I judge her by, but the ones what came afore. Our wee lassie has killed a man."

The idea of that child taking a life stunned me. "At least she might hae killed him," he continued. "David Bowser's cousin did not wait to find out afore bringing her away."

"Miss Douglass brought that girl out of Virginia?"

He laughed like I'd told the funniest tale he ever heard. "Bowser has got himself more than one cousin. This one is a free man doun in Richmond, locates baggage needing to come North."

McNiven's revelation about the girl caught me quiet for the better part of the day, until the sliver of moon rose, and we pulled off the road. He tended the horses, and then we exchanged places, so he could rest in the wagon bed while I kept watch.

I settled onto the plank seat, listening to the creaking of the buckboard as he lay down. I looked ahead, my eyes searching the deepening dark. "Why? Why did she kill him?"

"Fear as much as hate, I suppose. 'Twas her owner coming after her, and she were scared. He awready had one baby on her, sold it off the very day, then come after her again that night. He was drunken enough, she had a brick and hit him on the head. A fighter that one be, for certain."

I imagined the weight of a brick in my hand, the force it would take to bring it down hard enough to kill a man. The hate I'd have to have in my heart to do such a thing, and the sorrow that could make a person hate like that.

I wondered how many more there were like the girl, who didn't have a brick to take up in their hands, or a free colored man to send them North if they tried.

Eleven

I felt Mama's presence most days, soothing and advising me all sorts of ways. As I closed my eyes to doze off for the night, I found myself holding confidences with her, just as I had when we shared the husk pallet in the Van Lews' garret all those years before. But come autumn of 1859, she was as agitated as could be with me, and making me agitated, too.

Mary El, school teaching's a job, not a Calling.

But, Mama, aren't you proud? Miss Mapps picked me. Only one she wanted of all the girls from the Institute. Not just from there, she could have hired anyone from anywhere, and she picked me, because I'm the best.

After Zinnie left Richmond, Mistress V went on about she was the best cook the family ever had. But you know Zinnie meant for freedom, do for her own family, not just cook for the Van Lews.

But teaching colored children isn't like slaving. It's for our own folks. Don't you remember when you taught me?

I just showed you what you half knew already,'cause of your Gift. Gift from Jesus. And He knows what He means for you to do with that Gift, so don't be telling me or Him either that you're already doing what He wants.

If this isn't what I should be doing, how am I supposed to know what is?

When I traced letters and words in the fireplace ash, you mastered them fast enough. You so good at reading, didn't you learn to read His signs, too?

I thought I was going mad, arguing with a voice in my head. Mama sure could drive a person crazy, she was that persistent, that insistent, that loving. I had seen it in the way she played the Van Lews, the way she managed me and Papa both. But now only I heard her. And I needed to know if it really was her, or just a voice in my head.

"Jesus, if Mama's with You, and she must be up there, good a soul as she always was, then she's probably got Your ear, and You're hearing all about me from her. But Mama's telling me—at least I think it's

Mama—that I set myself at the wrong task. But what else can a colored lady do? I'm teaching, I sew and sell for the fair, I help Mr. Jones with the Railroad. If there's something else You mean for me to do, send me a sign. And since Mama says I'm not so good at reading Your signs as reading books, which I suppose is true, make it a sign I can't miss."

I guess that prayer got answered, because the very next week came a sign nobody, North or South, could ignore.

Zinnie Moore and I were making an inventory of the worsted yarn supplies, and the other ladies were sewing, when the elderly butler entered the Fortens' sitting room, addressing Margaretta Forten with an urgency that made us all look up from our work.

"Madam, a messenger just brought this note."

Any servant with so much as a whiff of literacy would read such a missive before bringing it to the lady of the house. We in the house wouldn't have missed such an opportunity, and I didn't expect the Fortens' butler to, either. But what surprised me was how clear it was to all of us who sat looking at him that he had perused the note, the tenor of its contents written all over his vexed features. No servant I ever knew, either when I was on their side or since crossing over, would let the mistress see that he'd been in her correspondence.

All this flashed in my mind as Margaretta Forten took up the slip of paper. I didn't have time to puzzle over it, though, because the moment she read the note she fell back in a faint.

Abby Pugh, one of the Quaker ladies, had done a bit of charity nursing, and she was on Miss Forten in a heartbeat, undoing the buttons on her bodice and loosening the stays of her corset. She fanned our hostess vigorously while the butler fetched smelling salts.

As the crystal vial was passed beneath her nose, Miss Forten blinked her eyes open. She glanced about uncertainly until she noticed the page in her lap and asked Mrs. Pugh to read it aloud.

The Quakeress took up the note. *"My dear Sister-in-Law. Reports have come of a slave revolt in Virginia. The telegraphs there are down, all is still rumor. Mob violence expected here as soon as news of the uprising spreads. Please keep the ladies in the house until the Vigilance Committee can escort them home. Robert Purvis."*

Strands of carmine yarn oozed like blood between Zinnie Moore's pale fingers. "Virginia." It was all I could say, and all she could do was nod back.

I was born long after Nat Turner was killed, but his name, Gabriel Prosser's, too, were bywords from my childhood. I don't remember ever being told right out who those men were, how they plotted to rise up. Just a slow seeping knowledge of the hate with which white people spat those names, the pride and fear together with which black folks whispered them. Even when Mama and Papa talked of freedom, they never dared speak of such rebellions. To utter a word on it was death, as surely as to try it.

Only two of the ladies took up their sewing again, Quakers both. I knew how they spoke of worthy tasks and idle hands, but I wasn't up to needlework just then. Neither was Zinnie. She sat beside me, clutching my hand in her lap as though her fear were as great as mine.

Not a woman in the room wasn't frightened, of course. We were thinking of those slaves, but of our own safety, too. It had been some while since Philadelphia's last big race riot, longer than I'd been in the city, though not much longer. Time and again, mobs had burned down businesses owned by negroes, beaten colored temperance marchers, killed and destroyed in mad frenzies while the police stood by and watched. If slaves were rising up, maybe even killing whites, down in Virginia, there was no telling how mobs in Philadelphia might retaliate.

"The rain will keep the mobbers at home," Mrs. Catto said, with as much hope as a person could muster just then. But wet streets were no safer for us than dry ones, really. I stared up at David Bustill Bowser's eagle painting, marking each detail of the predatory beak and pointed talons, as we sat wondering what dangers lurked in the October night. At last the brass knocker fell on the broad front door, and the butler announced Mr. Passmore Williamson.

A gaunt white man entered the sitting room. Miss Forten extended her hand to him. "Mr. Williamson, thank you for coming. Have you any more news?"

Only four years earlier, Passmore Williamson had stormed onto a boat moored at Philadelphia's Walnut Street wharf, seized a slavewoman named Jane Johnson and her children from their owner, and sent them off to freedom. He went to jail for that, though eventually the judge released him, ruling Johnson's owner had as good as freed her himself when he brought her through Pennsylvania on his way to a plantation in Nicaragua. Mr. Williamson had safeguarded Miss Johnson and her family when he might have rotted in Moyamensing Prison for the privilege, and he was as respected and trusted, even loved, as a white man could be among colored Philadelphia.

Now he stroked the muttonchops that formed a dark frame around his narrow face. "It is the hero of Osawatomie, John Brown. Leading a band of some two dozen followers, negro and white. They've seized the arsenal at Harper's Ferry, to arm the slaves he hopes will join them. There is word of killing on both sides, although Brown's men yet hold their ground. They mean to extend the rebellion into the neighboring counties, though it is too soon to tell whether they shall succeed."

Mr. Williamson spoke with a surety of detail that told me he had foreknowledge of Brown's plan, or at least had heard about the plot from someone on the Vigilance Committee who did. Such propinquity shocked me nearly as much as the news itself.

Was there some great conspiracy afoot, so large it stretched from Virginia to Philadelphia, maybe even to Kansas and Canada? Who around me had known what was to come to pass, and had looked at me without the slightest hint in their eyes?

Was this what we had waited for, worked for, prayed for all these years? Were all the slaves freedom bound at last?

Dear Mary

I presume you have less news of this than we have— though to tell fact from rumor is nearly impossible. Brown of Kansas fame—or infamy as the slavehold- ers would have it—was captured at dawn Tuesday.

Richmond is thirsty for blood—but all the bluster is just cover for her fright. SLAVE INSURRECTION—the two most fearsome words to a Southerner! All talk of master and servant alike benefiting from the paternal institution is forgotten now—nerves on edge awaiting the tocsin tolling another uprising. Virginians are as terrified of whites in the North as they are of the negroes among us—if there is anything to be glad for these days I should say it is their dread.

Will send more as soon as it is known.

Yours
Bet Van Lew

Dear Bet

There is much excitement here. The telegraph brings the news & the news-sheets turn it all to rumor. No mobs yet though they are feared.

If you can send a word or two from Papa it would do much to ease my mind. Please give him all my love.

Yours
Mary Van Lew

Dear Mary

I am sorry for the delay in responding. The curfew here is quite strict—Lewis could not come to me during the week. This morning I set out to find him—had only a vague notion of the location of his cabin.

When he opened the door he took quite a fright about the reason for my visit. I assured him that I only came because you asked me to bring him your regards. I did not stay long enough to take down any message. But I give you my word he is well and knows he may come to me for any aid a lady can offer should he need it.

Mahon will not let any harm come to him—for selfish reasons perhaps but those may prove as strong a motivation as the very milk of human kindness could be.

Yours
Bet Van Lew

Learning that Bet had gone all the way down to Shockoe Bottom to hunt up Papa's cabin turned me topsy-turvy. White people passed up and down that block of Main Street all day long, but only laborers, tradesmen, and shopkeepers. Never a Church Hill lady. I was sorry to have caused Papa such alarm. But relieved, too, that Bet knew where to find him, that she pledged her protection of him, even.

When I returned from the Institute one afternoon the following week, I heard men's voices debating hotly in Mr. Jones's back parlor. "We warned Brown the raid would be a death warrant. This madness is only more of the same."

"Faugh! Brown has fowk ready to fight at lang and last. We maun strike now."

I hurried up the staircase and found Mr. Jones, McNiven, and David Bustill Bowser in the front parlor. Mr. Jones frowned at my arrival. "Gentlemen, we will need to speak of this matter at some later time. I'm sure you understand."

McNiven wouldn't be put off. "We need not be protecting Mary from our talk. The lass is as brave as any man when danger is at hand."

I looked to Mr. Bowser to see if he would agree. "McNiven's plan is folly. What harm can there be in speaking of it in front of her?"

"No folly in it," McNiven said. "So long as I can find a route to Charlestown without coming from the North."

Charlestown was where they were holding John Brown while Virginia's highest civil authorities and the jeering mobs gathered outside the prison plotted his demise. "They're going to Charlestown by the train-load from Richmond," I said.

"How ken you so?" McNiven asked.

"A letter, from my— from a correspondent in Richmond."

"If I go first to Richmond, there might be a way to Charlestown that will not raise suspicion."

Mr. Bowser shook his head. "My cousin says Richmond is too hot these days. We cannot ask him to take on such a party as you suggest."

"Your cousin need not hazard himself to join me in liberating Osawatomie Brown."

I let out a little cry, the idea was so audacious. Mr. Jones slammed his fist down on the mahogany table, glaring at McNiven for saying so much in front of me.

"The lass can be trusted, I tell you. Awready she has given me the notion o' Richmond. I need but find a place to bide there, till I can slip up to Charlestown."

"Bet Van Lew would have you," I said.

Mr. Jones raised his arched eyebrow. "You suggest we send McNiven to a white lady?"

"McNiven is a white man, going to save another white man. I don't suppose the aid of yet one more white person would be so strange," I said.

"But a Virginian," Mr. Bowser said. "And female to boot."

He almost had me with Virginian, but when he added the part about female, something caught in me. I stomped upstairs to my writing desk, searched out the most recent missive from Bet, brought it down, and read it out to them.

"*Things here do make my blood boil! Governor Wise carries on so they say he means to ride this to the White House. The slave-owners are in such a frenzy they would give him the Democratic nomination— they demand no less than a Southerner for the Presidency now. They say Brown's correspondence is proof no Northerner can be trusted. For my part I should like to tell them there is a Southerner or two who thinks Brown more wise and Wise more yellow than the other way around. I do hope to have my part in this before all is said and done.*" I held the pages out to Mr. Bowser. "There is more, if you care to see it."

"No need," McNiven said. "I am the one what will go, and I hae heard enough. Write to your friend, ask will she help me or no."

"The mails are being searched," Mr. Bowser reminded him. "To write anything hinting at such a mission will get us all hanged."

"Mary is one what can fool fowk with her words." He nodded at me. "Scrieve the letter so only your friend will ken the meaning."

Dear Bet

I am sorry to hear your Uncle John has almost no one to care for him but yourself. I hope you will not take offense when I say that though I am not partial to many of your relations he is a great favorite of mine. Indeed others I know admire him & one in fact might wish to tend him to prevent any severe incapacitation. Though you have voiced fear that his confinement will prove fatal perhaps with the aid of this caretaker he might live many a year from now.

Would you be willing to host such a visitor come to tend your Uncle? His name is Thomas McN & he is a nearer relation to you than to me I should suppose from the physical resemblance. Will such a visitor upset your Mother & Brother terribly? I shall send him with a note in my hand so you will know him. He will see if your Uncle can be brought to a location where he might be better cared for.

I look forward to swift receipt of your reply. I hope I have not said too much nor too little as you know this matter is quite delicate inside both of our families.

> *Yours*
> *Mary Van Lew*

Dear Mary

Thank you for your note concerning Uncle— I had trouble making it out at first but of course if there is someone who might aid the dear man please send him immediately. It is my fondest wish to see Uncle recovered.

We have plenty of room for such a guest. My Brother has let a house of his own near the stores and Mother can be urged to take a trip to White Sulphur Springs—her nerves are worn so by the situation with Uncle it would do her good. Your friend should not expect much of a social visit in town—the men-folk here mostly marching with their militias in case of any more excitement from Harper's Ferry.

Please let me know how soon I might expect the visitor. Uncle is not well at all—some say he will not last even to the end of the month.

> *Yours*
> *Bet Van Lew*

Bet had freed me and Mama and the rest of her family's slaves, spent her own money on that and on subscribing to lots of abolitionist groups, too. But this was different than just spending or subscribing or making do without her favorite cook and butler. This was risking her own life just as much as McNiven was risking his. As much as I'd ever risked mine tending to the baggage. More even, if half of what everyone said about the panic in Virginia was true. Hang them first and convict them after—that's how it would be, if they caught anyone at what McNiven meant to try. White or not, woman or not. And still Bet wanted to help.

McNiven spent his time in Richmond walking about and pretending to look for work, all the while picking up information about most anything that might prove useful, especially the excursion trains to Charlestown. That's what the ticket barkers called them, as though people were taking a ride to the seashore or an agricultural fair for an afternoon's entertainment.

On the eighteenth November, McNiven boarded one of those trains, rode it all the way to Charlestown, and hunted up Mr. George Hoyt, Brown's attorney. Hoyt wasn't much of a lawyer, really, at twenty-one hardly older than I was by then—not that it mattered, since Virginia hadn't given Brown a trial so much as a

284 • LOIS LEVEEN

showpiece for the slaveholders' hate. Hoyt was more of a spy for the wealthy New England abolitionists who financed Brown, sent to suppress any evidence that implicated them. And to secure Brown's release through extralegal means, if possible, since surely that was the only way to save him.

All this we heard later, from McNiven, who told it with such relish, we had to believe all of it was true. So when McNiven told us Brown refused to be rescued, it seemed we might as well believe that, too.

"*Let them hang me! I am worth inconceivably more to hang than for any other purpose.*" That's what Brown told Hoyt. That's what Hoyt reported to McNiven. And that's what McNiven repeated to Mr. Jones, Mr. Bowser, and me when he returned to Philadelphia in the last fading days of November.

"I found a remembrance for each o' you, on how important our work is," McNiven said, as he finished telling us about John Brown's final stand. "Bowser, you hae yours awready. Jones, yours will come in good time, brung by a more bonnie hand than mine. And Mary, yours I hae right here." Reaching into the leather haversack he'd slung over the back of the parlor chair, he drew out an iron cross.

A cross whose maker I knew right off, it was so like the one that hung in Papa's cabin all the days of my childhood. "How is he?" I asked, taking the rood from McNiven.

"I canna say if he is better or worse, having only seen him the once, as any customer might. But he is a good smith, any can look on that and tell you so."

I rubbed my palms against the well-sculpted scrolls, nearly feeling the fire with which Papa had worked the metal. It was easy enough to see what McNiven meant for me to make of the memento, given as purposefully as Brown was giving up his own life.

I didn't need John Brown nor Thomas McNiven to make me hate what kept Papa from me. But McNiven had chosen wisely enough, setting me wondering what yet kept me from Papa.

On the last day of November, Miss Forten called a special meeting of the Anti-Slavery Society to hear a resolution proclaiming the club's position on John Brown.

"*The Philadelphia Female Anti-Slavery Society has long worked to end the dreadful institution of slavery throughout this nation and its territories. Although we deplore any use of violence in plan or practice, we commend Mr. John Brown's heroism in sacrificing himself and his sons for the cause of abolition.*"

Mrs. Pugh frowned. "I should think we would want to dissociate ourselves entirely from anyone who does violence of any sort."

"Mr. Frederick Douglass wrote about how he *repelled by force the bloody arm of slavery*," I reminded her. "If force was good enough for him, why should we condemn it?"

Sarah Mapps Douglass had always been especially proud of the former slave who shared her name, though he was no relation to her. "Mr. Douglass is a noble man in many ways," she said. "But like many men, he falls to violence too easily. We ladies must be a corrective to the male impulse."

I recalled the girl I helped transport two years earlier, imagined again the weight of a brick in my hands, the emotions that could make me bring such a weight down hard against a man's skull. That brick was plenty enough corrective to the male impulse, so far as I could see. But I couldn't loose that girl's secret, nor Mr. Jones's, in the middle of the Forten sitting room. "I thought we meant to be a corrective to slaveholding."

My former teacher nodded in her prim way. "That is why we sponsor lectures and publications on the wrongs of slavery."

I'd attended plenty of those lectures without noticing any slave-owners in the audience. Much as I enjoyed the speakers and the pamphlets and whatnot, I knew they only brought our cause before those Northerners who were mostly like-minded to begin with. "I've worked as hard as anybody to make our fairs a success. But do any of us really believe such things can raise money enough to buy out every slave?"

"It shouldn't matter if they did," Mrs. Pugh said, offering me a gentle smile. The kind of smile the Friends were always putting on, which mostly I delighted in but which could truly irk a person sometimes. "We would not purchase a single slave, not every slave even if we could, to set them free. To do business with slave-owners is a vile thing, and to engage in slave-trading only encourages the buying and selling of human souls."

"So I should be a slave rather than a free woman?" I asked.

"Bless thee, no," Zinnie said. "Thou was manumitted by an owner who came to see the evils of slavery. May she be a model to other slaveholders."

"Bet Van Lew wasn't my owner, her mother was. Bet bought me so she could manumit me." I looked around the room, catching each of the ladies' eyes with my own. "I assure you, it is no small thing to know yourself bought and sold that way. But I don't regret that Bet made trade with a slaveholder. I wish she could trade with another, so my father might have his freedom, too."

"Your feelings on this matter are quite understandable," Miss Forten said. "But our group has certain principles we hold dear, and we shall see, by vote, whether those beliefs lead us to adopt the statement in regard to Mr. John Brown."

While she called for a show of hands, I gathered my things. As I headed for the front door, Zinnie came trailing along the hall after me. "Will thou not stay and sew with us?"

I shook my head. "The time for sewing is past. It's time for something else now."

Zinnie's gray eyes didn't show a bit of the merriment that first drew me to her. "We want the same thing," she said, "though I suppose none of us knows how we shall get it."

As I hugged my friend good-bye, she must have sensed something in me that I'd only barely begun to make out for myself, because she added, "Do take care that neither a blow to thy body nor a mark on thy soul will be the consequence of whatever work thou chooses."

Walking out into the dark ocean of night, I turned my back to the North Star and began my journey home.

"**Our own** church, putting us out." Hattie was furious the morning of the second December, as we walked with her family to a memorial service for John Brown.

"Wasn't us they meant to turn away," her sister Diana said. "Just whatever pro-slavery mob might be coming along to meet us."

The trustees of Bethel African Methodist Episcopal weren't about to risk their church building, not for John Brown or anyone. And so we hurried past Mother Bethel and all the way to Passyunk Road, then turned west toward Shiloh Baptist Church. Mr. Jones traced this route often, directing his hearse to the Lebanon burying ground across from Shiloh. It was strange to catch sight of the headstones there, knowing the man we were remembering that day wasn't yet dead. He was set to hang at eleven that morning, and hundreds of folks were crowding into Shiloh's sanctuary before then.

"You sorry you're here and not over to National Hall?" Hattie asked as we slid into a pew.

I shook my head, looking about at negroes of every shade and age gathered together. "Nothing there could be more to me than what I see here." The speakers at the meeting organized by white abolitionists would be more famous, and the audience in the National Hall would be larger—with Sarah Mapps Douglass, Zinnie

Moore, and all my other friends from the Philadelphia Female Anti-Slavery Society turned out in full. But it just wasn't where my heart was anymore.

At Shiloh, it was mostly colored ministers speaking. They could all talk their talk—John Brown was their common text, but the sermons each went their own way, condemning slavery, Philadelphia's race prejudice, and every level of American government.

Reverend Elijah Gibbs took the pulpit first. "We hear folks telling the slave-owners they have a moral responsibility to free the slaves. But when have any but a handful of slaveholders heard the call of moral responsibility?"

Murmurs of "Amen" broke out among the crowd.

"We hear folks talk about the Underground Railroad, call the name Harriet Tubman and say she's the Moses of our people. Brought out fifty or more her own self. But how many Harriet Tubmans, what army of Moseses, how many lifetimes of Railroad work, will it take to free four million slaves?"

"Too many, brother," shouted a man in front of us.

"How many of us here today have loved ones over on the other side?" Reverend Gibbs asked, and I raised my voice with the rest. Seemed more of us did than didn't, and even those who didn't, like Hattie and her family, all knew someone like me who did.

"How many of us here today," he repeated, the spirit of the congregation moving along with him, "live our freedom a little less, knowing our loved ones have none? How many of us think every day of those held as so-called human chattel, to be worked, whipped, beaten, bred, and sold, all at the whim of the slaveholder?" The chorus of responses grew louder.

"We hear folks speaking of compromise, and containing slavery, and preserving the Union. But what is to be comprised, contained, or preserved, for the husband who has a wife in slavery, the mother who has a daughter in slavery, the brother a sister, the child a father?"

His voice rose. "I have more family in slavery than out, and I have no time for compromise, no heart for containment, no desire to preserve anything but my family's right to freedom. I do not know John Brown. But I know that what he has done to free our people is a great thing. And we must each of us be prepared to do no less. God bless us all in the struggle."

Shouts of approval rang out all over the room as Reverend Gibbs stepped from the lectern. Other ministers stood one after another to preach their piece. I leaned back against the pew, letting their words pour over me like the rush of the James over the boulders studding its falls.

But I sat bolt upright when a familiar voice boomed out from the pulpit.

"I'm not a minister, and I'm not here to mourn John Brown," David Bustill Bowser began. "I want to speak today of another man. A negro man. A man whose mother was a slave and whose father was her master. A man whose father freed his own slave children, but only after he had lived a lifetime on the proceeds of their labor. Only after his son was grown to manhood and married to a slavewoman, property of another master.

"This man took the freedom his slaveholding father gave him, and what did he do with it? He set out to buy his wife and child.

"I say wife, though for a slave there is no legal marriage, no bond the slave-owner is lawfully bound to respect. I say child, though this man had more than one. He and his wife had six precious children, all in slavery. But the wife's owner said he would sell him one, the youngest, and the wife herself, for no less than one thousand dollars, cash."

Cries of "Tell it, Brother" and "That's always the way, ain't it?" erupted around the room.

"What is it for a negro, who can earn so little at the jobs we are suffered to have, to save one thousand dollars? It is years, and it is tears. But this man did it.

"He returned to his wife's owner, and handed him the money. The owner counted it out, felt it in his hand, and said, *it is not enough.* This owner of human flesh and blood held the wages of a loving husband's labor and said, *I told you one thousand dollars, but now I believe I can make fifteen hundred at least if I sell them to a trader. So that is what I will do.*

"The colored man went off to see if he could make another five hundred dollars, a half again as much, to satisfy the white man who called himself the owner of this colored man's wife. And all the while, the wife in slavery kept writing to her husband."

Mr. Bowser unfolded a few loose pages and began to read. "*Dear Husband, I want you to buy me as soon as possible, for if you do not get me somebody else will. It is said Master is in want of money. If so, I know not what time he may sell me, and then all my bright hopes of the future are blasted, for there has been one bright hope to cheer me in all my troubles, that is to be with you. If I thought I should never see you this earth would have no charms for me. Do all you can for me, which I have no doubt you will.*" He looked up from the pages. "The wife wanted freedom, for herself and her child. But that's not all she wanted. She wanted the love and comfort of her husband. She wrote that, too. *Oh, Dear Dangerfield, come this fall without fail, money or no money. I want to see you so much. That is the one bright hope I have before me.*

"So the husband went back, not with money, but with a gun. Not by himself, but with John Brown. Not to take his wife and one child, but his wife and all six children. John Brown set out to free the unknown mass of slaves. Dangerfield Newby set out to free his own family. And it was Newby they shot down first."

Mr. Bowser drew something from his jacket pocket and held it high in the air. A piece of metal about the size of my cross, though it had only a single shaft, sharpened at one end.

"The mad dogs of Virginia were not satisfied to shoot Dangerfield Newby with a bullet. They shot him with a railroad spike, splitting his throat from ear to ear. They were not satisfied to shoot him dead, but ran to the body and stabbed it over and over again with their rusty knives. They were not satisfied to stab a corpse, but cut it to pieces, hacking off bits of the man's ears, his fingers, his flesh. They were not satisfied to mutilate the corpse themselves, but left it in the street that hogs might feed upon it. These are the good people of Harper's Ferry, of Virginia, of the United States.

"And oh yes, they found Harriet Newby's letters on her husband's disfigured body. And they brought them to the man who called himself Harriet's owner.

When he read them, he sold Harriet south. Maybe to Louisiana, maybe to Alabama. We do not know. But wherever she is, Harriet knows and we know, too, there is no one left to love and rescue Dangerfield Newby's wife and children. Unless we do it ourselves.

"A friend of ours has lately been to Virginia. They are selling the railroad spikes, along with pieces of what they say are Dangerfield Newby, as souvenirs. He brought this stake to me, that I might feel the weight of the thing that killed Dangerfield Newby." He raised the spike above his head. "But this is not the thing that killed Newby. It is slavery, and greed, and race prejudice that killed him. And it will kill us, too, if it gets the chance.

"John Brown dies this morning. But Dangerfield Newby is already dead. John Brown did a great thing in the name of justice. But Dangerfield Newby did as great a thing in the name of love. John Brown is an exemplar to many in the struggle to end slavery. But Dangerfield Newby is a hero of our own. It is his death we must mourn, and must honor, and must be ready to die ourselves, if need be."

I hadn't heard about Dangerfield Newby before then, and Mr. Bowser's preaching on him hit me strong. I was sad and angry and proud all at once, teary eyes and pounding heart and a mouth torn between resolution and a frown. Harriet Newby, Papa, Dangerfield Newby, me—everything seemed all tangled together.

Hattie laid her hand on mine. Though her touch steadied me, I felt more distant from her than I ever had. She sat with husband, father, sisters, and brothers-in-law, a whole family together. Nieces and nephews kept home, protected from what they might hear at the service. But for my family there had never been a together, never been a protection. For Newby's family neither. That's why Mr. Bowser's words resounded for me especially, made me ask myself what I was ready to do, to take up the Calling that Mama insisted was mine.

What started as a rumor around the edges of the memorial service on Friday morning was by Friday evening known fact all over Philadelphia—Mary Brown was bringing her husband's body home for burial on their farm way up in New York State. Which meant that on Saturday, they'd be coming through Philadelphia.

People all over the city were planning to turn out. Those who thought Brown a hero and a martyr, and those who thought him a hell-fiend and a madman, all were expected to line the streets around the train depot come the next morning.

Hattie, her sisters, and their husbands crowded in the front parlor of Mr. Jones's house to discuss the news. Mr. Jones stayed quiet, even as everyone else talked a storm over the Widow Brown's funebrial journey.

"She's lucky to have the body," Stephen, Charlotte's husband, said. "I hear they've mutilated the others, given them to medical students to dissect, dumped them in unmarked graves, or just left them to rot. Even Mary Brown's own sons."

Emily's husband frowned. "Don't talk about such things in front of the ladies."

"Daddy always says ladies ought not be so protected they are ignorant," Hattie said. "Ignorance of our enemies is just endangerment of ourselves."

"Our enemies?" Emily repeated. "We don't even know these people."

"We know they hate us," George said. "Only one they hate more is John Brown, because he acted for us."

Stephen nodded. "They say Mary Brown can have his body, but it will molder in his coffin before his grave is dug. No man in Virginia, colored or white, dares prepare the corpse."

Something knotty sprang root in my stomach, and in an instant I knew why Mr. Jones sat so tacit in his horsehair armchair. If Mrs. Brown was bringing her husband's body to Philadelphia to be embalmed, surely there was one man in the city determined to do the job.

Emily shrieked, and it flashed on everyone, all of them talking at once. "No, Daddy, you can't mean to."

"Of course he will, he's got to."

"It would be madness to try it. They say there will be a mob for sure."

"Don't say try, like he might fail. He will do it, and it will be an honor."

Through all the shouting and the arguing, I shared Mr. Jones's silence. He always said that when the wind blows from the South, there isn't a thing you can do to stop it. The wind that was blowing now wasn't going to cease until it knocked down either all the slaveholders or all the abolitionists. Maybe both.

A log fell in the fireplace. I drew my shawl tighter around my shoulders, as though the south wind was blowing right through the room.

It wasn't a cold December wind that troubled me once I took to my bed. It was a dream. Mr. Jones was in the backyard of the Van Lew mansion, digging a grave. Just when the hole was deep enough for him to stand in, someone laid down railroad tracks across the top, trapping him underneath. From above the pit, I tried to reach between the rail ties to pull him out. But

Mr. Jones yelled for me to help the other man, behind me. I turned and saw two giant metal spikes, fused together in a cross seven feet high. A crowd of white men led a negro to the cross. The mob all had hogs' heads as pale as their hands, and they made horrid noises like rutting pigs. As they tied the colored man to the metal spikes, one of the hog-men called out, "Well, Nigger Newby, what do you say, now you're gonna die?"

"Lost my wife and child," came the anguished reply. "What I got to live for anyway?"

When I heard the voice, I realized it wasn't Dangerfield Newby they had. It was Papa. I couldn't see his face, hidden as he was by the line of hog-men, who were loading their rifles with the fire-pokers Papa had made for the Van Lews. As I tried to run to him, a gust of wind blew hard against me. I heard a pop and smelled rifle smoke. Papa was gone.

I woke with a start. Daylight filled the room. The bodeful stillness in the house told me Mr. Jones was already next door, waiting for John Brown's body. I threw off the counterpane, dressed, and hurried outside. Though the day was bright and clear, few people milled about on errands, shutters pulled closed on homes and businesses alike.

Blocks before I reached the intersection of Broad and Prime, I heard the crowd. Hundreds of people, maybe even a thousand or more, ringed the rail station. As I got near, a clump of young white men sang out the latest coon-show song. *"In Dixie land whar I was born in, early on one frosty mornin, look away, look way, away Dixie Land."*

I skirted wide around them, hastening to the far side of the rail platform, where negroes and whites stood together, Quaker bonnets dotting the crowd. Some of the gathered were reciting Bible passages, some were singing spirituals, some whispered among themselves. Most were quiet.

Before I could search out a single familiar face in the press of people, a whistle pierced the air, and the train chugged into the station. As it braked to a stop, the crowd pushed forward.

The conductor stepped from the lead car. "Back, damn you, or you'll shove the train right off the track."

"Where is our John the Baptist?" a woman on our side cried out. "Where is our John the Baptist?" All around me, people took up the call.

The conductor shook his head. "Dead, just like the first one. Like we'll all be soon enough. Now step back. We've freight to unload."

Two dozen uniformed men poured down from the train, forcing the crowd from the platform. The door to one of the cargo cars slid open, and six guards carried a long pine box out to a cart at the far end of the station.

"Follow them," someone shouted. "They can't leave us behind."

"You best hurry," a man on the other side yelled back. "We've got a real warm welcome waiting for you at the nigger undertaker's."

The crowd surged forward, sweeping me up as it lumbered north and east. Later I noticed that I'd turned an ankle along the way, somewhere else a gripping hand had torn my cloak. But I didn't make out any of that as it happened. All I marked was the press of people suddenly slowing, and the pine smoke curling into the cool air. And then through the smoke, a glimpse of flames, licking their way up the walls of the undertaker's shop and the wooden barn beside it.

The heat from the fire made the air wave before my eyes, as a knot of white men dragged Mr. Jones out before the crowd. Three held him, a fourth put a burning torch to his feet, and the last smacked the butt of a pistol hard against his face.

"Where is it?" they asked, one after another. "Where is the body?"

"You've broken his jaw," shouted someone in the crowd. "He can't speak."

The man with the pistol whirled toward us. "Another word, or a step forward, from any of you niggers or nigger-loving sons of bitches, and I'll shoot the lot of you." He turned back to Mr. Jones and smashed the gun into his face, again and again. "Goddamn you, talk!"

I felt all the heat and the hurt they had loosed on Mr. Jones, feared for what more they might do to him. I didn't know how I might aid him, but I vowed I wouldn't just stand witness. I suppose I was as much foolhardy as fearless, steeling myself to break from the crowd and try what I could to make them stop, when a shout came from the north, arresting the thug midswing.

"By crivens, we been tricked."

The man who shouted came galloping toward the rowdies on North Star, yelling out his report. "The box they brung here was sent to hornswoggle us. They brung John Brown's body direct to Walnut Street wharf. Hurry or he will be gone afore we get there."

"Lord help us. Looks like the devil himself here now," muttered an elderly woman beside me. But it wasn't the devil. It was just a Scotsman with hair the color of hellfire.

"Led 'em on a merry chase, I did," McNiven told us later. "Almost a sin, to be preying upon fools so." He acted as though it had been a lark, diverting the pro-slavery mob away from the area while taking care they didn't reach the wharf before the boat with Brown's body set sail. But from what Doc Weatherston said, Mr. Jones would be dead if not for McNiven's quick thinking.

Even now, the old man barely clung to life. Sending a decoy coffin to the undertaker's shop gave the Widow Brown time enough to transport her husband's corpse through Philadelphia undetected, but Mr. Jones's part in the plot cost him dearly. The torch scarred his feet so badly he couldn't stand. His jaw was shattered from the pistol whipping, his tongue too swollen to speak or eat. Hattie and her sisters tended him day and night, taking turns spooning him pot liquor or porridge, praying he might recover.

We gathered around him at Charlotte's house. The undertaker's shop and the fine home that stood beside it had burned to the ground before the fire company bothered to arrive. Everything of mine—letters, books, keepsakes, every stitch of clothes except what I put on that morning—was gone. Even Papa's iron cross was buried amid the great heap of ashes. All the time I'd spent listening to Zinnie Moore laud the virtues of simplicity must have had its effect on me, because when I found myself without possessions, I felt more of a sense of being lightened than of loss.

The fire and the beating had wrought their changes on me, just as they had on Mr. Jones.

Fire tempers metal, beating shapes it. A blacksmith's daughter knows that well. Whatever I had been before—a young lady, a schoolmarm—I was something different now. Stronger, and with a purpose, like the tools Papa shaped at the smithy. I had no place in Philadelphia, nothing of my own. And that would make it easier to leave.

BOOK THREE

Richmond
1861–1865

Twelve

"I don't like it, not one bit," he insisted, for about the one hundredth time.

I opened my mouth to answer that it was my choice, not for him to like or dislike either way, but McNiven flashed me a look. "Not she nor I am asking you to like it, Bowser. If you do it, 'twill be a courtesy I shall remember and repay."

David Bustill Bowser, gruff and dark and broad, would have said no once and been done with it. But his cousin—I had to keep reminding myself they were cousins, for this slender, copper-skinned young man was so unlike the Mr. Bowser I knew—was more argumentative.

Weak sunlight streamed through the copse of leafless sweet gum and tulip trees. It was none too warm a

January morning, and I was still more than forty miles from where I meant to be. So though Wilson Bowser was anxious to convince me of the folly of my request, he couldn't. I was going home. And I needed him to take me there. "You've forwarded plenty of baggage through this area. Surely it wouldn't be so difficult for you to carry me on."

He acted as though my speaking of the Railroad confirmed I was a fool. "Baggage moves from the South to the North. Not the other way." He looked to McNiven. "She always this contrary?"

"Just be glad she is on our side. Elsewise we maun find her contrary nature even more troublesome." McNiven hid his mouth beneath the orange fringe of his mustache, but I saw enough of his devilish smile to know that between us, we would convince this Mr. Bowser to take me after all.

When I decided to come back to Virginia, I put my plan to McNiven and told him the part I meant for him to play in it. I never had need to ask a white man for a thing until then. This was a gift fate had given me, Old Master Van Lew dead when I was so young, Young Master John hardly grown enough to head the household before I left Richmond. The colored men I knew in Philadelphia always treated me the way they treated any colored females, as though they were our

protectors. Fearing any of them would make a different choice for me than I wanted to make for myself,
I turned to a white man instead.

"You ask mighty a wild thing," McNiven had said.
"Are you truly ready to go, whenever and however
I say?"

If he'd told me we were leaving right then, it would
have been none too soon. I'd already waited through
all the politicking of 1860, pinning my expectations on
Mr. William Seward. Senator Seward had opposed the
Fugitive Slave Act when it was first proposed, had even
defended fugitive slaves in the court of law. He helped
found the Republican Party, vowing it would be the
party of abolition. I thought for sure he'd garner this
new Party's nomination that May. Even thought of it as
a present for my twenty-first birthday.

So I was devastated to see the nomination go instead
to Mr. Lincoln, of whom we negroes knew so little.
Hattie's sister Gertie kept mistakenly calling him
Ephraim Lincoln, he was so foreign to us, and we all
thought it a grand joke. But we sobered up quickly
enough once the Republicans chose him for their
ticket. We knew all our hopes rested on him, whatever
he turned out to be.

When those slavery-loving Democrats split their
party right in half, nominating two different candidates

for president because the Southerners found Stephen Douglas not slavocrat enough, I saw this Abraham Lincoln would win the election. Just as soon as the ballots were counted, South Carolina announced it was seceding. As 1860 slipped into 1861, Mississippi, Alabama, and Georgia followed suit. Other Southern states were lining up to do the same. Some of them didn't even bother to secede before sending their militias to seize a Federal arsenal. Though they'd been mad as rabid hounds when John Brown tried that, they turned greedy as hogs at feeding time doing it themselves. But no one seemed to know what way Virginia might go. At least, no one up in Philadelphia.

All we knew was that though James Buchanan was spending the final months of his presidency hemming and hawing over all of it, surely Mr. Lincoln wouldn't stand for what was happening. And if he didn't, it seemed likely we were headed for war. If war was coming, I wanted to be in Richmond, with Papa, before it came to pass, and for as long as it took to see it through. To help it through, as I meant to do.

So when McNiven asked if I was truly ready to leave, I nodded and said just as soon as we could.

"I'm glad for it," he said. "Richmond will be much to us in the next years, whether Virginia secedes or no. Your talents will be a great help in our labors there."

When I first met McNiven, I couldn't have imagined I'd take pride or comfort in knowing he meant for us to ally together. But back then I couldn't have guessed I'd ever connive to travel back across Mason and Dixon's line, either.

We were halfway to Baltimore before McNiven informed me he could go only so far as the distant bank of the Rappahannock, that David Bustill Bowser's cousin would have to carry me on from there. And only after we met up with Mr. Bowser, at the regular rendezvous point for their Railroad work, did I realize McNiven hadn't yet told him about me.

We spent the better part of that morning hour arguing, until at last McNiven was directing his buckboard wagon back toward Maryland while we rode south to Richmond. Mr. Bowser's conveyance was much smaller, a cart barely big enough to haul three sacks of flour, though at five foot by three, large enough to hide a fugitive slave or two. As I sat beside him on the driver's bench, I reminded myself that Mr. Bowser's reluctance was understandable, given my unexpected presence and unusual request. Perhaps now we might begin to be acquainted without so much consternation.

I offered up some comment about how picturesque the winding road was against the wintry landscape.

But all Mr. Bowser answered was, "No one will believe it. Do you realize that?"

"What won't they believe?"

"That you're a slave."

It was the only way I could come back home. To do as Mama had done, use my freedom to play at being bound in slavery.

"Whites in Virginia look at a negro, they don't see anything but slave," I said. "Even if that person is free. I'd think you of all people would know that." My words came out snappish as I said that last piece. I told myself it must be the fatigue of the journey, although deep inside I felt there was something about Mr. Bowser that brought out such petulance in me.

"Anybody white or colored looks at you, they'll see a woman who carries herself proud. A woman whose clothes are fresh and whose face is soft. A woman without a chafe, callus, or bruise. Not so much as muscle well formed from hefting. How many slaves don't work all day? How many slaves' bodies don't bear the mark of that work, one way or another? Forget how quick you are to speak your mind. Even before your mouth gives you away, the rest of your body will betray you."

I drew my merino shawl fast around my shoulders and kept my mouth shut tight. I'd proven in the Railroad work I could keep mum, even play dumb, as well as anybody. But when I looked down, I saw that even against the dull brown skirt of my new linsey-woolsey dress, the unblemished hands folded in my lap were clearly those of a woman who didn't cook or clean, even for herself. Let alone for a master and his family.

Late in the afternoon, Mr. Bowser steered his cart off the road and down a narrow lane to a lone cabin. Without a word of explanation, he jumped to the ground and made for the door. Wondering if I was meant to follow or no, I decided to stay where I was. If he wants me with him, let him ask, I thought, stamping my feet against the cold.

An elderly negro, positively ancient in appearance, answered Mr. Bowser's knock, accepting some coins before disappearing back inside. When he returned, he handed Mr. Bowser a pair of birds. From their long, curved beaks, I recognized them as woodcocks, a species I hadn't seen in all my years in Philadelphia. Mr. Bowser returned to the cart, holding what I supposed was our dinner.

When I reached for the purse pinned against my skirts, Mr. Bowser waved me away. "I pay my own way in the world. And you best hold on to your pennies just as well as your dollars. I wager you'll get yourself in a heap of trouble before too long and need everything you have to get yourself out." He flicked the reins, and the noise of the horse and cart covered the silence between us.

We stopped that evening at a small brook a half mile off the main road. While Mr. Bowser set about feeding and watering his horse, I gathered what kindling I could find, piling it on a patch of bare ground.

Mr. Bowser took his time tending the bay, so I stepped to the cart and lifted out some split logs he had there, figuring that if they weren't meant for the cookfire, he could very well stop me. When he didn't, I brought them into the clearing and laid them with the kindling. It took me three trips to fetch all that wood out, and my arms were aching by the time I took the bucket from the cart to draw water from the stream. Just as I was thinking how lucky I was that the brook hadn't frozen up, my foot slid along a mossy stone. I slipped into the frigid water, soaking myself up to my skirts before I regained the shore.

"Mr. Bowser," I called in the sweetest voice I could summon, "would you be so kind as to light the fire?"

"I'd wait to light it," he said. "But if you insist, I suppose I should oblige." He drew a match-safe from his frock coat, and in a moment the fire was blazing.

As I warmed myself before the flames, Mr. Bowser brought out the woodcocks. I insisted on cooking them, though I was relieved he didn't inquire about my culinary experience before handing the birds over.

Plucking the carcasses took rather longer than I expected. So many feathers on those two little bodies, with now and again a plume breaking off in my hand. My fingers stiff with cold, I struggled to pry the remaining portion of those shafts from the puckering flesh.

When I had the birds more or less prepared, I brought them to where Wilson Bowser had laid out the iron rods of his cookspit. Two were the same length and had forked ends, with a third longer crosspiece fitted to lay inside the forks. I poked the crosspiece through the first bird, meaning for the pole go into its rear and come out its mouth, like all the skewered carcasses I'd ever seen. Only, it was harder to tug the body onto the pointed rod than I expected. The speared tip came out the neck instead of the mouth. The near-severed head dangled off at a horrible angle, dripping bits of giblet onto my skirt. I took greater care with the second bird, without much more success.

Putting the cookspit together was even more difficult. The end pieces could only stand with the crosspiece in place between them, but I couldn't lay the crosspiece inside both forks because one side or the other kept falling down. And the weight of the skewered birds made it even harder to balance the crosspiece. The woodcocks' eyes seemed to gawk at me from their lolling heads the whole while, making me all the more jittery.

When at last I had the pieces assembled, I turned to the fire. The only way I could maneuver the spit over the flames without setting my skirts ablaze was to ask for Mr. Bowser's help. He let out some comment about how awfully much easier it is to get a spit over a fire that hadn't yet been lit, though between the two of us we finally managed to stand the contraption in place.

I rested from all the hauling and plucking and poking while the first side of the birds cooked. When they looked about done, I rotated the spit to roast the other side. Mr. Bowser brought out a lone tin cup and tin plate from the cart and offered them to me. "If I'd known McNiven was going to ask me to escort a lady to Richmond, I would have brought place settings for two."

"I can cup my hands to drink," I said, "and I'll take the plate once you're done."

He considered my proposition. "I'll use the tin cup, if you take the plate first. After all, you should have the earliest opportunity to enjoy the delights of your cooking."

I started to argue with him, but he nodded toward the fire. The blaze was licking at the underside of the birds. I jumped up to turn the spit, but in my hurry I caught the iron bar too near the flames. Before I could even cry out, Mr. Bowser grabbed my wrist, submerging my scalded hand in the water bucket. While the water cooled my blistering flesh, he deftly removed the crosspiece from the spit, slid the first woodcock onto the plate, and handed it to me.

It was the singular most awful thing I'd ever tasted.

One side was burned to a crisp, positively inedible. The other was already cold, and so dry I thought the woodcock must have been dead a week. I chewed and chewed on the tough meat, now and then catching a tooth on a bit of feather shaft. After only a few minutes, I gave up. Hunger was better than choking down any more of that bird.

I expected some comment from Mr. Bowser about how little I ate, but he was waiting in silence for his own supper. Which wasn't going to be much satisfaction once he had it.

"I'm sorry," I said. "The woodcock doesn't seem to have turned out. Perhaps the other one will be more savory."

"I doubt it. A bird that small shouldn't be drawn before it's cooked. And it needs to be rubbed with fatback or butter or some such thing before roasting. And anything on a spit must be turned constantly, to roast evenly." His deep brown eyes held my own. "You've never cooked a meal in your whole life, have you?"

"No, I never have." I gestured at my skirt, damp and stained, and then held up my singed hand. "But at least I look a bit more like I've cooked or cleaned for somebody, don't I?" My pride was even harder to swallow than the burnt bird meat. "I'm sorry I spoiled your supper."

"I suppose I knew you would. But you were about as entertaining to watch as any traveling tent show, and that's more satisfaction than even the best roasted game bird would be." From a bag in the back of the cart, he drew out two large sweet potatoes. He was still chuckling as he nestled them into the embers to cook.

I had more on my mind than Mr. Bowser and his woodcocks when we turned down Mechanicsville Turnpike into Richmond the next afternoon, me directing him to head east, up Church Hill, rather than continuing into Shockoe Bottom. It tore at me to go to Bet before Papa. But Papa could no more leave off working the forge at the smithy to celebrate my arrival than he could have walked away ten years ago to come to Philadelphia with me.

I wasn't exactly sure celebration would be his response, anyway. I hadn't sent Papa word of my plan to return to Richmond, telling myself I wanted to surprise him. But the truth was, what little I'd been hearing from him sounded so angry and defeated, I feared what he might say.

As we rode along Grace Street, I was startled by the ornate hodgepodge of buildings that had sprung up during my absence. Italianate cupolas, Greek Revival mansions, even a Gothic Revival church—it seemed wealthy Richmonders all wanted to pretend they were in some other time and place. Only the Van Lew mansion appeared unaltered, setting by itself on the family's block of property. The other houses seemed to shy away from it, pulling together to avoid their imposing neighbor, just as the ladies of Church Hill had always shied away from Bet.

When I directed Mr. Bowser to stop, he jumped from the driver's bench to help me down. Then he reached into the cart and drew out my lone satchel, the stark reminder I was returning to Richmond with fewer possessions than when I left.

Mr. Bowser's reddish brown skin gleamed in the afternoon sun. "My barbering shop is over at Broad Street and Seventh, right across from the rail depot. I live upstairs. Whatever trouble you find yourself in, you come by or send word. If I'm away, pass a note under the side door. No one will find it but me."

Holding myself from protesting that I knew better than to get myself into trouble, I thanked him for transporting me. He nodded one final time, took his seat on the cart, and drove off.

Looking up at the mansion where I'd passed more than half my life, I felt as out of place as when I first stood before the Upshaws' apartment building. There were plenty of places I didn't go in Philadelphia—didn't because negroes couldn't. But where we did go, we walked in the front door, same as whites. Even into white families' homes. Knowing no colored person, free or slave, presumed to mount the front steps of a Church Hill house, I gathered my flimsy skirts in one hand and my satchel in the other and walked around to Twenty-fourth Street.

The Van Lews' garden and arbor lay bare and frost covered. I marked how much smaller they were than I remembered, how barren against the sharp-sweet odor of rabbit soup and marrow pudding emanating from the kitchen. I knew Zinnie was long gone. I even remembered reading about Terry Farr in Mama's long ago letters. But I didn't take time to think much on this stranger before the cookfire as I made my way to the servants' entry at the rear of the mansion. Before I even had a chance to knock, Bet swung open the door, looking as altered as Church Hill itself.

When she brought me to Philadelphia, Bet was a spinster of thirty-two. Now she was an old maid, already forty-two. Nearly the age her mother was when Old Master Van Lew died. Her features looked pinched, her once light curls fading to a dull gray.

She studied me as though she couldn't believe I was truly standing there. Then she pulled me toward her, her embrace almost desperate in its ferocity.

A white lady hugging a negro right where anyone walking by the yard might see us. That vexed me. My safety depended on Bet, and I doubted she had sense enough to know how such conduct put me in jeopardy.

But I was grateful, too. Though Bet wasn't quite family, wasn't quite friend, that hug was the first welcome I had.

"It's so good of you to come." She spoke as though she'd summoned me.

Figuring I might as well let her believe my return was her idea, I answered, "Of course I came, Miss Bet. We need to be ready for whatever happens."

She nodded. "We shall show those seditious Carolinians. Come upstairs, see what I've prepared for you." She led me through the house and up to my old garret quarter. A feather mattress set upon a new mahogany bedstead, Mama's chipped wash-set replaced by a rose-patterned porcelain pitcher and bowl.

Bet stood behind me in the doorway like a ruffian guarding the mouth of his treasure cave. "If there's anything else you need, I can obtain it."

"I appreciate your offer of a place to stay," not that it had been an offer, just a presumption on her part, "but I will be living with my papa."

She held steady. "It would be best if you reside here. Your father's circumstances are not what you think."

"His circumstances aren't what I wish, but I suppose I know them as well as anybody." How dare she lecture me about Papa? "Perhaps I should go to his cabin now, to wait for him."

"No." Bet answered so quickly, it startled me. She tried to make her voice less sharp as she added, "You're tired, and it will be some hours yet before Lewis is done with work. Rest here, have something to eat, and I'll send word for him to come as soon as he can."

I remembered how long it had been since I'd taken a proper meal, and how good Terry Farr's cooking smelled. Walking down to Shockoe Bottom wouldn't get Papa away from the smithy any sooner. Besides, it would be perilous for me to move about Richmond without the protection of a white person, so it made sense to appease Bet. Especially since I had no intention of staying on once Papa came. I agreed to wait there, and her smile returned.

Once the afternoon light began fading from the sky, I took up a post at the garret window, straining to make out Papa's figure. More than once I thought

I saw him, only to watch the person I set my sights on pass down Grace Street. At last my eyes lit upon him. Maybe I wasn't any more sure at first than I was with the others. But I surveyed this figure closely as he turned the corner of the lot, disappearing toward the servants' entry to the Van Lew property.

His footsteps sounded out slowly as he mounted the servants' stair, achy limbs finding trouble with each riser. When he reached the landing and we caught sight of each other, his face turned into a mess of confusion and anger. "How long she been keeping you up here? Ain't you free after all that?"

"Bet didn't bring me here," I said, hugging myself to him. "I came to be with you." I wasn't about to set him worrying by mentioning McNiven and our plans. "I'm still free, though I have to pretend otherwise. Like Mama did."

He pulled away, his words as pointed as a leather-punch. "Minerva died no different than if she was a slave. I don't want that for you. Not that anyone asked my idea on it."

Time had worked its way along his face in angry gashes, leaving long, deep creases in its wake. His hair was all white, as though a permanent frost had settled on him. Hardest on me was seeing his eyes. I still thought of the eyes I found gazing back at me every day from the looking glass as Papa's eyes. But the ones I saw now were missing the light, the fight, the play I remembered.

First I left him, then Mama did. Alone, Papa had become a different man. His letters had hinted as much. But it meant something more to stare it in the face than to read it between the scant lines of correspondence written in someone else's hand.

"Papa, I've missed you so. My coming home without telling you, I meant it for a surprise. Like a great big just-because, from me to you."

"Just because they keep me here year in and year out, like a lame horse wondering when someone gonna have the decency to shoot it, you throwed away fancy Philadelphia?"

"Just because I love you, I came back home."

He stared past me, out the window. "Curfew's coming on. I best be getting back to the Bottom."

I reached for the stiff handle of my satchel. "We best, you mean. I'm going to live with you, in your house. Our house."

He kept his eyes on the darkening pane. "Got no house now. Greerson Wallace put me out."

"When? What for?" Resentful as he'd grown toward Mahon, still I couldn't imagine my sweet, good-natured papa offending his old friend and landlord.

"Since that John Brown, white people worrying us all the time. This damn curfew was the first of it. Then they passed a law, no free negro can rent to a slave, even with the owner's permission. Free colored caught renting liable to a whipping, one stripe for each day the slave was there."

All through my childhood, nearly every slave in Richmond except domestics boarded out. And it wasn't too many white people who rented to them. "Where are all the slaves living?"

"Whites allow for free negroes to lodge relatives who are slaves, and the big factory owners, they can pay someone in the government to look the other way when the slaves they hire board out. But Mahon says he ain't got money for that. Told me I'm welcome to do what I like, but Wallace and me be taking our chances on the law finding out. Wallace weren't about to risk it, and I weren't gonna ask him to."

I knew how proud Papa always was of his little cabin. "Why didn't you tell me?"

"You always tell me everything happen to you up in Philadelphia?"

There was much I omitted from my letters, wanting to shelter him from the daily humiliations that reminded Pennsylvania negroes we might not be slaves but we sure weren't equals. But now I realized my trying to protect him, his trying to protect me—it had opened a breach between us I didn't begin to know how to fill.

"Where are you living now?" I asked.

"In a shed, back of Mahon's lot."

I told him I'd stay there with him, but he wouldn't hear of it. "That shed ain't big enough for but one person, barely even that. And it ain't mine to offer you."

I set my satchel back on the floor beside the mahogany bedstead, realizing why Bet had been so insistent. I wouldn't prefer the finest rooms in Richmond over residing with my own papa. But even if I couldn't live with him, I'd find a way to do for him. Find a way to cheer him back to his old self. And try to keep him from finding out my other reason for coming back to Virginia.

As he hugged me farewell, he whispered, "I want better for you than this. But it does a body good to see you so grown up." I bowed my head, and he kissed it just like he always had. Then he turned down the servants' stair and headed back to Mahon's.

When I lay down in my old room that night, I felt as far apart from Papa as I had all those years I was away in Philadelphia. The half mile that separated us now widened into the chasm between slave and free, age and youth, despair and determination.

Thirteen

As the slant of morning light streamed through the familiar gap between the shutters, I reached out for Mama, hoping the warmth of her body would brace me for the chill air before I got out of bed.

Out of bed. Not off the pallet. The difference pulled me from my drowsy slumber, made me realize there was no Mama here with me. Yet I sensed I wasn't alone. As I blinked my eyes open, I saw Bet hovering in the doorway.

"Did I wake you?" She didn't wait for an answer. "Terry will have breakfast up by now. I shall have Nell set it out for us while you dress."

"Miss Bet, if you want me with you, I can serve your meal and clear it after you're done," I said. "But if you sit down to table with a negro, it won't set right with your mother, nor your servants. And it will be trouble for both of us before too long."

"Nonsense, Mary. Surely Terry and Nell have better things to do than go about Richmond telling tales on their employer." She spoke as though she hadn't read a single of those leather-bound volumes of Mr. Shakespeare's plays down in her father's library, nearly every one with some maid or manservant playing pranks or plotting intently against master and mistress. "We shall do as we please."

"We should do as we must, not as we please, if we mean to keep from attracting any notice. You know it yourself, expecting me to call you Miss Bet, while you call me Mary."

She colored a bit, her only acknowledgment of the truth of what I said. "But I cannot have you waiting on me, when you're better educated than most white ladies on Church Hill."

"So far as anyone here is concerned, I'm not free and I'm not educated," I reminded her. "And any labor my mama performed in this house I won't consider beneath me." I put that part about Mama in there to show her that when she talked about servants and their work, she was talking about me and mine. Time, schooling, even death, couldn't change that.

"I see you are quite obstinate on this matter," she said. "Still, so long as we are not in public, I insist you call me Bet, not Miss Bet."

I fingered my burned hand and shook my head. "I need to practice Southern comportment every moment I can."

Bet puckered her mouth tight, the closest she ever came to admitting defeat. "I suppose we do want to keep up appearances. I shall tell everyone I've brought you here to attend Mother, she won't mind. She's a true Philadelphia patriot, as horrified by all this talk of secession as are we."

My hopes about secession were not at all like Bet's or her mother's, but I knew well enough to keep them to myself.

She went down to her solitary breakfast, leaving me to dress. It felt strange to go about without a corset, hose, and the rest of a proper lady's undergarments, as though I were wearing my nightclothes about for everyone to see. Stranger still to find myself listening for the ringing of my old mistress's handbell, the long ago summons that set me at whatever the Van Lews desired.

When the delicate porcelain peals finally called me downstairs, I couldn't have been more shocked by what I found. A fetid smell permeated the close air in the bedroom, punctuated by my former mistress' heavy wheezing. One side of her face hung limp with apoplectic palsy, dragging her features into a lopsided grimace.

Bet hadn't said a word to warn me about her mother's condition, and my horror must have been wide-eyed apparent to the old woman.

"So you really have come back to us," she said. "I didn't expect there'd be much to draw you here these days."

"My papa is here, ma'am." I took a cloth from the washstand and wiped spittle from her chin. Her pale skin was papery thin, delicate even on the side untouched by stroke. I dipped the cloth into the washbasin and bathed her face and arms. Her flesh wasn't putrefied, and I wondered at the source of the room's stench, until I pulled back the covers.

Her eyes swam up in her drooping face, milky with shame. "It's hard for me to reach the chamber pot most nights. I'm sorry."

I'm sorry. In all the years I lived in that house, I never heard a Van Lew apologize to a slave. What they did they had a right to do, what we in the house did we had an obligation to do. I met her unwonted humiliation with my own unwonted sympathy, the two of us sharing silent discomposure as I cleaned at where she'd soiled herself.

She stayed quiet while I guided her to her feet, led her to her dressing room, and helped her don the garments I brought out from her armoire. It reassured me to see her seated and dressed, more the lady I remembered. I tried not to stare at her palsied features, but as I pinned back her hair, she caught my gaze with her own.

"Whatever happens, you've a place with us, just as Aunt Minnie always did. Same as if you never left us."

She meant the words as welcome, I suppose. But as I stood tall in the room, remembering how as a child I hid behind a doorway or beneath a bedstead to spy on the Van Lews, I didn't think anything about me and my place in Richmond would ever be the same.

Without saying a word aloud on it, Bet and I connived a routine that kept me from spending much time around her hired servants. Most days, I accompanied her mother to gatherings of the Ladies' Auxiliary of the Union Guard. As we walked to the Carringtons' or the Catlins' to join the other stitching matrons, I carried my former mistress's sewing kit, minding she didn't twist an ankle despite her cane. Her slow physical recuperation seemed a steely testament of her Philadelphia patriotism. Stitching for the Union Guard, even iterating the militia company's name, had become her talisman against secession. During those gatherings, I sought talisman for something else entirely, keeping my head low but my ears alert for any news of whether Virginia would abandon the Union. But the white ladies of Church Hill hardly knew about such things themselves.

"What bluff and bluster from our men." Mrs. Carrington tut-tutted her way through mending a tear her son had put into his uniform during a drinking party that passed for the militia's shooting rally.

"I tell my Henry, sun will still rise in the East and set in the West, for all your grand talk," Mrs. Whitlock agreed. "Millie will still plead for a new ball gown every other week, and Carter will do more card playing than reading up at the university. And I'll still have a time trying to keep the house in order with such servants as we have. Mistreating my china and misplacing my silver, hiding out to avoid their chores." The matrons nodded at the apish male notion that such things could ever change.

But I marked how one of the younger women tipped up her nose at them. "Father says Virginia's bound to secede and join the new Confederacy."

"Secession, pshaw," said Mrs. Randolph. "Let the North secede from us, if they find respecting States' Rights so disagreeable. But cede the nation founded by our Washington and our Jefferson to them? Never."

I took care not to show how such declarations set my eye-teeth on edge. So long as the free states made Union with slaveholders, Congress would continue carrying on with its compromises. The Missouri Compromise, the Compromise of 1850, the Kansas-Nebraska agreement. Decades and decades of them, and every one made to protect slaveholding.

Secession was a gamble, to be sure. If the South succeeded at tearing itself away, there'd be less of a check on slavery than there even was now. But for folks with nothing to call their own, not even themselves and their children, a gamble with long odds and high stakes was the only possible way to win.

Secession, then war. War, then defeat. Defeat and then, finally, emancipation. John Brown's raid convinced me it could be so.

Meanwhile, the ladies of Church Hill kept at their sewing. One small, careful stitch after another, each push and pull of the needle rending a hole in the fabric and then filling it with thread.

All through my childhood, Mama turned just about any errand into an adventure, picking her way through Richmond streets with me at her side whenever she was sent to do the Van Lews' business. Though these outings took us all through the city, we only went once to Mahon's smithy. I was very, very young when Mama brought me by, on a day when

Papa must have known Mahon would be away. As Mama and I stepped from the bright Virginia morning into the smoky dark of the smithy, the stifling heat caught me in place. More than that, the noise stunned me. Metal hitting on metal, so loud I thought the world was coming to an end, with a host of ungodly monsters bent on breaking it apart. One of those monsters, muscles bulging and hammer in hand, looked up at me, and I let loose a scream. I kept on screaming, so hysterical the only thing for it was for Mama to pick me up and hustle me out, hushing and soothing me all the way back up Church Hill.

My parents never mentioned that visit. It became one of my private remembrances, stored away for months at a time until I'd take it out and toy with it a bit, the way a child runs a tongue along a loose tooth every now and again. The memory frightened me for years, scared me more when I turned old enough to understand Papa had to sit among those monsters every day. Perplexed me when I was older still, wondering why Mahon, who had so much power over Papa, didn't do something about those monsters himself. I felt mighty foolish once I was grown enough to realize those figures weren't monsters, just slaves made to work the glowing metal all day long. Ashamed about shrieking at my own papa that way, mistaking him for an ogre just because he was strong and sure at his task.

Now that I was back in Richmond, I went by Mahon's lot most mornings, carefully choosing the earliest hour of the day for my visits, before Papa's labors at the forge and mine tending Bet's mother. But what I saw when I stopped there vexed me almost as much as the monsters I imagined all those years before.

Buildings of all sizes choked the property. The largest by far was the smithy itself, a cavernous brick room anchored by three chimneys so powerful their smoke hung in the air day and night. At a back corner of the lot stood the barn for the horse and delivery cart. In the other rear corner sat the two-story wooden quarter that housed the apprentices. Smaller sheds for storing various supplies dotted what remained of the tight tract. It was in one of those that Papa slept.

The cabin Papa had shared with Mr. and Mrs. Wallace was by no stretch of the facts luxurious. But the bare stall he now occupied shocked by comparison. Four walls so close there wasn't room enough for him to stretch full out on his narrow sleeping pallet. Frigid air whistled through gaps in the wall planks, which in warmer weather must have been a passageway for vermin. Windowless, the shed lacked not only light but also the colorful tattersall curtains Mama made for

Papa's cabin so many years before. Worst of all, Papa's sculptured cross was nowhere to be seen.

Sundays of my childhood, I spent hours gazing upon that twisted metal form and marveling at my papa's ability to bend iron to his will. Now it seemed he had no will at all. Whenever I suggested small improvements we might make to the shed, he replied with the same defeated air, "Ain't my place to fix up, it's Marse Mahon's."

I cursed Mahon for relegating my dear papa to a workshed that wasn't even fit to stable an ox. This man, who always held such prepotency over my family, was in truth a stranger to me. I avoided the smithy property while he was around, lest he find reason to object to Papa passing his scant free moments with me. But I worked my nerve up like a skillet warming to a fry, positioning myself on Franklin Street late one afternoon to intercept Mahon as he made his way home for the night.

"Marse Mahon, sir," I said as I stepped into his path, "I'm your Lewis's daughter. I been gone out of Richmond for a while, my owner just brought me back lately."

Mahon didn't care to be kept waiting. "What is it, gal?"

"My papa, he's not so young anymore. I fear the chill air might weaken him. Keep him from being able to work so good for you, sir. If I could fill the chinks in his sleeping shed with rags or mud or what-not. And maybe if I could pretty it up a bit, to cheer him. Only if you think it would help keep Papa strong for you, sir."

He squinted into the distance. "Don't know why he insists on sleeping there rather than in the quarter with the rest of 'em." Could he really mean that Papa chose to dwell in that nasty shed? "Hardly been him-self since Aunt Minnie passed. Maybe should have sold him then, before all this talk of secession made prices so unstable."

That single sentence loosed all that had been build-ing in me for the decade past. I wanted to scream at Mahon, rage at him. Obdurately holding Papa all those years, in the face of unnamed profit from the sale. Keeping both my parents from building a life together, with me, in the North. And now, saying he would let Papa go, once it was too late for him to be with Mama until they met again in Glory. Once it was too late for my family to make a home in freedom.

I bit my tongue hard and kept my eyes low, thinking of what a colored woman's outburst to a white man on a Richmond street would cost her.

Mahon must have taken my downward glance for sub-missive gratitude. "You best do something to improve

Lewis's attitude, gal." He pushed past me to make his way home to his supper.

I felt vain and silly, thinking how I wanted to make myself out to be a great liberator with a heroic part to play in some grand plan for abolition, when I hadn't so much as managed to help my own papa. Now that I had Mahon's leave to meddle with his property, I promised myself at least I'd fix the shed up in short order, never mind whose aid I'd have to enlist or how Papa might protest afterward. I wanted to do right by my papa. And I needed to prove to myself that I really could, and would, do even more in Richmond than I had in Philadelphia, to counter slavery.

In the seven blocks beyond the Van Lew mansion, Church Hill slopes down into the Shockoe Creek ravine. Most streets dead-end against the creek, starting up again on the other side. Traveling by foot or cart or carriage, you have to pick your way across by heading some ways upstream or downstream to one of the rickety bridges that traverse the creek bottom. Residents of Church Hill always spoke about Shockoe Hill, which rises up on the far side of the creek, as if it were a foreign land. Since I never had business at Court End or Capitol Square, I had scant sense of the Richmond that stretched west of the creek.

Making my way toward Shockoe Hill, I had to pass through the long blocks of slave pens and auction houses that constituted Richmond's topographical and moral low point. Omohundro's slave jail was right on Broad Street. So were smaller slave-traders like Faundron's and Frazier's. Clustered on side streets off Broad all the way to the Canal were more than a dozen similar establishments, Lumpkin's Alley the worst of them. Little wonder colored Richmond called the area Devil's Half-Acre.

"Servus est." Sed fortasse liber animo. "Servus est." Hoc illi nocebit? Ostende quis non sit: alius libidini servit, alius avaritiae, alius ambitioni, omnes spei, omnes timori. I silently declaimed the passage from the Stoic philosopher Seneca that I translated my first year in Miss Mapps's class, as the rapacious white men gathered outside Omohundro's looked me over just as though I were standing half-stripped on the auction block. *You say, "He is a slave." But he is a person with a free spirit. You say, "He is a slave." But how shall this harm him? Show me who is not a slave. One man is a slave to his lusts, another is a slave to greed, another a slave of ambition, and all are slaves to hope and fear.*

I told myself that the men ogling me were slaves to lust, greed, ambition, hope, and fear all together. They saw me only as an ignorant slave. But surely that was better than being a slave-trader or his lackey, who chose ignorance for themselves.

The noise of the slave pens fell away by the time I got as far west as where Broad Street crosses Seventh. On one corner was the train depot where I said good-bye to Mama. On another was a two-story clapboard structure painted dove gray. Through the six-paned windows that framed the front door, I spied two tall chairs set before a counter laden with all manner of barbering tools. One of the chairs was taken, though all I could see of its occupant were the hirsute hands holding the newspaper that obscured his face.

Mr. Bowser was stoking the fire in the small stove at the back of the shop, and as I opened the door, he called, "Right with you in a moment, sir. Only but one gentleman ahead of you, wait shouldn't be long."

When he turned and saw me, he started, then looked to his customer, who remained ensconced behind his news-sheet. "Mr. Saunders, I must step out for a moment, be right back."

Following me outside, he took my elbow and steered me through a gate by the corner of the building. "What's the trouble?"

Hearing his worry made me feel funny all of a sudden. "No trouble, only I need a favor of you, if you please."

Which it didn't seem he did. "What do you mean coming into a barbering shop, short of a genuine emergency? A lady doesn't belong any such place."

"I'm not supposed to be a lady," I reminded him.

"Contrary Mary, do you ever fail to disagree with something a person says to you? Don't bother objecting, I have a customer waiting and no time to argue. So tell me what's brought you here."

Swallowing my umbrage at being called contrary, I explained about Papa's living situation. I told him I needed some way to lure Papa off the lot come Sunday, so I could patch and clean the shed. "I don't know you well, but you've been kind to me once already, and I thought maybe we could come up with some excuse for you to invite Papa off someplace for a few hours."

He shook his head, but I wasn't about to be refused. "If you're busy this Sunday, then perhaps next week—"

"Not a thing to do Sunday I can't put off," he said. "It's just that what you're asking doesn't make a lick of sense."

"Doesn't make sense to want to do for my papa? Man's got rheumatism, shivering his nights away, and it doesn't make sense to want to fix up that nasty shed? You call me Contrary Mary, but you're nothing but a—a Willful Wilson."

"I don't know that I'm so much willful myself as I have a tender spot for willful women. Aren't I lucky one's fallen into my life, asking me favors one after another without ever meaning to let me decline?" He smiled like he'd been pleased all along, knowing I'd come to plead for his aid. "Fixing up your papa's place makes plenty of sense. But you can get him away from there easier than a stranger can. So you do that, leave the fixing up to me."

I didn't know quite what to make of what he said about willful women, so I just sniffed a bit over the part about him fixing up the shed. "I can do the work myself, you know."

"No doubt you're eager to try. But you just worry about distracting him, let me round up a fellow or two who owe me a favor, and we'll handle the furbishments. What time shall I have them over at the smithy?"

He didn't leave me much chance to say nay. "We'll be gone by ten o'clock, and I can keep him out for most of the day. I'll leave a bucket of mud plaster and another of whitewash for you in the hollowed tree at the edge of the lot." I gave him my most decorous nod. "I appreciate you showing such kindness to a man you haven't even met."

"You're welcome for it. Just don't thank me by cooking me any more suppers."

It was well more than two miles from Mahon's smithy to the colored burying ground on the northern edge of Richmond. Papa's rheumatism slowed our walk, but he came along without the protestations with which he greeted most anything I said to him these days. He even stopped at one frosty lot on Jackson Street to snap off some sprigs of winterberry holly, "To have something pretty enough to bring to Minerva."

Most of the graves in the colored burial yard didn't have any markers. Others had just sticks or rocks that mourners used to set off their beloved's resting place. The expense of a wooden tablet, let alone a true gravestone, was well beyond the folks who buried someone here. Many couldn't read anyway, so a gnarled branch or impromptu cairn was as good a monument as any. But I could pick out Mama's grave from a dozen yards away, distinguished as it was by one of Papa's metal crosses.

Papa bent low when we reached the plot, laying holly along the cold ground. His voice was so quiet, I had to lean close to hear him. "You recognize her yourself, I suppose. Strong-headed just 'cause she grown. She come back without a word of warning, Minerva. What do you think of that?"

"She knows," I told him. "It was her idea, me coming back here to be with you."

He rose slowly and looked me in the eye. "From the day we decided to send you North to the day she passed, Minerva never talked on anything for you 'cept your freedom, how you was gonna have a different life in Philadelphia. You want to defy that, don't you be saying it was her idea."

"This was after she passed. She used to come to me, going on about what plan Jesus had for me, whether I was at the right task or no. You know Mama always liked to tell a person what to do."

He gave a nod of agreement. "Do sound like Minerva. But why she tell you come back here, when she always say North the only place for you?"

I didn't want to worry him, but I couldn't keep all that was happening from my own papa. "Since the election a few months back, people have been saying the country might be going to war, South against North." I wrapped my hand around his, taking care not to bother his achy joints. "I couldn't let a war come between us. Mama wouldn't abide it either."

He looked at the hard plot that was all he had left of his beloved Minerva. "Miss that woman so, every minute of every day she been gone. Mary El, why she never come talk to me like that?"

My heart ached, for him and me both. "Since I came back to Richmond, she hasn't said anything to me, either. I don't know why not, but then Mama never did feel the need to explain herself."

He hugged me to him with one arm, reaching his other hand to lay hold of the iron cross. "Minerva, we got each other again, but we sure still miss you."

We stayed there a good long while, until Papa dropped his arm from my shoulder and gathered my hand in his. We walked back down Second Street and across the city, feeling how Mama had pulled us close together again, without even saying a word herself.

The easy rhythm we settled into clapped to a halt when we came up Franklin and Papa marked smoke rising from Mahon's lot. "One of them damn prentices, got the smithy fire up on a Sunday. Man can't get a moment to his self, got to watch them like they children." He picked up his labored gait, and I hurried along with him.

As we drew near, we saw that the smoke that caught his worry wasn't coming from the smithy but from farther back on the lot. My heart was thick in my throat as we rounded the big building and saw the plume rising out of Papa's shed.

"Papa, I'm so sorry. There must have been some accident. I'll explain to Marse Mahon it was all my fault, I only meant to fix things up for you." I silently cussed Wilson Bowser for being so tomfool careless as to set the shed on fire.

Except, I realized, the shed wasn't on fire. Though a steady wisp of smoke was trailing into the sky, no flames licked at the building. Papa must have perceived it, too, because he slowed his pace. If he noticed the shed had been whitewashed, the holes between the boards plastered over, he didn't mention it. But once we got inside, neither of us could overlook the changes we saw.

Mr. Bowser and whoever he'd brought along to help him had cut through the far wall, nearly doubling the length of the narrow structure. They'd dug a fire pit, lined it with loose stones, and even lit a small blaze. The new back wall sloped toward a hole they put in the roof, creating an old-fashioned smoke bay to draw smoke from the shed.

Papa took it in with wonderment. "You got all this done, Mary El?"

I nodded. "I know this place will never be home like your cabin was, but you don't mind me getting it fixed up, do you?"

"Why should I mind?"

I didn't dare mention that he seemed to mind just about anything anyone said or did these days. He was happy now, warming himself over the fire. No need to stifle that.

"How'd you do all this up so quick?"

"I asked the help of a free colored man I know."

He turned from surveying the room to surveying me. "You only back here a few weeks, already keeping company? Minerva's daughter for sure." The old sparkle was back in his eyes.

Glad as I was to see it, still I couldn't let him believe what wasn't true. "We're not keeping company. Mr. Bowser is just an acquaintance I asked for a favor."

Papa chuckled. "I may be old, but that don't make me simple-minded. Man goes about doing such favors for a young lady, ain't just the kindness of his heart. I know you like to carry on how you all grown now, but 'fess up. Don't a father have a right to know when his daughter's keeping company with some man?"

Before I could answer, Wilson Bowser's deep voice rang from the doorway behind me. "Mary's a contrary gal, sir, likes to deny just about anything you accuse her of. But she's telling the truth now, I give you my word. We're not keeping company."

I felt like something sharp struck me in the chest, hearing how he sounded. As though it was his dearest wish to refute the charge. The jab was so intense I almost didn't make out what he said next. "I wouldn't dream of keeping company with Mary, until I had your permission, sir."

By then, Wilson Bowser was standing next to me, reaching to take my hand in his. Papa looked from one of us to the other. I was so flustered I couldn't meet his gaze, certainly not Wilson's neither.

"Why, you got her so she's speechless." Papa gave Wilson a happy nod. "Mary El met her match in you, I suppose. I got no opposition to that, and wish you best of luck. I expect you gonna need it."

Fourteen

And so Wilson and I set to courting, with him calling me Contrary Mary all the while.

I wasn't about to object to that, knowing he'd only tell me that was just such contrariness as he was referring to in the first place. I didn't much mind it anyway. Hearing him call to me, that Virginia timbre to his voice, rich as the sound of a grand concert piano and just as moving to my ears. It was something I missed all those years in Philadelphia, the call of a Southern voice.

Keeping company with Wilson touched something deep inside of me I'd forgotten existed. The thing that makes you giddy when you first wake up, hoping maybe you'll see him sometime that day. That gets you humming to yourself while you're mending a hem or walking to market, without you even knowing there's a melody in your head. The thing that seeps so sweet and warm it makes you feel like every day is the first day of spring.

Wilson wooed Papa right along with me. He'd bring a cabinet or chair by the shed and convince Papa he'd be doing Wilson a favor to keep it. The two of them would fish Shockoe Creek all Sunday afternoon and laugh about how they didn't trust me to cook up their catch. And when I fetched round some crushed prickly oak bark for Papa's rheumatism, it was Wilson who convinced him to drink the decoction. He couldn't buy my papa, nor build a whole wing of a magnificent mansion to keep him in high style. But he had respect instead of riches, and when he paid it to Papa as well as to me, I couldn't help but care for him.

So I smiled to myself when Wilson called me Contrary Mary while he fixed Sunday dinner in the three-room suite above his shop for me and Papa both. When he closed the shop an hour early on a weekday, just so he could stroll with me up to Church Hill before curfew caught us on the street. When he waltzed me around his little parlor, my spine atingle at his touch and me happier than I ever was at any grand colored ball in Philadelphia. When he read to me from one of the books he kept in the case tucked beneath his parlor window, his meager library positioned so no white Richmonder might catch sight of it. Or when I recited things to him I'd read in Philadelphia years before, abolitionist literature a negro in Virginia couldn't possibly lay hands on for himself.

"It's a gift, that memory of yours," he'd say, in awe at all I could recall.

Maybe, I thought.

Gifts come scot-free. But Mama's talk of Jesus's plan always made me feel special and indebted all at once. And now my talent for remembering meant I had more to do than just admire my new beau. By the middle of February, white men from all over Virginia were pouring out of Richmond's train depot, filling Powhatan House and the Exchange Hotel and such establishments all around Shockoe Hill. They were delegates to the convention that was to decide whether Virginia would secede.

Bet fumed when the convention was called, saying Virginia had no legal sovereignty to break from the Union. She made a grand show of refusing to attend the convention sessions, even though white ladies from all over Church Hill were crossing Shockoe Creek to fill the gallery at Mechanics Hall. But she was curious enough to convince her mother to go, so I could be sent along to attend her. I was to absorb every word the delegates said, then repeat it all to Bet each night.

There were plenty of words, too. Such blustery pontification those first weeks, it didn't seem they'd ever get around to settling the question. It drove Bet to fidgets, though I could tell the delegates were just waiting to see what Mr. Lincoln would do about the self-proclaimed Confederate States, whose Jefferson Davis had taken his own oath of office down in their capital of Montgomery.

The more I read the news-sheets and listened to the convention delegates, the surer I became that although Lincoln might not be Seward, still he was all the man we needed. Why else had all those other states already seceded, if he wasn't a threat to slavery, that thing they held most dear? And secession was the very thing that might provoke Lincoln to shake loose the stranglehold of slavery.

At last, on the fourth April, the Virginia convention called a vote. The Richmonders who crowded into Mechanics Hall that morning had sat through six long weeks of speeches by hot-headed politicos jangling to break from the Union. Though my hatred of slavery was as deep as their attachment to it, I suppose I was as crushed as any of them when the delegates' ballots got counted out two to one against seceding. Virginia had set her white knights and rooks and bishops on the chessboard, yet still they were looking to Mr. Lincoln, the Black Republican they called him, to make the first move.

But I had no patience for waiting. So I searched out my own gambit to play.

That very evening, I repaired early to my garret room, placed a long, slim taper in the brass candlestick, and put a fresh nib on my pen. The hour was late, the candle burned low, and the nib worn dull by the time I'd worked through my many drafts, satisfied at last with what I had.

The question of peace is not before us. Civil war must now come. Sectional war declared by Mr. Lincoln awaits only the signal gun from the insulted Southern Confederacy to light its horrid fires all along the borders of Virginia. No action of our Convention can maintain the peace. Virginia must fight. She may march to the contest with her sister States of the South or she must march to the conflict against them. There is left no middle course. War must settle the question. We must be invaded by Davis or by Lincoln. Virginia must go to war—and she must decide with whom she wars—whether with those who have suffered her wrongs or with those who have inflicted her injuries. Let every reader demand of his delegate in the Convention that Virginia join with her sister States of the South so that we may decide the question of Our Rights once and for all.

I copied those lines over in the most mannish hand I could muster and signed them *Virginius Veritas.* Rousing myself early the next morning, I crossed the city to Twelfth and Main, to slip my factious prose beneath the door of the *Enquirer,* Richmond's tin-derbox of Secessionist sentiment. Jennings Wise, the paper's editor, was ever eager for more inflammatory to set before his readers, and I was gratified to give it to him.

After all that watching and listening and wonder-ing, I was glad to finally be doing, and mighty hopeful that my words could incite Wise's abolitionist-hating, slavery-loving readers to just such a Secessionist fervor as I wanted the city to show. Eager to tell about what I'd done and figuring there was but one soul in all of Richmond in whom I could confide, I made my way to Wilson's shop.

But I caught myself quick as soon as I got there. Though businesses up and down Broad were already open, the shutters on the barber shop were shut tight.

A sign in Wilson's hand was tacked to the door, dated the day before. CLOSED TODAY AND TOMORROW. WILL OPEN SATURDAY FIRST THING.

I went through the side gate and knocked at the door to his residence, pounding harder and harder still. Just as I gave up, I heard white men's voices coming from the street in front of the shop.

"Now what will the Missus say when I arrive home for one of her infernal luncheons with these whiskers untrimmed? These free negroes are too damn free about the hours they keep."

"I'd heard the barber got himself a gal in town, thought that would keep him from going off to see his other ladyfriends." The men chortled. "But I suppose he's got a hankering for variety same as any man."

For all his calling me Contrary, I'd believed Wilson cared for me in a way that would've kept him from even looking sidewise at another woman. Yet here I was, listening to a gaggle of white men snickering over the gal who didn't have sense enough to notice she was being two-timed, or three- or four-timed, by a colored barber with a caustic tongue and copper skin.

Lovely copper skin, I thought, remembering how it shone in the sun and glowed in candlelight. I didn't know if I was more mad or sad, keeping my head low and my route to the alleys as I made my way back up

Church Hill. But I forced myself to put on as brave a face as I could once I got to the Van Lews'. I wasn't about to let on to Bet about Wilson, any more than I'd confide to her about what I'd left for Jennings Wise.

Bet hadn't much taken to the notion of me courting. I hadn't felt any need to ask her leave on the matter. It didn't even occur to me. She wasn't my owner, wasn't my people, wasn't even a friend to gossip and giggle with like Hattie was. But she made her disapproval clear all the same. She pursed her lips each Sunday morning when I left for Wilson's shop, and poked her nose between the drawing room curtains to watch as he walked me back up Church Hill at the end of the day. She'd steal up on me about the house and say I'd been right to keep up appearances around Terry and Nell, since we couldn't trust just anyone, even anyone colored, about what we might have to do if all this dreadful secession talk came to anything. Now it seemed she was right enough, at least about the trusting part, if not about how dreadful secession might be.

The next day, tongues wagged all around town about the *Enquirer*'s latest call to secede. Knowing my false words were published and passed about like that made me all the more sorry I couldn't set my true thoughts down in a letter to Hattie. A supposed slave might risk the occasional posting to a free black in the North, but risk it would be—even if the missive said no more than *Howdy do?* and *All are well here.* Before I left Philadelphia, Hattie and I agreed that such correspondence would court too much danger. It had seemed sensible enough at the time. But now, between Abraham Lincoln raising one set of hopes and Wilson Bowser dashing another, having no way to communicate with my friend was awfully difficult to abide. While Bet grew madder that secession seemed closer, I grew sadder that Hattie was so far.

Though it was warm on the afternoon of the twelfth April, I marked the menacing gray sky as I helped Mistress Van Lew down the front steps and into Mrs. Catlin's coach, and then took my place on the box beside the driver. As we descended the Hill, heading to the afternoon convention session at Mechanics Hall, fat drops of rain began to fall. I kept my face tipped down, wishing I had a proper bonnet rather than just a slave's kerchief to cover my head. Feeling the rainwater soak through the back of my collar, I reminded myself how Mama used to say the smell of spring rain was a promise of flowers soon to bloom. I closed my eyes and breathed deep, trying to smell something besides the heavy odor of the carriage horses.

That's why I heard the commotion before I saw it. When I opened my eyes, a crowd was already forming into agitated groups right in the street, so thick that Mrs. Catlin's driver had to stop the carriage nearly a full block from the hall.

The ladies exchanged worried glances before extending their gloved hands one by one for the driver to hand them down. One of the matrons recognized her nephew in the throng and pushed toward him. I held Mistress Van Lew's umbrella over her head, as the rest of us followed. "They've locked everyone out of the hall without a word of explanation," the young man told his aunt.

While the ladies frowned at this news, I listened hard to the snatches of rumor circulating around us. Lincoln had persuaded the Confederates to come back to the Union. Lincoln had recognized the Confederacy as a sovereign nation. Lincoln had been killed. Though everyone was ready to hazard a tale, no one knew which to believe.

In all the jolt and jostling of the crowd, Mistress Van Lew's breathing grew strained. I led her across to Capitol Square, hoping to find a place on the green where she might rest while I sought the truth among all the tittle-tattle. As I maneuvered her around the Bell Tower, a small man, his bowler tipped down over his face, rushed right into us.

It was illegal for a negro, free or slave, to set foot in the square, thanks to one of the laws passed after John Brown's raid. But before I could think what to do, the man lifted his hat, and I saw it was McNiven.

I kept even the slightest flicker of recognition from my face. Even so, the shock of finding him in Richmond paled compared to the shock of what he had to say.

"Apologies for such clumsiness." He took care to hold his eyes on Mistress Van Lew as he spoke. "I am rushing to get word to a friend o' mine. The Confederates hae fired on Fort Sumter. They are giving Mr. Lincoln his war, whether he is wanting it or no."

The news sent Mistress Van Lew into a faint. I was fast enough to get behind her, and McNiven's quick tug kept her upright. I held her propped against the base of the Bell Tower while he fetched a cab.

Once she was installed inside the hack, he took off his overcoat and hung it over my wet shoulders. "I'll take her up to Bet, lass. Go tell Bowser all what's passed."

I watched the cab roll off through the rain, knowing I had no mind to pass any news to that philandering Wilson Bowser. So I turned in the opposite direction from the barber shop and headed down to the smithy. It would be hours yet before Papa was done with his day's labor, but I figured I could wait until then. Only, before I even cleared the block for Mahon's, I saw I wasn't going to be waiting alone.

"What are you doing here?" The words were out before I even knew I was uttering them.

"Hoping to see you. Same as I've been doing every afternoon this week, ever since you didn't come by my place on Sunday. Don't you have so much as a hello for your Wilson?"

"Not my Wilson." I hated him for assuming I could still be duped. "Leastwise, not mine alone."

He shifted his cap back on his head. "What's gotten into you?"

"The truth's gotten into me, thanks to some of your customers. Bad enough to be treated so by you, but to be laughed at by white men. The soft-headed gal who doesn't know her Lothario's got a string of sweethearts."

He let out a low whistle. "Who told you what about me, exactly?"

I kept my arms crossed tight in front of me. "You expect me to tell you what I heard, then let you prevaricate some lie to explain it away?"

"I never lied to you, and I never will." His voice was a soft drawl compared to how hard mine was. "I swear it, Mary. Never."

"Never lied, but didn't exactly tell me the truth. The truth about how many lady friends you're courting."

"If I never told you you're the only one for me, I'm a fool for keeping quiet, since I've known it ever since I first laid eyes on you. You're the only one I've got and the only one I want."

"Only one in Richmond, maybe. But someone called you away Thursday last, and you went running. Left your customers standing in the street guffawing about your romantic conquests."

"Don't you know me better than that? What's the first thing you knew about me?"

The remembrance of chill January air streaming sunlit through a stand of leafless trees wasn't going to cool my April anger. "You didn't want to bring me to Richmond. Thought you had a right to tell me what to do."

"I did bring you here, remember? But think back before that. What'd you know about me when you were up in Philadelphia?"

I remembered taking that cataleptic girl over toward New York with McNiven, him telling me it was David Bustill Bowser's cousin who brought her out of Richmond. "Working for the Railroad doesn't give you the right to two-time me."

"I never said it did. What took me away yesterday was another woman, sure enough. Her and her husband.

He's already up in Canada, sent word of where he is so she could get to him." Wilson took a single step toward me, holding his hand out, palm up, in peace offering. "I let out it's lady friends keep me heading all over the Virginia countryside, because it's the best cover I can get to do Railroad work."

I worked the strand of his words over, slowly hooking myself a lace of renascent trust, before slipping my hand into his. "Why didn't you tell me?"

"The need to take this woman came on so fast, I hadn't the chance. Figured you wouldn't even miss me. But you did miss me, huh?"

"Why do you stay?" I'd wondered it often enough but never dared to ask, never wanted to set him thinking about leaving Virginia. "You've sent so many North, and you're free to go yourself any time you want."

"Free to stay as well as go. Come, let me show you." He kept tight to my hand as we walked all the way back to his house, rain falling in soft drops on the two of us. He led me up to a pair of hand-drawn portraits that hung in his parlor.

"My family's been free so many generations nobody's sure we ever were slaves, and they haven't hounded us out of Virginia yet." He pointed to the sketch of an elderly black man. "James Bowser, my grandfather, fought for Virginia in the Revolutionary War. He made his appeal for a bounty land-grant with the rest of the veterans in 1833, same year I was born. A year after they made him give up preaching because of a new law passed in response to Nat Turner's rebellion, meant to intimidate free negroes and slaves alike. Older sons, like David's father, they'd get restless and leave. But my grandfather insisted the youngest in each generation stay. He taught me, and my father before me, that he'd earned our right to be here, just as much as any white man."

He turned to the other portrait, of an Indian lady. "Of course, my mother's mother would have had a fit to hear such things. No person owns the land, that's how her people saw it. Through her, I've got a legacy here longer and stronger than any white Virginian." He gave off looking at his grandparents' pictures, took up looking steady and warm at me instead. "And now I found a woman tenacious enough to talk me into bringing her here, and wonderful enough to make me fall in love with her. To my mind that's the best reason yet to stay."

I smiled as he took me into the kitchen, where he set to chopping onions and carrots and turnips, claiming I was so soaked through he best cook me a stew. I waited until he turned his back to me to put the vegetables in the pot before asking, "So you never saw fit to court anyone until I came along?"

"I wasn't about to take up with a slavewoman."

"Like my papa did? You too good for that?"

He faced me in surprise. "I respect Lewis, you know that. But I can't imagine how it must have been for him, seeing you and your mama owned by a white family. I couldn't troth to a woman whose children would be bound in slavery. I'd risk my neck to send any such woman North, but I wouldn't partner with her here, knowing how things could end up for her and for our babies. Your folks made a life like that, it's a tribute to them, but it wasn't something I could take on for myself."

"What about free colored ladies?" I asked as he unwrapped a hunk of salt pork from his cupboard and set it in to stew. "They have a few of those here, too."

"I said I'd risk my own neck to send a slave North. But it's a different thing entirely to risk a wife's neck, a child's neck, because husband and father is working the Railroad. It always seemed best to keep to myself." He smiled and pulled me to him, slipping his arms around my waist and running a line of kisses down from my earlobe to my collarbone. "At least it did, until I found a lady contrary enough to give me reason to think otherwise."

It was an explosion. Then a chorus of explosions, echoing, repeating, seemingly a hundredfold. Wilson's body, warm and soft and welcoming as it curved around my own, grew taut and tense in an instant.

"What the hell is happening?" His words brought me fully awake.

It was strange and wonderful to sleep beside Wilson, to have my head and heart so filled with the nearness of him. I'd convinced myself over the week past that he was vain and vile, but the things he told me in those last precious hours reminded me he was valorous—and also vulnerable, a man who'd taught himself to live in the service of countless strangers he helped bring to freedom. I wanted nothing more than to be with him, and I savored every word in all the hours we talked, curfew long forgotten. When finally, near dawn, drowsiness overtook me, Wilson carried me from his parlor like I was his dearest treasure, and lay down fully clothed beside me atop the coverlet of his bed. I cherished the way we clung to each other in slumber, closer than I'd ever felt to anyone, all my life.

But strange and wonderful as it was to sleep so, it was strange and awful to hear the thundering report that roused him, drew him awake and away so fast, as he scrambled startled to his feet.

Listening to the bursts and bangs, I thought at first it must be some great fire taking out every window in the city. But then above the shouting in the street, I made out a brass band, playing the same tune over and over.

I sat bolt upright when I recognized the melody. "Dixie"—the coon show song they sang at the rail station when John Brown's body arrived in Philadelphia.

"Sumter," I said.

Wilson, already halfway to the window, turned and looked at me in confusion.

I'd forgotten the news from McNiven, that Sumter was under fire. Now the yelling and singing outside told me the Federal fort must have fallen to South Carolina. And from the celebration in Richmond's streets, the cannonade salute ringing from her armory, I could tell Virginia's mind was made up. She would secede.

Though the sixteenth April was a Tuesday, Papa was wearing his Sunday suit when he arrived at the Van Lews' lot. The green vest was long faded, the trousers patched, and the frock coat frayed. But he looked as proud as he had every Sunday of my childhood.

I was waiting for him in the yard, marking how the bright blue sky matched the color of my new tarlatan dress. Though it was a cheaper fabric and a less fashionable cut than any I wore in Philadelphia, I beamed with joy when Papa told me I was the most beautiful sight he'd ever seen.

"You ready?" he asked.

"I feel like this is something I've been ready for, been waiting for, my whole life."

"Was like that for me, the day I married Minerva." The memory made him happy and sad, both at once.

"You think she would approve?" I asked, slipping my arm through his as we walked out to Twenty-fourth Street, then across Grace Street to St. John's Church. It was the day every bereaved daughter most misses her mama.

"Of the lady you become, yes. Of the man lucky enough to wed you, no doubt. Of the place you gonna do it, I'm not so sure."

His joke took me back to the only other time I ever set foot inside St. John's, fifteen years earlier. Bet had somehow gotten it into her head that I should be baptized at the Episcopal church, a rare occasion indeed for a Richmond negro. The suggestion terrified me. I saw the white wooden building whenever I looked out from the Van Lew property, and the two windows and the transept door between them always seemed like the gaping eyes and mouth of some ghostly apparition hovering over the church graveyard.

Mama was furious with Bet, sure I didn't need some baptism in a white church when my soul and I were doing just fine in the surreptitious prayer meeting our family attended every week. "Baptize my child in a church that won't welcome her to regular worship? No thank you."

This she said not to Bet but to Papa, who surprised Mama and me both by answering, "That woman respectful enough to ask your leave 'bout the baptism when she might order it. Why not oblige her?"

Making mud pies in front of Papa's cabin that warm Sunday afternoon, I shuddered to hear him suggest Mama let the goblin building swallow me up. "You usually too wise to let a chance for Mary El's advantage pass," he added.

"What advantage is there in our child being paraded around a white lady's church, when Henry Banks already gave her all the baptism she needs?"

"Yes, she's already baptized, among our folks and in our faith. Whatever happens ain't gonna undo that. So if Miss Bet want this, why not use it to get something from her?"

Mama's mouth curled down, the way it always did when she started scheming. "I do what I can to teach the child to read, but educated folks need to tally numbers, too. If she'll give Mary El lessons in figures, we'll go to St. John's."

So the next time Bet raised the subject, Mama went into action, saying how kind she was to offer but how shameful it would be to bring an ignorant slave child into St. John's, when the white children there were all so smart, even knowing their figures. Bet took the hint, musing that though it was illegal for her to teach me to read, there wasn't any particular law against her teaching me arithmetic in the afternoons while Mistress Van Lew was napping. Bet was as glad to defy her mother's prohibition as she was to have me baptized in her church. Though Mama wasn't delighted about that last part, she was satisfied enough with the arrangement to bring me to St. John's the following Sunday.

Now I was heading to St. John's again, but with Mama gone and Bet the one bristling at the idea. When I stayed that one night with Wilson, Bet lectured me all the next day about how I'd worried her. As though she were more vexed over my keeping company with him than over the attack on Sumter.

Which was no small part of why Wilson and I were marrying so soon, not wanting to be separated by Shockoe Creek and Bet's brazen meddling. We chose St. John's purposefully, knowing that if our names appeared in its official marriage register, Wilson and I would be regarded as family in the eyes of white Richmond, and thus exempt from the law against slaves lodging with free negroes.

As Papa and I entered the churchyard, I caught sight of my betrothed standing proud beneath the white clapboard of the spire, formal and dignified in his deep brown suit.

"Morning," Papa said.

Wilson's response was a distracted, "mmm hmmm," as he gazed at me.

I unhooked my arm from Papa's and reached out to my intended. Wilson leaned forward to kiss me, but I turned my head, shy in front of Papa. I felt Wilson's lips in my hair, sensed him breathing in the scent of the lavender I'd bathed in that morning.

"You're like spring itself, after a winter of my loneliness," he whispered. "I just hope you won't be feeling too contrary when Reverend Cummins asks if you take me for your husband."

I remembered how I'd taken a dislike to Wilson the very first hour we met, his cocksure manner turning me awkward and inept. Nothing like how special Theodore Handsome Hinton made me feel when he contrived and connived to meet me. Theodore doted on me right from the start. But he hadn't been so much interested in who I was as who he wanted me to be. Seeing how attentively Wilson's eyes met mine, knowing he always listened with care to what I said, even when he didn't agree, I shook my head at his teasing.

We were both sure of how I'd answer the reverend's question.

But as we stepped inside the church door, I felt my joy flicker. The interior of St. John's was dim and dismal, the dark wood absorbing what little light stole through the windows. Besides the minister, the only figure in the cavernous room was Bet. Seeing how rigid she sat within the high walls of her family's pew-box, her back to us, I missed Hattie so. I longed to share such a day with her and her sisters, and with Zinnie Moore and the ladies from our sewing circle. But it was more than geography that separated me from all of them. Even in the solemn quiet of the sanctuary, occasional shouts and shots could be heard from outside, marking the city's restless wait for the next day's vote of secession.

As Papa walked me and Wilson up the aisle, I moved through a commixture of happiness and fear that few brides ever know. I couldn't imagine what a marriage set against the background of war might be like. But I couldn't imagine not marrying Wilson, either. And, with all respect to Mama, there was another reason this church seemed the right place for us to wed.

Richmonders learn young that St. John's was the scene of Patrick Henry's famous speech urging his fellow colonists to war. I knew Mr. Henry was like the rest of the FFVs, not much caring for colored people's freedom. But when we took our places before the altar, his famous words seemed to echo through the church, as though they were meant for me that very April morning. *Gentlemen may cry, Peace, Peace. But there is no peace. The war is actually begun! The next gale that sweeps from the north will bring to our ears the clash of resounding arms. Is life so dear, or peace so sweet, as to be purchased at the price of chains and slavery? Forbid it, Almighty God! I know not what course others may take, but as for me, give me liberty or give me death!*

As the minister asked us to troth our love until death did us part, I thought of what Wilson said about risking his own neck to do the Railroad work, but not risking a wife's as well. It was risk to me and Wilson both I'd be courting, if I were caught doing anything seditious to Southern interests.

But the liberty at stake wasn't simply mine and Wilson's. It was the liberty of Papa, who hovered behind us, finding his long-lost hope in the shadow of our joy. It was the liberty of all enslaved negroes, whose chains and slavery were all too real, not just a rhetorical turn of phrase like Patrick Henry's. Neither love nor liberty could be so sweet without the other. Wilson and I meant to enjoy both. And we meant to see Papa and all the other slaves freedom bound at last.

As my husband and I crossed the city after the ceremony, we passed many a building already flying the Palmetto flag. It turned both of us somber, and we walked in silence along Broad Street.

Virginia and her massive ironworks were an irresistible jewel for the Confederate crown. Rumor had it that just as soon as the convention delegates cast their votes to secede, the Confederates would move their capital to Richmond. And so as Wilson held my hand in his, I made my second vow of the day, silently swearing to be ready for whatever happened.

Fifteen

That spring, Richmond bloomed in a riot of color. Military companies from all over the South poured into the new capital, each donning its own gaudy hues. Reds and purples and yellows were festooned with every sort of cockade and ribbon, as though the Confederates' strategy were to blind the Federals. The State Fairground on the far end of Broad was given over to the troops, renamed "Camp Lee" in honor of the Virginian who'd turned down Mr. Lincoln's offer to head the Union army. Drumbeats sounded through the city, a driving rhythm for the buzz of marketplace gossip as people pushed themselves along the jammed streets, eager for what they said would be a glorious sixty-day war.

Up on Church Hill, Bet paced and wrung her hands while Mistress Van Lew stared dull-eyed out the window at the neighborhood matrons passing by on their way to endless rounds of sewing parties. The Union Guard was now the Virginia Guard, and nothing would do but to outfit them all over again in flamboyant new uniforms. Though the maiden daughters of Church Hill made a show of sewing, too, mostly they flirted and waved their handkerchiefs at passing soldiers, welcoming the war as an opportunity to court more beaux than their elder sisters ever had.

In Shockoe Bottom, factories and foundries prepared for the grim reality of battle. The clang of metal from Mahon's smithy rang stronger and longer each day, and I watched exhaustion eat away at what happiness Papa had found during my courtship with Wilson.

As the days stretched hot into summer, Papa grew so sullen, I tried to guard him from all I was thinking. "What you done to Mary El?" he asked, eyeing us across a platter of cold chicken at Sunday dinner on the twenty-first July. "She never this quiet."

Wilson frowned as he reached for the lemonade, pretending Papa's question made no sense. "Day as warm as this, flies can't even be bothered to buzz."

"Don't much care about the flies. Mary El ain't bothered to talk to her papa, is my concern. Just set there with her face all pinched up in worry, staring at the parlor window."

"Whole city's quiet today," I said, lifting my fork toward my plate.

Papa wasn't about to be put off. "Don't start pushing them taters round again. You been at that for near a quarter hour, ain't so much as took a bite. What's the matter?"

I laid out the truth in such a way as I hoped would keep him from catching my worry. "Reason it's so quiet is the soldiers are all gone from the city. They're fighting a full-on battle, Secesh against the Federals, way up near the Maryland border. If the Federals win, they may be able to take Richmond. But if they lose, the Secesh say they'll march right from Manassas on to Washington."

"Manassas, molasses, what it matter?" Papa replied. "Don't see how that's gonna change the fact that it's Sabbath day, a daughter ought to have two civil words to say to her own papa."

"Lewis does have a point," Wilson said. Meaning, Sunday was Papa's only time away from the smithy, from the labor that bent him and bent him until I thought for sure he would break. The day for Wilson and me to dote on him, give him a decent meal and love enough to last through the week. "You bought that big basket of strawberries for dessert," my husband reminded me. "And I have a mind to get my share, so hurry up and eat that dinner."

Worried as I was that the Confederates might get their sixty-day victory after all, I did what I might to oblige my menfolk, nibbling and conversing, even wresting out a smile at Papa's amazement when Wilson set down our biggest wooden bowl brimming with fruit, alongside a tin cup full of cream. The price of strawberries was the lowest anyone in Richmond could remember, farmers from the nearby country-side crowding the markets with rich, ripe fruit that couldn't pass any farther on account of the Federal blockade.

I chattered with Papa as best I could while we savored the sweet tang of the berries. My fingernails were still stained red with their juice the next morn-ing. But all my delicate fruit and cream hopes soured when word reached Richmond from Manassas that the Confederates had won.

"What do you want with going out there?" Wilson asked as I wrapped a scarf around my head late the next night. "It's raining to beat the Flood, hours past curfew, and the streets crowded with Secesh."

I searched through our clothes-chest for my merino shawl. Though the thick night air was plenty warm, I needed something to guard against the downpour. Just as surely as I needed to make sense of the Confederate victory. "Whatever they're unloading from those rail cars, it's more true war than all the marching and carrying on we've seen in Richmond these months past. I want to see it for myself."

"Then I'll come with you."

I settled the shawl onto my shoulders and looked my husband in the eye. "A negro couple would catch more trouble out there at this hour of the night than a slave-woman will alone. If anyone stops me, I can say I'm with my mistress, got separated from her while looking for my master." Not waiting to hear more of his disapproval, I kissed him with all the passion of a three-month bride, then hurried down the stairs and out into the night.

The rain hit me as soon as I pushed open the door, stinging hard as pellets and soaking through my sleeve. The deluge had turned the dirt of Broad Street into an oozing brown mass. It pulled at my ankle boots as I crossed to where the dead and dying Confederate soldiers were being unloaded from the train. Knots of white Richmonders and their slave attendants struggled against the mire like flies in molasses. They surged forward and circled back, echoing the eddying mudriver in the street, as here and there a wounded man called out from a stretcher, or a lantern was held up to identify a motionless form.

Somewhere along the dark depot, a familiar voice kept repeating, "My cousin is at the Spotswood. She heard it from Mrs. Davis herself, by telegram from the president. Dreadful news, but he died a hero for Our Cause."

I heard the refrain two or three times before I placed the speaker. Mrs. Whitlock, one of the ladies who sewed with Bet's mother for the Union Guard. And who shunned her once the group became the Virginia Guard.

Mrs. Whitlock pushed through the mass of people, presenting herself to the soldier attending one of the cars. "I am here on behalf of my cousin, Mrs. Gardner. The colonel is to be laid in state at my home on Marshall Street. Please see to it."

"I don't have orders to see to nothing but the unloading of the train." The soldier's voice weighed heavy with whatever part he played in the battle.

"All I am asking is that you send the . . . the . . ." Mrs. Whitlock seemed unable to finish. "Colonel Gardner is to be laid in state at my home on Church Hill. Is that clear?"

The soldier turned to answer a call from inside the car, leaving Mrs. Whitlock to shove her way up and down the length of the platform, peeving out the same demand to anyone assigned to the train detail and

380 · LOIS LEVEEN

waxing more indignant with each refusal. She went on about her poor cousin and the telegram, and clearly these soldiers were no Virginians, and wouldn't she see to it they were reprimanded for such impertinence. She moved oblivious to the cries of the injured, and the howls of grief from those who found their menfolk already dead.

As I turned to take myself home, I caught sight of Palmer Randolph. Only a few years my senior, Palmer tramped about Church Hill tagging after Bet's brother John when we were children. Now he wore the uniform of the Virginia Guard, and he stared at me, a glimmer of confused recognition flashing across his face. As I backed out of the circle of light cast by his lantern, Mrs. Whitlock bore through the sodden crowd to him.

"Palmer, is my husband about? I am sure he will attend to the arrangements at once."

His face paled. "I guess you haven't heard the news, ma'am."

"Yes, yes, of course I've heard. My cousin received the news by telegram at the Spotswood. She is proud of his sacrifice, but dreadfully distressed. She asked me to see to the arrangements. But no one will assist me."

Palmer laid a hand on her arm. "Mrs. Whitlock, I'm sorry. Sorry for your loss."

"Thank you," she said. "Colonel Gardner, though only my relation by marriage, was a man for whom I had a great affection."

"I didn't mean the colonel, ma'am. I meant"—he paused, coughing a bit—"I meant Mr. Whitlock. Major Whitlock. He took only a flesh wound at first, led us back into the fighting almost immediately. But they hit him again, right in the face. We carried him from the field quick as we could, but it was too late. I'm sorry."

Mrs. Whitlock stared at him. "You must be mistaken. I have received no telegram."

"I don't know anything about a telegram. I only know your husband served, and was brave, and was lost. My condolences."

"But I have received no telegram."

"Mrs. Whitlock, I'm sorry."

She kept repeating her refrain about no telegram, he kept apologizing. For all the pathos in the little scene, no one else in the crowd noticed them. And they were equally unmindful of the gangrenous smell of rotting flesh and the shrieks of misery all around them.

"Out the way there, gal, coming through." The man addressing me was one of a pair of negroes who were maneuvering a stretcher off the cars. "Marse Randolph," the other called out, "where'll we put it?"

Palmer shook his head, his mouth shut fast. Mrs. Whitlock turned to see the cause. Slowly, as though everything around her were stopped in time and she was wading alone through the heavy mud molasses, she moved to the stretcher. When she drew back the winding sheet, her scream ran up my spine like a razor, swift and sharp and sure.

There, frozen in death, was what was left of Henry Whitlock. Half his face blown away, bone and muscle left exposed. An empty eye socket gazed up at his wife.

War had come to Richmond at last. And victory though they called it, Manassas took its toll.

The horror of what I saw on the train platform replayed itself in one nightmare after another until Wilson woke me just past daybreak, pulling me close and murmuring words of comfort. But as my lips found his, a pounding sounded through our house. Someone banging on the door with force enough they might have meant to shake the building down. And just as insistently calling out, "Mary, are you there? It's urgent."

"That damn Bet can't have nerve enough to call my wife from our bed, without so much as a good-morning and by-your-leave," Wilson said.

"You think that, you don't know Bet." Sure she'd keep shouting until I let her in, I extricated myself from the bedclothes, pulled on my summer shift, and hurried down to unlatch the door.

"They have them in one of the tobacco factories." Her torrent of words hit me like the downpour of the night before. "I heard they've not been fed nor tended, not even the injured."

"Come upstairs, where we can talk." I pulled her inside, hoping to snatch a minute to make sense of what she was saying.

She climbed the stairs right on my heels. "I've filled the gig with provisions. We must go to them at once."

"Them who?" My hastily dressed husband stood in the parlor, arms folded across his shirt front, scowling.

"The Federal prisoners. The so-called Secessionists brought them in by the trainload all night, hounding them into a factory with no food or water."

Wilson's scowl deepened. "Usually it's only slaves they shut up in those factories, working all day without food or water."

I shot him a look. "Miss Bet has no part in that," I said. "Now, Miss Bet, you set down just for a minute while I get my hair covered, then we can go."

I gave her a gentle push toward the sofa and brushed past Wilson into the bedroom. He followed, standing close so Bet couldn't hear. "So you jump up whenever she orders you to, never mind you're already scared half to death by what you insisted on seeing last night?"

I tied an apron over my skirt, to make it look like I was a house servant called away from her chores, and peered into our looking glass to plait my hair. "She didn't order anything, she just asked for my help. At least, that's about as close as she gets to asking."

Truth was, I didn't need ordering, nor much asking, from Bet or anyone. I felt something catch inside me when I thought of Mr. Lincoln's soldiers. Not kinship exactly, but some sort of camaraderie. If I could figure something to do for the captured Federals, I was ready enough to try it.

But Wilson wasn't yet going to understand all that as he gazed at our empty bed. "There are times I wish you'd be a little less contrary, for your husband's sake."

Pinning my kerchief over my plaits, I gave him a smile. "Husband, I love you, and you know it. But I better see if I can be any use to those prisoners, at least." Though he didn't object, I marked how neither he nor Bet would look the other in the eye as I bid him farewell and followed her out.

Bet raced her gig to where factories lined Main Street, two blocks from the York River Rail Line and the Canal Street locks. The name LIGGON'S TOBACCO was painted in large black letters against a white field on the three-story brick building where she stopped. A young soldier lounged before the door, observing with lazy curiosity as Bet tied the horse to a post and I unloaded our baskets of provisions.

"What you got there, ma'am?"

"Charity for the prisoners. If you will be so good as to let me pass." Bet issued it as a command rather than a request.

He ducked his head, perplexed. "Nobody said anything about visits to the prisoners."

Bet tipped her chin, looking at him across her long nose, eager to play the scold. "Young man, hasn't your mother raised you as a Christian?"

Whatever enemy that boyish fellow expected to encounter when he enlisted, it sure wasn't Bet Van Lew. " 'Course she has, ma'am."

"Doesn't Christ teach us to love our enemies?"

"But these are Yankees we've got here, ma'am, damnable Yankees."

Bet nodded in triumph. "All the more in need of Christian charity. Think of how proud your mother will be of your aiding such a pious act. Why, I daresay your company chaplain will commend you for your participation." She turned to me. "Come along, we mustn't dawdle when there's charity to be done."

I bowed my head, stifled my smile, and followed her past the bewildered guard.

Once inside, we found ourselves in a cavernous room, some seventy feet by forty. Massive machinery for pressing tobacco took up most of the floor, with scores of Union soldiers crowded among the menacing contraptions.

"Good morning, gentlemen," Bet said. "We have brought you food, and some lint and bandages for the wounded. A few books, as well, for you to pass the time. But now I see so many of you, I fear we haven't nearly enough to feed you all."

The unkempt men surged forward, extending their hands to beg like street urchins, until a sudden banging called them to a halt. The clattering came from the middle of the room, where a short soldier had taken off his boot and was striking its heel against the long handle of a tobacco press.

"Gentlemen, remember, we represent order in this land of rebellion." He spoke in the hard Yankee accent I knew from the New England abolitionists who visited Philadelphia on their lecture tours. "Dear lady, forgive this uncouth welcome, but we've had nothing to eat since we entered battle on Sunday."

He looked ridiculous making such a formal speech in his stocking foot, his boot held up like a saber raised to lead the charge. But Bet was entranced, all gallant Federal that he was in her mind. "It is I who ought to ask forgiveness of you, on behalf of all the loyal Unionists of my native state," she said. "What may I offer you from our meager supplies?"

He waved his boot to indicate she needn't bother. "Someone else can have my share of the provisions. But can you get a message to my family? The Rebels refuse to report our names to the Federal commanders, and I cannot bear to think that Mother would believe me dead on the battlefield."

"I will be honored to send a missive. What is your name, and where is your family?" Bet glanced my way, meaning for me to memorize whatever the man might say.

But before he could answer, the door was swung open by a stout man in a heavily decorated Virginia uniform. Announcing himself as Brigadier General John Winder, he demanded to know what we were doing in his prison.

"I am Elizabeth Van Lew, and my servant and I are on a Christian mission of charity." Bet smiled and coquetted, though the general was twenty years her senior. "Surely a man with the intellect I see in your eyes will understand that such kindness on our part will impress the world with the worthiness of the Southern cause."

General Winder ran a hand through his silvered hair. "This influx has been so sudden, your contribution could be of some use to us." He called to the guard, who skulked in red-faced. "Private, see to it that this lady has an escort whenever she enters this facility. I would not trust so charming a creature to these ruffians."

The New Englander's face seeped disappointment as he realized he'd have no chance to dictate out a message for his family. Never one to look her own failings in the eye, Bet turned away from him to distribute food on the far side of the room, with the lanky guard at her elbow all the while.

I wasn't about to give up so easily. After all, Mama raised me on a steady regimen of stealth and surreption, especially when it came to doing right by those in need, and Mr. Jones took up where Mama left off. I worked my way through the group of prisoners, dispersing the contents of my basket until only one item remained. By then I'd reached the place where the bootless Federal leaned against a tobacco press, struggling to hide his chagrin. I drew out the small book I'd kept in reserve and offered it to him.

"Marse, take this book instead of your breakfast. Only be mindful once you got it. Mistress takes such care with her books, she's sure to notice any little mark someone makes in it." I pressed the leather-bound tome into his hands with a nod. "Any mark at all," I repeated, hoping my meaning was clear.

Bet fumed so hard as we took our places in the gig, she didn't notice me worrying my sleeve over the prisoner. Nor did she mark my distraction as we made our way among the stalls at First Market, laying in another round of comestibles for our charges. When we returned to the impromptu jail, a new guard had taken over the watch, one with enough experience soldiering to demand a pass from Bet. Which meant we had to spend an hour or more chasing down General Winder, and then another quarter hour while he flirted with Bet, before we had the pass in hand.

By then I'd thought on the guard enough to realize we might do well to bring him a little something to ease the way for our visits. I persuaded Bet to stop on Church Hill for some of Terry Farr's gingerbread and a bottle of buttermilk. While she muttered resentment about feeding lawless Secessionists when the Federal heroes were being half-starved, I seized my chance to slip into her father's library for a few more books.

Once we were back inside Liggon's, my hands shook so I thought the guard or Bet or one of the prisoners was bound to comment on it. I bided my time distributing food until the guard became distracted with reprimanding a prisoner who dared to utter a "Bless you, ma'am," when Bet handed him some pudding. As Bet reproached the Confederate, I sidled up to the New Englander.

"Brought some more books for you, Marse." I handed over the volumes I'd tucked into my apron pocket. "Still need the one you already got?"

"I'll take the ones you have there, and return this." He held out the book I'd given him that morning, his eyes shining. "I always say there's a great message in books. A careful reader should find the one in there right off."

I fairly hustled Bet out of the makeshift prison, I was so anxious about what might lie inside those leather covers. I settled into the gig while she untied the reins from the hitching post, biting hard on my tongue to keep from urging her to hurry.

I sat silent as Bet careened along Main Street and then up Seventh, jabbering about the dreadful treatment of the Federals. I didn't let out a peep about the book nestled inside my apron pocket, determined to keep my plotting just as secret from her as from Brigadier General Winder himself. When she let me off just shy of Broad Street, I rushed into the side door to our house and up to the stifling heat of the parlor. Taking my seat in a straightbacked chair, I flipped open the book.

It was Mr. Ralph Emerson's *Essays*. I'd read them years before, in Philadelphia. Though I found the style somewhat ponderous, Mr. Emerson's theme of following one's moral purpose rather than succumbing to the weight of social convention was inspiring. I turned the title page now with more interest than I ever had before.

There is one mind. These opening words of the first essay were underscored with a smudge of some brownish substance that served as the prisoner's extempore ink. What did the phrase mean? My eyes tripped down the page to the second paragraph. A portion of its first sentence was marked as well. *of this mind history.* The word *mind* was crossed through, and there was a double line under the *y*. I stared in wonder at the two sentences, until I noticed that in the opening sentence *one* was struck through as well, so lightly I hadn't noted it right off.

I closed my eyes, arranging the words in my mind just as I had when Mama first taught me to read, or when I began my Latin lessons at Miss Douglass's school.

There is one mind of this mind history.

There is mind of this history.

T— i— m— o— t— h—y.

The prisoner's Christian name was Timothy! My eyes flew open, and I turned the page, anxious to test my theory. *The Sphinx must solve her own riddle. If the whole of history is in one man, it is all to be explained from individual experience.* The name leapt right off the page. *Sphinx must if the history,* Smith. Timothy Smith. From the underscoring and cross-outs on the next page, I learned that the 3rd Maine was his company, and he hailed from Augusta.

Somewhere in Augusta, Timothy Smith had a mother, and she was worrying on him. Had they heard word of Manassas there yet? Did she know the 3rd Maine had taken the field? Surely if she did, she was anxious for her boy.

But it was more than one mother's worry I could answer now. The Confederates were being deliberate in holding back the names of their prisoners. Unable to march on to Washington like they'd hoped, they knew for now Manassas was all the victory they had. The more Union soldiers who were believed dead on the battlefield, the grander that victory seemed. Maybe Timothy Smith realized that, or maybe he just wanted to assuage the fears of as many mothers and fathers, wives and children, as he could. Because on page after page of Mr. Emerson's *Essays,* he'd encoded the names and companies of the men who were held prisoner in Liggon's tobacco warehouse.

When Wilson's footsteps sounded on the stairs an hour later, I folded my copied-out list of soldiers and tucked it into my apron.

"For once, my wife looks contrite," Wilson said when he saw me sitting with my hands clasped in my lap. "I suppose she's hungry, doesn't want to start up until after I cook supper."

"I'm not much hungry for supper." I rose and kissed him hello.

He hummed with pleasure, moving his lips up to my ear to whisper, "Perhaps you'd rather get right back into bed, return to where we were when Bet barged in?"

Though I thrilled at the warmth of him, I shook my head. "We need to find McNiven."

"McNiven? I can name a thing or two I need right now, and he sure isn't one of them."

"This is important, Wilson. It's about the battle, and it can't wait."

"So much for my wife's contrition." Not one for sighs of resignation, still he loosed a deep exhalation to cool his passion. "What exactly can't wait?"

I told him about the prisoner's request and Winder's edict, how I managed to find a way to communicate with the New Englander after all. How I decoded the names of prisoners the Confederates wanted kept secret. How we needed to bring the list to the house McNiven had let over on Eighth Street and Clay, in the hopes he could somehow get the information to Washington.

"You managed all this just since morning, not even knowing you were going to the prison till Bet arrived here?" Wilson scanned the lengthy list I held out to him. "I don't suppose you could have done much better if you planned it for a month."

"Wasn't me who planned it. It was Jesus." It felt strange to say it aloud, even to Wilson. I wasn't sure I could make him understand. I wasn't quite sure I understood it myself. But he was my husband. I had to try.

So I told him about Mama insisting on Jesus's plan, explained how her insistence sustained me and mystified me both, through my whole childhood and then even more in Philadelphia, until it brought me back home to Richmond. How I never fully believed it myself, but when I opened Mr. Emerson's *Essays* and deciphered the Yankee's markings, the meaning came to me so easily it felt like maybe it really was His plan.

My husband let out a low whistle. "What can a man say when he learns his beautiful wife is an angel sent from Heaven?"

"I'm no angel, Wilson Bowser, as you of all people should know." I didn't mind conceding as much to him, pleased as I was with what I'd done. "But this all-too-human wife of yours has got yet more work that needs doing. So we best find McNiven before the sun goes down and curfew comes on."

Even as we crossed into the Richmond summer evening, a warm wind urging us along, I couldn't quite be sure what path I was setting myself—and my husband—on. But I knew it was one I couldn't put off taking, for all it might mean to the Federals, and to the slaveholding Confederates who fought them.

Sixteen

For the next week, we kept up our charity visits, Bet trumpeting over all she was doing to aid the Federals, and me careful not to let on that I was doing much more. Timothy Smith kept slipping me information—names of new prisoners, gossip overheard from the guards, ship movements on the James observed from the windows of the prison's upper stories. And I kept passing what I learned to McNiven, to be smuggled North. It might have felt like I was no more than playing a riddle-me-ree parlor game, memorizing whatever scenes of possible military interest I observed at the prison or puzzling out another of the New Englander's encoded messages—except for my recollection of the Manassas dead, the agony of the living wounded, and the Confederates' foaming determination to do yet more damage to the Union, all of which served as stern reminder of the twin import and imperilment in what I'd taken up.

Wilson, long accustomed to the Railroad work, insisted we carry on as same old, same old, as we could to avoid suspicion. Which meant that on the twenty-ninth July, I was doing our laundry, just as I did every Monday. All through our scant months of matrimony, I took a secret satisfaction from seeing the variegation of my husband's things intermingled with mine as they hung on the line behind our building. But that morning I was too harried to savor any domestic bliss as I struggled to get everything pinned in place so I could head up to Church Hill.

There were near to a thousand Federals in Richmond by then, spread across a range of converted prisons, and Bet meant to tend as many as she could. General Winder's men were providing the meagerest of rations, so she concentrated on procuring dainties and savories, scaring up linens and clean garments, and supplying such diversions as the Federals might enjoy. The last meant a goodly share of the books from her father's library, which she was glad to lend, little imagining how valuable they proved to me and Timothy Smith and anyone else he let in on our system of communication. But the rest of it meant sewing, lots of sewing. Bet set her mother on it, knowing it did the older woman good to have a task to distract her, when everything she held dear was being crushed under the boots of the troops mustered around the city. And Bet stitched away as though she were Penelope herself, pestering me for every minute I wasn't pulling a needle with them. Knowing my entree to the prisons depended upon her good graces, I gave whatever time I could to oblige her.

But as I rushed to get my washing done, everything went wrong. Water spilt and soap run low and misplaced pins and not room enough on the line. Just as I was hanging the last of Wilson's shirts, he came barreling around the corner of the building, waving one of the daily news-sheets.

"What do you mean, giving me such a fright?" I asked, hand over my palpitating heart.

"I'm the one who's had a fright. One of my customers was cussing over the *Examiner,* so upset with what he read that he recited it aloud to the whole shop. Plenty of others were just as angry when they heard."

"Heard what?"

He thrust the paper at me, pointing to the headline SOUTHERN WOMEN WITH NORTHERN SYMPATHIES.

Two ladies, mother and daughter, living on Church Hill, have lately attracted public notice by their assiduous attentions to the Yankee prisoners confined in this city. Whilst every true woman in this community has been busy making articles of comfort or necessity for our troops, or administering to the wants of the many hundreds of sick, who, far from their homes, which they left to defend our soil, are fit subjects for our sympathy, these two women have been expending their opulent means in aiding and giving comfort to the miscreants who have invaded our sacred soil, bent on rapine and murder, the desolation of our homes and sacred places, and the ruin and dishonour of our families.

Out upon all pretexts of humanity! The Yankee wounded have been put under charge of competent surgeons and provided with good nurses. This is more than they deserve and have any right to expect, and the course of these two females, in providing them with delicacies, buying them books, stationery and papers, cannot but be regarded as an evidence of sympathy amounting to an endorsation of the cause and conduct of these Northern Vandals.

I folded the news-sheet so the screaming headline wouldn't show. "I best take this to Bet. Who knows but they'll be hurling bricks through the windows and her not even realizing she needs to close her shutters."

Wilson caught my wrist, as though to tether me to our yard. "Are you mad? I show you this, your first thought is to go up there and put yourself in harm's way. For what?"

I thought of Bet's mother, still weak with palsy but thanks to the news-sheet more at risk than I was, for all I'd done against the Confederates. "After John Brown's raid, Bet did what she could to assure me Papa was safe. If the Van Lews are in danger, the only right thing for me to do is let them know. Just like the only right thing to do is help those Federals, who are fighting our fight. You know that."

"All I know is, since Virginia seceded it's been harder than ever to get baggage out of Richmond. And while you have it in your head that this war is going to end slavery, Lincoln himself says otherwise." Before I could argue back, he added, "I don't care for my wife endangering herself over some white lady."

I pulled free of his hold. "And I don't care for my husband telling me what to do." I turned and hung the clothespin purse on the line, keeping my back to Wilson as I headed around the building to Broad Street.

Up on Church Hill, I found the Van Lew women in their sitting room, sewing away like nothing on earth was the matter. "Good of you to join us at last," Bet said, as reprimand for my tardiness.

I chose my words with care, not wishing to frighten her mother. "Miss Bet, there's something I must show you, out in the yard."

"This is no time for distractions," she said. "I should like to get to Liggon's before too long." But she set down the Federal jacket she was mending and followed me outside.

Peering around the lot, she asked, "What is it?"

"Have you seen the *Examiner* today?"

"Hardly. I wouldn't let that rag into the house, even to line the slop pail."

"Perhaps you ought to have a look at it." I drew the news-sheet from my apron and handed it to her.

Her eyes darted over the article, a broad grin breaking across her narrow face. "I hadn't realized our good work attracted such notice."

"Attracting notice means attracting trouble. It doesn't take but one or two rowdies, they could come here and do who knows what."

"I should like to see them try." She raised herself up straight. She meant the gesture to be defiant, but it looked ludicrous, short as she was. "I am proud to have these uncouth Rebels know all that we are doing for the Union. I only wish we could do more."

It wasn't just the thick heat and the fast walk up Church Hill that had my head swimming. "Miss Bet,

I'm already doing more." I was Mama's daughter—I wasn't about to mistake Bet's interests for my own. But I resigned myself to telling her about my espionage, knowing I needed to keep her from doing anything that would draw more scrutiny from the Secessionists.

She must have been mighty surprised, because she didn't say a word to interrupt as I explained how I made the daily exchange of information. But when I got to the part about how McNiven rode what I gathered to some distant corner of northern Virginia, from whence my messages were secreted into Maryland and then to Washington, she said, "Why that's foolishness."

Anyone calling me a fool to my face might have been taking as much risk with me as I'd taken with the Confederates. But Bet didn't give a moment's pause to consider my feelings. "Mother and I have a pass for travel to our market farm. I shall ride the messages there, and they can be sent down the James to the Bay and out to Fort Monroe in a matter of hours." She frowned at the *Examiner*. "I suppose we must be more discreet concerning our work among the prisoners, for the sake of the Union. I shall write up a cipher for our messages, and we can commence at once." She strode back inside. Within a quarter hour she presented me with a card on which she gridded out letters and numbers for me to use to code my messages, no matter that it would take me at least an hour more each night to write them out.

That was Bet a hundred times over. So full of sanctimonious effrontery she'd seize on whatever might be someone else's and make it hers, without offering so much as a nodding at-your-sufferance. I dawdled at the wash line when I returned home that evening, not wanting to admit to Wilson that he was right. But he read the news on my face just as soon as I brought the basket of laundry inside, and I didn't bother keeping any of the details from him.

For once, though, he wasn't ready to be angry at Bet Van Lew. "Maybe it's for the best, her getting involved with the messages."

"I thought you'd be fuming over it, saying how you knew all along she wanted to put herself in the middle of everything."

"'Course she does. So let her." I wasn't quite ready to do that, until I heard what he said next. "Long day in the shop, gave me lots of time to think. That article wasn't railing about any negro servants, just about the Van Lews. If the Confederates ever notice messages in those books, Bet will step right up to tell them proudly it's her doing. They'll be so infuriated that a proper white lady's been up to such things, they won't ever suspect you're the one who's really behind it. If she puts herself in danger, she pushes you out of it. I can only be happy about that."

I kissed my husband, supposing he was right. And relieved that we were loving and not quarreling, the way we'd been doing all too often because of secession, and of Bet.

Many was the game of I-spy that Mama and I played during my childhood. Each Sunday, I made a grand report to Papa of how many of Mama's riddles I solved in the week previous. But what I was doing now was no game, and much as I hoped Mama was watching over my work, I didn't breathe a word of it to Papa. I didn't want him to know anything that might endanger him, or even give him more to worry over than what he already had to bear.

Wilson and I appeared at the smithy early each Sunday to escort Papa back to our house, fearful of letting him walk by himself, now that he moved so unsteady through the city's teeming streets. It was more than rheumatism that constrained him. The constant press of strangers, all come to fight for the Confederacy, for slavery—Richmond was whipped week by week to the same rushed pace that so disconcerted me when I first arrived in Philadelphia. And every swell of population seemed to squeeze a little more of the breath from Papa.

"Inch-worm get there just as surely as a March hare, even if it ain't as quick," he said as we traced our route one Sunday in September. That was Papa's way of letting me know that even my deliberately slowed pace was too swift for him. As he walked between me and Wilson, there was no denying he was caught by something weightier and more worrisome than what had held me, giggling with pleasure, between him and Mama as they caught me on all those long ago Sundays when I was a child.

"Maybe I should close my eyes," I said. "You can lead me about, like you used to do at Christmastime. See if I'm still able to tell just where in the city we might be."

But Papa didn't have my heart for reminiscing. "Don't see how a body could tell. Things here don't ever sound or smell right no more."

It was true—the sound of drilling troops filled our ears, and what filled our noses was more distressing still. Even with the worst of the summer's battles over, wounded soldiers crowded Richmond. By the time they were borne to the hotels and homes that served as Confederate hospitals, or to the factories where the wounded Federal prisoners were kept, those men gave off the same sickly stink, no matter which uniform they wore when they took the field. Much as I wanted to give Papa back the hope he'd lost, and the freedom he'd never yet had, I had a harder time spying out how to do that than I did secreting intelligence out of the military prisons.

Much grumbling by guards the Secesh may rout Union troops in Virginia for good. One Stevenson has brother at Leesburg under commander Evans says they can push the Union off the Potomac. Accuracy of claim unknown. Man a regular braggart but—

A knock on the front door sent my pen jerking across the page. I tucked the message I was scribing in Bet's cipher into my chemise as Wilson headed down to answer the door.

"I must speak with Mary at once," Bet said by way of greeting. Wilson didn't bother to respond, just turned and came back upstairs with Bet following.

"I'm not half done with the transcribing yet, Miss Bet." For three months, we'd had the same routine. After each of our prison visits, I copied my intelligence into Bet's code. She waited up on Church Hill for me to bring the day's message to her, so she could ride it out to her farm, where William Brisby, the free colored man who'd long been Wilson's Railroad contact in

New Kent County, collected the report and brought it farther east. But now here she was, upsetting the very regimen she demanded I follow.

"Mother has had another stroke." Worry edged tight around her eyes. "Dr. Picot is with her. I must fetch John. You will have to carry the message to the farm yourself."

"Let McNiven do it."

Wilson's words surprised Bet. She'd probably forgotten he was even there. "The pass is for Mother or myself or our servants. A white man cannot use it. Mary will go."

"She will not. It's too dangerous."

I looked from one to the other, wondering that each was so certain of commanding me. I didn't much care to transport the message out through the Virginia countryside. But I couldn't tell how urgent it was, what the cost of a delay might be. A gust of autumn wind rattled the window, sending chill air through the panes.

"It's only a few miles," I said, as though stating the distance might keep me safe for the length of it.

"Through territory patrolled by Secesh," Wilson said. "No place for you to travel by yourself."

"I've done it every day." Bet was proud and indignant all at once.

"Those soldiers don't have to show a negress the same courtesy they do a white lady." Wilson let the unspoken threat of what could happen to me settle on all of us. "If she goes, I go with her."

"I don't see the need—" Bet began, but I cut her off.

"Wilson's right. If he and I travel together, it will be the surest way to get the message there. Leave me the pass. You must want to get back to your mother." I claimed the precious slip of paper and led her back down the stairs.

The steaming breath of the Van Lews' grand white carriage horse curled into the late afternoon air as we rode through Henrico County, the mare swishing her tail back and forth as though expressing dissatisfaction at drawing Wilson's humble cart. Osborne Turnpike was nearly deserted, and when we reached the checkpoint at the fork with New Market Road, we found ourselves alone with two Confederate sentries. One plucked on a Jew's harp while the other sneered and spat a sodden wad of tobacco, demanding to see our pass.

"What trouble you darkies up to?" The soldier stood so close he covered me in a spray of spittle, his eyes shifting from the pass to rove over me.

"Like de paper say, suh," Wilson answered. "Got to get Mistress dem things from de farm."

The sentry kept his lusty gaze on me. "They need two of you to rustle up a day's worth of taters and turnips? This Eliza Van Lew must breed her slaves special to keep them that stupid."

I swallowed hard, kept my gaze low, and prayed Wilson was doing the same.

"Maybe you so stupid, you gonna try something like to get you killed." The sentry drew his pistol, nudging my belly with its barrel. "You ain't planning on running off now, are you?"

Fear closed my throat, as surely as if the sentry had put those tobacco-stained fingers around my neck and started to squeeze.

"Us ain't gonna run, suh," Wilson said.

The muzzle dug farther into my gut. "I'm talking to the wench, she can damn well answer me."

I willed my words past the obstipation of worry. "I's a good girl, sir. Come along like Mistress tell me, pick out the food Cook need." I nodded toward Wilson. "He don't know, bring back all the wrong things. Mistress have a fit."

"Mistress have more of a fit if such a fine gal as yourself were to run off. But you wouldn't do nothing like that, would you?" The metal jabbed in again, hard. "Unless some young buck been talking sweet to you, telling about the fine things he's gonna do once he gets you out to Fort Monroe."

Before I could conjure out a word of reply, he raised his sidearm, aimed it right between Wilson's eyes, and cocked the trigger. "That what you been up to, nigger? Talk sweet to this gal, how you gonna run off?"

"No, suh. Promised Marse I look aftuh Mistress, help her make de other slaves mind. Not about to run to no Marse Monroe. Don't even know who he be."

"Promised Marse? Don't say anything about no master on this pass."

Wilson shrugged. "Don't know what de pass say. But Marse sure say plenty he hear we ain't back by curfew."

Desperate to shake that pistol loose from my sweet husband's brow, I did the only thing I could think to do. I straightened up with feigned pride. "Marse a great man these days. One of them corn tenants they made up for the war."

"Corn tenants?"

The other sentry gave off twanging his Jew's harp with a guffaw. "I suppose she means Lieutenant."

I nodded. "That's it, yessuh. Only not just one them regular loo tenants. He that corn kind. Cob tenant, maybe Mistress say."

My interrogator spat another lump of tobacco and turned to his partner. "Can you translate that bit of darky as well?"

The soldier plucked a few notes before responding. "I don't suppose this corn tenant of yours is a colonel?"

I clapped and grinned like I was about to jump Jim Crow. "That the one! Loo tenant kernel. Only he sure do get mad, he hear anyone make supper late for his wife and daughter."

"You can bet the lieutenant colonel ain't stuck out in the middle of nowhere, nothing to do but keep idiot darkies from running off." The chaw chewer leaned nearer, his breath hot and stinking. "Get a move on. If you ain't back here within the hour, I'm going to get on my horse, ride out until I find you, and shoot you both. That clear?"

"Yessuh," Wilson and I said together. The soldier crumpled the pass and tossed it in my lap. My husband flicked the reins, and we pulled away.

We rode a quarter mile or so, until the turnpike curved around a stand of trees, before I dared speak. "You were right, Wilson. We shouldn't have come out here, risked ourselves to a brute like that. I'm sorry I let Bet talk me into it."

He reined the mare to a halt. "You that frightened?"

"Of course I am. I thought he'd shoot you and— And make me wish he'd shoot me, too."

"Not him. I've seen the type plenty of times before. Takes his pleasure being blustery cruel when he can, but not one to risk his own neck just to shoot someone else's negro. Especially not when there's another white man around to witness it." Wilson wrapped me precious in his arms. "I don't care to see my wife subjected to a man like that, it's true. But he didn't stand a chance against a woman as clever as you. Corn tenant indeed."

Though I held myself proud at the compliment, that dread stayed with me until the sentry waved us past as we crossed the checkpoint on our way back to Richmond. Bet could have her fun, riding through the countryside with those messages sewn in her hem or tucked in a false heel on her shoe. I had Papa to care for, and my husband and my own free self to worry on. I wasn't about to submit myself to such a man again.

If I were caught smuggling messages from the prisons, I'd likely face hanging—but at least it wouldn't be on some lonely country road and at the whim of a leering Confederate picket. It was Richmond I'd come back to. Much as I was willing to risk to serve the Union, still it seemed safest to pass the war within the city limits.

Seventeen

North and South, men had volunteered for a sixty-day war. By the time anyone realized it would be not days or weeks but death-filled years, those volunteers were hardened into something even more indurate than any professional soldier trained to battle might be. Some of the Federal prisoners wouldn't so much as lift their eyes when I passed them what provisions Bet and I brought. At first I took it for the same negro-hating with which many a white man cussed his rebuke as he passed me on a Philadelphia street. Until one day when I came upon a sandy-haired prisoner, a boy of no more than fifteen, whose pale eyes were as weak a watery blue as an early winter sky. Though he brought those troubled eyes to mine, in an instant I wished he hadn't, for all I read in them of the things that sandy-haired boy had seen on the battlefield. Those eyes would never look upon another mortal soul the same way, although whether what haunted him were the things he'd done himself or just what he'd watched others do, I couldn't tell. There were tent hospitals and army surgeons for the ones whose injuries were physical. But for the others, it didn't seem there was a balm in this world that might salve the wound.

More troubling still came the slow, seeping truth that the battlefield wasn't the only place where folks were being schooled in suffering. Soldiers go to battle, but it is whole nations that go to war. There was no missing what that meant for the South, including my own sweet papa, who was working harder and waning more wasted by hunger than ever. It was like watching fruit wither on the vine, to see a man so strong go weak, not all at once but bit by daily bit. By February of 1862, the Federal blockade had taken such a heavy toll on market prices in Richmond, Wilson's earnings could barely keep the two of us, let alone provide for Papa. I was glad enough for whatever orts and leavings I might take from Bet's table, to see my papa fed.

"Brought you a bit of sweet potato pone, some mock turtle soup as well," I said when I stopped by Papa's shack one noon hour to supply the meal for his midday break from the smithy.

"Keep it for you and Wilson. You young people need your nutriments."

"And you need to keep strong for all the work you're doing."

Papa rubbed a palm along the half-plank table Wilson had put up the spring before. "Not much to do, these days."

That wasn't any comfort. Slow business is bad for the slave-owner but worse for the slave. The master makes his profit one way or the other, and the slave is always the source. "I can barely push my way down Main Street, Richmond's so swollen up with new people. Surely Mahon must have customers enough among them."

"Customers or no, smith ain't gonna do much unless he got metal to do it with. And these days, we don't."

"Better for you though, huh?" I set a piece of pone on the rickety half-plank. "You keep to supervising the others while they work, less ache in your bones."

"My bones ache whatever I do or don't. Ache even in my sleep. Ache no matter what awful-tasting things I drink or awful-smelling poultices I lay on," he added, eyeballing me before I could even reach for the packet of prickly ash decoction I'd brought.

I tried to seem more sanguine than I truly was, eyeballing him right back and waiting for him to take a bite or two of the food I'd laid out, though I knew whole pharmacopeias could not remedy all that he suffered. "Weather this cold is hard on everybody," I said. "But spring will be on us soon enough, you'll feel better then."

"Till summer comes, hot and bothersome. You in your spring now, you and Wilson both. Young and full of blooms. But I'm in winter for good. Last of the seasons a person gets."

"Winters can turn mild, melt into a new spring without a person even noticing," I reminded him as I kissed him farewell, not wanting to let on how his despondence gnawed at me.

Winter had yet to turn mild, I admitted to myself as I headed home. Crossing west along Broad Street, the cold gashed against me, numbness in my toes and chilblains in my hands. I pulled my neckcloth tighter as I passed through Devil's Half-Acre.

A whimper, more animal than human, sounded from Silas Omohundro's slave pens.

"Damn wench is froze in place." A young pen-hand jabbed his toe at a rag-clad form on the ground. "Omohundro ain't gonna care for no damaged merchandise."

"Ain't his merchandise," replied his workmate, rubbing his hands together against the frosty air. "Just a runner caught outside town. Holding her for the bounty."

"Maybe won't be any to collect," the younger man said. "Ain't likely this one'll make it through another night out here."

Between the city's crowding and the state's inflation, Confederate clerks were so pinched that they were reduced to laying their heads down in whatever accommodation they could find. Every cell at Omohundro's slave pen had long been rented over to these white men, leaving only the exposed yard for Omohundro's stock of slaves.

"What it ain't is ain't your concern," the older hand said. "Now help me get this wench up. He's got someone coming by, gonna turn her in for the bounty, down to the Scuppernong River."

"North Carolina? My cousin writ Yankees took them parts last week. Satan hisself couldn't get through there now."

The pen-hand jerked his shoulders back like he was proud to do a demon's dirtywork. "What old man Omohundro say, this catcher's mean as Satan, rich as Satan, too. Running slaves all over the South ever since the War started."

One man is a slave to his lusts, another is a slave to greed, another a slave of ambition, and all are slaves to hope and fear. There was nothing more hateful than making bounties off runaways, battered souls who'd gotten that much closer to freedom only to have it snatched from them. I tacitly cursed the slave-catcher. But before I could hurry off, I witnessed something that froze me in place just as surely as the long February night had frozen that slavewoman.

"Bi crivens! I told Silas to hae her ready. If you two canna get her to her feet, step aside for one what can."

McNiven's whip cracked the air within an inch of the woman's face. He stormed over and grabbed her short nap of hair, yanking her to her feet. Omohundro's hands unlocked the chain that held the woman to the pen. Wrenching her arm behind her, he pushed the slave through the gate. "Tell Silas I will be back within the week, with his bounty share."

I shook myself into movement, meaning to scurry away before he saw me. But in the moment that I passed him, McNiven's eyes met mine.

I spent the sixth anniversary of my mama's death at her graveside, hoping she might have a word or two for me, of comfort or warning or plain old directive about what I'd witnessed at Devil's Half-Acre the week before. But after passing the whole day without the slightest sign from her, I crossed out of the burying ground. As I made my way along the hard-packed dirt of Coutts Street, a man's shadow came up from behind me. He caught my arm, pulling me round to face him.

"I been searching on you, lass. Found a use for you."

I yanked myself free of McNiven's grasp. "Like you found a use for that captured slavewoman?"

"Ay, a mighty ugly business, that. But it needed doing."

"Dragging a fugitive back to a master never needs doing." I spat the words at him.

"Union forces camp but ten miles from that plantation. I sent an agent to be looking for the slavewoman, and any others nearby what are wanting to escape. She is probably free again by now."

"So why return her in the first place?"

"She was half starved and froze near to death in a slave pen here. If she be taken as Union contraband doun in North Carolina, she'll be fed and clothed and maybe schooled some. Surely the slave be none the worse off for that."

"And you are rather the better off." I eyed the silk lapel on his new wool frock coat. He couldn't have afforded such a fine garment a year ago, and in the interval clothing had grown ten times more expensive, thanks to the blockade.

"An operative need look the part he intends on play-ing, doun to the very silver o' his buttons. As long as Omohundro and the rest believe me a slave-trader, it gives me means to rove about the Confederacy. 'Tis important for our work."

"Our work is to free slaves," I said. "Not trade in them."

But McNiven answered me just as I'd been answer-ing Wilson the whole year past. "If we want to win the bigger prize, we need be making a gamble or two along the way."

Still, I wasn't ready to shake off the risk to that fugi-tive. "You're gambling with the lives of colored people."

"And with none whiter than myself, for what the Confederates would do if they discover what I am really about."

I weighed his words carefully. Hattie's father had long entrusted McNiven with Railroad baggage. Mr. Jones's own life had come safe, and only barely so, because of the Scotsman. And for nearly the whole year past, McNiven had set himself to living clandestine in Richmond, just as I had—without the pull that Papa's presence had on me. The risk he took was every bit as real as my own.

I wasn't sure I was ready to forgive the part he'd played at Omohundro's. But still I asked, "What did you mean, when you said you have a use for me?"

" 'Tis some work for our side, and you are just the one for it."

"I already have work, in the prisons."

"Bet can do such by herself. This will be something only you can do, for you are dark, and smart, and they never expect the two together. None will suspect you for copying out the things you hear and see for Mr. Lincoln's army, when you be in the Gray House."

The Gray House, Richmond slang for the Shockoe Hill mansion where Jefferson Davis lived. The building perched pelican sure above Butchertown, its back to most of the city. Since I had no call to pass down Clay Street, that rear wall was about all I ever saw of it. "Why would I be there?"

"Waiting on Varina Davis, what has run an ad in the *Enquirer* this very day, for a serving gal and maid. She maun be a cruel one, she canna keep free nor slave working for her long. But the slave she's hired for from me will last the whole war through, I wager."

It was one thing to play-act at serving Bet, who knew me free and educated. Who gave me both those things herself, when no one else in the world but Mama and Papa thought I deserved them. But to serve the First Lady of the Confederacy, cleaning and tending all day, was something else again. "So while you play the wealthy slave-trader, I'm to be the misused slave?"

"We'd not have much sense to try it the other way round, would we, lass?" Though McNiven wasn't much for kindly gestures or comforting phrases, he added, "We maun be doing so, for the sake o' them that canna yet do for themselves."

I'd come back to Virginia with only the vaguest sense of what I was meant to do, had carved conviction from danger to secret the prisoners' communications out to the Union, never doubting I'd set myself the proper course. That same surety told me now that McNiven was right—Bet could manage on her own in the prisons. Whether I could manage walking back into the lows and depths of slavery, I wasn't nearly as certain. But I thought about the woman from Omohundro's, and about Papa. About the millions of bondspeople that I'd been telling Wilson this war would free.

If my being a slave might hasten the day when Papa and countless others weren't, I had to try my hand in the Gray House, whatever the risk might be.

I barely had time to take to the plan myself, before I was back home telling Wilson about it. And he made his opinion on it quite clear.

"How am I supposed to feel about my wife working as a slave to some white family?"

"I'm none too keen on it myself. But there's a war on, and—"

He didn't so much as let me finish. "Don't start with all your *the war's going to end slavery, Mr. Lincoln just doesn't know it yet* business. I'll believe that when it comes to pass, and not a moment before."

"What if I mean to have a part in making it come to pass?" I put all the indignance and insistence I could muster into what I said out loud. But that was just blustery cover for what I felt deep inside, which was utter trepidation. Not trepidation over what it would be like to wait on the most powerful white man in all of the Confederacy. Trepidation my convictions might cost me Wilson, like they did Theodore. "I thought you loved me because I'm contrary enough to favor doing what's right over doing what's easy."

"I do love you, more than I've ever loved any person on this earth. But can't you see it's hard for a man to have a wife he can't protect?"

Looking into my dear husband's eyes, I couldn't help but see it. But I could see, too, that Wilson was no easy-smile Handsome Hinton, who adored me only so long as I was willing to be his adornment. "I love you, too. And it breaks my heart to think that though my mama and papa loved each other, they never could look after each other like we do, that so many slaves today still can't." I took his hand in mine. "I'm not loving you any less if I work to change that."

"And I'm not loving you less if I don't much care for all the worry you put me through when you do."

We left it that way—neither of us quite satisfied, though at least we each begrudgingly understood the other.

Two mornings later, I had my first good look at the facade facing out from Clay Street and Twelfth. Square and plain, the house was built of gray stucco cut to look like masonry. Bigger but less comely than the Van Lew mansion, and likely to stink all summer long, with the stables set just behind a low wall on the side of the residence.

There wasn't a soul in the yard, but as I passed through the servants' entry into the basement, cries and yelps sounded off the whitewashed walls and brick floors. I followed the noise to an unornamented room where three olive-skinned children were shrieking at each other. The eldest, a girl of about seven, had porridge in her hair. Brandishing a lob of butter, she chased her two brothers around a long plank table. As they rounded the corner, the smaller of the boys careened into my legs, howling and flailing against me.

"Where is Nurse? Where is Nurse?" A tall woman in a purple broché morning dress appeared in the opposite doorway, shrilling out the question. Her mannish height and her coloring, as olive as the children's, set her off from any Richmond matron I'd ever seen. Her eyebrows pinched in permanent glower, and her dark brown hair was pulled back from her face as severely as a plaited mane on a show horse. Though younger than Bet, she was already thick around the middle, with jowls that shook as she spoke. "I have told Nurse a hundred times that she is to keep you quiet while the president is in the house."

The children scrambled to their places on a low wooden bench before the table. "Nurse says she has too much to do tending Billy, and we are to look after ourselves," the older boy said.

"She has too much to do?" The woman scowled at the notion of an overworked servant. "The president has too much to do running the Confederacy, and I have too much to do running the household that runs the Confederacy, to have the president's children tearing about like wild Comanches."

The girl inspected a spoonful of porridge. "Yesterday you said we were as wild as African savages, Mother. Which is wilder?"

At the mention of African savages, Varina Davis took her first notice of me. "Who are you?"

Before I could answer, the older boy pushed the younger off the wooden bench, sending a creamer tumbling after him. I snatched up the crying child, using my apron to wipe the milk-white splatters from his face.

"She's as fast on the cream as kitty," the older boy said.

The observation set his sister whining. "I miss kitty. Why couldn't we bring her to this dull old house?"

"Kitty could not be brought all the way from Brierfield to Montgomery and then here, as you have already been told. I will not have the president's children complaining about that animal anymore." The woman's eyes bore hard on me as I gathered up shards of porcelain and set them on the table, then passed her the slip of paper McNiven had written out.

"Marse say you hired for me."

"Hired, indeed. These Richmonders should be glad to give their servants to tend the president's house, instead of charging us a fortune for such barest of necessities. Richmond grows rich off the Confederacy, while the president himself grows poor."

I marked the yards of periwinkle silk ribbon that crisscrossed her full skirt. The trim on her jacket alone must have cost more than an army private or a government clerk made in two months' time.

She tucked McNiven's note into the clip on her chatelaine. "Go on up to the parlor, you'll find the rest of them there." As I passed toward the doorway, she asked, "What do they call you?"

"Mary."

The girl wriggled along the bench toward her younger brother. "That's aunt's name, and Mrs. Chesnut's as well."

"Indeed, it will not do to have a negro named Mary about," her mother said. "We shall call her Molly."

I hadn't even set to work for the Davises, and already I felt as used-up as my crumpled, cream-soaked apron. A mistress who took every other sentence to bray about how important her husband is. A gaggle of children competing to be the most ill behaved. A nursemaid no one could find. And not even my own name to see me through. I ticked off all I had to contend with, as I made my way through the basement and up to the dining room, then passed through the entry hall to the parlor.

The ostentatious furnishings on the main floor told me as much about the Davises as the set piece of domestic relations I'd witnessed among the cellars. Every inch of every wall in those rooms was papered, the flocking swirled in garish greens or crimsons. The wall colors clashed with the elaborate patterns of the carpets, which warred in turn with the gaudy uphol-stery, the ornate brocatelle curtains, and the gilt edging on the mirrors, paintings, and gasoliers.

I found the housekeeper kneeling over a bucket of vinegary liquid, washing the bottom panes of the parlor window. "You the new one, I suppose," she said with a Deep South accent. She was a dark string bean of a woman, bones nearly poking through her ebony skin. "You can stop staring. Like to burn off what little flesh I got on me, the way you looking."

She squeezed out the rag and draped it over the edge of the bucket, then stood and looked me hard in the eye. "She keep the food locked up and everything weighed out to the ounce. Be glad you live out, take your own meals stead a eating her scrap." She leaned over and pinched my upper arm. "Still, she like to work even that much fat off you."

"My name is Mary, though she say she gonna call me Molly. What's yours?"

"I outlasted all the rest a her servants ten times over, that's enough for you to know. Ain't about to learn your name till you been here a month or more. She run through your kind too quick for me to bother." She clucked her tongue. "Unless she take a fool's liking to you, like that shanty Irish nursemaid Catherine, laziest thing I ever seed and them chiljen running raggedy through the house. Or snobby little Betsy, carry on like she royalty herself just cause she dump Queen Varina's chamber pot."

Queen Varina—Richmonders were handy with that appellation, some using it with pride at the First Lady's regal bearing, others with complaints of how snobbish she was. I didn't have to guess which way the emaciated housekeeper meant it.

She nodded toward a girl gawky with adolescence who was cleaning the mantel dressing. "Sophronia, show this one how I like things done. Don't look as though she know too much, standing there hanging on to a soiled apron like it were a ten-dollar note." The housekeeper picked up her bucket and left the room.

"Don't . . . mind . . . Hortense." Sophronia's words came out in tiny gulps, like bubbles of air struggling to the surface of a pond. "Plain hates Catherine and Betsy. 'Cause she can't boss 'em. But she boss me and you. Plenty."

For the next hour, Sophronia and I cleaned our way through the center parlor and the drawing room, laboring in silence except for her occasional hiccups of instruction about how Hortense insisted a particular chore be done. It had been more than a decade since I'd been set to such grueling work. The intervening years had imbued me with more determination than bodily strength, though the former kept me careful to hide the lack of the latter, even from this Sophronia.

But mine wasn't the only false front amid the swash and swagger of the Gray House. When I laid the dusting rag along the library mantel, I discovered the seeming marble was nothing but painted cast iron. As I wiped the fakery clean, a hacking started up in the adjoining entryway.

"You're not going out in this weather, are you, Jefferson?" Varina Davis chirped like a mother robin trying to ward off whatever might upset her nest.

"I must get to the Treasury Building. I've meetings all"—a deep voice I took for Jefferson Davis's twisted into a cough—"day long."

"The president needs to take care of his health, for the sake of the Confederacy. And the president's wife needs to take care of him."

"I must go. The news of the Virginia has everyone hopeful. I must be ready, before that damn Joe Johnston rushes in and takes the credit for himself."

I thought of the Virginia Guard, the Virginia Infantry, the Virginia Howitzers, and at least a dozen similarly titled military companies that had paraded through Richmond since the war began. Which one did Jeff Davis mean? And what were the Confederates hoping it would do?

"Sophronia," Hortense cut into my rumination like a jagged-toothed rip-saw, "didn't I tell you to show that gal how I want things done? She like to smash them Chinee doodads the way she carrying on."

I looked down and righted one of the large Chinese vases flanking the fireplace, which my skirt had snagged when I turned to hear the exchange between the Davises. "I was just–"

"Ain't talking to you. Daydreaming and backtalking, another one ain't gonna last, look like." Hortense turned back to Sophronia. "Get upstairs and do his office, quick. Who know how long we got before Queen Varina drag him back here, convinced he about to keel over just from a bit a cough and spit."

Sophronia led me up the narrow servants' stairs, gurgling out a word or two on each step. "Hate that office. Papers everyplace. Move 'em, he has a fit. Don't, and she hollers it ain't clean. Like to burn them all."

We set to work in the upstairs hall, which with its ornate coat rack and array of straightbacked chairs served as the receiving area for visitors to the president. From there we advanced into a tiny pass-through of a closet that had been commandeered for the secretary's office. Though the calendar of appointments lying on the drop-front desk piqued my interest, I didn't dare to more than glance at it with Sophronia crowded so close. She dawdled over the room as long as she could, until finally we stood in one corner, staring through the open door into Jeff Davis's office.

"Hortense scared to do it herself," Sophronia said. "That's why she makes me. Makes us." A flicker of realization crossed her face, and she pushed me into the room. "Yeah, Molly. Us better get to it."

Davis's office seemed nearly stark in comparison to the decor downstairs, with a simple red and brown fleur-de-lis pattern on the beige wall paper, and repeating diamonds of gold and maroon on the carpet. A pair of crossed swords and scattered paintings of military scenes adorned the walls. The walnut and black horsehair furniture sat dark and spare and heavy. An Empire couch, a desk and tufted chair, and a round table with two straightback chairs, all set purposefully around the room. Writing papers were scattered across the desk, and larger pages, probably maps, covered the table.

Sophronia crossed to the far wall. Her face was flat and round as a fry pan, her eyes set wide like the raw yolks of two eggs cracked in to cook. "I better watch you. Make sure you get it right. Go on."

Like a child forcing himself through his haricots and saving his cake for last, I began dusting the sofa, the paintings, and the large globe and stand, then polishing the wood with our mix of beeswax and turpentine. By the time I finished sweeping the fireplace and cleaning the long, thin tube that connected the desk lamp to the ceiling gasolier, Sophronia had turned her back to me to nod and wave out the window. Watching her pantomime, I guessed she must be carrying on a romance with the groundsman. That was all the opening I needed. Nudging the spittoon that stood sentry beside the desk, I leaked an ooze of brown onto the carpet.

"Hortense have a fit if she see this," I said, calling Sophronia's attention to the tobacco juice. "I best run downstairs, fetch a fresh bucket of water to clean it. Is the sink in the cellar?"

"Cellar water too rusty. Got to draw it in the yard. Go myself." She scurried out of the room, delighted at the prospect of a rendezvous with her groundsman.

I didn't waste a tick of the mantel clock before I was studying the correspondence scattered on Davis's desk.

Gosport Naval Yard, Va. February 28,

President Jefferson Davis,

My design for the former Merrimac has been fully executed. The CSS Virginia sits in Norfolk fully clad in iron, awaiting only her coal before she attacks the Union fleet at the mouth of the James.

Our naval men look forward to their historic voyage on behalf of the Confederacy.

Very respectfully yours,
Jn L Porter

Sketched on the bottom of the missive was the oddest-looking maritime conveyance I'd ever seen. She had no sails, and most of the hull sat below the squiggly marks meant to show the water-line. Atop the water, the ship rose into a trapezoid, with slits drawn in for gunnery windows.

On the back of the letter, someone had scribbled technical particulars.

L: 270ft
    Armored casement: 24in oak and pine clad with 4in iron plate
    Prow: 1500lb iron ram
    Armament: 3 9in smooth-bore Dahlgrens, 1 6in rifle on each broadside.
    Single pivot mted 7in Brooke rifle in stern and bow gun ports.

This *Virginia* was an iron-clad monster of the sea. Surely able to decimate the Federal navy and destroy the Union blockade.

Before I could search through the next letter, a loud crash sounded through the house. I hurried from the office and down the curving center stair toward the commotion.

In the entry hall, two ornate mahogany chairs were toppled onto the brawling Davis sons, a silver dish and a dozen calling cards scattered across the floor. Queen Varina stood above the boys, howling about how the president's wife must be able to have her nap without the household going to bedlam. Catching sight of me, she snatched an umbrella from the hallstand and cuffed it hard against my ear. "Infernal servants, too busy prancing about to get their work done."

As she turned to bark at a befreckled white woman who appeared in the far doorway, I slipped into the library.

Hortense, huddled behind the door, sent no comfort my way. "One a them chiljen like to kill the other, way they fight. Let that Lazy Irish have 'em, we got 'nough to do cleaning up after it all." Though my ear ached, all she offered was stern command. "Keep to the back stair and keep out of trouble. I got plenty a grief without needing to train a new maid every other day."

Through the long, labor-filled afternoon that followed, the only way I could distract myself from a nagging tinnitus was by damning Varina Davis and her umbrella. Damning McNiven for expecting me to put up with her. And damning what intelligence I had gathered about the CSS *Virginia*, for making me feel it was my duty to come back to the Gray House the next day and the next, even if I were beaten for the privilege.

Wilson was sweeping the stoop of the shop as I came up Broad Street. Or pretending to, moving the broom back and forth as he squinted to make out my arrival, his face ashen with worry.

He shepherded me through the side gate and inside our door. "You heard?"

"Haven't heard a thing but ringing." I slid off my head wrap, exposing my contusion.

"How did that happen?"

"Same way most things happen to slaves. Hot white anger, looking for a place to land."

I worried over what he would say, seeing my body bruised by Queen Varina. But he curled into me and kissed my ear, the nearness of him soothing the ache. "I suppose you're safer than if you'd been on Church Hill."

I pulled back and peered into his eyes. "What do you mean?"

"They've been arresting Unionists, all last night and this morning. Richmond is under martial law."

Something pulled tight in my chest. "What about Bet?"

"I don't know. A man came into the shop just after dinner, boasting to the other customers about all he'd done. Captain Godwin, he called himself, bragging on how they renamed McDaniel's negro jail Castle Godwin on account of all the white Unionists he locked up there." Wilson rattled off what names he could remember of those who'd been arrested.

I recognized some of them, John Botts, Franklin Stearns, Burnham Wardwell. Men I'd waited on at Bet's table way back during my childhood. "If they have her . . ." I couldn't bring myself to finish.

Bet had been a part of my life as long as I could remember. Not exactly family, not quite friend. Still, there was a bond between us unlike any I had with anyone else.

Outside our parlor window, the last rays of sunlight were disappearing from the sky. With curfew on, there'd be no news of Bet's whereabouts unless we had a white person to seek her out, and there was only one to ask. Provided he wasn't locked up in Castle Godwin.

"Where's McNiven?"

Wilson shrugged. "I wager no one's thought to arrest him. He hasn't given anyone reason to think he's a Unionist."

"And given them plenty of reason to think otherwise."

"Still, there isn't any suspicion raised on him, or you." Seeing there was yet more worrying me, he added, "Probably not on Bet, either."

I nodded. But I sat hunched with apprehension while Wilson cooked supper. Wrong as it was to be wasteful with food grown so dear, still I no more than picked over my meager portion before setting all my intelligence about the *Virginia* down in Bet's code. Staring at the strange pattern of letters and numbers was like seeing how tangled up everything of mine was with her, as though we were Mr. Barnum's twins of Siam. My intelligence, her cipher, my hand. One twin of Siam couldn't dance or ride or even rest without the other doing the same. Without sure word of Bet's whereabouts, I couldn't drift to sleep, no matter how late it grew.

A knock sounded on our door near two o'clock in the morning. We found McNiven on the step, his breath warm with alcohol. "Where have you been?" I asked once we got him upstairs to our parlor.

"I passed some hours over to the faro parlor favored by the guests o' the Spotswood Hotel. Partwise to see what I might hear there, but mostwise waiting for the streets to empty enough that I could come here without any taking notice." Gambling houses, drinking houses, even houses of ill repute had sprung up all over Richmond, filling the streets with rowdies long after decent people had gone to bed. McNiven's tippling among them provided him with more details than we'd yet had. "Two spies are among those what are arrested."

Spies. The word seemed sharp and waspish as he said it. "Who are they?" I asked.

"Strangers to us. There is a fellow in Washington, Pinkerton. Worked on our Railroad back when in Chicago, and now runs some operations for the Union. From what I gather, these fowk be his."

Wilson looked to the hyssop leaf compress he'd bound to my ear. "What does it mean for Mary?"

"These men hae naught to say on us, even if they wish to tell to save their own necks." That was all the reassurance McNiven offered. If he marked my injury, he didn't bother to mention it. "What have you learned over to the Gray House?"

Passing him the cipher message, I related the information it contained. But he didn't show even a hint of surprise about the CSS *Virginia*.

"We heard such a thing was being builded, from a slave what escaped from the engineer some months ago. The Union has been trying to make a like ship for herself."

Wilson frowned. "If this Pinkerton has agents here in Richmond, and the Union already knows about this ship, what need is there for Mary to put herself in danger?"

"What Mary tells here," McNiven patted the pocket where he'd tucked my message, "is o' great use. They hae been building on this *Virginia* for many, many months. If she be ready for battle, the Union's *Monitor* maun be sent straight away to meet her. A day or more delay and the Union would lose ships and men and the hard won surety o' the blockade."

He reached for his wallet, peeling off a half dozen Confederate notes and holding them out to me. I marked how the silver buttons on his frock coat shone like beady rodent eyes as I told him I didn't want his money. "I'm no mercenary. Whatever I do in the Gray House, it's only to end slavery."

McNiven kept his outstretched hand steady. "Still and all, the payment be yours, what Varina Davis give for the first month's hire. 'Twill help keep you and Bowser both."

Much as I didn't care to take the bills, I knew he was right. Already Wilson and I passed evenings hungry, food prices had gone so high. Even the sum McNiven insisted was mine would have to be stretched and strung, to last any time at all at the market stalls.

As I folded the Confederate notes, McNiven consulted his gold pocket watch. "I ride to the Rappahannock in a half hour's time. Dibrell's tobacco company has hired me to go to Baltimore and see what product I may arrange for selling. I can pass your news while I am there."

"What about Bet?" I asked.

"There is no talk of any women what are taken in. Any more assurance than that, you'll need to find for yourself."

I had to be in the Gray House all day and was kept penned in by the curfew all night. McNiven knew that, but it was Wilson who spoke to it. "Tomorrow when I close the shop for dinner, I can head over to Church Hill, check on Bet. I'll stop in on Lewis, too."

I knew he put that part about Papa in just to convince me. And much as I always tried to keep Bet and Wilson apart, still I was relieved that he offered to go to her.

No need to fret over Bet. That woman is crazy," Wilson reported when I returned from the Gray House the next day.

"So much for you feeling more kindly toward her."

"I mean no hostility. But she is acting crazy. Be the first to tell you so herself."

He explained how he'd come upon her wandering along Grace Street, done up in a calico bonnet, a cotton dress, and buckskin leggings, as though she'd just meandered down from the hill country. Muttering to herself in a little sing-song, scratchy and high.

"She was doing such a fine job with her play-acting, I might have fallen for it myself. Only, when she looked straight at me, the wildness in her eyes cleared away. Just for a moment she seemed sharp and certain, and then she mumbled in her crazy way"—he raised his voice and intoned in a fine impression of Bet—"*Mary had a little lamb, and the lamb were the peacemaker. But we are at war so the lamb is gone. Who's gonna bring Mary's lamb back here?*" He chuckled and lay off imitating her. "Then she shrieked a little laugh that scared off some neighborhood children who'd come out to stare at her."

I couldn't make sense of what he said. "Why is she carrying on so?"

"First lesson of the Railroad. The best way to sneak about is to hide in plain sight. Looks like Bet's lit on a way to do that." Just like McNiven, playing the part of the cruel and cunning Confederate slave-trader. And me, the simple-witted slave.

I shook off the thought by inquiring after the aroma that was coming from our kitchen. "Where'd you get a chicken to roast?"

"Bet gave it to me, one of the scraggly hens pecking all over that yard of hers."

She must have been crazy after all, offering charity to a free negro as proud as Wilson. "Did she just happen to slip a chicken out from under her calico bonnet?"

He smiled. "No, ma'am, I suppose not even she would make that much of a spectacle of herself. Once she scared those children off, I followed her into the carriage house at the back of her family's lot. She showed me a little compartment she fitted out under the seat of her gig, where I'll store your messages."

"You?"

"Fastest way to get what you learn in the Gray House to the Federals is for me to ride your message out to her farm first thing in the morning, while Bet fusses with her prisoners."

"But what about the shop, all your customers?" What about your wife, fretting over you?

"I can open the shop a little later, no one will be the wiser." He dropped his voice so low, I barely heard what he said next. "The money from McNiven is more than I make anyway. Negro labor is worth more enslaved than free."

I felt his ache of crushed pride myself. The sum Queen Varina paid for my hire was far more than I'd earned as a schoolteacher. But I was troubled by more than just pecuniary resentment as I recalled the bully of a picket at the junction of Osborne Turnpike and New Market Road. And I told my husband so.

"Riding out those messages is no riskier than moving baggage, and I did that long enough." He'd been restless ever since Virginia's secession disrupted his Railroad runs. "Who knows but once the sentries see me regular, I might even be able to slip some baggage past without them noticing."

I set my safety in jeopardy by working in the Gray House. I knew I hadn't any right to tell him not to risk his own by carrying my messages, maybe even transporting fugitives along with them.

Uneasy though I was, I nodded in agreement when he suggested it was best I didn't tell him what was in the ciphered messages—and he didn't tell me if he moved any baggage down the James. The better part of intelligence is pretending ignorance. I proved that in the Gray House just as surely as Mama had shown it to me in the days of *we in the house.* But that wasn't much comfort to a woman who was a loving wife as well as a Union spy.

Eighteen

Any house slave can tell you there's more to a neat parlor or a laid table than meets the eye. Whatever master, mistress, and their guests take in doesn't begin to account for all the labor that's been put out. I'd known as much my whole life, known before I was ever old enough to think on it. But I also knew it was more than just hard labor that escaped the notice of the slaveholder. Every now and again in my childhood, rumors circulated about some slave cook who spitefully snuck emetic, purgative, or worse into her owners' meals. Maybe it wasn't many who ever did so, but still we knew they could. Poisoning was an enslaved cook's prerogative, even if it was seldom exercised. Every house of bondage was webbed with such prerogatives. Serving in the Gray House, I tugged and tightened each possible strand, meaning to unravel slavery's hold once and for all.

From the start, Hortense made her prerogative clear. She learned my assigned name quick enough once she was sure it would serve her, calling out "Molly" faster than I could remember to respond. "Too slow to know who you is, or what," she'd say, if I didn't snap to servile attention the moment she summoned. But I saw from how she treated Sophronia that slow- witted suited Hortense just fine, so long as being slow-witted kept other slaves subservient to her. Hortense reigned tyrannical in her role as housekeeper, and she hated anything—and anyone—who challenged it.

Neither the ladies' maid Betsy nor the nursemaid Catherine were subject to her authority, and, just as Sophronia said, Hortense hated them both. She never even uttered Catherine's name, calling her "Lazy Irish" as surely as she called me Molly. Lazy Irish slept in the second-floor nursery, but that didn't rile Hortense nearly so much as the exceptional arrangements made for Betsy. Though she was dark as Dahomey, Betsy had her own small cell of a room on the third floor, right across the hall from where Jeff Davis's secretary, Burton Harrison, slept and adjacent to the guest chambers kept for whichever of Queen Varina's pride-rich but cash-poor relations happened to visit. Betsy might be up half the night most days, tending Queen Varina through whatever nervous illness she conjured for herself, but still it galled Hortense that when Betsy finally laid her head down, it was in her own quarter on the very top story of the house, while Hortense, Sophronia, and the rest of the living-in slaves were all crowded together in the cellar. Hortense refused to set foot on the stairs leading to the third floor, and she declared within my first week it would thereafter be my duty to scour and sweep, wipe and wax the entire story, and most of the one below it as well. I didn't flinch or fuss over such decrees, glad as I was that Hortense's prerogative gave me leave to exercise my own.

All those months in the prisons, I'd meticulously recorded what Timothy Smith and the other prisoners sent out, embellished whenever possible with things I observed myself. But seeing and telling weren't the half of spying, no more than poking the parlor fire or refilling the guest's wineglass is all there is to house service. Just as a slave cook might slip something into the white family's fare or a housekeeper might wage a war of resentment over the rest of the servants, even the supposedly simple serving gal could manage her own prerogatival campaign. This was the truth I relished and relied on. It rendered even the most loathsome tasks bearable. And before too long, it let me see new ways I might set the slaves freedom bound.

Some of my best days in the Gray House were when the portly, bearded Judah Benjamin called on Queen Varina. "Secretary Benjamin" was how she always addressed him, fawning over his every word. Even if she'd spent the whole morning in bed with a sick-headache, she perked up as soon as he arrived, fluttering down to receive him. He complained constantly about how hard he worked to serve the Confederacy, and she always responded with a *tant pis*, thinking herself quite cosmopolitan for uttering her sympathies to a Louisianan *en français*. I imagined the fit Miss Douglass and Miss Mapps would have if they heard her Mississippi accent mutilating those delicate French syllables, *tant pis* coming out more like *tante piss*.

Aunt Piss was secretary of war when I started at the Gray House, though from his visits with Queen Varina, I could see he meant to be more than that. The two of them would sit in the library, she arrayed on the meridienne like a roast goose served up with trimmings, he rocking furiously away in the president's favorite chair, plotting to advance his own career.

Queen Varina adored being confidante to a cabinet member, and she shone with self-importance whenever she promised to intercede on his behalf with the president. Despite her grumblings that the president's wife must guard the meager resources bought with the president's paltry salary, she lavished indulgence on Aunt Piss.

I was grateful for the way he gobbled down Jeff Davis's pecans, drank Jeff Davis's whiskey, and puffed Jeff Davis's cigars. All that gluttony meant someone was needed to clear away pecan shells, refill the whiskey glass, and clean up cigar ash. Hortense wouldn't do anything she could order Sophronia or me to, and Sophronia cowed so around whites she was glad to be scrubbing Queen Varina's boudoir while the serving fell to the new maid. So I came to pass an hour or more most afternoons listening to whatever news Aunt Piss shared with Queen Varina.

On the ninth March he told how the CSS *Virginia* had attacked the USS *Cumberland*, the USS *Roanoke*, and the USS *Minnesota* the day before. He boasted of it as though he had personally captained the lethal ironclad. But on the tenth March he neglected to report that the USS *Monitor* had arrived from New York and engaged the *Virginia* to a draw. I'd nearly let out a peacock's caw of joy when I saw the telegraphed report on Jeff Davis's desk, knowing the part my very first Gray House report had in the Union victory. But it didn't surprise me not to hear a whiff about it down in the library. Though Aunt Piss moaned over how his rivals criticized his work as secretary of war, he never acknowledged a hint of his own failings.

"Such censure I face, my dear Mrs. Davis, when all I do is for the good of our Confederacy. My enemies, like those of our president, show no shame." He waited just long enough for Queen Varina to murmur *tant pis* before continuing. "After all, with a president who is as fine a general as your husband, what is there left for a secretary of war to do?"

Queen Varina wallowed in his flattery. "We all know Mr. Davis would be proud to lead his men to battle, but the president must serve in the capacity that has been thrust upon him," she answered, conveniently overlooking how she preferred the First Lady's life of hosting receptions to the worry that plagued generals' wives.

"The battles are important, but I do not believe that is where the war will be won, or lost. It is diplomacy we need." Aunt Piss swirled his tumbler of whiskey before taking a sip. "Britain must be made to recognize the Confederacy."

"Britain needs us as much as we need her," Queen Varina said. "Why, without Confederate cotton, what use are English mills?" It was the same argument she'd heard a cocksure South Carolinian make to her husband at dinner the day before.

Aunt Piss smiled as though he were explaining to a child. "You might say the same for the New England mills, yet the Yankees make war with us." He scooped up a handful of pecans and reached for the nutcracker, which he used to emphasize his words. "It would be a terrible thing" (crack) "*tant pis pour tous*" (crack) "to ignore the threats" (crack) "that come far from the battlefield" (crack). He rocked back in calculated detachment. "Such as this latest ploy by Lincoln."

Queen Varina's face twitched in surprise. "What threats? What new ploy?"

I swooped forward to empty the silver bowl of nutshells, eager to hear his answer. "I have reliable word that Lincoln has proposed a bill to his Congress." He paused to fume out a ring of cigar smoke. "A bill of emancipation."

I could have kissed Aunt Piss, stinking cigar and all.

Queen Varina was shrieking in dismay. "Didn't Jefferson Davis know that Lincoln wanted to take our slaves, even though that Black Republican lied and lied about it?"

"Not take, and not our slaves," Aunt Piss corrected. "Lincoln proposes to pay four hundred dollars a head to slaveholders in the border states, if they agree to gradual emancipation."

"Four hundred dollars per slave? Is the Union so rich as that?"

"Four hundred dollars for every slave in Delaware is but half the cost of one day of war for the Union. Four hundred dollars for every slave in Maryland, Missouri, the District of Columbia, and Mrs. Lincoln's own Kentucky would be the cost of eighty-seven days of war. Lincoln gambles that compensated emancipation will shorten the war by that many days or more, by ensuring the loyalty of the border states."

Queen Varina puffed up, parroting what she heard her husband say so many times. "We do not fight for slavery, Secretary Benjamin. We fight for the right of States to govern themselves. If Lincoln is too much of a fool to see that—"

"He is no fool, of that we can be sure. He gives the border states the option of compensation and says it is their choice whether to accept. Thus he makes emancipation a grand show of Federal respect for States' Rights." Queen Varina squawked an objection, but he continued. "You are correct. We do not fight for slavery. Neither does Lincoln. We fight to win, and so does he. But he is willing to sacrifice slavery in the process, while we are not."

As far as my espionage went, the conversation was of no consequence, because it revealed something the Federals already knew all about—a presidential proposal that never ended up passing into law. But I was gladder for Aunt Piss's report than for a stack of Confederate battle plans, proof as it was that I was right. Slavery might at last be done, if all went right with the war.

Not a week after the battle between the ironclads, the Gray House was abuzz with news that Union forces were amassing at Fort Monroe, planning to make their way up the Peninsula toward Richmond. Although Jeff Davis shuffled his cabinet like a deck of cards, appointing Aunt Piss secretary of state, for the next two months it was the Union General McClellan who held the deal.

But this was no card-parlor diversion. Come the twenty-second April, five simple sentences in the Richmond *Dispatch* reminded me of all there was to ante, in what I was playing. Those sentences reported that Timothy Webster, one of the alleged Unionists being held in Castle Godwin, was set to die. The first American to be hanged in nearly one hundred years for spying.

I'd never laid eyes on Timothy Webster, couldn't have told him from the king of Prussia. But once that article appeared, I seemed to breathe my every breath with his, to echo his numbered heartbeats with my own. Not just during my wakeful hours, but also the long, awful ones at night. Sleep, if it came at all, brought such horrid, vivid visions that nightmare was not grisly enough a word to describe them.

There were rumors the execution would never happen, that the Confederates wanted to make Webster's life a mere chit in their next round of chaffer and haggle with the Federals. But rumors were like dandelion puffs, they sprung up everywhere those warm spring days, only to prove as delicate as they were plentiful, dissipating in the first hard blow of truth. No one knew when the next blow would come, or what truth it would bring.

By Sunday the twenty-seventh, I was agitated as much with what I didn't know about Webster's imminent demise as with what I did. I was so anxious I couldn't wait for Wilson to return from riding my previous day's missive to Bet's market farm, before I set out to see Papa.

"What's the matter?" Papa asked when I appeared in the doorway of his tiny shed hours earlier than usual.

I longed for the sweet words of Sunday comfort he offered all through my girlhood, whenever I recounted receiving a reprimand or the rare slap from Mistress

Van Lew during our week apart. But all I answered was, "Not a thing."

I bent to loose some mud from my shoe, just to keep his large eyes from meeting my own. "Wilson had an errand to run, made such a ruckus getting ready he woke me. Once I was awake, I didn't see any reason to wait around by myself, when I could be with you instead."

Though Papa didn't reply, he regarded me as if I were a child caught filching a pinch from the sugar jar. I could have cussed myself for giving him reason to wonder over what I was concealing, as we closed up his shed and crossed to the front of the lot, then traversed the blocks between Mahon's smithy and my home—blocks that seemed so much longer when I took them at Papa's pained pace.

"You go on upstairs," I said when we arrived. "I'll be up in a minute, just need to draw some water to boil up supper."

"I'll get the water." He made for the well at the edge of our lot.

I wanted to stop him, but I didn't. I knew no father wants to be told he's too debilitated to take care of his own daughter.

But I also knew Papa didn't have half the strength he once had, between the rheumatism that ached him and the hunger that afflicted all of us. Hungry or not, I grew stronger with each week I slaved in the Gray House. Still, I couldn't let on to Papa how I spent my days laboring, lest he ask me why.

The secret I kept weighed heavy as I watched him reach for the windlass on our well. Just the week before, I'd asked Wilson to lubricate the crank, but grease and time were both in short enough supply that he hadn't yet gotten to it.

Papa turned more slow than steady, the bucket creaking out its long climb. The taut rope appeared to twirl as it rose. Though I knew it was only a visual illusion, it made me think of another rope, the one the Confederates might slip around Timothy Webster's neck that very day. I watched the woven hemp, felt it thick against my throat. Imagined the snap and felt my own body fall.

"No!"

So caught was I in my own gory imaginings, I wouldn't have realized I'd cried aloud, except for the way Papa whipped round to see what was wrong. The windlass slipped his hand, and the full bucket crashed to the bottom of the well.

"Sorry, Mary El," Papa said, though what I read across his face was more shame than sorrow, at finding he hadn't held the windlass sturdy.

"I'm the one who's sorry," I said. "Calling out like that, just because a crow flew by and startled me. Making me startle you."

There didn't seem to be much more for us to say on it. Just as there didn't seem much to do about the wooden water bucket, splintered to pieces against the well bottom. Wilson returned within the hour, and the three of us passed a waterless Sunday that seemed to me a dry and certain omen of what the Confederates would finally do to their convicted spy.

Two days later, Webster was hanged at Camp Lee. Wilson and I learned all about it the morning after, when the news-sheets gave out every detail of the event. They took especial care to relate that when the trigger for the drop was first drawn, the hangman's noose slipped, sending the condemned man falling all the way to the hard-packed earth. *Half hung and partially stunned,* was how the *Dispatch* described him, the reporter telling with greedy, eager words how Webster was raised up a second time, a new rope laid around his neck, and then let to swing in the air, until the very last of life was choked from him. Dead as John Brown was for trying to free the slaves, and Dangerfield Newby for wanting to free his own family. I still couldn't tell Webster from the king of Prussia. But what worried me was whether I could tell his fate from my own.

I was careful to carry on about the Gray House as though I took no notice of the war, had no inkling of how either soldier or spy was meeting his demise. So I set myself to giggling with Sophronia as we beat the carpets clean on the twelfth May. Mama always made a game of the chore, when we changed the Van Lew mansion over to its summer appurtenances each year. She would pick a bright Saturday morning to hang the carpets in the yard, Daisy and Lilly and I shouting and laughing as we clapped at the heavy weaves. I'd tumble into our pallet more exhausted than usual that night, but happy, too, as I anticipated the scent of the lavender Mama would bathe in the next day at Papa's cabin.

The memory lightened my vexed mood, and Sophronia met my exuberance with her own. It was easy enough to play frolicsome, with the intoxicating smell of spring in the air. That was a rare joy, given how the odor of rotting flesh clung to the city most days, reeking reminder that in skirmish after skirmish along the Virginia countryside, the Federals were vanquishing the Confederates.

Far as the horror of war seemed from the Gray House yard that warm morning, still it was close. When we carried the parlor carpet inside to the storage

THE SECRETS OF MARY BOWSER · 459

cupboard in the basement, a loud clap marked precisely how near.

"Just the front door slamming," I reassured Sophronia. With the woolen floor coverings taken up from the hall overhead, any noise came down to us.

"What is it, Jefferson?" we heard from above. "You look a fright."

"They are near, my dear, very near. You and the children must leave Richmond at once."

"But it would take a month to pack up the house! And we couldn't leave you, why who would—"

"You will go," Davis cut off his wife with a rare firmness. "I am putting you on the train to Danville tomorrow morning. I was lucky to get the tickets, with the number of people fleeing the city."

Furniture legs screeched against the bare floor. Queen Varina must have slumped hard into the hall chair.

"We have lost Yorktown and Norfolk, Portsmouth and Gosport, all in a week." Jeff Davis intoned the names like a preacher pronouncing a funereal benediction. "Our navy has destroyed the *Virginia,* to keep it from falling into their hands. We expect Federal boats at Drewry's Bluff within the week."

Drewry's Bluff was all of eight miles, nine at most, from where we stood.

"What it mean, Molly?" Sophronia whispered.

I blinked at her, as though I were as addle-headed as she was. "Who knows what half they say means? He put Mistress in a tizzy, make more trouble for us. And Hortense have our hides if we don't get the rest a them carpets inside."

I strode purposefully back out to the yard, hoping Sophronia hadn't read the interest on my face.

The final day of May was stormy, claps of thunder indistinguishable from the cannon fire that rang outside Richmond. But the morning of Sunday the first June dawned clear. At half-past seven, I made my way past the bodies piled around the Broad Street train station, dead and wounded evidence of the latest Confederate defeat. I was still queasy by the time I crested Church Hill. Though Bet's note said she had a delightful surprise, the visit didn't bode much pleasure for me. Not when it took me away from my only time with Papa.

Bet was pacing the back veranda when I came into the yard, and she fairly pulled me after her into the house, through the hall, and up the stairs. Her pinched face shone with pride as she pushed open the door to what had been her brother John's room. The dark curtains and bed hangings had been changed for new

brocatelle in a bright floral pattern, and a vase of olean-
der stood on the night table.

"Wasn't Mother clever for purchasing the fabric and
storing it away all these months? I never would have
seen the need. But General McClellan must long for a
decent room, after living in camp all this time."

Musket fire crackled in the distance like corn ker-
nels popping in a skillet. How could Bet worry about
window dressings, with battle raging so close by? Did
she really expect Lincoln's general-in-chief to reside
with her if Richmond fell?

She nodded toward a spyglass that stood before
the window. "I had Thomas McNiven bring that a
month ago, and it's been such a use the past day. Do
try it."

I crossed the room and leaned to the eyepiece. It
reminded me of Theodore's treasured opera glasses,
which he loved to show off but had little chance to use,
since Philadelphia's Music Academy didn't allow colored patrons, no matter how rich, among its audience.
Bet had better opportunity to put her ocular device to
service. She might have been instructing me in some
ancient religious rite, her tone was so reverent as she
showed me how to aim the scope.

My gaze swept over the acres of low buildings at Chimborazo, the massive army hospital the

Confederates pitched up a half dozen blocks from the grand homes of Church Hill. Beyond them I saw a strange little globule hovering in the sky due east of the city, just above the Williamsburg Road. A square form dangled beneath it. I wondered to Bet over what it could be.

"Another great work of Union ingenuity," she told me. "A balloon big enough to lift men into the air and carry them over the battle lines, so they may observe the Confederate defenses."

I'd found notes among Jeff Davis's papers about such a thing. A Confederate detail was hastily piecing together precious swathes of silk and varnishing the resulting form, hoping to make a balloon that equaled those of the Federals. But they couldn't master the chemistry to maneuver their aerostat aloft. The Confederates filled their balloon first with hot air, then with gas from the city gasworks, but nothing they tried could give it the rise of the Union air-craft that had Bet beaming so. She might have believed McClellan was up in the balloon himself, admiring the linens she'd put out for him.

"Soon enough, Richmond will surrender," she said. "The Union will be reinstated, and everything will return to how it was." She shook her head, her graying curls swaying like a choir of amen-singers.

"This horrid interim will seem nothing but an awful dream."

I thought of Theodore's opera glass, and the Music Academy. This fine room decorated over for a white man, the shabby shed from which Papa could barely hobble forth to do his work in the smithy. Bet never so much as mentioned Timothy Webster, though I presumed his execution troubled her just as much as me. I was living proof of her opposition to slavery, yet even she thought of the war only as a matter of preserving the Union. *Everything will return to how it was.* Her words set me wondering what colored Virginians might gain should McClellan take the Confederate capital. And what they stood to lose.

With his family away, Jeff Davis turned the Gray House dining room into his military headquarters. So while the rest of Richmond wondered when the snake of a Union army encircling the city might make its venomous strike, I studied Confederate strategy. Outnumbered and surrounded, with little hope of posting a successful defense of the capital, General Bobby Lee sent word from the front informing Davis he meant to do what only a madman or a genius might try. He would put his troops on the offensive, hoping to bluff McClellan into believing the Confederates had superior manpower and munitions.

"Does Lee really have the audacity to manage it?" a young aide-de-camp asked as Sophronia and I served dinner one mid-June day.

A soldier whose high, broad brow offset the raging bush of his beard nodded. Passing behind him with the serving tray, I smelt the scent of horses that hung about his uniform. "Their forces are larger than ours," he said. "But not so large I couldn't ride round them, taking prisoners and supplies where I might."

"But what surprise can we hope to have, General Stuart?" one of the older men asked. "I don't sneeze but I expect some damn Yankee off in Washington responds with a God bless you, they have so many spies among us."

"General Lee knows just what to do with their spies," the corporal who'd brought Lee's missive answered. His words set my heart pit-a-patting so, I struggled to keep the serving platter steady. "We will march two brigades through the streets of Richmond with much hullabaloo. Lee will ask the Richmond news-sheets not to mention a word of it, lest the Union learn that he has troops to spare to send to Jackson. Of course they will print it immediately." Chuckles broke from around the table. "The Federal spies will send word North, and when McClellan receives it, he will never suspect troops are coming to Richmond from the Shenandoah, and not the other way round."

The sternutatory gentleman remained skeptical. "And are the Union field commanders so blind they won't notice Stonewall Jackson leading fifteen thousand troops to join Lee?"

"Magruder will feint an attack from the south. As McClellan moves troops to respond, Jackson's men can slip into place through the gap, then charge from the north."

That would more than dash all Bet's certainty of Richmond's surrender, and the Union's reinstatement.

Aunt Piss gestured for more whiskey. "A bold plan, if it is successful. But in case it is not, perhaps it would be prudent for some of the key government functions to remove to Charlotte." Such a move would place the Louisianan hundreds of miles from advancing Union troops.

"We shall not evacuate the government, nor do anything else their spies may report as weakness," Davis said. "God willing, it will all be over soon."

"They say the same in Washington," Aunt Piss muttered, so low that only I heard him, as I refilled his glass.

———————

Back when I was a girl, one of the most astonishing sites in Richmond was the fisher's stall at First Market, as odiferous as the very depths of the James. It was stocked by a slave as broad as an oak and seeming nearly as tall. His left hand had but a thumb and three fingers, the little pinky gone with not so much as a stump-like remnant left behind. How and where that lost finger went I never knew for sure, though there were whispers his owner made the slave take the saw up in his own right hand to cut it off, punishment for some transgression.

Nine-Fingered Nate, that's what Lilly and Daisy and I set ourselves to calling him, as we shrieked out stories of where his tiny pinky lay, severed and wriggling and bringing a haint's worth of harm on whatever creature it could. We'd screw our voices into kitten yowls and puppy yelps and the cries of helpless children, tormented as we imagined them to be by the diabolical wayward digit. Mama caught us at it once, and when she asked what all the fuss was, Daisy told her it was Nine-Fingered Nate's missing tenth. Mama didn't know what or who she meant at first, till I put in something about the fisher's stall. When Mama realized what we were saying, she got sore as she'd ever been at any of us.

"That man is some mother's son," Mama lectured me. "When she brought him into this world, he had ten fingers and ten toes, and a name she gave him. Not a person on this earth ought to take any of that from him. Just because some slave-owner did, doesn't mean any child of mine better try the same." She made me promise I'd never so much as utter the moniker Nine-Fingered Nate again, nor abide anyone else doing it either. "His name is Shiloh," she said. "And I expect you'll not forget it."

Shiloh was a name no one could forget these days, as stories seeped back from that battle-stead of how high the piles rose of legs and arms hacked off by military surgeons. Pit after pit dug to bury nameless pieces of what had once been whole men, every one of them some mother's son. Each wasted limb lost over the claimed right to cut off another man's pinky, the right to call that other man property. No childhood imaginings could have suffered one negro's pinky to be worth that multitude of pale arms and legs, all that bloody loss.

No one could say what more bloody loss might come if the war continued. Or what might come to negroes especially, if it didn't.

If McClellan learned what I knew of Bobby Lee's ruse, he would surely attack as Aunt Piss feared, capturing Richmond and toppling the Confederate government—returning things to how they were before the war, just as Bet predicted. If the Confederacy fell now, slavery would still stand. But if McClellan, lacking this intelligence, fell for the ruse and retreated, Lee might well seize the great and final triumph that Davis's advisers believed was within his grasp, bringing the war to an altogether different end.

My breath came shallow, as I felt the awful alternatives squeezing in. But still I sensed something deep and near-resolute within me. Some quaverous inkling of another possibility, if I could only determine how it might come to be.

If we want to win the bigger prize, we need be making a gamble or two along the way. McNiven had uttered the words with confidence, justifying all he did to deceive the Confederates and urging me to do the same. Was I ready to take such a gamble now? Could I trust myself with such a choice, keeping my latest intelligence from the Federals to prevent a decisive, ultimate Union victory, knowing I was risking a decisive, ultimate Confederate victory instead?

If the war came to a close now, there would be no emancipation, no matter which side won. But if the war stretched on—what if I lost my espial wager, as Webster lost his?

"You haven't heard a word of what I'm saying, have you?" Wilson's question poked right through my contemplation as he crossed to where I stood by our parlor window.

I gestured toward the panes, pretending it was the latest wagonload of casualties lumbering up Broad Street that had me distracted. "So much suffering and death."

Wilson and I watched a weeping white woman step forward to embrace a ragged, uniform-clad amputee. "That's all the violence of slavery, visited right back on them," he said. "The way you tell it, what gunfire we hear is the very angels singing of liberation."

"But what if the war ends before Lincoln frees the slaves?"

"I do believe that's the first time I've ever heard you entertain the possibility you might have been wrong about anything." He rapped on the window frame to mark the rarity of the occasion. "You know I'm still not sure secession can do the slaves much good. But if this war is meant to bring emancipation, I suppose it's bound to last until it does."

The war might indeed last, if I let it. And so I pressed my lips tight and held his words dear for the next quarter hour as I picked over what trifles I might put into the evening's cipher, resolved not to give any of Lee's plan away.

The Confederate ploy succeeded, and in the weeks that followed, the sounds of battle drew farther and farther off, until by summer's end Richmond heard them only in her dreams. The Federals retreated from Drewry's Bluff. The tocsin bells no longer tolled. Queen Varina and her children returned to the Gray House. Union prisoners swelled the population of the city between flag-of-truce exchanges, Bet tending them as best a woman playing at dementia might. And I kept my role in what I'd wrought secret, even from my husband.

On the thirtieth August, McNiven brought me a tattered clipping from the *New York Tribune,* already a week old and obtained the devil only knows how. He was sitting with Wilson in our parlor when I came home from the Gray House, and he pulled the slip of news-sheet from his pocket before saying so much as good evening to me.

It was a letter Lincoln had written to Horace Greeley, the editor of the *Tribune,* who published it for all the world to see.

> My paramount object in this struggle is to save the Union, and is not either to save or to destroy slavery. If I could save the Union without freeing any slave I would do it, and if I could save it by freeing all the slaves, I would do it; and if

> I could save it by freeing some and leaving
> others alone I would also do that. What I do
> about slavery, and the colored race, I do because
> I believe it helps to save the Union; and what
> I forbear, I forbear because I do not believe it
> would help to save the Union.

As I read aloud, Wilson sank deeper into his chair. "We best accept what this means."

"It means we have to make certain the Union cannot be saved unless the slaves are freed." I made my voice as sure as I could.

"Ay, we maun, and I do believe the lass has awready been seeing to that."

I searched McNiven's face to see what hint he might have that I'd withheld what I knew of General Lee's plan. But his pasty features revealed nothing.

"Plenty of hubbub in the Gray House today," I said, to distract him and Wilson both. "The Confederates have beaten the Federals at Manassas, same as they did last summer. This time, Lee will ride the army into Maryland. He means to invade the Union."

McNiven weighed the threat. "'Tis a ragged force Lee leads, after all this summer's fighting."

I nodded. "Half of Lee's motivation to invade is to raid the farms and shops of Frederick County, to feed and clothe his troops."

"And the other half?" McNiven asked.

"According to Aunt Piss, the Confederate victories of late have impressed Great Britain. He has persuaded Jeff Davis that taking the offensive may yet convince Queen Victoria to recognize the Confederacy as a sovereign nation."

McNiven swatted at the idea like it was a gnat aflight in the late summer evening. "England canna support a war to preserve slavery."

Wilson pointed at the *Tribune* clipping. "Lincoln says the war is for the Union, not for slavery."

"Lincoln will make it a war to end slavery, to keep England from aiding the destruction o' the Union."

I hummed out my hope that McNiven was right, as I set the latest message between the Confederates and Queen Victoria's envoy down in Bet's cipher. I chose each word with especial care, meaning to show Lincoln just what he need do to save his precious Union.

When next I saw McNiven, only ten days later, what he had to tell me wasn't in any newspaper. It was something Lincoln hadn't yet made public knowledge. Even McNiven seemed anxious to hold it secret, intercepting me on my way to the Gray House early one morning.

"He has it writ awready, and gotten his cabinet to agree. A proclamation emancipating all the slaves in the territories in rebellion."

"When?" My heart quickened so, I barely heard my own words over it. "When will they be free?"

"It becomes law the first o' the new year. But Lincoln means to be announcing his plan far sooner than that, for all the world and Queen Victoria especially to hear. All he is awaiting is a Union battle victory, so it seems a move o' strength and not a desperation."

With emancipation at last hanging in the balance, such a victory was just what I would give him.

I was laying the supper table when the telegram arrived at the Gray House on the afternoon of the eighteenth September. Just after the messenger's heavy boots thudded up the curving stairs, Burton Harrison, Davis's secretary, called down for whiskey.

I'd served plenty of liquor at the Davises' dinners and receptions, and during Queen Varina's near daily tête-à-têtes with Aunt Piss. But I'd never known Jeff Davis to take a mid-day tipple. I rushed to fetch the crystal decanter, then hurried up the servants' stairs, anxious to learn whether he wanted the drink to mourn or to celebrate.

When I entered the office, Davis sat ramrod straight, tall even in his desk chair. His bad eye was filmed over, and the steely gray good one stared into space. His face had gone so pale, his high cheekbones might have been chiseled from white marble. I poured out a measure of whiskey, and he drank it in one swallow.

"Read it again," he ordered.

I refilled Davis's glass as the messenger shifted under the weight of his butternut uniform. *"Sharpsburg, Maryland. Mr. President. I have lost well over ten thousand men, dead, wounded, or captured in yesterday's fighting above Antietam Creek. We retreat tonight under cover of dark. General Lee."*

"Ten thousand men," Davis repeated, once he swallowed the second glass of whiskey. "One quarter of Lee's entire army. McClellan couldn't have done much more damage if he'd authored Lee's attack himself."

McClellan may not have written the plan of attack, but I'd ensured he'd read it. I stepped forward to fill Davis's glass a third time, but he waved me away.

"Shall I send a note to the hospitals, to expect the wounded?" Burton Harrison asked.

"And to Hollywood Cemetery, that they will need more gravediggers," I heard Davis answer as I made my own retreat to the servants' stair.

"**Mary El** look like the cat what got the canary," Papa observed as he and Wilson dangled their fishing lines into Shockoe Creek the last Sunday of September.

"Your daughter doesn't care about getting some old canary," my husband said, "so much as she likes getting her way."

Papa gave a harrumph of agreement. "What you let her get her way over this time?"

"Wasn't me, Lewis. It was President Lincoln. And doesn't she look glad about it."

I grinned over at them from where I sat, mending Papa's workshirt. I took frugal care with the thread, which had grown wildly expensive because of the blockade. But I wasn't so parsimonious with my joy, which I was eager to share. "Wilson's just sore that I've been right all along, and now everyone knows it."

"Right about what?" Papa asked. "You two might stop talkin' nonsense long enough for a person to make out what you got to say."

"I've been telling Wilson that President Lincoln meant to free the slaves. And now Mr. Lincoln has finally announced it himself. A proclamation of emancipation, is what it's called."

Papa looked at us as though this were proof we were both mutton-headed. "What it matter what Lincoln is proclamating over to Washington, when I got to do Mahon's bidding here in Richmond?"

"I know it doesn't change anything right away, Papa. But it puts slaves in a new legal standing. As of the first January, all the slaves in the Confederacy will be considered free. Once the war is over—"

"As of the first January?" Papa cut in. "Once the war is over? Mary El, I see you mighty impressed with that Mr. Lincoln fellow for all this proclamating. But maybe somebody should tell him it don't do much good to take out the bit if you leave on the bridle."

"I don't suppose it does." Wilson spoke softly, worried Papa's sharp words had hurt me. But they hadn't. They just strengthened my resolve to shake the bridle off.

I knew full well the many ways that being free, or slave, meant more than just a word written out here or there on legal parchment in someone else's hand. All those years apart from Mama and Papa in Philadelphia, I'd never felt my freedom quite the way I did these days in Richmond, play-acting at slavery as I worked to make Lincoln's proclamation become true liberation for my papa.

Nineteen

There I was, a grown woman of twenty-three, looking forward to Christmas with the same delicious anticipation I had as a child. In my girlhood, Richmond always slowed its pace the final week of the year, hired-out slaves gone home to the plantations, whites and free blacks alike keeping to their families. Not so in 1862. The city's population was swollen to three times what it was before the war, and you didn't have to be a census taker to note the difference. White and colored, everyone was crowded in. The noise and press of the place wasn't about to let up, no matter what the calendar said. But Papa would have the whole week off, same as always. And posing as a hired slave, so would I.

Spending Christmas week with Papa promised to be sweeter than all the molasses seized in the Federal blockade. I beamed as the days of December fell shorter and shorter still, knowing that as Papa's holiday with us neared, so did the day Abraham Lincoln would proclaim him legally free.

I wasn't credulous enough to believe the Emancipation Proclamation would change much of anything for Papa, so I took it upon myself to do for him what Mr. Lincoln couldn't. The Monday between Christmas and New Year's, I left him with Wilson, crossed Shockoe Creek, and turned south toward the Bottom, passing factories all along Franklin Street and Main Street that had been turned into hospitals. Blocks once fragrant with tobacco now wreaked of wasting flesh, the slaves and free blacks who manned the tobacco presses before the war these days tending wounded Confederates. Richmond newspapers made much ado over the white ladies who visited the hospitals, never mentioning that the nastiest work there was left to negroes.

Where the factories gave way to residences, I searched out Mahon's house. Two stories topped by a half attic, the brick building was just wide enough to show that its owner had a successful business, yet plain enough to suggest he still worked with his hands. Only two steps separated the front entrance from Franklin Street, and when I mounted them and rapped the brass knocker, Mahon swung the door open himself. His face lengthened in surprise at finding a colored woman on his stoop.

"Marse Mahon, I'm Mary Bowser, Lewis's daughter. If you can give me a moment, sir, I'd like to discuss some business with you."

He crossed his arms and leaned against the doorjamb. I'd have to say my piece right in the street, if I wanted to be heard at all.

"My papa is too infirm now to be much good at the forge. My husband and I would like to buy his time from you, sir. We can pay in advance for the year, no guarantee of refund required from you in the case of—"

"Can't be done," Mahon interrupted.

I'd known he might well refuse, had schemed and planned about what I'd say if he did. But Mahon didn't give me a chance to utter any of the persuasives I'd prepared.

"They've conscripted him, along with the rest of my slaves, to work for the defense of the city. He's theirs as of next week."

I could make no sense of what he was saying. "What use could Papa be to the government? He can barely cross a room, how is he supposed to—"

"No one asked your opinion of it. No one even asked mine." His voice rang with the angry rhythm of anvil blows. "Man can't make a living without trained laborers to work his smithy. But President Davis and Governor Letcher don't give a good goddamn about an honest man's ability to provide for his family."

I bit my lip, thinking of all the years Papa had provided for Mahon's family rather than for me and Mama. Thinking, too, that there'd be no appeal, no bargaining over the conscription. Wilson and I might have had every dollar in the Confederate Treasury, and still we couldn't have bought Papa's time. I pulled my shawl tight and turned to go.

"Lewis don't know yet," Mahon called after me. "You might as well tell him yourself."

One more chore a negro can do for you, I thought as I headed back to Broad Street.

I hadn't told Papa I was going to speak to Mahon. Wilson and I agreed to hold it for a surprise, neither of us saying what we both feared—best not to raise his hopes in case Mahon refused. Now the news I bore was worse than a refusal. Mahon had reason enough to look after his slaves, property as they were to him. But what did the city of Richmond or the Confederate military care for the well-being of an aging bondsman, when with an order of conscription they could call up a dozen more to replace him?

Wilson saw with a single glance that I hadn't succeeded with Mahon. Prevaricating came so easy to me by then, I didn't even have to think before the words came out. "I got all the way to the market, only to realize I'd forgotten my purse. Would you go back to get the things we need for dinner while I warm up before the fire?"

He nodded at my falsehood, understanding that I wanted to be alone with Papa.

Once Wilson left, I pulled two chairs up before the hearth. Sitting beside Papa, every ounce of joy I felt over the Emancipation Proclamation seeped away. Conscription laid bare the one truth I wasn't able to make untrue. So long as we lived under the Confederacy, my own flesh and blood remained a belonging to change hands among white men, same as a mule or a hog.

I held my gaze on the fire, unable to meet those eyes that were so like mine. "What was it like for Mama, knowing she had her freedom but had to act like she didn't?"

"Minerva always was one to follow her own mind, slave or no," Papa reminded me. "She figured out long before then how to be one thing in her heart, though she was something else in the eyes of them Van Lews."

"Was she sorry she wasn't living free, though?" What was I asking? Did she die a bitter, regretful woman? Did she berate herself for the decision she agonized over for so long? Was she sorry she chose Papa over me?

"Every damn day of her life. 'Course she was sorry, we both was. I still is. What kind of fool wouldn't be sorry to be a slave?"

Marking how heavy his words fell on me, Papa gave out a "Look here, Mary El," in that tone I'd heard all through my girlhood. The one a father takes when he needs to convince his daughter of something he fears she is too much a child to understand. "The greatest hurt of Minerva's life was when she got took from her family. They didn't know then freedom time was coming for slaves in New York, just that Virginia was far off, and they never seed anyone go that far and come back again. But much as that hurt her, Minerva never said a word on losing her family to me, till after you was born."

This revelation caught me in surprise. I wouldn't have guessed there was a thing in the world my parents didn't share with each other. At least that's how it seemed when they carried on together every Sunday, me scheming to make out what they were saying.

"You come just past dawn on a Friday," Papa said. "I didn't even hear about it till after. Josiah brought word to me down at my cabin, but it weren't like I could leave off from the smithy and appear on the Van Lews' doorstep, asking to see my wife and child." He shook his head at the memory. "After all them years we didn't have no baby, I was crazy for them first two days to pass, till I could see you. Minerva was late coming on Sunday, worrying me the whole while. Mistress Van Lew didn't want to let her away, say she take sick walking so far right after her lying in. Minerva throwed a fit, saying she was well enough to bring her baby to its Papa.

"When I seed you that first time, it were like seeing how much I loved Minerva and she loved me, all add up to a whole new person. She was sore from the nursing, sent me to fetch her some sugar of Saturn for the pain. When I come back, I heard crying from the cabin. Not a baby, a grown woman, howling with grief. I went wild, thinking something happent to you. Thinking maybe we wasn't getting a child to raise up after all. I bolted inside and saw you was fine, setting right in her arms with a look of perplexation on your face, like you was trying to make sense of what was happening."

He swallowed hard, living it all over again. "Minerva was sobbing for her own mama, her sisters and brother, too. Sobbing at the thought she was gonna lose you like she lost them. Sobbing at the thought she wasn't, and you'd live and die slave to the Van Lews, just like her." Tears welled his eyes, mine, too. "Ain't a slave in the world don't wanna be free. But there ain't one wouldn't rather stay slave to know their baby don't have to."

"But she was free, Papa, those last five years. And come next week, you will be, too. Union troops are two days ride down the James River. Wilson could bring us out there in his cart."

He frowned at me. "Mary El, I don't know what all you got yourself mixed up in since you come back here. Don't know if you got Wilson in it, maybe even that Miss Bet you still running off to see so much. I don't ask 'cause I see you don't wanna tell. But I know you come back for that as much as for me."

I ducked my chin, ashamed I hid so much from him. Even more ashamed that he guessed the pull of my work was just as great as the pull of loving him. He leaned over and kissed the top of my head, just like when I was a child.

"I don't lose no love for Mahon, but I can do my work for him till the good Lord take me home. Got you to comfort me till then, and Minerva waiting to welcome me on the other side."

I curled my fingers around his rheumatic hand, steeling myself to the task of relating what Mahon wasn't man enough to tell Papa. "You aren't going to work in the smithy anymore. You'll have to work for the Confederates. Digging trenches maybe, or building earthworks. Tending the soldiers at Camp Lee. Could be anything. Maybe harder even than what you did for Mahon." Though it made my heart ache, I knew the choice I had to make. "So maybe we should think on leaving Richmond after all."

He went quiet a long moment, weighing the full measure of what I'd said before he spoke again. "Whatever you up to here, you believe it's Jesus's plan for you?"

I sidled my way toward all that was contained in that question. I never knew how much true heed Papa gave Mama's talk of Jesus's plan, though she professed it loud and long and strong enough for all of us. I still wasn't sure how much heed to give it myself. "If He has one, then I suppose this must be it."

He stared hard at our entwined hands, like he didn't quite recognize which was part of himself. "Seem like I lost Jesus, somewhere back when Minerva passed. But I ain't no husband to betray the one thing his wife prayed on most. Ain't no father to tell his daughter not to do what she meant for. Seems we best stay."

I might have argued it with him, but instead I loosed my fingers from his and rose to lay another log on the hearth fire, watching it catch flame as I settled back in my chair.

———————

After Papa reported for conscription, I hounded McNiven until he somehow discovered that Papa was assigned to the blacksmith shop at the Confederate Arsenal. The Arsenal was eight blocks from our house, down Seventh Street on the south side of Kanawha Canal, just above the James. But Papa, held behind the heavy walls that enclosed the Armory, might as well have been a thousand miles away. There'd be no more Sunday visits, no supplementing his meager rations, no remedies for his rheumatism. No way for me to tell if he was faring well or ill.

Wilson tried to comfort me, saying we were lucky even to know where he was, when most families of conscripted slaves didn't have that much. Lucky he had a skill worth something to the Confederates. Lucky he wasn't worse off than he was.

But none of it seemed lucky to me. Papa was likely working sixteen hours a day before the forge, making bayonet stocks for Confederates to use to impale the very men who were fighting to make him as free in fact as he was by law. It was like a cruel joke, the way everything turned worse for him once the Emancipation Proclamation was signed. His liberation seemed to be slipping ever further away, like a trick of light refracting along some distant and unreachable horizon.

The last day of January had me on my knees, scrubbing streaks of who knows what the children had grimed along the wall of the nursery. Hortense and Sophronia were downstairs, laying the table for another of the martial dinners Jeff Davis now hosted with such frequency. Queen Varina must have caught sight of all the places they were setting, because she stormed into her husband's office, her flint-and-steel temper striking loud enough to be heard right through the wall.

"Jefferson, do you realize that a turkey costs thirty dollars these days, and coffee is twenty times what it was three years ago? How am I to run this household with a hundred-dollar dinner three times a week, no income from Brierfield, and only your meager salary to keep us?"

"Our soldiers are living on eighteen ounces of flour and four ounces of pork fat a day. Do you suppose there is a one of them who wouldn't give his month's wages for a turkey?" Davis hacked liked a whole ward of lung disease patients. "You spend twice what this meal costs to host luncheons for Mary Chesnut and the Preston girls."

"If I entertain the wives and daughters of important men, it's only so the people might have a chance to love and admire their president. You are so much a general, and not enough a politician. I must tend to the difference."

"There will be time enough for politicking when the war is won. But so long as the recapture of Fort Donelson, the skirmishing at Mingo Swamp, and the protection of the Yazoo Pass occupy me, military men shall occupy our dining room."

Queen Varina couldn't have known half what he was talking about. She probably couldn't even have pointed to those places on a map. But I smiled and set myself back to leaching the Davis children's dirt from the cream and rose clusters of the wall paper, satisfied that my afternoon's service in the dining room would furnish me with plans of the Confederate forces in Tennessee, Missouri, and Mississippi.

The day's snow had turned to rain by the time I left the Gray House, but I hardly marked the downpour as I made my way among the crowds on Broad Street. General Joseph Wheeler was preparing to move two brigades of cavalry on Dover, Tennessee, in an effort to overtake the Federals who held Fort Donelson. I rushed upstairs to set down the day's report, as though my haste could marshal the Union forces that much faster. Only after I finished encoding the message did I trouble myself that Wilson wasn't home, wasn't in his shop either.

I ran my finger along the stack of writing paper McNiven brought me the week before. Paper was such a dear commodity these days, Wilson joked the pickets along Osborne Turnpike could arrest him just for finding a sheet of it on his person, whether they could decode the message inscribed on it or no. I hadn't seen the humor in such jesting, and his absence now didn't have me any more amused.

With the last bit of light disappearing from the sky, I tried to occupy myself by starting supper, as though all that was fretting me was the thought of Wilson coming home tardy and teasing me about my poor cooking. As the pot of dried peas came to a boil, I heard the door swing open and my husband's familiar footfall on the stairs. But when Wilson entered our kitchen, the vexation tugging at his face told me there was yet more to worry about.

He hung back, holding fast to his news. Whatever he didn't want to tell, I didn't want to hear. The silence pulled on both of us like a leaden weight, until at last he said, "McNiven just got word, Lewis is at Howard's Grove."

The hospital out on Mechanicsville Turnpike was where they put smallpox patients, hoping it was far enough beyond the city limits that they wouldn't spread the epidemic. "How long has he been there?"

"Heard it was a week Tuesday."

Today was already Saturday. Papa'd probably been infected two weeks before anyone realized he had smallpox. And then he'd lain suffering eleven days, without me even knowing. "Please don't let tomorrow morning be too late."

I didn't realize I'd said the words aloud, until Wilson answered. "You can't go up there. It's too contagious."

"Mama and I were vaccinated, back when the Van Lews were."

Wilson found faint comfort in that. "Maybe you've noticed there's no vaccination scar on my arm."

I told him I would stay with Bet while I nursed Papa. The Van Lew mansion was a mile and a quarter closer to Howard's Grove anyway. "Will you find McNiven first thing tomorrow, tell him he needs to come up with a story for Queen Varina about why his slave won't be serving her the next little while?"

"From what you say, that woman doesn't have the patience to wait for a hired girl." Wilson's eyes searched mine. "How are you going to feel if you go to Lewis and then lose your place at the Gray House?"

"How am I going to feel if I don't?"

The next morning, I gripped my satchel in one hand and my skirts in the other, navigating the mud of

Mechanicsville Turnpike as the earliest dawn lit the sky. When I arrived at Howard's Grove, I searched out the row of buildings flying white flags, the sign for smallpox wards. I was halfway to them when a dog came barking at me.

Before I could get it to hush, a voice called, "Halt there."

Maybe the potbellied private was happy at first to draw homeguard duty, rather than being sent into battle. But turning to face him, I could see he didn't much care for watching over a contagion, nor for being woken early on a Sunday. He'd jumped out of bed so fast when he heard the barking that he forgot his cap, and rain cascaded down his bald pate.

I bowed my kerchiefed head. "Morning, Marse."

"What do you mean, sneaking about this here facility?"

"Come to tend one of the patients over to the colored hospital, sir."

He snorted. "We got doctors for that. Don't need no darkies coming by, stirring up trouble, spreading the pox."

"I's vaccinated. Mistress done it years ago."

"I don't care if Mistress jigged with the cow that had the pox." He gestured toward the turnpike with his rifle. "Now git."

I might have told him it had been decades since anyone used cows to vaccinate against smallpox. But I didn't suppose he'd take kindly to a medical lesson from a negro. As the white flags flapped in the rising wind, I turned from where Papa lay and headed back to Richmond.

It took me three-quarters of an hour to reach the Van Lew mansion, and not much more than three-quarters of a minute for Bet to pronounce her solution, once I told her what had transpired. "William Carrington is a fair man. He always sees to it the Federal prisoners in his charge get adequate medical care." To her, that was the singular mark of a person's decency, but I knew it was no guarantee a prominent FFV would have sympathy for a slave. Still, I was relieved when she marched over to Carrington Row, the austere block of Church Hill, intent on securing me a pass from her neighbor, the surgeon inspector of Richmond's hospitals.

She came back just as the St. John's bell was tolling for the morning service. Her pursed lips and pinched brow confirmed what I already feared—though some people survived the smallpox, Dr. Carrington's prognosis for anyone lying in the colored ward at Howard's Grove was grim. When I thanked her for the pass, she waved my words away and tramped out to the carriage house, harnessing the horse to her gig so she could ride me back to the hospital.

We arrived to find the private huddled beneath a lean-to that served as the hospital guardhouse. I raised the umbrella so that Bet could sit up a bit straighter as she reined the horse to a halt. She handed down the pass as though she were General Beauregard presenting the man with his marching orders. "Here is a letter from Dr. Carrington, directing that my servant is to nurse a patient in the colored hospital."

The private pulled out a soiled handkerchief and mopped at his face. "I don't take my orders from anyone but Captain Babkan, usually."

"Perhaps you would care to find out for yourself whether the surgeon inspector of Richmond outranks your captain. You would have ample time to review the order of command if you were sentenced to a month in Castle Thunder for insubordination."

At the mention of the military prison, he squinted at the pass, waving his handkerchief like a flag of surrender. "She's welcome to tend the lot of them. Skittish as most darkies are, I don't suppose she can bear the stink in there for long."

Bet smiled, pleased as ever to get her way with a Confederate. And so long as it served me and Papa, I was pleased enough to let her.

But not even the sentry's taunting prepared me for the misery of the negro ward. It was a dreary, windowless shed of ten foot by twelve. The air so fetid with rotting flesh, the scented flannel I held over my mouth and nose barely kept me from gagging. Dozens of pox sufferers lay in miserable heaps on the dirt floor. Hideous bumps distorted their features so, it took me several minutes to recognize Papa.

"It's Mary El," I whispered, kneeling beside him.

"What you doing here?" His voice cracked as he strained to make out my face in the darkness.

"I've come to tend you."

"I don't want you here."

"Don't worry, Mama and I were vaccinated against the smallpox years ago. Remember?"

He moved his head, just barely, toward a wretched woman huddled about two feet away. Papules crusted across her skin. "I look like that?"

I nodded. Truth was, he looked worse.

"Don't want you remembering me like that. Go on now." He grimaced and closed his eyes, slipping into a delirium so deep he didn't realize I was still there.

In the long hours that followed, I saw that his condition was even worse than I'd feared. Pustules coating the inside of his mouth and throat kept him from drinking the water or swallowing the pot liquor I'd brought. Giant scabs of pus encrusted his arms and legs—confluent smallpox, the deadliest form of the disease. If he shed a massive scab, he would surely succumb to an infection of the exposed flesh. That would mean a miserable, rotting death, though I didn't know if it would bring him more suffering than dying of thirst would.

Immune though I was from contracting smallpox, I felt sick with grief when I emerged from Howard's Grove that evening. It wasn't much comfort to find McNiven waiting for me. "Take this to Bet, lass," he said, holding out a small brown bottle labeled laudanum.

Queen Varina and her friends resorted to the drug every time they had so much as a sick-headache. But I could hardly imagine Bet desiring to grow dull and languid as a laudanum user.

"What use does she have for this?"

"Not she, he"—McNiven jerked his head in the direction of the hospital—"what she will be tending. Tomorrow be Monday, and Varina Davis will be wanting her maid. Likewise the Federals will be wanting word o' the Confederate movements at Vicksburg."

"I don't much care what Varina Davis wants," I said. "Nor the Federals. I'll be spending the day nursing my papa. And as many days more until he passes."

496 · LOIS LEVEEN

"Aye, so he is dying. What need you to sit watch as he does, when he will not be the better for it, and others will be much the worse? Since Fredericksburg, the tide has changed to favor the Confederates. We maun gain the Mississippi, or all will be lost."

What more did I have to lose? Mama was long dead. Papa lay ravaged by smallpox. Wilson and I had passed a worrisome year, prickling with apprehension as one after another, supposed spies were hanged in Richmond—after Webster, we never even spoke of the executions, though each of us marked the news-sheet reports closely. And now McNiven thought fit to order me to give up my last days with Papa in order to slave to Queen Varina. I didn't say another word before walking past him to head down Mechanicsville Turnpike.

When I arrived on Church Hill, Bet led me up to what nine months before she'd declared General McClellan's room. The vase beside the bed stood empty, and the spyglass was put away. The bright floral pattern of the appurtenances made a mockery of Bet's hope for Union victory—and mine for Papa's freedom.

She lit the fire, then brought me some supper. I didn't care much for eating, and when she left me, I dozed fretfully, haunted by nightmares of orange-haired ogres whose monstrous bodies were riddled with stinking, pus-filled protuberances. I awoke confused, reaching for Wilson, until I remembered how I'd quarantined myself from him. Lonely in the dark, still mansion, I slipped up to the garret that had been Mama's and my quarters.

I was startled to find the room stripped bare. Mama hadn't left anything worth wanting when we moved to Papa's cabin after Bet gave us our freedom. And I'd been glad enough to quit the newer furnishings when I married Wilson. But still, it jarred me to see the space empty, as though all memory of me and Mama had been cleared out along with the scuffed table or the brass candlestick.

Finding no comfort in the empty attic, I stole back down the servants' stair. A taper flickered in the second-floor hall, and I made out the broad form of Bet's mother.

"I hope I didn't wake you, ma'am," I said as I came along the corridor.

"I am more awake than asleep, most nights. It is the curse of age. Perhaps you would care to sit up with me a while, as long as you are wakeful, too?"

It was a request, I reminded myself, not a command. And her company might at least distract me some. "Thank you," I said. "I suppose I would."

I followed her into her dressing room, and we settled into the matching hunter green armchairs. "How is Lewis?" she asked.

"Very bad off. I don't expect he can recover."

She stared at the reflection of the candle in her dressing table mirror. "I lost my own father to an epidemic. Yellow fever." The disease had ravaged Philadelphia years back, coming in nearly annual outbreaks. "He was the mayor, and he stayed in town out of a sense of duty. Sent his family to the country, but didn't think to save himself."

"At least he had the choice to stay or go." It was the only time in all my life I ever sassed her. But her response came in a defeated sigh.

"Do you think that was much comfort to his widow? Or to his infant daughter, who never knew her own father? Be thankful you'll have memories of Lewis to carry with you after he's gone."

What I wouldn't give to forget the memory of him today, I thought, watching the molten wax of the burning candle form into a bulb, round and swollen like the pustules on Papa's skin. The curved mass burst, sending a stream of wax to settle at the base of the candlestick.

The same brass candlestick that had been removed from the attic quarters.

I polished the silver so often in my childhood, I could still recall every detail of the ornate candleholders that had graced my mistress's dressing room, a wedding gift from the weathiest of Old Master Van Lew's New York aunts. "Where are your Boelen candlesticks?" I asked.

"Sold. Along with the rest of the silver, all my china, and half the furniture from the drawing room. It is for the best, I suppose. Less to keep up, now that we are on our own."

I recalled Bet kneeling to light the fire hours earlier, carrying the supper tray to me herself. The plain dishes on which the meager fare of boiled turnips and potatoes were served. On the other side of Shockoe Creek, the auction houses along Main and Cary streets put household lots to sale nearly every day, because so many families on Church Hill were reduced to selling off their most treasured heirlooms just to keep from going hungry. I hadn't realized the Van Lews might be among them.

My former mistress forced her mouth into a tight smile. "At least we haven't yet had to take in boarders, like half the neighborhood has. It's their just deserts for rushing us into this war, though I suppose we all suffer its costs."

I knew the costs she meant were more than financial. The war had become a living hell to the men who fought it and the women who mourned them, North and South. Even more soldiers succumbed to dysentery and cholera than to gunshot wounds or cannon fire. And soldiers weren't the only ones dying of disease.

We all got to die. Suddenly I heard the words Mama had used to scold and comfort me after she left this world for the next. *What matters is what comes first. That's what a child's for, living long after her mama and papa are gone. And if you don't start living again, how you gonna do Jesus's work?*

Mama had known plenty about living through suffering. All slaves do. And now white Richmond did, too.

I shivered as though the stench of death that permeated the city had seeped right inside me. What was smallpox but another form of suffering in a world full of pain and misery? What was I but another woman left to make sense of the devastating loss that left no family untouched?

But Mama's words reminded me that I had something to sustain me that the denizens of Church Hill did not. The hope of better days for my people, if not for my papa.

Bidding Bet's mother good night, I crossed the hall. I kept a sleepless but certain vigil through the next lonely hours. Before dawn's earliest streaks even touched the eastern sky, I woke Bet, asking her to do for me what no one else could, so that I might be at the Gray House as usual that morning. It was the second greatest gift she'd yet given me, after my freedom—her promise to sit beside my father just as devoutly as eighteen years earlier she'd sat beside her own.

I came home the following evening well versed in the latest reports of grain shipments to Vicksburg, evidence that the Confederates there were preparing to endure a siege of many months. But I could barely endure telling Wilson what harrowed thoughts I had of Papa.

"You think I did wrong, not taking him out of Richmond to his freedom when I had the chance?" I asked as we sat upon our sofa.

"I don't imagine there was a right or wrong to it."

I wanted to believe him. But I'd agitated for the war, had deliberately held back information to prolong it, and never fathomed the toll it might take on Papa. "You can't understand what it's like, feeling responsible for my own papa's death."

"I understand it better than you know. I never told you how my parents died."

Never told were words that signaled something dear for Wilson, given all he held secret of what he saw in his years of Railroad work—and all he held in of the petty hurts and humiliations that piled up for a free man in slavery-loving Virginia. I hated being reminded of any anguish my beloved husband kept from me. "You said it was an accident, when you were just a child." I'd never gotten him to yield any more detail of their deaths than that, aside from the fact that his grandparents raised him after his parents were gone.

"I was a child, all right. Only seven, but already old enough to fish and love it. One fine Sunday, I begged my father to take me fishing. My sister Lucy was just turned five and wanted to come along, too. So my mother packed a picnic lunch, and we walked up the James, above Mayo's Bridge. From the Manchester side, you could wade right in until you came to a nice flat rock, big enough to hold a family." Something shifted in his voice as he uttered that last word. "We were having a fine old time, eating and laughing, my parents clapping with pride whenever I caught a fish, until out of nowhere the waters started to rise. Happened so fast, we noticed the shouting of the other people on the river before we marked the flood itself."

He rubbed his palms against his trouser legs, like he was trying to hold himself in place. "My father grabbed Lucy, told my mother and me to swim for shore as best we could. Young as I was, somehow I made it across. But the weight of my mother's skirts pulled her under. I got to the riverbank in time to see a twelve-foot log float hard against my father as he clutched Lucy. It pushed them down the James until they disappeared from view."

I laid my hands over his, wishing I could comfort the boy who stood alone on that riverbank.

"More than twenty people died in the James that day, a crowd watching in horror from the shore not able to do a damn thing to save them. But only three of the drowned were there because I'd begged and pleaded to go fishing, when the rest of my family would have been content to stay at home."

"That flood wasn't your fault," I said.

Wilson nodded. "Just like the smallpox epidemic isn't yours."

"But I knew the risk when Papa was conscripted, and still I chose to stay in Richmond rather than take him away."

"That's what it is to be free. Free to make a choice, not knowing all that's going to happen once the choice is made. That's the hardest part of it."

Hard didn't begin to describe how heavy it weighed on me. "Nearly two years of war and still no end in sight. I feel too tired to go on."

"All those trips I brought baggage North, I damn sure grew tired of it. But I'd given up something of myself to serve those people, and tired didn't give me the right to stop." Wilson settled a soothing kiss on me. "Everyone's tired of this war, from Mr. Lincoln on down. Hell, I wager even your Bet is tired of carrying on crazy, and I never thought I'd see that day come."

I smiled despite myself at that last part, just like he knew I would.

But Bet was somber and wan when next we saw her, and I sure wasn't smiling then. It was just two evenings later, when she came to tell us Papa was gone. The cold fact of it was all she could bring back to me. Colored or white, the infectious corpses of the smallpox dead met the same ignominious end—the incinerator at Howard's Grove. Fire vanquished the blacksmith at last, leaving me nothing to bury beside his precious Minerva.

Twenty

Many a slave lived a whole lifetime never knowing her own papa, nor her mama. Sales tore countless others from cherished families, with no way for parent or child to know thereafter how the other fared. I knew my childhood was a rare respite within bondage, me losing my parents only to death, when most slaves, even my own mama and papa, lost theirs long before. But *many* and *countless* and *rare respite* proved scant comfort in the months after Papa died. Whatever deception I put on in the Gray House, I couldn't deceive myself about how bitter the draught of mourning, how much it burdened. As the yoke of slavery chafed more terrible, I resolved to find a way to do yet more to rout the Confederacy.

———————

"Do you have it?" Aunt Piss was barely inside the library of a February afternoon, before Queen Varina made her demand.

"My dear Mrs. Davis, does a gentleman ever break his word to a lady?" He bowed and handed her a gold-leaf and leather-bound volume. "It came through the blockade just today."

"You are too kind, Secretary Benjamin." She signaled me to unlatch the humidor as he set himself in her husband's rocker. "I declare I have been as lonesome for Jean Valjean and Cosette as I have for my own people in Alabama. To think the Yankees should have the pleasure of Mr. Hugo's *Les Misérables,* when all we have is—"

"Lee's miserables," Aunt Piss finished, his greedy fingers picking a selection of Jeff Davis's finest cigars while he and his fawning hostess chuckled at his joke about the half-starved troops.

Aunt Piss rocked forward. "But I am afraid I must keep you from your literary diversions a few moments longer, in order to discuss some important business I have for the president." He reached for the nutcracker and the bowl of pecans. "I have authored a proclamation" (crack) "for a day of prayer and fasting" (crack) "on behalf of the Confederacy" (crack). "Once I have secured your husband's signature—"

A commotion in the entrance hall cut him off, a voice that struck me as half-familiar shrilling, "I must see Mrs. Davis."

The library door burst open, pushed in by a white lady whose aging face was red with exertion. "Mrs. Davis, I'm sure you will pardon the intrusion. I believe my cousin, Mrs. Gardner, may have mentioned me to you. My name is Mrs. Whitlock."

I started in surprise. The intruder hardly resembled the elegant woman I remembered from Bet's mother's sewing circle. Faded patches on her green grosgrain dress revealed that the once stylish garment had been made over twice at least. Her features appeared even harder worn than her gown.

Fearing she might mark my presence and recall my connection to the Van Lews, I repaired to the fireplace, kneeling to poke at the coals while Queen Varina admonished her for the unwanted interruption. "I receive visitors every second Thursday, Mrs. Whitman. In the drawing room."

"Not Whitman. I am a Whitlock," she said. "And I wish to make a personal request in confidence, not in front of other guests you might receive on Thursday."

"I am speaking with a visitor of great importance to the president," Queen Varina answered, but Aunt Piss was already standing to go.

"Mrs. Davis, please allow me to take my leave. It is clear this lady"—he turned and made a bow to Mrs. Whitlock—"must have business more urgent than mine. I shall come see you tomorrow."

Once he was gone, Queen Varina offered only an impertinent, "Well?" without bothering to invite her visitor to sit.

"I understand a number of ladies have taken posts in the Treasury Department, as clerks in the note signing room. I should like one."

"Places are very hard to get," Queen Varina said. "I cannot secure one for just anybody who barges into my home." She couldn't secure one at all, really. She had no influence at the government bureaus. But she was too conceited to admit that, and Mrs. Whitlock was too desperate to realize it.

"Surely you will help me. My cousin Mrs. Gardner was a great intimate of yours, when you first arrived in Richmond."

"I have many intimates. I tell you, there are no places in the Treasury."

"Well there must be something somewhere. Here in the house, perhaps? You can use a housekeeper, surely?"

A Church Hill matron, begging to take Hortense's place? Queen Varina scoffed. "You don't expect the president to take a white lady to labor in his household."

"What I didn't expect was that I'd see the day when niggers would be given food and shelter by the very leaders of our people, while widows from the best families in Richmond are left to starve."

Queen Varina took quick stock of Mrs. Whitlock's green dress. "What widow goes about in such attire? How am I to know who or what you really are?"

"Do you know how hard it is to find black cloth in Richmond? Last month I sold the summer mourning I'd worn since Major Whitlock was killed at First Manassas, so that my daughter and I might eat for another fortnight. I'd already given the winter mourning put away from when my mother passed some fifteen years ago to my daughter, to make over for herself." She smiled an ugly, awful smile. "I have lost a husband and son. She has lost a father, a brother, and a betrothed. Don't you agree her grief outranks even mine?"

"I should think if something were to happen to my own dear husband, my heart would be too broken to go about insulting decent ladies in their own homes."

"The only hearts left unbroken in Richmond are the many that have stopped beating." Mrs. Whitlock's eyes narrowed hard on Queen Varina. "Or those whose blood has always run cold. Good day, Mrs. Davis."

She stormed out, leaving Queen Varina to settle back on the meridienne with Mr. Hugo's novel.

Queen Varina departed for Montgomery first thing on Friday, the thirteenth of March, to visit her ailing father. She'd whined and repined ever since her family had to leave Louisiana, as though the Howells were the only refugees in the whole of the Confederacy. It was a relief once she was off, her supercilious lady's maid Betsy, the ill-disciplined Davis children, and their indolent nursemaid Catherine along with her. After a three-week illness, Jeff Davis was feeling well enough to return to his office at the old Customs House, on the far side of Capitol Square. Which left Hortense, Sophronia, and me plenty of time to scour the empty Gray House.

It wasn't quite noon when we set to straightening the nursery. "Look like bedlam broke loose in here. Smell even worse," Hortense said. "Molly, open them windows."

I pushed against the sash until the swollen wood frame slid a few inches, letting the first fresh air of the season into the room.

"Too cold," Sophronia said as she righted the doll's tea set.

But Hortense showed no sympathy. "I'm sure I don't hear no moaning from no one got fat enough on 'em to keep warm." She never seemed to notice cold nor heat herself, and she had little patience for those of us who did.

We worked wordless after that, until a sudden rumble sounded outside.

"Yankees?" Sophronia asked.

"Never mind if they is," Hortense said. "Till them bluecoats is in the parlor, don't mean nothing to us." But I saw the curiosity writ across her face.

The noise wasn't cannon, the booming low and steady, not like the angry bursts from the big field guns we heard the previous spring. Not letting on that I marked the difference, I turned to stripping the bed linens, musing over what the thunderous sound might mean.

I discovered the rest of the city was just as curious, when I pushed my way through the crowds lining Richmond's streets that evening. Rumors hung in the acrid air along with smoke that stung my eyes and throat. An explosion, someone said. Down at Brown's Island, in the Confederate Ordnance Laboratory. Scores of workers killed. Some crushed to death under the collapsed building. Others burned alive. Still more drowned after throwing themselves afire into the James. Most of the rest scorched and scarred so badly, they weren't likely to survive.

I slowed alongside a crowd of whites gathered in front of Broad Street Methodist Church. A boy stood atop the church's rounded steps, dwarfed beneath the soaring spire. Soot coated his face coonshow black. Pulling at his smutchy shirtsleeves, he described what he'd witnessed of the blast from his post at the Armory, across the channel from Brown's Island. "I'fe nefer seen nuffink like it," he declared. "Conflagramation like that, deffil himseff must of set it."

The whole of Richmond seemed to share that harrowed boy's horror as news of the explosion spread. The next day, Wilson's shop was full of talk of the nearly forty women and children who died horrible deaths in the ordnance fire. But there was a bigger shock still in store for my husband and me, when McNiven turned up at our house Saturday night.

"'Tis a mighty advantage we take for oorselves this time." He spoke with the closest I ever saw him come to glee.

"We?" I asked. I couldn't place what he might mean.

"The disruption to the Brown's Island manufactory," McNiven explained. "Wasn't our Mary Ryan a fine one, to think o' jostling a case o' friction primer, to ignite whatever gunpowder was floating in the shop."

"Mary Ryan?" I recognized the name from the list of injured workers published in the *Enquirer.* "She's not expected to live."

" 'Twould be plenty more dead from the munitions, if the wee lasses had finished their morning's work."

Neither Wilson nor I wanted to believe anyone we allied with could be proud over instigating such a thing. Wilson told McNiven so, rationing out his words in a low, quiet anger. "You start killing children, are you any better than what you're fighting?"

"They say this war is become a true hell on earth, the most horrid thing what man has ever made," McNiven answered. "But I suppose there be those of us what might still say slavery be the greater hell, the greatest sin. One what we maun destroy, the cost be what it will."

Listening to this man I'd longed looked to as my comrade, I couldn't apprehend whether I had more in common with him, or with the females he'd had a hand in killing.

When I first arrived in Philadelphia, Hattie told me whites could be as nasty to one another as they were to us. I'd been too wide-eyed to believe it, until Miss Douglass's history lessons taught me it was true. Now McNiven's scheming to kill girls and women proved it all over again.

But I wanted no part in such peccancy. Whatever animosity whites might feel for one another, at least I might make better use of it. And in such a manner as wouldn't cost the lives of children.

Perhaps wealthy Richmond was too proud to acknowledge what poor Richmond muttered every day, but rich or poor, all had grown weary of war. Yet in the two days since the explosion, two years of discontent was suddenly forgotten, Virginians once again rallying to their Cause, vowing to sanctify those girls' martyrdom.

Knowing we'd gain better advantage for our side if we played on white Southerners' disgruntlement, I related the details of Mrs. Whitlock's visit to Queen Varina. "There are more like Mrs. Whitlock, hungry and angry, than like your noble and self-immolating Mary Ryan," I reminded McNiven. No one knows better than a slave how such festering hatred can explode. "Let the starving women and children be their own army against Jeff Davis. They may do yet more damage to the Confederacy than all the battering of Union mortar and cannon."

The tocsin rang loud on the morning of the second April. It had been the city's most feared sound before the war, meant to toll a slave uprising. Since '61 we heard it often, whenever Union troops came near to Richmond. But when the clang of metal came that morning, it was neither slaves nor Federals that threatened. It was the fairer sex of Richmond.

I was in the Gray House yard, midway through hanging the wash. Hortense had gone up to Second Market, and Sophronia was scrubbing the front stoop, no doubt dawdling over the task to flirt with Tobias, her beloved groundsman. Likely not to notice if I slipped through the yard and down toward the Governor's mansion.

I dried my hands on my apron as I hurried toward Capitol Square. McNiven had connived with two females to rile the crowd up, and as I came down Twelfth Street, I saw the pair standing before the white mob. One was about Bet's age, though taller, with a long white feather in her hat. The other was younger and shorter, clutching an antiquated flintlock pistol. She raised it into the air and her sleeve fell back, revealing an arm no thicker than a broom handle. I wondered how many of the frayed and faded dresses in the crowd covered figures as wasted by hunger.

"Governor Letcher says he can't speak with us just now," she shouted. "He asks that we come back after breakfast."

"My children haven't got breakfast in six months," someone in the crowd called out. Others jeered in agreement.

The older woman flashed an open-mouthed grin. "Well then, let us take our breakfast while the governor takes his."

Her companion fired the flintlock into the air. The mob roared, pushing past Thomas Jefferson's legislature building and the great bronze statue of George Washington astride his horse. They poured onto Ninth Street, jostling to make their way to Main.

I ducked along Tenth Street as frenzied mothers pushed their children down Shockoe Hill. By the time I turned onto Main, rioters had overrun a bakery. As they greedily devoured loaves of bread, others ran toward the grocers, seizing any foodstuffs they could grab. At the sound of breaking window glass, many forgot their hunger, turning instead on the clothing shops and fancy goods stores. The throng swarmed down side streets, onlookers joining the pillaging. Here or there, a soldier appeared but drew back quickly, unwilling to make a solitary attempt at restoring order.

"They are like jungle beasts, ready to tear the meat from their living prey." Bet appeared at my side, clad in the calico bonnet and buckskin leggings she wore about the city. "To think Thomas could imagine such destruction."

"It wasn't McNiven who imagined it," I said. "It was me."

"You?" She was as surprised as if I'd sworn I'd been to the moon and back. "How ever did you get the idea?"

"*A fat rat is as good as a squirrel,*" I said. "That's Jeff Davis's response whenever someone complains the poor of Richmond have no meat. The Secessionist version of Marie Antoinette's *s'ils n'ont pas de pain, qu'ils mangent de la brioche.* It put me in mind of Mr. Dickens's *A Tale of Two Cities.* Hunger festering into anger, anger to malice. Malice to lawlessness."

I pointed to a familiar figure in the crowd, and Bet turned to see Mrs. Whitlock shoving her way through the street, clutching three pair of shoes in one arm and a tub of butter in the other. A flicker of recognition touched the distraught woman's ruddy face when she saw her Church Hill neighbor. But she laughed and hurried on her way.

"And is that Virginia's own Madame Defarge?" Bet asked.

Before I could respond, the Public Guard turned out in earnest. Jeff Davis struggled through the mob, climbing atop an overturned wagon to shout, "You must stop." His words were barely audible over the hoots and cries of the looters. "The farmers won't bring food to the city if they fear violence. And the Federals will hear of it and know we're weak. It will be the end for us."

As the crowd continued to push and shove, snatching up whatever was left to plunder, Davis ordered the

Guard to load their rifles. Once the guns were readied, he shouted that the mob had better disperse or they'd be fired upon. He drew out his pocket watch and counted off three minutes. When he announced that time was up, the troops raised their rifles.

They clicked their guns to full cock, sending the women and children stampeding off in all directions. Amid the shrieking, I made for the James, pulling Bet along beside me.

"Would the Guard really have shot them?" she asked, once we'd taken cover against the brick wall of a foundry building on the canal.

I couldn't know for certain. The Public Guard was paid in the same worthless Confederate currency as everyone else. Some of them may even have had wives and children among the rioters. But so long as both the Guard and the public believed Jeff Davis might have given the order to fire, he'd surely lost something of their loyalty, and their respect. And thus the victory was ours.

When Queen Varina returned to Richmond later that spring, she was wearing black for the father she'd just laid to rest. Though I knew full well the devastation of a daughter's loss, I preferred to believe her melancholy might be premonitory mourning for the demise of her husband's government.

Twenty-one

"Dammit, what are you saying?" Jeff Davis's mood was so foul, I quite nearly pitied whoever climbed the staircase of the mansion to see him the afternoon of the eleventh July.

When word came four days earlier of the fall of Vicksburg, Davis had taken sick. When a telegram from Lee on the ninth confirmed the Confederate defeat at Gettysburg, his illness hardened into irascibility. Once Lee's official report arrived late on the morning of the eleventh, Davis ordered his wife and children, even his secretary Burton Harrison, out of the Gray House. Hearing him cuss, I left off cleaning the third-floor rooms to creep down to the narrow office where Harrison usually worked, hoping the unexpected visitor was sharing yet more glad tidings for the Union.

"Do you not find the coincidence of twin defeats at Vicksburg and Gettysburg otherwise inexplicable, Mr. President?" Judah Benjamin's voice startled me. The calculating Aunt Piss seldom petitioned Davis directly, preferring to make his appeals through Queen Varina.

Whatever brought him here set Davis barking so loudly, I didn't need strain to make out his every word. "Johnston has made such a bumbling ass of himself since First Manassas, I am not surprised that he floundered the defense of Vicksburg."

Aunt Piss usually disdained the braggart Joe Johnston just as much as Jeff Davis did, but for once he defended the general. "How could we expect otherwise, when Grant appears to have had clear knowledge of all attempts to reinforce our troops there? Just as Meade, one thousand miles away, appears to have known precisely when Early and Lee were taking their men into Union territory. Such information must have come from someone with access to the highest levels of Confederate correspondence."

My heart lurched hard in my chest, and I squeezed myself tighter into the cubby-hole gap between Harrison's writing desk and his bookcase. As though I could hide myself from what Aunt Piss must mean.

Davis's reply confirmed my worst fears. "I am vilified in Congress, in the press, even in the streets. Now you say you think me such a simpleton as to be duped by a spy employed among my own household."

Aunt Piss's eager response drove icy thorns of fear deep into me, pricking me inside and out. "Do I have your permission to pursue the matter?"

"My honor is at stake if you do."

Aunt Piss didn't bother with any of his usual obsequience. "Your nation is at stake if I don't. Good day, Mr. President."

I watched Aunt Piss's well-polished boots storm out from Davis's office, half believing they'd sense my presence and kick me from my hiding spot.

"Investigate as you wish," Davis called out. "If what you say is true, the culprit must hang."

The Louisianan departed, and Davis returned to whatever occupied him at his desk in the adjoining room. But I remained huddled on the floor of Harrison's office, my legs too weak to support me.

Jeff Davis never seemed to take notice of the house slaves. Such obliviousness, shared by all but the most lascivious Southern gentlemen, had afforded full protection for my indagations. Or so I'd always let myself believe.

I cudgeled my memory for any minor slip I might have made of late. But I was certain that every page I ever lifted from Davis's desk, I'd taken care to return just as it was found. Perhaps that was my mistake. It flashed on me how Dulcey Upshaw used to leave my schoolwork out of order, illiteracy rendering her unable to hide that she'd been in my things. Maybe the risk was in always getting it right. Maybe I'd given too much intelligence to the Union, until the victories became otherwise inexplicable, as Aunt Piss said.

Aunt Piss. Immutably sly and scheming, it was no surprise he was the first to turn suspicious. Having gambled Davis's goodwill to level his accusation, he'd hunt hard to deliver a culprit. And Davis would be swift enough to mete out punishment, if Aunt Piss's charges proved true.

If—or when. For I knew Benjamin was right. The intelligence that brought Federal victories at Vicksburg and Gettysburg had come from the Gray House itself.

"Don't tell me nothing's the matter," Wilson insisted when he found me in our kitchen just past dawn the next morning. "Your one day of rest, and you keep yourself up all night rather than sleeping in. What's troubling you?"

I didn't care to lie to my husband. But I couldn't bring myself to tell him what I'd heard. As though my repeating Aunt Piss's suspicions would somehow bring the investigation to a faster and even more furious end.

"I'm feeling a bit poorly," I said. That was true enough, trepidation cramping me up.

"Perhaps you should take some tansy."

I shook my head at the thought of the bitter medicinal. "It's just the heat. Richmond July wears on me more each year."

"Some fresh air, then. We'll pack a picnic hamper, walk up to that stretch of creekside past Coutts Street. You deserve a pleasant Sunday, much as you did to help the Federals in their two grand victories."

"Fifty thousand or more casualties, just at Gettysburg," I said. "It hardly seems decent to be celebrating that."

"I'm not celebrating anyone dead or wounded. I just think my wife needs some respite after all our working and worrying. I know her husband does."

I supposed he was right. It was a relief to think of getting even a half mile away, just for a few hours. And stopping by Mama's grave might help me feel sure again, even give me courage to tell my husband what was vexing me.

We filled a basket with what fruit we had from the Van Lew arbor, fly-ridden though it was, along with the last of our share of boiled eggs from their chickenhouse. Grateful we had that much to eat when many in Richmond didn't. "What a wise husband I have, to

524 • LOIS LEVEEN

think of such an outing," I said, putting on my hard-worn shoes.

"And what a wise wife I have, to acknowledge it." Wilson hoisted our basket of comestibles and followed me down the stairs. But when we opened the door, we found Bet, her fist poised to knock.

She surveyed Wilson's attire. "I need a pair of pants, such as a farmhand might wear."

"Aren't any farmhands here," he said.

"Doesn't matter. You're too tall anyway."

"Then maybe you ought to find some short farmer whose pants would suit you. As though them buckskin leggings aren't crazy enough."

I shot Wilson a look. I wasn't any too pleased by Bet's arrival. But she had a bound and determined way about her this morning, and that might mean something important. "Why don't you come upstairs," I said, "and tell us what's brought you?"

"I don't know that I should stay, if you haven't the right trousers. But where can we find such a thing on a Sunday?" She pursed her lips and turned her head, as though she were listening for something outside. "Very well, you wait upstairs. I'll be back directly." With that she disappeared out the door.

"Why are you letting her spoil our outing?" Wilson asked as we ascended to the parlor. "Surely she can hunt up trousers or trombones or whatever other non-sense she needs, on her own."

"Just give her a few minutes to explain. If it isn't important we'll be on our way soon enough. And if it is . . ." I let my voice trail off as Bet appeared, leading a figure nearly as small as herself. A hunched-looking colored woman with large, fidgety hands, who kept her head bowed so low all we could see was the top of her bonnet.

"Miss Bet, I don't believe we've met your companion."

"Of course you haven't. My companion is only lately arrived from Chambersburg."

A colored woman, come all the way from Pennsylvania clear into Richmond? "How did she get here?" I asked.

The stooped figure straightened up and corrected, "Not she. He." Pulling off the bonnet, the stranger revealed his face. "I came by invitation from the rebel cavalry. If you consider a bayonet prod an invitation."

Wilson forgot his irritation at Bet, gesturing the man to our armchair. "Please, have a seat. Can we bring you anything?"

The visitor sat, folding the bonnet nervously. "A drink of water would be welcome."

I fetched a cupful from the kitchen, and he drank it down. Then he recited his story, as though he were telling it as much for himself as for us.

"They rode into town in the middle of June, spent three days rounding up all the negroes they could find. Claimed every one was a fugitive slave. No matter if there were whites there willing to testify they'd known us our whole lives, that we'd been born in Pennsylvania and our mammies and pappies before us. Two hundred, maybe two hundred and fifty of us they took. Marched us with them to Gettysburg, then down to Richmond after the battle. Put us all to sale once they got us here."

Even with the Union victories, the Confederates had found another way to make negroes suffer. I hadn't heard even a word of it in the Gray House. I wondered what else was happening to colored folks that I didn't know about.

"And your clothes?" I asked.

He didn't look at me, holding his gaze on Wilson. "They took everyone, women and children along with the men. Wasn't much I could do to protect my wife, but at least I managed to trade clothes with her. Whatever they'd do to a colored man, can't be worse than what they might try with a negress. First day of my life I've been glad to be this small, knowing at least we could fit into each other's things. Even so, not much comfort in it."

My husband's eyes flashed sympathy. "Where is she now?"

"I don't know. Dear God, both of us born free and thirty years married, I never imagined my own wife could be sold away from me. I just pray McNiven can find her."

"It was Thomas who interceded on Mr. Watson's behalf," Bet explained. "They are acquainted from some work Thomas did in Pennsylvania before the war."

I thought of the many trips Hattie's father made to Chambersburg to collect baggage. "Perhaps you are similarly acquainted with Alexander Jones? Or David Bustill Bowser?"

Mr. Watson nodded. "Know them both. Good men."

"My name is Wilson Bowser. David is my cousin." Wilson offered his hand to our guest. "I used to send him things before the war, by way of Chambersburg."

Mr. Watson shook Wilson's hand. "I believe I may know what you mean. I received items from this area and forwarded them to Jones and Bowser, from time to time."

Bet clucked her tongue, impatient at all this talk she couldn't understand. "Our first matter of concern is

528 • LOIS LEVEEN

finding Mr. Watson some proper attire. And then figuring out how to get him back home."

I could hem up a pair of Wilson's pants well enough
to fit our guest. But how we'd get him and his wife
across the lines to Pennsylvania, I couldn't guess. Nor
could I imagine how they'd feel returning home, when
so many of their neighbors would still be gone. Folks
born free but made slaves by war. My worry over how
spying in the Gray House threatened me seeped into a
new dread terror, as I realized how vulnerable negroes
were, even in their own houses in the North.

I was so distracted at the Gray House that week,
Hortense reprimanded me at least three times a day,
and Queen Varina had a slap for me nearly as often.
I could barely maintain my composure come Thursday, when Aunt Piss called on her. But it was fury
more than fear that had me shaking as I walked home
that evening.

"It's over two hundred miles to Chambersburg."
I heard Bet's harangue the moment I stepped inside. She
was lodging Mr. Watson at her house while McNiven
tried to locate his wife, Mag. "Fort Monroe is less than
half the distance. And with my pass—"

Wilson cut her off. "Your pass isn't going to get
the Watsons any closer to their home. Maybe you

haven't noticed, but Fort Monroe is southeast of here. Chambersburg is due north."

I held to the bottom of the stairs. The ugly things I'd learned that afternoon haunted me so, I suddenly wanted to flee. Flee from war and worry and death, from the horror of it all. But where could I possibly escape all horror, with things as bad as they were? I forced myself up to our parlor to deliver the latest news.

Bet, who sat facing the landing, caught sight of me first. "Mary, tell Wilson that what matters is getting the Watsons to Union territory as soon as possible."

"We need to get these people home, not to some army camp." Wilson turned to me for confirmation.

"I don't know that it matters whether you take the Watsons to Chambersburg or Fort Monroe, or just keep them in Richmond. Seems there's no place safe for us." I swallowed down a mouthful of bile. "They're killing negroes in the North, right in New York City."

"New York?" Bet was incredulous. "No rebel troops are anywhere near there."

"It's not the rebels who are doing it. It's the Yankees." I shivered over the pleasure Aunt Piss took in relating the details to Queen Varina. "All week long, they've been beating and burning and killing. Rioters set fire to a colored orphanage, lynched colored men in the street. They're angry at being drafted to fight for a bunch of slaves, so they're murdering every negro they can find."

Wilson sank back into his chair, but Bet teetered forward on the sofa's edge. "This cannot be," she said. "Your source must be mistaken."

I reminded her I'd had the same damn source for a year and a half, bringing news of Confederate battle plans, and she never thought to question it. "Just because you don't like what I've learned now, doesn't make it any less reliable."

"There is no need to snap at me."

"No need?" Wilson repeated. "And what need is there for whites to harass colored folks, North and South? To deny us a single half-acre of this country in which we might be left peaceably to ourselves?"

Bet didn't dwell long on such questions. "All I know," she said, "is that Henry Watson is relieved enough to have word that McNiven is bringing his wife back to him. And it's our responsibility to find a way to ensure their passage to freedom."

Freedom from slavery, maybe, but clearly not freedom from harm.

Bet bent to upturn the hem of her skirt. Tucked inside was a folded bit of paper, an old letter that had been turned sideways so a new message could be written over it. The method was common enough, with paper in short supply throughout the Confederacy. But when she passed me McNiven's missive, I marked how queer the content was.

Friend Eliza,

Between the Denizen o' Paradise and the Mad is One, made to hail a man for who the Main brought Missery. Henry will be finding his dear Mag in a place o' Strength. If the name o' the Riverway is the first and the place o' the man is the last, what son and will son maun be arrived and the happy Mag awaiting.

Yours,
Thos. McN.

"Why doesn't he tell us where they are, when they'll be back?" I asked.

"It is odd, I'll warrant you." Bet peered at the note. "But of course for Henry Watson the main has been misery, to be kidnapped by slave-mongers and have his wife sold away. I suppose that is why Thomas describes him as between mad with grief at losing her, and in paradise at the news that she is found. At least we know she has remained strong through her ordeal." She pursed her lips into a smile. "And perhaps the last bit means that Mag is *enceinte,* and Henry may have a son before long."

I tried to imagine a colored lady telling McNiven she was expecting, if her own husband didn't know already. It hardly seemed likely. Just as unlikely as McNiven waxing poetical just to write such a circumlocutory note, given how spare with words he always was. But I knew I wouldn't be able to puzzle through what it all meant with Bet about.

"It's getting late, and Mr. Watson may be worrying on your absence. Why don't you go home? There's no need to settle on a route until McNiven and Mag return."

She nodded and stood. "Yes, surely Thomas will tell us what we are to do."

I suspected he already had. And so I pondered his note as I lay in bed that night, rearranging the words in my mind just as I had Timothy Smith's first message in Mr. Emerson's *Essays.* But McNiven hadn't struck out any words or letters, hadn't underscored any either. The words were all set down regularly, no marked clue to reveal a hidden meaning. All set down regularly, I repeated until sleep began to overtake me. Except for that one odd spelling.

I was full on awake in the next moment, imagining the Scotsman pronouncing *for whom the Main brought Missery* in his heavy brogue.

I shook Wilson from his slumber. "Maine and Missouri."

"Ohio and Oregon," he answered. "What kind of game are you playing now?"

"When Maine became a state, they brought Missouri into the Union, too. One came in free, one slave, to keep the balance in Congress."

"Thank you for the history lesson. But couldn't it wait until morning?" He rolled over, turning his back to me.

Henry Clay was the man for whom the Maine brought Missouri, I knew that thanks to the thoroughness of Miss Douglass's history instruction. Clay brokered Congress' passage of the Missouri Compromise back in 1820. And he shared a given name with Henry Watson. But what could McNiven intend for me to make of that?

I pictured the whole of the note again. *Main. Missery. Denizen of Paradise. Mad is One. Strength. Riverway.* All capitalized, these words were the oddest bits of the message, which meant they were the ones McNiven had chosen most carefully. Adam and Eve were the denizens of paradise, so I started puzzling over all the Eves and Adams I could recall. And before too long I thought of John Adams and John Quincy Adams, presidents both.

Then came *Mad is One*. Madisone. Madison. James Monroe held the presidency between John Quincy Adams and James Madison. Back when the Missouri Compromise was passed.

One more reason to damn Henry Clay to hell, confusing me like that. But I didn't dwell on him, now that I had Monroe in my mind instead.

In a minute I was shaking Wilson again. "I've got it now."

He groaned, pulling the summer coverlet over his head. I pried the blanket loose. "Mag is waiting at Fort Monroe. You're going to bring Henry to her."

He blinked awake. "You're worse than that damn Bet, you know that? At least she only acts crazy, not clairvoyant."

"I'm no mind reader. More of a sign reader." Like Mama, I thought proudly. I explained about the place of Strength being the fort, right from the French. About Monroe being President between Madison and Adams, during the Missouri Compromise. How his Christian name, James, was also the name of the river at the mouth of which stood Fort Monroe. And that Henry was the Watson who would arrive to find Mag waiting, and my own husband was the Wilson who would take him.

"Am I having some peculiar dream right now, or is all of this really happening and making sense to you?" he asked when I finished.

"You're crotchety when you wake up, you know that?" I kissed him. "But you best get what rest you can. You're going to have to figure a way to ride out farther than usual tomorrow, to bring Henry Watson all the way to Fort Monroe."

Which meant I was going to fret about him even more than ever. As though fretting over Aunt Piss's investigation, the plight of the rest of the Chambersburg negroes, and now the slaughter in New York wasn't worry enough.

Wilson and Henry Watson left early Friday morning, while I was gone to my day's labor. Coming back to our three empty rooms made my heart ache, and after passing the night alone, I was nearly relieved to have the distraction of returning to the Gray House come Saturday.

As soon as the nursemaid Catherine took the four Davis children down to breakfast, Hortense ordered me to make up the nursery. Crossing to the servants' stair, I caught sight of Aunt Piss pacing nervously in the entry hall.

As I drew back from the doorway, Queen Varina came down the curving center stair. "Secretary Benjamin, what are you doing here at this hour? I'm hardly ready to receive visitors." Meaning she still wore her morning dress, and she'd barely finished her breakfast cakes and coffee.

"Dear Mrs. Davis, I wouldn't think of paying a social visit at this hour, even to so charming a hostess." Agitation tinged his words. "It is rather serious business with your husband that brings me so early."

Queen Varina nodded with importance. "Let us step into the library, and the president will join us in a moment."

"That will not be possible. I am afraid this is a most delicate matter, and it demands complete confidentiality. My report must be for President Davis's ears alone."

Never one for being excluded, Queen Varina hardened her voice. "Then you ought to go upstairs and see him in his office. Good day, Mr. Benjamin."

I hung where I was until I heard Aunt Piss's footsteps on the main stairway, then made my way up the servants' stair. Once I was sure he'd disappeared into Jeff Davis's office, I inched into the waiting room.

"I don't see the need to make a scene," Aunt Piss was saying.

"It is a point of honor for the accused to be allowed to face the accuser," Davis answered.

The notion of such a confrontation sent me scurrying toward the nursery. But before I could duck inside, Davis stormed out of his office and called, "You there, come here."

I turned to him, my heart so full in my mouth I could barely force out a "Yessuh."

"Go upstairs," he ordered, "and fetch Burton Harrison."

I mounted the stairs to the third floor, muscles up and down my legs twitching with fear. Knocking at Harrison's bedchamber, I repeated the summons.

Then I stole back down to the nursery, wondering if I should try to slip away. Bet could secret me in her mansion until Wilson returned with the pass to her farm. But by then Davis would have gone to McNiven about his wayward slave, and who knows how many intelligence operations would be endangered.

I wouldn't flee. I couldn't save myself, if it put everything I'd worked for, everyone I worked with, at risk. I would stay and spin some tale to convince the Confederates that McNiven knew nothing about the espionage.

Standing before the nursery window, I looked south past the Gray House yard to the makeshift military prisons and hospitals that dotted Butchertown. The war had already cost countless lives. The realization curled rope-heavy around my throat, that mine might well be next.

Hearing Harrison pass into Davis's office, I cupped an ear against the nursery's communicating door and listened to Davis's clipped command. "Tell him, Secretary Benjamin."

"As you know, Mr. Harrison, the security of our military depends on eternal vigilance. To that end, a man with my responsibilities in the government must bear the burden of some rather indelicate matters. It is certainly not something I relish, but for the good of the Confederacy—"

Davis had no patience for Aunt Piss's pontification. "Dammit Benjamin, out with it."

"Mr. Harrison, for the past week, you have been under investigation for suspicion of espionage."

"I?" Harrison's bewilderment matched my own.

"Certain information reached our enemies that appeared to come directly from this office, so suspicions naturally arose." Aunt Piss's usual sycophancy crept back into his voice. "My investigation has cleared you of any wrongdoing, just as the president and I knew it would." Davis coughed violently, causing Aunt Piss to add, "I apologize for any insult to your honor."

"As I have nothing to hide, I take no offense at the investigation," Harrison said. "Who is the true culprit?"

My heart pounded so heavy, I barely made out Davis's answer. "Secretary Benjamin seems unable to find him. Do you know of anyone else who is privy to my correspondence?"

"No one, sir. Neither friend nor foe could reach this floor of the house unobserved."

"Then the turncoat must be in the War Department. Benjamin, I trust your investigations will take you there henceforth."

"I already have a trap in place to expose the scoundrel," Aunt Piss replied.

Just don't expect to spring that trap any time soon, I thought. As my hammering fear subsided, I turned to make up the Davis children's room.

It was so late I was nearly abed when McNiven came knocking. "The Confederates' suspicion is raised upon us," he told me.

"Their suspicion may be raised, but not upon us." I related Aunt Piss's accusation of Burton Harrison, and Davis's insistence that the espionage was in the War Department. "They'll look there a long while and never find us."

He frowned, his mouth disappearing in the down-turned curve of his mustache. "The intelligence maun pass out o' Richmond somehow, and that is how Benjamin now looks to uncover it. 'Tis the reason I sended for Wilson these two days past."

"Wilson needed to bring Henry Watson to Fort Monroe."

"The Watsons were only a part to the whole, or I might hae brung Henry out myself today. There was a trap to be waiting for any what rode along Osborne Turnpike yesterday. I had to get Wilson to Fort Monroe afore then."

In all my worry for myself, I hadn't ever thought my husband might be in danger from Aunt Piss. I might have saved his life if I'd realized it—or cost him his life because I didn't.

"But he's safe now?"

"Ay. 'Tis you I worry over. Crowded as Richmond be, a vacant storefront right on Broad Street surely will be attracting notice, so I hae arranged with Robert Ballandine from Leigh Street to let the shop. One colored barber or another will not make a difference to them what come for a hair-cutting or a shave."

Wilson's shop was more than his livelihood, it was his pride and his joy. There weren't too many businesses Richmond negroes managed to keep for themselves.

I couldn't imagine my husband consenting to have another man take up his barbering tools, even for a few days, and I told McNiven so.

"'Twill be more than a few days afore Wilson is returned from Fort Monroe. None ken the countryside so well as he, from moving baggage these many years. Better than a company of scouts to the Union command, he is."

He was still more than that to me. But it didn't matter what we were to each other. Didn't matter that we hadn't even said a proper farewell before he'd gone.

My husband wasn't coming home, not any time soon.

Loneliness stung me so hard, I could barely pay much mind as McNiven instructed me on how to secret my daily reports in our alley, where they would henceforth be collected.

The next evening, the massive rosewood table in the Gray House dining room was crowded with military officers and government officials, along with their wives. Food shortages had grown so severe in Richmond that even those who cursed Jeff Davis behind his back, blaming him for the bad fortunes of the Confederacy, didn't refuse an invitation to dine in his home.

The talk was mostly of Vicksburg and Gettysburg, the two-week-old Confederate defeats. But while I served the guests a sad little spice cake made with sorghum syrup in lieu of sugar, the raven-haired Mrs. Chesnut steered the dessert conversation to a new topic. "What about this business in our own South Carolina? I find it most shocking."

Her sallow-faced husband didn't bother lifting his eyes from the plate I placed before him. "Our forces at Fort Wagner repelled the Union attack. No shock to that."

"But that regiment from Massachusetts," Queen Varina said. "Who would have thought the Federals could stoop to such a thing?"

Colonel Chesnut snorted. "Doesn't surprise me in the least. This Shaw fellow, his father is the worst kind of Yankee. An abolitionist and a Unitarian. Just the type to send his son on a fool's errand like that."

Any time the Davises and their guests cursed abolitionists, I paid careful attention.

"From what I've heard of the attack," observed a scrawny chief from the postal bureau, "the 54th acquitted itself quite bravely."

There was a rustle of disapproval from Queen Varina and Mary Chesnut. One of the military men leaned back, peering through his spectacles to address the bureaucrat. "Do not confuse ignorance for bravery. Darkies are simply too dumb to know any better than to run headlong into death. The reports we heard of these troops terrorizing women and children, burning civilian possessions in Darien last month, prove they are all of them brutes." He paused to suppress a belch, then waved his fork for me to bring another serving of cake. "Our men wiped out nearly half the Massachusetts regiment, once they presumed to meet us on the battlefield. As for Captain Shaw, he got what he deserved, shot down dead among the niggers he and his abolitionist kind adore."

A sudden crash came from the sideboard. Hortense had dropped the tea service.

Queen Varina shouted a blue streak of oaths, cussing over how hard things were for her with not a decent servant to be had.

Jeff Davis let out a coughing fit, presumably as much to cover his wife's coarse language as to clear his throat. "We gentlemen had better repair to the parlor," he said. "All of our talk seems to be upsetting the ladies."

As the company stood up from the table, Colonel Chesnut said, "You see, we who must live with the niggers know their incompetence. What Lincoln expects will become of them without masters to care for them,

I don't know." Murmuring agreement, the Davises and their guests made their procession out of the dining room.

I hurried to the sideboard. Hortense's face had gone gray, her usually fiery features slumped in despondency. "I got a son up in Massertooset, always thanked Jesus he made it that far," she whispered. "Could be him they's talking 'bout, killed by Secesh." All the time I'd been in the Gray House, it was the first she spoke of having any family—and the only sign she gave that she listened as keenly as I did to the Davises' conversations.

"What all it mean?" Sophronia asked.

"Means white folks don't care to see no negro with a gun," I said. "Ain't much surprise in that."

I knelt and gathered up the pieces of the tea service, hiding my face from Hortense and Sophronia. I hated myself for cutting them off like that. The news that colored soldiers had fought and died for the Union made me proud and scared and sad all at once, and truly I wanted to talk out the shock of what we'd just heard. But I'd felt the threat of exposure too keenly to risk speaking so in the Gray House.

First the draft riots in New York, then the defeat of the Massachusetts 54th in South Carolina. The Rebels slaughtered our men when they fought, and the Yankees slaughtered us when they didn't. And the Watsons were proof you couldn't even keep to yourself without some Confederate hauling you out of your home, your life, into the living hell of slavery. Alone that night and many a one thereafter, I worried over Wilson, knowing how little protection the Union command could give the colored men who served them.

Twenty-two

O ne night in the summer of '45, a barn swallow flew inside the Van Lew mansion. It made such a racket, it woke the household. Old Sam chased that bird from room to room, waving a broom to shoo it outside. When I asked Mama why it was flapping and swooping and flying around so, she said, "Lonely for its kind. It knows there are other birds out there, but it can't figure how to get to them."

I thought about that bird for the first time in years as I drifted about our three little rooms while the summer of '63 cooled to autumn, and then autumn chilled to winter. I was lonely for my kind, too. Wilson, of course, but Papa and Mama also. Hattie, even Zinnie Moore.

Queen Varina and her friends had taken to attending starvation parties, singing and dancing all night long as though the death and devastation of war weren't all around them. It put me in mind of Emperor Nero fiddling while Rome burned. But as the year drew to a close, a part of me understood it, envied it even. Because waking alone, slaving for the Davises, and coming home to those same empty rooms, I felt like a bird who might beat and beat its wings, but would never soar free again.

With Papa passed on and Wilson passed across the Union line, I was dreading Christmas alone. So when Bet insisted on having me to Church Hill for Christmas dinner, I accepted gladly. But as soon as I arrived, I began to doubt my choice. I'd braced myself for the effusive Bet, who'd hug me to her for the holiday, speechifying on the great role we were playing. Instead I discovered a woman as gaunt with worry as any of the hollow-cheeked crowds I saw on the city streets, and longing to share her vexation with me.

"They are holding somewhere between ten and twenty thousand of them," she said as soon as I came through the servants' door into the basement. "I cannot get things enough into Libby Prison. And nothing to Belle Isle." The giant island in the James was where the Confederates kept all the non-commissioned Union prisoners.

"I know, Miss Bet."

"But you have no idea of the suffering. Dysentery, cholera. Fifty of them dying every day. Do you realize that is fifteen hundred a month?"

I was full ready to remind her I knew my multiplication, maybe she recalled teaching it to me herself, when a fearsome thudding sounded above our heads. "What's that?" I asked.

"Only Frances Burney." Bet wasn't ready to leave off her litany. "We can hardly smuggle our own apothecary into the prison hospitals, now can we? So there's nothing for me to do but watch them dying—"

"Your carriage horse is in the house?" It had taken me a moment to realize that's who Frances Burney was.

"The Confederates will confiscate any horse they can find. They've come two or three times to search for her. Never thought to look in Father's library, the fools," she said, though I didn't suppose anyone keeping a horse in the house should be calling somebody else a fool.

It had been thirteen years to the day since the Van Lews first sat down to dine with negroes. Neither Bet nor her mother marked the anniversary as we pulled our chairs up before the table a half hour later. Just as they didn't mention how meager the fare, just partridge stew and potatoes, we had this Christmas. Didn't even acknowledge the occasional nickering and stomping from the library. The mother was grieving over her son John, who'd fled North to avoid another round of the Virginia draft, and the daughter was too occupied with her prisoners.

Though I was ready to rush back across Shockoe Creek right after the meal, Bet insisted there was some matter she needed to discuss with me. I half expected to find a shoat and some laying hens as she led me into the drawing room. But the space was bare of livestock. Bare, too, of nearly all its furnishings, sold off to support her beneficence to the prisoners.

"You must find out what's to become of them," she said, as if she read my thoughts about the captured Federals. "There are rumors that they are to be moved from here, taken down to Georgia. If it is true, we must find a way to prevent it."

I could no more interrogate Jeff Davis on a particular point of policy than she could hold twenty thousand Federals safe from their Confederate captors. But she was as much a mule as Frances Burney was a mare. Having no husbandry to talk sense into so obstinate a beast, I only nodded, glad at least to have my own empty rooms to repair to. I took my leave of the desolate Van Lew mansion, making my way home beneath a yule sky so overcast, it offered no star that might guide a wise, nor even just a weary, traveler.

A brutal cold spell quieted most of the military campaigns, so come January 1864 about all I discovered of interest in Davis's office was a letter from Zebulon Vance, complaining over how frequent women's mobbing was growing down in North Carolina.

Richmond's Bread Riot had sparked months of similar uprisings throughout the South, and I was mighty pleased that what I'd instigated was at last bursting to full fruition. Vance hadn't been much for secession back in '61, though once he became governor of North Carolina he proved to be as States' Rights as they come. When Confederate cavalry units rode roughshod through his state, seizing supplies from civilian farms, he even threatened to set the state militia on them. "It will be writ upon the grave of the Confederacy, 'Died of a Principle,'" Jeff Davis muttered whenever Vance and the other governors flouted his presidential authority in the name of States' Rights. Now Lincoln had announced that he'd recognize the return of any state in which one-tenth of the citizens pledged their allegiance to the Union and forswore slavery. Which had Vance writing Davis to declare North Carolinians so discontented with the war, peace negotiations might be his only recourse.

I clung to Vance's words like they were warming stones as I made my way along the crowded and cold-hard streets that frosty evening. If North Carolina took Lincoln's terms, robbing the Confederacy of its greatest source of soldiers and its most plentiful ports for blockade running, surely the war would—

Someone pushed hard up against me, knocking the thought from my head and my feet from the icy ground. A hand reached out and grabbed me as I fell. A white man's hand. It gripped me hard, remaining fast on my wrist even after I stood steady again.

"Clumsy in these new shoes, I am." The man was tall and burly, his voice low. "Sorry to knock down a servant to the Davises like that. You are the gal from the president's house, aren't you?"

"Yes sir, a maid."

He winked and kept his hold on me. "Plenty of interesting goings on over there, with the military officers and the government officials and all. I wager you could keep a fellow up all night, with stories of what you hear."

I didn't dare glance about to see if any passersby heard him. "Don't know nothing 'bout all that, sir. I just do like Mistress say, cleaning and what."

"No need to play shy with me. Wouldn't a fine gal like you want to tell what she's seen to some nice people who'd help her go North and be free?"

I pulled hard out of his grasp. "Don't know nothing worth telling, sir, and my home here in

Richmond. Don't make me go North. I's scared of them Yankees."

He stepped so close, his chestnut whiskers nearly brushed my brow. "Can you read, gal?"

Though I shook my head furiously, he shoved a folded page into my hand. "My name's Acreman. I have a room at Carlton House. It's written on that paper, my name and the hotel's. You forget, have someone read it to you. Come see me there. Money and a nice trip North, just waiting for you."

He turned, disappearing into the crowd. I hurried off, barely able to hold from running as I crossed the street. Once I was home, I slammed the door fast, my hands trembling so as I set the latch that I dropped the man's note. Out fell a hundred dollars in Federal greenbacks.

Union currency had become a rare sight indeed in Richmond. But I wasn't certain whether this Acreman was a Northerner, or just pretending to be.

His accent didn't sound familiar, one way or the other. But he made sure I noticed his shoes were new, even the most accomplished blockade runners weren't bringing leather like that into the Confederacy. There was something else, though, that didn't sit right. He bumped against me on Marshall Street, just past Ninth, a good four blocks from the

Davis residence. With the shortages at the municipal gasworks, Richmond's streetlamps barely threw off any light, and I was well wrapped against the cold. How could he recognize me as a servant from the Gray House?

Much as I'd quavered and quaked the summer before over Aunt Piss's eagerness to find a spy, I'd taken comfort for the last six months, believing he never thought to suspect me. Neither did Jeff Davis nor Burton Harrison, though I passed all three as I slaved in the Gray House. What made this stranger take notice of what they ignored? Was he their enemy, or their ally? Whatever the cause, his colliding into me was no accident.

After that, I kept one eye over my shoulder as I navigated the city's dim streets. When I arrived unannounced at McNiven's sixteen days later, I was especially wary. Any negro caught dallying about Richmond after sunset was still subject to jail and whipping. And whatever deviltry McNiven was up to—pretending to be a slave runner or a tobacco smuggler or what—I didn't care to put myself where any associates who called upon him might see me. But I didn't know what greater risk there'd be, if I didn't speak to him about what I'd learned that day.

"Has Vance come to acting after all that talk?" McNiven asked as soon as I was inside.

I shook my head. "It's Georgia, not North Carolina, that we need to worry about. Sixteen and a half acres, some place called Andersonville, to be built into a massive prison. They'll send the Federals they're holding in Richmond there, as soon as it's ready." I detailed the plans I'd found on Davis's desk, then recounted how Bet had carried on at Christmas, threatening to obstruct the relocation of the prisoners. Expecting me to join in whatever folly she set herself upon.

" 'Tis no folly to fear that half-starved men canna survive a five-hundred-mile journey."

I didn't have much patience for McNiven taking her side. "The way she carries on about the ill treatment the prisoners get here, why try to keep them in Richmond?"

"Two and a half years Bet has looked after the Federals. If they go, what is left for her to care on?"

"So we should let her try who knows what disruption, never mind how she might raise General Winder's suspicion?"

McNiven marked my agitation enough to promise, "I will send Butler a caution against acting anyway rash."

I suppose I should have held myself triumphant for persuading him to forward my counsel to the Union general. But I was no less apprehensive when I arrived at the Gray House the next morning. And I wasn't the only one in a state by then.

"So you here after all," Hortense said when she saw me.

"Where else would I be? Mistress have a fit, dusting and polishing ain't done like always."

"She ain't gonna notice today. Her little Betsy run off North. Some sap-head Yankee gived that dicty nigger two thousand dollars to tell what she seed around here. What she gonna see 'sides herself putting on airs?" Hortense rolled her eyes at the fool ways of Yankees and Betsy both. "Queen Varina howling a fright, like no other darky can dress her hair. You go on up tend her, Sophronia can mind the dusting."

I would rather have dusted the whole of the Sahara than face Queen Varina. Growing heavy with a new pregnancy, she howled even more histrionic than usual over the loss of her personal maid. "What won't the Yankees stoop to, to humiliate the president's family? The sacred bond between master and servant means nothing to them." She fumed her agitation as I combed out her hair. "And that Betsy, after all I have done for her! Why, she ran off wearing one of my own gowns!"

Truth was, I nearly shared her surprise. The way Betsy always doted on her mistress, I never supposed

she'd plot to go North. Knowing the seemingly obse-
quious Betsy had put on as false a face as I did about
the Gray House nearly made me smile—until I thought
how the revelation of her play-acting threatened to
expose my own.

As I secured Queen Varina's recalcitrant locks with a
tortoise-shell comb, her eyes met mine in the dressing
table mirror. "Has anyone said anything to you about
leaving us, Molly?"

In the two years I'd slaved for her, Queen Varina
never once called me by my right name. She never
seemed to give a thought to who I was or what I did
outside the Gray House, and I didn't much care to have
her musing on it now. But lying outright to her might
bring who knew what risk to me, if she began nosing
around, asking who'd seen strangers talking to her
servants.

"Oh Mistress, a horrible man with a funny way a
talking say something to me once. He grab me in the
street and don't let go. Ask me to meet him in his hotel.
Mistress, you know I's a good girl, never do no such
thing. He say he take me North, but I won'ts never
leave my husband for nothing, or run off from my
marse. I breaks away fast and runs home."

I dropped my eyes, all desperation and deference.
"Ma'am, you ain't gonna say nothing to nobody, is you?

My marse, he be right furious if he hear. I's a good girl, ma'am, never run off from no one."

Queen Varina nodded, glad enough for evidence of the evil of Northerners and the loyalty of her negroes. "To think of those un-Christian Yankees, trying to corrupt a gal like you. Forget that man ever spoke to you, and if any of his like come around again, you tell me right away and I will see that they are punished." She turned her head this way and that, admiring her half-dressed hair in the looking glass. "Hurry up, now. You still need to press out my orange pekin, for my luncheon with Mrs. Chesnut."

That afternoon, Sophronia sidled up to me in the second-floor waiting room. "Us go, too?"

The way she grinned, she seemed to think we might follow Betsy's tracks right then and there. "Go how?" I asked. "Sleep where? Eat what? Just cause Betsy ain't here, don't mean she any better off where she is."

Sophronia's smile withered to a frown. She turned away, running her flannel dusting-cloth across the maple window bench. I saw her glancing furtively out the glass, worrying herself over what lay beyond the Gray House yard.

I hated to snatch the hope from her. But I couldn't have Sophronia giving Queen Varina more reason to be suspicious of her servants. I told myself she'd borne slavery long enough, she'd survive it until the war was over and then have freedom aplenty.

I spent the first part of the tenth February cleaning up after Queen Varina's morning sickness, and the second part serving her and Jeff Davis dinner. The woman was glutton enough not to realize she wasn't going to keep down but half of what she ate. She might have waved me over to bring her second helpings, even thirds, if a flustered private hadn't arrived with an urgent message for her husband.

"Sir, I—I was sent to tell you—sir." The young herald's eyes darted about the dining room, as though the sideboard or the chandelier might remind him of what he had to say.

Jeff Davis was as anxious as I was to hear the news choking this military messenger. "Out with it, young man," he said. "Can't you see Mrs. Davis is waiting to finish her dinner?"

The soldier turned to Queen Varina, his face flushed as ruby as the French decanter that stood half-empty at the table. "I'm sorry to interrupt, ma'am."

"You should be sorry. The president is harassed morning, noon, and night with the work of the Confederacy. Why, if George Washington were alive, do you suppose he—"

"My dear, let the boy speak," her husband said. "Private, tell me what's brought you. That's an order."

"It's the men in Libby prison, sir. The Yankees. Some of them . . . they seem to have escaped, sir."

Davis choked over the news. "Seem to have escaped? Have they, or haven't they?"

"We've had a devil of a time counting and recounting them, took all morning. And it seems a little more than a hundred are gone, sir."

Jeff Davis drew his thin lips tight, his cheekbones jutting sharp as he pondered the escaped Federals scrambling toward the Peninsula, hoping to join up with Butler's troops. "I trust General Winder has set his men to looking for them?"

The messenger nodded. "Yes, sir. Found a few already, right on Dock Street. Drunk as could be at Nottingham's saloon. Sergeant says it's like a Yankee, can't make it four blocks without getting soused."

"And it's like a sergeant to blather on about someone else's faults, when his own company has failed in its duties," Davis answered. "Has anyone discovered how some hundred men happened to slip out of our best guarded prison?"

The private swallowed hard and looked at the floor. "Yes, sir. Shimmied to the cellar through a closed-off chimney, then dug themselves a tunnel fifty feet clear from the building. Popped up past the sentry and just went from there."

I supposed they'd been digging since Christmas. And the Church Hill lady who smuggled them the tools to do it must have thought it was quite a holiday gift.

"You should shoot every one of those prisoners once they're found," Queen Varina said. "To make an example for the others."

"I shall not," Davis answered. "Those men are prisoners of war, and anything we do to them, the Union may do to our own men who are held in the North. But residents of the Confederacy are entirely under my control. Any of our citizens who are found to have abetted this escape will immediately be hanged for treason."

There were even more Public Guard patrols than usual along the streets that evening, searching for escaped prisoners. I hung between buildings and darted across corners as I made my way down to Shockoe Creek and then up Church Hill.

My hands fumbled so at the door to the servants' entrance of the Van Lew mansion, I nearly started when someone swung it open from inside. "Miss Bet?" I called into the darkened cellar.

"She's upstairs." The man who gestured me in was pale and unshaven. His unwashed body stank inside his soiled blue uniform.

"Is that you, Mary?" Bet descended the servants' stair, launching into a fine speech about all we needed to do to tend the men she was sheltering.

As she railed on, I frowned at the stranger who'd let me in until at last Bet nodded at him to leave us. I waited until he was up the stairs and out of earshot, before I relayed Davis's execution edict.

Bet's eyes caught the fire of the candle in her hand. "I have no worries. I shall tell no one of this matter, and the prisoners certainly have no reason to reveal my involvement."

I wasn't quite ready to trust whatever score of strangers she had passing through her house, knowing that if one of them were recaptured before reaching the Union lines, he might well be willing to tell a few tales to ease the terms of his confinement. "What about your mother?"

She smiled. "Mother was most agitated when we heard a rumor that Federal soldiers were being hunted in our streets. I suggested a bit of laudanum might ease her mind. I daresay it has, as she took to her bed after dinner and hasn't so much as murmured since."

"Drugged or no, if the prisoners are found in her house, she'll hang as surely as you will."

A flush of anger, or maybe just of pride, ruddled Bet's face. "These men have risked death to fight for the Union. Surely our lives are not more dear than theirs."

My life wasn't so dear I hadn't hazarded it since the war began, hazarded it this very hour to warn Bet she was in danger. But danger was like show and ought to her, and she flouted it just as eagerly. And as imprudently.

Her haughtiness with the guard the first day we went to Liggon's, and her arrogance to the sentry at Howard's Grove—all that had served me well. But she'd grown so vain about her role in aiding the prisoners, she'd become a dangerment to them, and to herself. To her own mother, even. And to me, if I allowed it.

"I'd best go home," I said, "so you can tend your visitors." As I made my way from the mansion, I couldn't help but wonder if Bet was so defiant because she meant to be caught.

By the next day, the city was abuzz with the news of the prison break. I heard as much talk about the escape on my way home from the Gray House as I did while I was there, the tally of Federals recaptured increasing from one street corner gossipry to the next. Trying not to pay the rumor-mongers much heed, I searched out my parlor window as I came down Broad Street. The shutters were closed tight, though I usually opened them before I went to the Gray House, hoping the sun would warm the empty rooms. Unlatching the door, I smelled the smoke of the hearth fire. But I was certain I hadn't left so much as an ember still smoldering that morning, wood was in such short supply. Somebody had come in while I was gone, and like the three bears who discover a fox in their bed, I might well find he was still inside.

I had nearly edged back out the door before I heard that sweet-timbred voice humming a spiritual, then singing out the refrain, "O, yes, I want to go home."

"Wilson Bowser, no more wanting, you're already here." I ran up the stairs and into my husband's arms.

His kiss was like water to someone who's been wandering in the desert. The loneliness I'd carried during the seven months we'd been apart melted in the warm press of his body against mine.

"Is this really my beautiful wife?" he asked.

"It better be," I said as we ran our hands over each other, " 'cause you'd be in a mighty lot of trouble if you tried all this with another woman." For all the pleasure in our unexpected reunion, still I couldn't snuff out a flicker of worry. "Is it safe, you coming back here?"

"Those Confederates are so busy looking for Union prisoners, it was easier for me to slip into Richmond today than it was to carry the escaped Federals out to Butler's lines yesterday. Just be grateful to whoever got all those prisoners out at once, for distracting the Confederates."

I didn't bother responding to that. But as I admired my husband's handsome face, I saw a line or two of worry pinching between his eyes. "What's troubling you?"

He told me he was just achy from all he'd done the past two days. He put a kettleful of water over the fire, heating himself a bath as he described how he'd ridden cartload after cartload of escaped prisoners from New Kent County out to the Federal troops on the Peninsula.

Once he filled the tub and settled in, I gathered up his soiled clothes, meaning to wash them in the warm water after he was done bathing. I was fretting about where I'd find fabric enough to patch his frock coat, when I felt something stiff in the pocket. I drew out a carte de visite. It showed such a sight, my breath caught deep in my throat.

Sic Semper Tyrannis. The motto was emblazoned on the state flags that flew all over Richmond, I'd have recognized it even without Miss Douglass's Latin lessons. But the image beneath the phrase wasn't like anything I'd ever seen. It was a picture of a colored soldier, wearing the deep blue uniform of the Union. And thrusting his bayonet into a fallen Confederate.

"Wilson, what are you thinking? Carrying an image like this into Secessionist territory can get a negro killed."

My husband splashed his face. "I don't suppose it's any more lethal than spying on Jefferson Davis, or contrabanding escaped slaves or fugitive prisoners." It wasn't a joke to set my mind at ease. "Look at the picture. I do believe you'll know the artist."

I wasn't interested in the artist, agitated as I was. But as Wilson stood and took up a cloth to dry himself, sure enough I recognized the hand that created the image, as surely as he'd created the paintings that hung in Mr. Jones's dining room and Margaretta Forten's parlor— David Bustill Bowser.

"How did you get a picture of one of your cousin's paintings?"

"They're all over Yorktown. It's the battle flag of the 22d regiment of the United States Colored Troops, and that's where they're headquartered." He paused. "That's where I'll be, too, come Monday, when my enlistment takes effect."

My husband had only just come back to me, and now he wanted to leave. Leave for even more dangerment than we'd yet known. "Running around with incendiary materials isn't risk enough for you, you need to make good and sure the Confederates are going to be shooting bullets your way?"

"Contrary Mary, can't you see I'm owning you were right all along? The war is going to bring Emancipation. And every colored man who puts on a uniform is more proof that slavery is ending at last."

Proof or no, a negro in uniform faced more peril than even the white soldiers who'd been dying all through the war. I reminded him that the Confederates didn't take colored troops prisoner. They slaughtered them, or they sold them as slaves.

"Then the colored regiments have that much more reason to win." He nodded at the carte de visite. "This is everything I've worked for my whole life. You can't expect me to just sit through all of it now, not doing my part."

"You've already done plenty. You've smuggled my messages out of Richmond, smuggled out Henry Watson and the escaped prisoners, too."

"Those message are meant to serve the Union army, same as the escaped soldiers will. Hell, even Henry Watson has signed up to fight, though he's fifty years old or more." Wilson never was a beseechful man. But this once, there was true entreaty in the way he took me in his arms. "I thought you'd be proud of me for joining up. Like your friend Hattie."

What did he mean, putting her name in the middle of this? "You don't even know Hattie."

"Never met her, that's so. But I've seen a sweet little ambrotype of her, carried at the breast of one Private George Patterson, proudly serving in the 22d USCT."

"George is out at Yorktown?" I thought of Hattie's husband and his gapped-tooth smile. I couldn't imagine him carrying an army rifle.

Wilson nodded. "He's singing 'Do You Think I'll Make a Soldier', along with the rest of them. From the way he tells it, just about all the boys you went to school with have joined up, except for the most pompous and pretentious of the lot."

I knew just who he meant by that, though I didn't let on. I never mentioned my old beau to my beloved husband, though I always relished the difference between them, Wilson as conscientious as Theodore was conceited. But I wasn't about to remark on that now, as Wilson kept on about how excited he was to be soldiering. "George said he couldn't wait to write Hattie and tell her Mary had gone and got herself a husband, and he was going to serve beside him."

Hearing about Hattie and George tugged at my heart, it was true. But this wasn't some schoolgirl's lark Wilson was talking about. Battles were leaving bodies so mangled that all the words I knew could not describe them. Virginia had seen such things the year past as made the scene at the Richmond depot after First Manassas seem barely horror at all. "This war already cost me my papa. How should I feel knowing it might take you, too?"

Wilson laid a hand against my face, making a watery-warm impression on my cheek. "You told me how when Hattie's daddy was attacked, you knew you had to come back to Virginia, whatever the risk. George said Mr. Jones never did recover from that beating, though it took nearly two full years before he passed. When they put out the call in Philadelphia for the 22d, Hattie told George to go fight in her daddy's memory. Don't you want me to do the same for yours?"

I ducked my head, unsure. "I don't know how to be glad about you going off to battle, I just don't."

"Maybe you can be proud, even if you aren't glad."

I remembered when Mama taught me about pride. She was mighty proud of Papa, and of me, though she wasn't ever glad we were slaves. Nor glad she had to send me away to a distant, unknown city while she stayed on in Richmond.

I vowed to follow her example, as best I could. "I am mighty proud of you. So you be sure to be brave and smart and careful enough to be worthy of that pride. You come home safe to me, Wilson Bowser, you hear?"

"Yes, ma'am, I intend to." He put his hand across his heart like he was swearing an oath. Then he kissed me with all the passion one person can have for another, reminding me we only had a few days together, and there he was without a stitch of clothing on him.

Later that night, as we lay in the bed, he whispered, "I'm proud of you, too, Mary. For knowing a man needs to fight his own fight sometimes."

Twenty-three

George Patterson had his ambrotype of Hattie, and she had the nuptial picture the two of them had sat for years before. Even Wilson marched off carrying the daguerreotype I'd sent Mama and Papa all that time ago. But there was no David Bustill Bowser to take a negro's image in Richmond. Once my husband's footfall fell away, all I had left was the empty echo of our rooms. I'd cut the collar from his shirt, hoping for any scent of him, though it was hard to make out even a hint of it over the miasma of sickness and starvation that clung about the city.

February gave way to March, and my back ached along with my heart. I was endlessly scrubbing mud from the Gray House. Mud tracked in on the boots of the military men and politicians who came to see Jeff Davis, then tromped all over the house by the Davis children. Just shy of his seventh birthday, Jeff Junior had been given his own little Confederate uniform for Christmas, and all winter he made a regiment of his younger brothers, marching them about as much as a two-year-old and four-year-old can be marched. Those boys waged ferocious war against the carpets, walls, and windows that Sophronia, Hortense, and I struggled to keep clean.

"What she need with bringing 'nother a them hellcats into the world?" Hortense muttered as we scraped away the latest clods.

"Got to make sure us don't get a moment's rest," I answered.

As long as Queen Varina kept having babies, she got as much attention from her husband as any man struggling under the weight of a foundering government could give. She didn't tend her own children—even Catherine, the Irish nursemaid, barely bothered with that. So though Queen Varina carped and whined over her condition, she was pleased with being in the family way, her vanity swelling right along with her belly. And though her condition meant more work for those who waited on her, I seized what opportunities it offered to audit Jeff Davis's conversations.

He stormed into the house the afternoon of the third March without bothering to scrape his boots outside the door. Before I could even take a rag to the trail of footprints he left across the entry hall, he shouted from the library for someone to bring smelling salts.

I fairly galloped up to Queen Varina's dressing room to snatch the crystal vial from her bureau, then dashed back down to the library, where she lay collapsed on the meridienne. I held the aromatic spirits of ammonia beneath her nose until she blinked at me and then at her husband, unsure why we were huddled over her.

"What is it? What's happened?" she asked.

"I gave you some news that was too much for you to bear in your delicate condition, I'm afraid," Davis said. He ordered me to pour some claret, then held the glass of burgundy liquid for his wife to sip. The alcohol brought a flush to her cheeks, as she demanded to hear the news again.

He coughed out his hesitation before telling her, "Ulric Dahlgren is no more."

She frowned. "I remember when Commodore Dahlgren brought his family to visit us in Washington. That little fair-haired child in his black velvet suit, fussing at his Vandyke collar. Why, he couldn't have been much older then than our Joe is now."

"That little boy had grown to a man of twenty years and more, and traded his Vandyke collar for a Federal uniform. Colonel Ulric Dahlgren he is, or was. Our men routed him as he was trying to attack Richmond. They have shot him dead."

Queen Varina went pale again, but then she shook her jowls and swallowed hard. "If he was our enemy, I suppose I am glad he was killed." She fixed her gaze on her husband's good eye. "Did you come rushing home just to tell me a Yankee colonel was dead?"

Davis gestured for me to have the vial of smelling salts ready, in case what he had to say sent her into another faint. "When they searched the body, they found his orders. Fitzhugh Lee brought a copy to me not half an hour ago. It will be in the news-sheets by morning—Dahlgren and his men were to enter Richmond, free the Federal prisoners, and set fire to the city. But first, they were to kill me, and all my cabinet."

"Assassination? Jefferson, are even Yankees capable of so despicable a thing? Are we safe yet?"

Davis laid his long fingers across her mouth, though whether to soothe her or just to silence her I couldn't tell. "Dahlgren's men are all arrested, except for a handful who fled back to their camp. I suppose his death will give the Federals pause before they try such a thing again. But my dear, we must not forget that this is war. Whatever friends we had on the Union side, they are lost to us forever. Lincoln has taught them dishonor and deception, and we cannot trust even those we hold closest to our own bosom."

With that, he signaled for his devoted servant to pour another glass of claret.

A surprise snow came the first Saturday in April, melting away to raise Richmond's creeks all the higher. Which meant I had to walk west all the way to Second Street on Sunday, just to find a passable route up to Shockoe Cemetery.

Oakwood Cemetery and Hollywood Cemetery, the newer burying grounds where Confederate soldiers were interred, would be full of mourners of a Sunday. But Shockoe Cemetery was deserted, no one taking time to visit the grave of a grandfather when there was a brother or son laid freshly to rest across town. I picked my way among the sodden burial plots, until I found the marker for Old Master Van Lew's lying place. Nearly two decades' worth of weather hadn't marred the words etched into the stone. JOHN VAN LEW. BORN MARCH 4, 1790. DIED SEPTEMBER 13, 1845. MADE PERFECT THROUGH SUFFERING.

I'd seen enough suffering in war-time Richmond to know a wealthy man lying in a featherbed on the second story of his mansion didn't hardly compare, even if he was stricken with lung disease. As for perfection,

I hadn't met a person yet I'd mistake for perfect, and certainly no Van Lew.

Particularly not the one who asked me to meet her here this morning.

"I hardly know where else I can find a moment's privacy these days," Bet said when she arrived. She'd left off her buckskins and calico bonnet in favor of a mourning dress, the costume worn by so many Richmond ladies. "Every time I turn, I find a detective at my elbow." She leaned close before continuing, as though the very graves might harbor some unwanted auditor. "I have learned where they've left Colonel Dahlgren's body."

When the news-sheets published the report of Dahlgren's orders, the Confederates condemned him so, words weren't enough. They chopped the little finger off his corpse and stole his artificial leg. Buried him in a shallow grave, then dug him up and put him on display, before interring the moldering remains in some ignominious locale.

Now Bet declared we would retrieve those remains and lay them properly to rest. She spoke with such enthusiasm she might have been telling me we were to unearth a treasure of gold bullion rather than a month-old corpse.

"Why would we unbury and rebury someone who's long gone?" I asked.

"It is the very least we can do for him." She swept her hand toward her father's grave, as though she meant to set the colonel down right in her family plot. "He was a Federal officer. He deserves a decent burial."

"He was a cold-blooded killer." The *Richmond Examiner* was so enthusiastic about proving Dahlgren a scoundrel, they published a diatribe against his treatment of the man who tried to guide the expedition to the city. Now I cited it back to Bet. "How do you think your Colonel Dahlgren was going to find his way into Richmond? Like plenty of whites, North and South, he relied on some negro. But when the rains swelled the James so high that the Federals couldn't ford across, Dahlgren blamed the scout. As though colored people have the Lord's own power to make the waters rise and fall. He had that man hanged, stripped the reins off his own horse to do it." The tale haunted me, knowing Wilson had scouted for the Union army.

Bet flicked her hand, as though she were shooing away a gall wasp. "That cannot be. Why would any Federal officer do such a thing?"

I pursed my lips, thinking of George Patterson and Henry Watson and my own husband serving under who knows what chain of commanders. "Since when does being a Northerner, a Unionist, or even a

Federal officer preclude hating negroes? Your Colonel Dahlgren wasn't even decent enough to have that poor man's body cut down once he was dead. When the Confederates found it, they were glad enough to leave it swinging from the tree. A reminder to the darkies of how the Yankees mean to treat them." I bucked my chin up, daring her to respond.

"What you describe is a despicable act, and if it occurred as you say, there is no excuse for it. But there is no excuse for us to behave indecently, either." She cocked her head, trying to bring her chin up to mine. "The correct thing to do is to give any body, white or colored, a proper burial. That is what we must do for Colonel Dahlgren."

We must. I wasn't sure which of those words irked me more—the one that assumed I was indivisible from her, or the one that declared me bound to do whatever she deemed necessary. Though she rebelled against other people's ideas of show and ought her whole life, Bet was always glad enough to show me what she believed I ought to do.

I strode to the cemetery gate without a word of farewell. Bet could spend her Sunday plotting whatever foolishness she wanted. I'd spend mine at the colored burying yard across the way, tending Mama's grave.

———————

On the warm Saturday that ended April, Jeff Davis set out for his office in the old Customs House first thing in the morning, sputtering about the need for proximity to his cabinet. Queen Varina bustled after him at mid-day, half moaning and half boasting that her dear president wouldn't remember to eat a morsel of food unless she delivered it with her own hand. Hortense and Sophronia were scrubbing the first floor, and in the momentary quiet of the second story, I left off my dusting and sweeping to search through Jeff Davis's correspondence. The Union generals were positioning their forces for a great new confrontation with Bobby Lee, and they needed every detail I could supply about where the Confederate regiments lay in wait.

Just seven weeks earlier, Mr. Lincoln had installed U. S. Grant as head of the Army of the Potomac. Unconditional Surrender, the Confederates called him, for the terms he demanded when he took Fort Donelson, Tennessee, back in February of '62. They spat the appellation ruefully when he won the siege of Vicksburg in the summer of '63. By '64, after three long years of war and so many Federal generals come and gone from the Virginia campaign, it was hard for me to believe Grant could bring victory to the Union side at last. But marking how his appointment agitated the Confederates, I hoped Unconditional Surrender might prove true to his nickname once again.

Atop the pile on Davis's desk were three drafts of a plodding, ponderous speech he was to make to the Confederate Congress when they reconvened in the coming week. Beneath those lay a copy of a letter General Breckenridge sent General Bragg three days earlier. Underneath that I found another missive, dated the day before, in a crisp hand that by then I recognized as surely as I did my own.

Headquarters, April 29, 1864
His Excellency Jefferson Davis,

President Confederate States:

Mr. President: I received this morning a report from a scout just from the vicinity of Washington that General Burnside, with 23,000 men, 7,000 of which are negroes, marched through that city on Monday last to Alexandria. This report was forwarded by General Fitz. Lee from Fredericksburg, and I presume the scout to be Stringfellow. If true, I think it shows that Burnside's destination is the Rappahannock frontier, and that he will have to

580 · LOIS LEVEEN

*be met north of the James River. I would therefore
recommend that the troops which you design to
oppose him, which are south of that river, be drawn
toward it. I think there are sufficient troops in
North Carolina for the local operations contem-
plated there without those sent from this army, and
request that Hoke's brigade and the two regiments
attached to it be returned to me. I think it better to
keep the organization of the corps complete, and, if
necessary, to detach a corps than to weaken them
and break them up. I have kept Longstreet in
reserve for such an emergency and shall be too
weak to oppose Meade's army without Hoke's and
R. D. Johnston's brigades.*

With great respect, your obedient servant,

R. E. Lee,
General.

That was Lee's way. He played at humbly submitting
himself to Davis, all the while telling his commander-
in-chief what to do. Whether he was right about
Burnside or no, I couldn't gauge. But his great vexation at having Grant's men on one side, Burnside's on
another, with Butler's on yet a third, was some comfort
to me, knowing my own husband served among them.

I held Lee's letter before me, arranging all the details in my mind so I could write them out that night.

"What you think you doing?"

Hortense's question shocked a bolt from my heart to my head, and deep into my belly.

She'd come up behind me, seen the paper in my hand. Seen me squinting at it, too.

"Looking for cat ears." I turned the page sideways, then upside down. Moving it slowly and tilting my head like I was puzzling over it. "Missy, my first master's little girl, her name Mildred Ann. When they learnt her reading, she show me how one them letters look like cat ears. She say her name start with that letter, my name, too. Sometime I see writing, I try pick out that cat ear letter 'cause it the only one I know. But I don't see it nowhere here, do you?" I held the page out to her.

"Don't got time to be looking for no cat ear or dog tail. Got work enough to do 'fore Queen Varina come home hot full of holler." She stepped closer. "I don't know what trouble you up to in here but I know there some. Now you get to cleaning or I gonna—"

A shriek pierced the air. It came from outside, shrill and long. One of the Davis children—but with an edge of panic that distinguished it from their usual yelps of mischief.

"Where that Lazy Irish at?" Hortense strode to the open window and surveyed the backyard.

The nursemaid mustn't have been too far from her charges, because the next moment she was screaming, "Yiv killed 'im! Sweet Mary Mother o' Jesus, the boy is dead fir sure!"

Hortense whirled round and ran from the room. As she thumped down the stairs, I slid Lee's missive back into the stack on the table.

Shoving my hands beneath my apron, I made my quick way outside, where I found my fellow servants huddled around the brick pathway between the basement door and the kitchen. That's where little Joseph Davis, a child of barely five years, lay—bloody, twisted, and motionless. Fallen from the veranda balustrade twenty feet above, where he'd been playing with his brothers.

It was only later, after Catherine went to the Customs House to fetch the Davises, after Queen Varina arrived screaming and Jeff Davis praying, after the doctor came and confirmed the child would breathe no more, after we set the house in mourning for the stream of visitors who arrived that very evening to express their condolences—only after all of that, did I stop to realize that when I thanked Jesus for distracting Hortense from what she saw of my spying, it was the death of a child I thanked Him for.

I would not have harmed a hair on the boy's head. But still I carried with me the weighty truth of what slim respite I gained, solely because he was lost.

The Sunday morning church bells had all tolled their last before I noticed the letter lying on the floor just inside my door. Someone must have slipped it in from outside while I slept, like they'd done to Bet only a few weeks before.

Though she pretended not to pay that note any mind, I'd marked the way her face twitched when she showed it to me. On the top was a skull and cross-bones, the words beneath blocked out in the unsure hand of someone without formal schooling: *Dear Miss Van Lough, Old maid. White caps are arownd town. They are coming at nyte. Look out! Your house is going at last. FIRE. Is your house insherd? Put this in the fire and mum's the word. Yours truly, White Caps. Please give me some of your blood to wryte leters with.*

Picking up the unmarked packet that had been left for me, I considered burning it still sealed up, just to keep whatever image of harm it might contain out of my mind. But it was a warm May day, no fire lit, and matches a rare enough commodity I didn't care to waste one.

Or so I told myself as I walked slowly back up the steps and set myself down at the kitchen table. I closed my hand tight around the wood handle of my kitchen knife, slid the blade under the seal, and pressed the folded pages flat.

I quite nearly cried when my eyes fell on the first lines.

6 May 1864

My dearest Wife

How I wish you could see me this morning stand-ing in my uniform shoulder to shoulder with all the men of the company the regiment & division. Never was men prouder to serve. We have our first victory already though was hardly a battle to speak of the enemy scurrying off instead of meeting us on the field.

I hope to be as close to you in my person as I am in my heart soon enuff but for that all I can say in this letter is we are moving closer than the enemy would care to find us. Close enuff to hope the end may be at hand.

George is a great friend to me & many an evening entertains me with tales of a girl he used to know at school. She was quite something if only half what he says is true & I look forward to repeat-

ing such tales & seeing what you think could become of such a girl now that she is full grown. For my part I suppose her quite wonderfull as ever at least I hope her so.

I bear regards to you from George & throu him from your Hattie. He shows me the letters from her telling of their children Alexander named for her father Beatrice for her mother & a lovely little babe named Mary for a dear friend. That infant is quite colicky & proves a handfull for all who tend her perhaps a contrary nature in the child is why? George & the other men tease cause I havent any offspring to boast about but I tell them my wife has been very busy with important work we pray to be done soon so we can get to the business of raising a family in peace.

With that I bid you goodnight & trust that our friends will get this to you. Who knows when I may send another.

Ever your loving
Husband

The gut twisting fear fell further and further off with each line I read. But whether it was joy or sorrow that replaced it, I couldn't quite say.

For two and a half months, I'd pored ever more assiduously over Jeff Davis's papers, hanging all the more intently on every word I heard at the Gray House. Desperate for news of the USCT 22d, yet knowing any tidings the Confederates had might only be such as I didn't care to hear, of defeat and capture—or worse.

Glad as I was for word from my husband, I saw right off how Wilson wrote that letter as much for the eyes of any Confederate who might intercept it as for my own. It was hard to take comfort from such correspondence, long on longing for us to be together but short on information about where he was while we were apart.

I folded the pages and pinned them to the underside of my skirts, just below my waist. It was danger for a supposed slave to be caught with writing, even if the letter didn't suggest too directly it was from a colored soldier serving on the Union side. But the deadliest fighting was yet to be, and coming soon most likely. However many hundreds of thousands were killed already, more still would have to die before the war was done. I needed some talisman to carry close against me.

Friday, the thirteenth of May, seemed ill luck enough, for all Sophronia, Hortense, and I had to do readying the Gray House for the funeral reception for General J. E. B. Stuart, who'd passed the day before from a gunshot wound incurred at Yellow Tavern. All the Confederacy seemed to feel his loss. By late that afternoon, the Gray House was thick with guests. And choked with the heat held in by the blanket of smoke from the nearby skirmishes. "Fan them pullet hens till they done cackling at each other," Hortense said, pushing me toward the knot of ladies gathered in the central parlor.

Cackle they did, as eager to gossip as to grieve. A gray-haired woman was nodding toward the men clustered in the next room. "The president has aged ten years since his dear child passed."

A cannonade thundered outside, drowning out the murmurs of agreement from the half dozen ladies around her. But the youngest member of the circle told the others, "My aunt says some folks aren't sorry that at last the Davises know what it is to lose a son during war. Perhaps now Varina Davis won't hold herself above the rest of us."

A rotund lady dominating the sofa frowned. "Sally Buxton, you oughtn't speak that way."

The chastised Miss Buxton picked at a worn spot on the seam of her skirt. "I'm only repeating what my aunt said."

"Well you oughtn't repeat it, and she oughtn't say it. Oughtn't even to think such a thing. The South has seen enough death, we needn't make up accounting sheets to tally whose is worst."

But Queen Varina herself seemed eager for such computation. In the dismal fortnight since her son's death, she'd grown as bitter as the parched corn coffee sipped by her guests. Having stopped to seek the sympathy of the men in the adjoining drawing room, she now swept into the parlor, taking the seat closest to my fan.

"How good of you to open your home to Mrs. Stuart," said the lady who'd spoken last, eager to change the topic of conversation. She could hardly have imagined how Jeff Davis wheedled and pleaded, just to persuade his wife to allow another woman's mourning to eclipse her own, if only for an afternoon.

"It is hard for me even to think of her as Mrs. Stuart," another of the guests said. "For I knew her back when she was Miss Flora Cooke. What a figure she cut in her youth. She rode so much as a girl, she was nearly as deft on horseback as her husband."

Queen Varina clucked at the image. "One more indication of her father's queer ideas. To think of the way he turned his back on the South and rode against his native Virginia with McClellan's invading army in '62."

"If she rides so well as that," put in a young redhead, pointedly ignoring her hostess's harsh words, "perhaps she should take over her husband's command. We've few enough cavalry officers left."

"You mustn't make such jokes, Miranda," the rotund lady said. "There is no amusement in suggesting a lady take up such pursuits."

"No one would have thought ladies could serve in government," replied a prim mouse of a woman. "But our whole bureau of clerks is female, and the superintendent says we do as well as any males."

"Laboring in an office!" Queen Varina waved her handkerchief as though she were leading a military charge against the very idea. "I couldn't imagine it, with my nervous headaches."

"I haven't had a headache since I began working for the Treasury Bureau. Some of us clerks think perhaps it isn't effort but idleness that makes ladies ill. I shan't care to give up the position, when the war is over."

"Perhaps you won't have to," the ginger-haired Miranda said. "Far fewer of our menfolk will return than left. Someone shall have to take their places."

The eldest of the ladies set her cup onto its saucer with an imperious clatter. "You cannot expect us to believe you are in earnest. It is one thing for Southern ladies to exert themselves in this time of great sacrifice, but the female constitution simply is not meant for constant labor."

I didn't let out a flicker of contradiction as I held my gaze steady across the fanning of my aching arms, past the tables I dusted and the mantel glass I scrubbed, to where Hortense and Sophronia were toiling in the drawing room, diligently refilling whiskey glasses and deftly keeping cigar ash from the carpet.

"Why, here is Flora Stuart at last," one of the ladies called out. Shifting my gaze to the other doorway, I watched the guest of honor make her way from the entry hall.

The grief etched across her young face stung me. Through all the talk of the pitiable widow, I expected a woman equal to Varina Davis in years. It caught me quick to see Mrs. Stuart couldn't be more than two or three years past twenty-five—the age I was to turn that week.

Queen Varina rose. "My condolences. I am sorry we do not meet under happier circumstances, for either of us." She gestured at her own mourning attire, a lace-trimmed silk rather finer than her guest's worn black poplin.

"Thank you, Mrs. Davis, and my condolences to you. General Stuart and I lost our own little girl back in '62, when she was the same age as your Joe."

"They say there is no grief like that over a child, and I believe it is true." Queen Varina laid a hand on her swollen belly, an indelicate gesture she'd taken up to emphasize her maternal condition. "I only pray the next one will come to us healthy, and remain so."

Flora Stuart looked at her with red-rimmed eyes. "I suppose there is great comfort in knowing you are to have another child. For a widow, there can be no such solace."

The portly matron on the sofa fidgeted with her hoops, trying to distract Mrs. Stuart. "It was a lovely service today."

But Queen Varina wouldn't let well enough alone. "I am sorry I could not attend, but even the shortest refrain from the Dead March reminds me of how they played it for my little one only a fortnight ago."

"You needn't have worried," the widow said. "There's not a military band to be had in Richmond. With the Federals advancing so closely on all sides, there were barely half a dozen able-bodied men left in the city to bear my husband's coffin to the hearse."

Before Queen Varina could reply, Aunt Piss came into the parlor, bowing and greeting each of the women in turn. "I hope I am not interrupting you ladies."

One of the dowagers laid her hand on his arm, waiting for a round of cannon fire that rattled the leaden windows to die off before she asked, "Is Richmond in great danger?"

I shifted the fan from my right hand to my left, turning to hear his answer.

"It is the men serving under Grant who are in danger. Unconditional Surrender has turned into Unremitting Slaughterer. He sends his troops to their deaths like steers to the abattoir."

"Even the smallest skirmish can take lives on both sides." Flora Stuart's quiet observation sent chills up my spine.

"I'm sorry if my reference to casualties upset you. It is in contrast to such fine officers as your late husband that we see the inadequacies of the Union commanders." Aunt Piss turned to lecture the other ladies. "To the north of us, we have Grant the butcher, assaulting where he cannot win. To the south is the coward Butler, faltering even where he might win." He smiled and gave just such a prediction as he knew would keep the ladies cooing and praising him long after he joined the gentlemen in the drawing room. "I pledge to you on my honor, Richmond will stand as safe this spring as it did two years ago, when we gallantly repelled McClellan's forces though they so outnumbered our own."

But I smiled, too. McClellan lost Richmond in '62 because he didn't know he outnumbered his enemy—didn't know because I chose not to tell him. Now, with

Mr. Lincoln's Emancipation Proclamation written into law and my own husband serving in the Army of the James, I was more than ready to see the Confederacy face its final defeat. I'd make sure the Federals received every scrap and seed that could bring the war to a quicker end.

I set a hand onto my waist, meaning to let it rest against the fabric covering Wilson's letter. But when I felt my skirt, I realized his missive was gone.

That very day and every one thereafter, I searched the Gray House, my house, and each step in between, desperate to find the folded page covered with my husband's steady hand. I wasn't just worried over who might find the letter, whether they would link it to me—it was a deeper dread that held me. If I couldn't safeguard that single sheet, how could I expect that Wilson himself would remain unscathed?

More than a full month later, on the seventeenth June, Jeff Davis received a long report the Confederates had intercepted en route from Butler to Grant. It told of the initial Federal attack on Petersburg, twenty miles south of Richmond, and how the Union gains had come at a cost, to the USCT especially. The 22d alone had lost fourteen men killed, one hundred and sixteen wounded, and eight missing.

Every day Richmond's news-sheets would list out the wounded company by company. But only on the Confederate side. I knew my husband's name would never be among them, but still I sifted and scoured through those lists for what I knew I couldn't, prayed I wouldn't, possibly find. Many a woman woke in the morning thinking herself a soldier's wife, not realizing that sometime in the night she'd already become a soldier's widow. Weeks or months might pass before a dead man's family would get word. Some never heard at all, Union and Confederacy both more bent on slaying the other than on identifying who on their own side had been slain.

Twenty-four

"Jefferson! Don't leave me to die with these niggers, Jefferson!"

Not a one of us wanted to be with her, but still Queen Varina cried out like she was our captive. "Don't pay her no never mind," Hortense whispered, dipping a facecloth into the water bowl Sophronia held. "Birthing only kill some womens. This one ain't about to up and die, so long as she got all us to boss around if she live."

With the curtains closed and fuel too scarce to run the gasolier, the Davises' bedchamber was dark as a winter night, though still heavy with the stagnant heat of the June afternoon. I raised the oil lamp a little higher as Hortense laid the moist cloth across that proud forehead. "Doctor on his way," she soothed. "Hush now, Mistress, 'fore you scare the chiljen."

"Don't you dare hush me." Queen Varina clawed at Hortense's slender wrist. "Out, every one of you black hell-fiends! Get out!" She shoved Hortense into me. The lamp I held swung wild, sending a spray of oil scalding my arm and throat.

Hortense, Sophronia, and I fled to the hall. "Womens all suffer when they time come?" Sophronia asked.

"She ain't suffering. We is." Hortense ran a quick eye over the nailmarks patterning her forearm before turning to me. "You get downstairs, tend them guberment mens. Make sure Marse Davis don't be running up here, making her hiss and spit even more. All I need is menfolk tramping all over the house during a female time."

The arc of burns along my neck and arm felt like a thousand hot needles, each peppery point digging deeper as I made my way to the dining room, where Jeff Davis huddled with half a dozen advisers. They'd taken the china and glassware from the étagères, arranging the pieces across the rosewood table to demarcate the positions of the Union and Confederate forces. The porcelain punch bowl stood in the middle of one cluster, representing Atlanta. At the center of another cluster was the silver and crystal berry bowl, Richmond. One of the men adjusted regiments of goblets and corps of saucers, while Burton Harrison read out a dispatch regarding Joe Johnston's latest clash with General Sherman.

As I hovered about the room refilling glasses, my burns grew harder to bear. I stepped away to grip the sideboard as often as I could, fearful I might faint outright.

"If the mission succeeds," I heard Custis Lee say, "it will be an end to Lincoln for once and all."

Those words caught me quick. Forcing myself to listen through the nauseating fog of pain, I struggled to make out what Confederate plotting I'd missed.

"The Union failed at the very same gambit," Aunt Piss said.

The other men glanced nervously at Jeff Davis while Custis Lee answered, "The Union sent but two thousand men, relying on the command of that imbecile Dahlgren. Even as we speak, Jubal Early is amassing ten thousand of our finest troops, along with munitions to arm all the Confederates that we will liberate from the Federal prisons."

Rushes of pain swept across my seared flesh, as though the hooves of those ten thousand horses were thudding along each sharp pepper-point of my burns. James Seddon, who'd held the post of Confederate secretary of war nearly as long as his three predecessors put together, leaned forward to pluck a berry from the bowl at the center of the table. He suffered from strabismus, and his lazy eye seemed to linger on the tabletop, even as he fixed the other on Aunt Piss. "So long as Grant does not suspect Early is riding toward Washington, the Union capital and its president will be ours for the picking."

Despite all the poultices of beeswax and flaxseed resin I laid on my putrefied skin, that whole week just about any labor rubbed my burns raw. Sophronia and Hortense suffered right along with me, slaving extra hard to make up for my slowness. So long as they worked beside me in Jeff Davis's office, I stayed as far as I could from his papers, lest my curiosity betray me. Mid-day Friday, as we wrang out rags to wash the windowpanes, Queen Varina, still not recovered from delivering a bawling baby daughter four days earlier, shouted for Hortense.

Hortense sucked her teeth and disappeared into the adjacent bedchamber, nodding to me when she returned. "Get the cook to put up a basket a whatever she got for Marse Davis' dinner, you carry it over to him." She dropped her voice. "Queen Varina think he too stupid to eat if she ain't up to feed him herself."

When I stepped out of the Gray House, the thick July air felt nearly intoxicating. My head echoed from the preternatural quiet of Capitol Square, which stood empty in the noontime heat. White Richmond's hunger and discontent had grown far worse since the previous year's Bread Riot. But by now the residents were too weak and wasted to riot. No one even patrolled the Square to enforce the prohibition against negroes crossing the green.

Still and all, a soldier stood guard outside the central archway of the Customs House, and others were stationed on every landing of the stair. I lifted my basket to each one and muttered, "For Marse Davis, from the Gray House," keeping my eyes low as they waved me past.

When I reached the office that ran the length of the top floor, Burton Harrison gestured for me to set the basket on the massive desk, not even pausing in his address to Jeff Davis, who stood gazing out the window. "We have the report from Early's scouts today. He's ridden clear to Winchester with no resistance. He should ford the Potomac within the week."

Davis kept his back to the room, as though searching the window for a glimpse of his far-off lieutenant general. "A force of ten thousand men riding across Virginia, and Grant without the slightest knowledge of it. Truly, it seems too great a miracle even for us to hope for."

"Any miracle is but the will of the Lord," Harrison answered. "He has sustained the Confederacy, and now it seems He sees fit to end Lincoln's tyranny at last."

Though I fought to keep my features blank and my gait steady as I left the room, what I heard had me foundering. I'd taken even greater care than usual when I prepared my report the Monday previous. By Tuesday morning, what information I had of Early's planned attack on Lincoln should have been on its way out of the city. With Union troops only a dozen miles away, it would take no more than one day, two at the most, for the message to reach Grant's own eyes. Surely he had it by now. What could be keeping him from acting on my intelligence—and what would the price of ignoring it be?

For three years, Mr. Lincoln had prosecuted the war with a constancy that awed even his foes. The Union had lost far more men than the Confederates, was losing still more with every week of Grant's campaign, Unconditional Surrender sacrificing his own men corpse by corps. But Lincoln never wavered in his determination to preserve the Union, though it might cost deaths another hundred thousandfold. The would-be Confederate assassins knew that without Lincoln in command, Northern politicians might be done enough with death to choose peace over victory. And if they did, the Emancipation Proclamation would have no more force than a fistful of sand tossed into a hurricane wind.

Through every bloody season of the war, the Confederacy had clung to slavery even over the lives of its own sons. If Lincoln's successor accepted a peaceful dissolution of the Union, the Confederate States of America would never free their slaves.

As Bet pulled her gig up beside the darkened cabin that night, I gagged at the sickly stench of rotting fruit. The people of Richmond were slowly starving, yet here was some farmer letting his crop molder in the field. Bet didn't seem to pay the least mind to this wonderment, though hunger must have pinched at her stomach just as constantly as at mine.

I'd gone to her as soon as my day's labor was done in the Gray House, figuring I could count on her devotion to Lincoln. Sure enough, she shared my consternation over how Monday's report could go unheeded this long. But relieved as I was when she harnessed up her horse and rode us out to where we could get word to the Union command, still I braced myself for whatever she might do, given how reckless she'd grown.

Jumping down from the gig, she secured the reins to the split rail fence, strode to the door of the cabin, and let out a series of short whistles.

The door cracked just wide enough for a hard voice inside to ask, "What do you want?"

Bet answered with her usual self-pride. "I am a lady from Richmond whom Sharpe knows well."

The door shut, and we heard murmurings inside, low and unintelligible. A bearded face hovered at the cabin window and then disappeared. The door opened again, a pale hand gesturing us inside.

The three men occupying the little room were so scrawny I could tell none of them did a farm man's physical labor. The crop gone to waste in the field wasn't their concern. Whether the farm was abandoned, seized, or willingly lent, I couldn't say. But I guessed from their wary expressions that they occupied the farmstead solely because it sat halfway between the Confederate capital and General Grant's latest headquarters.

"Who is this Sharpe fellow?" one of the men asked.

"This is no time for nonsense play." Bet spoke as though the men were her servants, and it were her burden to order them about. "I am a true Unionist, and you know as well as I what that means to Colonel Sharpe." She let out how Sharpe, Butler, and the rest before them had been the glad recipients of the correspondence she left at the edge of her family's market farm, farther up the Osborne Turnpike.

The men showed no flicker of acknowledgment, though one of the three likely rode her missives out to City Point himself.

"A message was sent earlier this week, that we fear has been apprehended." Bet nudged me forward. "Tell them, Mary."

I didn't much care to be ordered to speak in front of strange white men. Searching for my voice in the close air of the cabin, I was as nervous as the day I made my first recitation to Miss Douglass. And even less expectant of an approving audience than with my stern schoolmistress.

"Jubal Early is riding north through the Shenandoah with ten thousand men, to attack Washington."

The men stayed quiet and still. They might have been a father and his two grown sons, the way they shared the same stony semblance.

"Early is within a week of Washington." Bet's voice turned high and tight, she was so agitated at their silence. "Grant must be informed."

"General Grant is quite aware of Early's location," the man who'd peered out the window at us said. "He is facing Grant's troops, before Petersburg. Along with the rest of Lee's army."

"No." I needed no prodding now, knowing how important it was to convince them. "He is past Winchester already. He means to kill Lincoln."

The man sneered, not at me but at Bet. "A Southerner comes to us from Richmond, driving a finer horse than many a Confederate cavalryman has these days, to bring news of Early that contradicts Grant's own observations." He grabbed her arm, twisting it behind her back until she cried out. "Do the Confederates believe we will fall for such deception? Do they send women and niggers to lead us astray?"

Another of the men yanked me from behind. "Did they tell you what would happen if you were suspected?" he breathed into my ear. "What happens to Confederate spies who are caught by the Federals?"

"Arrest us, then," I said, "only tell General Grant to send troops against Early. Once they find him, you can free us."

"I'm not about to send Federal forces on a wild goose chase, weakening our line and giving the Confederates a chance to break the siege at Petersburg. Or to tell General Grant he is wrong, because some ignorant darky appearing out of the night says so."

"She is not ignorant," Bet insisted. "She is—"

Hoofbeats thundering toward the cabin cut her off. The rider jumped down just outside the door, not bothering to whistle or knock before he pushed his way in. Shouting his news before he was even fully inside.

" 'Tis a mercy I hae reached you at last. I am riding two days and nights, over the Blue Ridge from Mount Jackson. Ten thousand rebels came through the very hamlet, telling that they were going on to Washington."

McNiven didn't let out a flicker of recognition for me or Bet. He just stood more wild-eyed than I'd ever seen him, as the older man asked, "You are sure of this?"

"As sure as the beating o' my own heart, rapid grown from journeying fifty hours with nary a rest, to bring the news." McNiven held out a sealed report.

The man tore open the packet and skimmed the page. "Grant will get this before dawn," he promised McNiven. He barely took time to order his comrades to let us go, before he stormed out the cabin door and disappeared toward the barn.

"How fortuitous that Thomas arrived just when he did." We'd ridden in silence for the first mile back to Richmond, McNiven slowing his horse to keep pace with Bet's gig. But now Bet seemed eager to converse, pleased as she was with the excitement of the evening. "It was most exceptional, don't you think?"

"Nothing too exceptional about being called a nigger and a darky." I was more than a little piqued that she could overlook such a thing.

She bristled stiff beside me. "The burden of race prejudice is a terrible one, as we both know. Once the threat to the Union has been put down, surely that grave problem will be addressed."

I was ready to address it right there and then. "Maybe you believe that. But I've seen enough race prejudice among Unionists, Northerners, even Quakers, that I can't agree."

She reined Frances Burney to a halt and turned to face me. "Race prejudice is nothing more than ignorance, something all people, white and colored, should and will be taught to overcome. Surely you know that."

I was in no mood for her telling me what I knew. So I bit my tongue, like I'd seen my mama do a thousand times. Mama who'd taught me that anyone trying to talk sense to a fool just makes himself a fool as well. And a winded fool at that.

Unsatisfied with my silence, Bet turned to McNiven. "Don't you concur that once the Union is preserved and the scourge of slavery removed, race prejudice will be eliminated?"

"I canna predict what is to come. But for now I ken that what be most easeful is to show people the very thing they want to see."

McNiven's bay snorted and pawed the ground, as if to agree. The horse hadn't settled well into the slow pace of our travel, and he seemed even more restless now that we'd stopped entirely.

Not at all like a horse that had been ridden hard for two days across the Blue Ridge.

Watching the eager hoof, I realized it wasn't a damn bit of fortuity that McNiven had turned up at that cabin. It was a bamboozlement.

I looked hard at McNiven. "How did you know where we might be?" I asked.

"'Tis my work to know what passes 'tween Confederate and Union lines, lass. The two of you were not so hard to track."

Track. That word put me in mind of how slave-catchers hunted negroes down with dogs. It didn't lighten the unyielding truth that already darkened my spirits: McNiven had shown the Federals the thing they wanted to see—a white man with a report purportedly from some garrison commander out in the Shenandoah—while Bet and I might have wasted away in prison without persuading them to trust my word. "So I should be glad a white liar is believed when a colored intelligence agent, ready to swear on her life, isn't?"

"Them what did not mind your words might just as well mind mine, though yours be true and mine false. 'Tis a thing neither for us to be glad nor sorry on, only to act upon as we maun." He softened his voice. "The wisest soul is one what takes a curse and disparagement, and makes an advantage o' them, as you have showed these last years."

These last years, I'd played the role of the ignorant darky well. So ignorant as to be thought incapable of literacy, of treachery. So dark as to seem nearly invisible to Jeff Davis and the men who came to see him. I took faint comfort as McNiven brought a boot against his horse and Bet flicked the reins on hers, with nothing for me to do but ride quiescent through the hot night.

On the twelfth July, a messenger to the Gray House interrupted Jeff Davis's supper with a telegram reporting that Union troops had turned out to oppose Early's force at Frederick, Maryland. Though the Confederates had won the battle, the delay gave Grant time to move his Sixth Corps to Washington, where any assault by Early would now be handily defeated.

"So much for your miracle," Davis told Harrison. "Some infernal scouting expedition from Martinsburg must have seen our men and telegraphed to Grant. It is as though the Federals stand among us, for all they know of our strategies."

He threw his napkin onto the table, and the supposedly ignorant serving girl stepped forward to clear his place.

Twenty-five

"**Y**ou gonna do something 'bout that Sophronia."

I was on all fours in the basement of the Gray House, the late September chill seeping from the bare floor through my frayed linsey-woolsey as I scrubbed what mess the children had made of their dinner. All the day before, cannonades sounded, auditory evidence of the Federal troops skirmishing a mere half a dozen miles away. With Jeff Davis gone south to confer with his field commanders over how to stop General Sherman's string of victories in Georgia, there was little for me to gather for my daily reports. So I was glad enough to find myself laboring in this empty room that seemed the only quiet corner in all of Richmond, with time to wonder over whether the latest fighting would come to anything or no. Or so I thought, until Hortense hunted me up with some new complaint.

I eased to a kneel, anticipating a report of some disaster in the parlor or the nursery. "What Sophronia done?"

"Ain't you got eyes in your head? Once the turkey's tail feathers begin to spread, it mean laying time coming soon."

All those years of private schooling in Philadelphia, even my time in Richmond, didn't leave me the least bit able to understand Hortense's countrified way of speaking.

She shook her head, not so much at my ignorance as at the burdens she bore as housekeeper. "I told her watch herself sneaking round with that Tobias. Now she in the family way."

By 1864 we were all so hungry, white Richmond along with colored Richmond, it was hard to believe anyone could grow thick around the middle. But Hortense ran her eyes over me and Sophronia all day long. She'd probably noted Sophronia's pregnancy before the poor slow child knew herself.

"She must be scared half to death."

Hortense rolled her eyes. "Scared a her own shadow, most the time. She so muddle-brained, she think just cause Queen Varina coo over her own brat she gonna coo over a pickaninny, too." She snorted. "Anyone with a spit of sense see Queen Varina gonna sell that pickaninny away faster'n Sophronia say 'please Missy don't.' Not even bat a eye worrying over what fiddle-faddle she spend the money on."

She was right. Queen Varina would sell a newborn slave just to feed her carriage horses another month. And that could kill a woman stronger than Sophronia would ever be.

"What you want me to do 'bout it?"

"Get her away from here, 'fore anyone know 'bout the baby." Hortense said it just as though she were directing me to dust the library mantel.

"You think I got some way to get a slave out a Richmond, I wouldn't be long gone myself?"

"Maybe you done stuck around, looking for something you dropped." She reached into her apron, drew out a wadded-up sheet of paper, and let it fall onto the floor between us, casual as you please. Without even reaching to smooth it flat, I knew what it was–the letter from Wilson that, months before, slipped out from where I carried it. Though Hortense couldn't read a single word on that page, she'd had sense enough to snatch it up and keep it, just to have something to hold against me.

"I don't know what you up to," she said, "the way you sneak round this house. But I know you up to something, and you like to keep it quiet. So you gonna see to it Sophronia get took away, or I gonna get real noisy to Queen Varina 'bout your sneaking ways. Or maybe to Marse Davis hisself, when he get back from carrying on down in Georgy."

I studied her inquisitorial eyes and that hard-set mouth, just as surely as I'd ever studied Miss Douglass's Latin lessons or Miss Mapps's geometry. What I saw was as certain an answer as I ever found in any school-book. I might have lied and denied about that letter, at least enough to connive Queen Varina or Jeff Davis. But Hortense wasn't about to be fooled. And not just about my misplaced missive.

The Gray House sure wasn't *we in the house*—but still and all, Hortense lived by the same code Mama taught me. She knew slaves saw things, heard things, did things without master and mistress ever suspecting. Knew I was doing something I needed to conceal.

"Federals real close," I said. "Hear them guns most every day. Likely they be here 'fore that baby."

"Them Federals been sniffing round Richmond since Marse Davis first drug us here from Alabam. Don't set much store by them one way or the other. But a bright gal like Molly, why I know she gonna take care a Sophronia, just like I tole her to." She plucked the letter up and tucked it into her bodice. "Queen Varina going to one a them starvating parties tonight, she gonna lie in bed all day tomorrow moaning over she so tired, she got a sick headache, and all that. That's Saturday, and no one spect you be here Sunday. You leave tonight, no one miss Sophronia 'fore Monday."

Leave tonight—even Moses himself had more time to lay plans for leading the slaves to freedom. Still, with Jeff Davis away, my being gone a day from the Gray House wouldn't hurt the Union any. "Why you fretting and fussing so much over Sophronia, all of a sudden?"

She puckered her face into a frown. "Last thing I need be some hysterical nigger gal about the house, carrying on over her sold away pickaninny."

Hortense put up a good bluff. But Queen Varina would be plenty hysterical herself when she discovered another of her slaves disappeared across the Union lines. So Hortense wasn't angling for more peace in the Gray House, whatever she said.

Maybe it was a desire to defy Queen Varina. Maybe revenge for some long ago hurt of her own. Maybe another hint of a child Hortense had, or more than one, that were taken from her and sold away. Whatever it was, I could sense it, even if all the details weren't for me to know for sure. Just as Hortense sensed enough about me to know I'd find a way to get Sophronia to Federal territory safe and sound.

I didn't know whether it was more sympathy or self-preservation welling inside me as I told her I'd see to it, no need for us to talk on it further.

Being in the family way must have exhausted Sophronia, because she drifted off to sleep just as soon as we passed Rocketts Landing, despite all the jostling of Wilson's cart. I wasn't sorry for the lack of company. While she was awake, she kept asking "Where Tobias at?" or "Tobias come soon?"—questions I didn't care to answer. How could I tell her I didn't know if she'd ever see her man again, didn't even know if I'd see mine?

Wilson had driven many a slave to freedom in this very cart. Those slaves had curled up small, a sack of flour or a cord of wood covering them. Knowing that if some white Southerner discovered them, all their hope of freedom would end in whipping, maiming, sale—or who knows what combination of the three.

Sophronia and I didn't ride like that. I sat and she lay right out in the open, our only cover the velvet black sky, and the propinquity of the white lady who drove us along the Osborne Turnpike and then down New Market Road.

Bet perched ramrod straight on the driver's seat of the rough-hewn cart, acting for all the world like that's where she ought to be. She was obliging enough when I appealed for her aid, eager to help transport a runaway slave. Glad to flash her pass at the Confederate picket outside Richmond, who warned her to be careful of the Yankee varmints who might be sneaking about.

For all her bold and brash, still I caught Bet frowning in consternation over how to fix upon a route to ride Sophronia to the Federals. With the constant skirmishing, even the Union troops pressing forward and the Confederates trying to regain lost ground couldn't know just where one side's territory gave off and the other's began. Bet and I both had our brows well furrowed over how we'd make our way, when a gunshot rang out a dozen yards away.

Everything happened so fast after that, I could barely mark it all.

Frances Burney whinnying and rearing up with fright.

Bet shouting and struggling to calm the horse.

Virginia air thick with the smell of gunpowder and fear.

And then on the road in front of us, the silhouette of a soldier, aiming his pistol right at Bet and ordering, "Hold there."

Bet grappled desperate at the reins, but that mare wouldn't stay still.

I saw a flash and heard the crack of a bullet. Frances Burney, the last of the Van Lews' grand team of six white carriage horses, fell to the ground.

Bet jumped down to kneel over the beast. She rubbed a hand ever so gently along its muzzle, as though coaxing it through its last pain spasms. Three and a half bloody years of war, all that death and mauling, and she could still mourn for a horse.

The soldier came toward us. As I made out his raggedy butternut uniform, Bet rose to a stand. "I shall report this act of wanton cruelty to your commanding officer, young man. You may be sure of that."

The soldier howled a maniac's laugh. "Tell the devil howdy-do when you do. 'Cause the captain's in hell sure as I'm standing here. Though mebbe like he said I'm headed there myself. Reckon I am, but I don't care."

He jerked his head a half-turn and nodded as though he were listening to a voice behind him, then darted his eyes back around. "Only, Sam and Becky and the baby is in Heaven by now. Never got to see em one last time like Becky wanted. If I go to hell ain't never get to see 'em agin."

"I am sorry for your loss," Bet said. I hoped she had sense enough to see the soldier wasn't in his right mind. He'd probably run off from his company after hearing tidings of sickness and death at home.

"I ain't much lost," he said, though he peered about as if he wasn't sure how he came to be talking to her. He waved his revolver toward me and Sophronia. "Who's that?"

"Those are my servants. I brought them to the city to tend Mother, and now I must take them back to our farm."

"We ain't got no slaves. No fancy city house neither. Paw said it was a fool shame to go off and get kilt for them that did."

He stepped to the cart, holding his sidearm steady on us. "Jethro says you can milk a nigger, same as a cow. Paw says nah. They ain't neither of them ever saw one, though." With his free hand, he pinched at where the fabric of Sophronia's bodice pulled tight across her bosom.

Bet was on him fast, whirling him around as Sophronia squealed in pain.

"Young man, in the name of decency, do not behave this way."

He rubbed the back of his hand against the stubble on his cheek, like an animal pawing its matted fur. "You awful careful a them niggers. You one a them abolesh started this damn war, maybe." With two quick clicks, that deranged Confederate cocked his gun, training it on Bet.

The only thing in the cart besides me and Sophronia was the basket of food Bet had packed along. I reached into it, then crept quick to the edge of the cart.

The water jug was heavy, still nearly full. I felt the heft as I swung it up in both my hands, then brought it down hard on the back of that man's head.

I thought I heard bone crack. Or maybe I felt it. Maybe I just mistook the breaking of the pottery jug for the smashing of that man's skull. But the next thing I knew, he was lying on the ground.

I jumped out of the cart, the earth hitting stiff again my soles. I raised my foot and brought it down hard against the same bloodied spot where the jug had smashed apart like an egg cracked against a skillet. I stomped his head over and over, until at last I made out Sophronia sobbing in terror, and then Bet's voice.

"My God, Mary! What have you done?"

Without even bothering to answer, I bent and took up the unconscious soldier's revolver, checked the hammer, and put a bullet right into his head.

Twenty-six

At least Bet was willing to forgo her notions about proper burial when it came to carriage horses and crazed Confederate soldiers.

Heavy as Frances Burney was, there wasn't much chance we could move her carcass. Wilson's cart would have to be left behind, too, no use to us without an animal to draw it. As for the Confederate, I slid a hand beneath each of his armpits, his arms dead weight against my knuckles as I dragged him off the road and a little ways into the woods, so whoever came across the horse and cart wouldn't find him as well.

Sophronia was still whimpering with fear by the time the three of us set off on foot. "He can't hurt you anymore," I told her. "Let's forget all about it, like a bad dream. Keep a lookout for sun-up and your first day of freedom."

But even as we walked along, I knew sun-up might bring still more trouble. I could make out spots of blood and who knows what all pulpy else on my skirt and shoes, thought I even felt it dried across my face and hair. We were without so much as a jug of water to wash me clean, and likely to chance upon more strangers come daylight.

"Is there a creek anywhere near here?" I asked Bet. We didn't dare make for the James, guarded as it was by Confederate troops.

"I believe Four Mile Creek is somewhere farther down the road," she said. "I've never had cause to travel there." When I'd gotten the soldier into the woods, I stepped away from the corpse and vomited so hard I shook from head to toe. Bet was just the opposite, her speech and movements mechanical with shock at what I'd done.

Not a half hour after we started walking, it began to rain. At first I was glad for it, hoping the water would wash away some of the blood, some of my fear, too. But the drops came hard and fast. The angry deluge soaked us through, Sophronia's teeth chattering from the cold. We left the road for what cover the woods offered, none of us remarking on the artillery rounds that burst out from time to time, thundering yet closer than they had in Richmond.

We made slow progress as we navigated the mud-thick tangle of trees. Just a quarter mile from the road the land was cleared, but we didn't dare edge along those fields. A Virginia farmer might not take too kindly to discovering three trespassers on his land, one a fugitive slave and another a killer.

A killer. That's what I was. What in an instant, I had made myself.

The razor-sharp realization cut at me, when from deep in the woods a man shouted, "Halt there. Identify yourselves, and state your business."

"My name is Elizabeth Van Lew, and these are my servants." Bet gestured for us to come stand beside her. "We were traveling on New Market Road when our cart horse went lame. We are trying to find Darbytown, but I fear we've gotten lost in this downpour."

I heard tree limbs sway and leaves rustle as the man pushed closer. But all I could see was the glint of a bayonet.

"Miss Van Lew? Is that really you?" Wonder curled the soldier's voice. "I wouldn't hardly have recognized you, you've grown so thin."

Bet squinted into the rain, frowning and shaking her head in confusion.

With another bout of rustling, the scout came into view, asking, "Don't you know your old friend?"

I gasped in surprise. "I'd know that gap tooth of yours anywhere, George Patterson. Only you ought to know by now, these days I answer to Mrs. Bowser."

Hattie's husband shouldered his rifle as he came up close to us. "I stand corrected, Mrs. Bowser. But I do suppose there's some correction warranted all the way around. You three look like you've had a sight more trouble than just a horse gone lame."

Bet was ready to spin him who knows what story, but I spoke up before she could, explaining that Sophronia was in the family way, and we needed to get her someplace she could have her baby in freedom. I told him that Bet was a Unionist and an ally, maybe Wilson had mentioned her to him. When he nodded, I added that I'd bloodied myself shooting our horse, to put it out of its misery. To keep him from questioning my tale, I asked what he was doing wandering by himself in the Virginia countryside.

"Reconnaissance." He drew himself up, looking more of a man than the boy I remembered. "We took New Market Heights yesterday, Fort Harrison as well. Spread the Rebel lines thinner than ever, giving us some vantage from which to push them back toward Richmond." But then the pride seeped out of him, and he seemed older still. "Only, I hate to have to tell you. Wilson's been shot."

Shot. The word hit me hard. Hard as the recoil from the bullet I put into a man hours before.

The uncertainty of all the months I'd feared my husband killed or captured was wholly eclipsed by the hellish surety of knowing he was wounded. All I could do now was follow, as George led us through the battle-weary Virginia countryside.

The sky brightened into day but held its grayish hue. We stopped at Four Mile Creek, where Bet tore a makeshift washing cloth from her underskirt. I stood numb while she cleaned my face and hair and hands. I felt like I was outside myself, watching everything that happened as though we were players on a stage.

From Lavinia Whitlock to Flora Stuart, these three years I'd witnessed a stunning sorority of grief. I wanted no part of that sisterhood. But it didn't much matter what I wanted, or what I'd worked for or prayed for all this time. Not now that my husband was shot.

The stun that had cloaked us since our encounter with the Confederate weighed heavier as we walked on, George's report choking not just words but also the very breath from me. Every minute he led us along might be taken from the death hour. The hour Papa sat with Mama. The hour Bet sat with Papa. An hour I didn't get with either of them.

That death might take my husband, this knowledge had been the ugly companion plaguing me these many months. That he might die with me so near but still not there, this was a new horror in a world I hadn't thought could grow more horrible.

Here at last was the singular truth of war: A hundred thousand soldiers might take the field together, yet each who fell could die alone.

At last we reached the Union encampment, rows and rows of low, bone-hued tents, hundreds of negro soldiers milling between them. Our foursome drew plenty of curious stares as we made our way along the trampled meadow grass to a larger tent, tall enough for a man to stand in and wide enough for several rows of bed-cots. Bet and Sophronia waited beneath the yellow hospital flag while I followed George inside. Followed to the cot that held my husband, the trouser leg of his uniform cut away, a bloodied bandage wound tight against his bare thigh.

Wilson lay still. Too still for my comfort. It seemed nothing could be so quiet and peaceful amid all these years of war. Seeing the lids closed heavy on his eyes, my brain made out the words *too late, too late.*

The air within the tent was an acrid distillation of the deathly stench that hung so often upon the streets of Richmond. Fearful my husband would never look on me again in this world, I touched the back of my hand to his cheek, a tender, tentative farewell. I nearly didn't believe it when those dear eyelids blinked slowly open.

He looked thunderstruck from me to George and back again. "Tell Doc I must be delirious. I'm having visions of a ministering angel."

"No angel here," I said. "Just a woman who loves you."

A woman whose each braced muscle eased again, though the fear of losing my husband was yet but palliated. I bent and kissed his brow, not bothering to hold to modesty in front of the nurses and the other injured soldiers.

George muttered something about seeing to Sophronia and Bet, and exited the tent. One of the nurses offered me a small stool, and I sat as close to Wilson as I could, willing myself courage to utter the question I couldn't hold from asking but wasn't sure I was ready to hear answered. "What does the doctor say?"

"The ball passed through my leg and right out the other side, missed the bone entirely. Figures I'll be fine, maybe just a limp if the muscle doesn't heal right." The seven long months since I'd last laid eyes on him might have been as many years, for all that time had worked upon him. "Hurts so bad, I didn't believe it when the surgeon told me I was a lucky man. But seeing you, I guess he's right. How'd you come to be out here just now?"

"Sophronia's got herself in the family way. Bet and I were trying to bring her out to one of the contraband camps. We lost our horse and were wandering around afoot when George happened upon us, brought us back here." Not wanting to dwell on what I wasn't telling, I leaned forward and kissed my husband again.

After promising me he wasn't suffering much, he grinned and told me I looked terrible. "I suppose that comes from having to eat your own cooking."

"My poor cooking can't do what little food there is much harm," I said. "General Grant's doing the best job yet of keeping Richmond hungry. Summer was hard enough, who knows what winter will bring."

"Winter might bring peace, if we take the city in the next month or two. If we don't, Grant will hold the line tight, then press it forward in spring." He squeezed my hand with all the strength a wounded man might muster. "It won't be any longer than that. Even Lee's men know it, you can feel it along the Petersburg line. Victory's coming, and freedom with it."

Coming and *already came* weren't the same, and in the difference between them, it was hard for a soldier's wife to rest easy. "Plenty more battles to be fought before then," I said.

"The worst thing I faced in this war wasn't in battle." He shifted, pain flashing across his face. "Back in May, when we landed at Bermuda Hundred and established Fort Pocahontas, one of our patrols came upon a local planter. Eppes Clayton—a true FFV and nasty as a slave-owner comes, from what folks said. One of the men in the 1st had been his slave, and when they brought Clayton into camp, General Wild ordered the private to whip him.

"That soldier must have given him twenty lashes. And then he handed the whip over to some colored ladies. Fugitive slaves who'd also belonged to Clayton, they'd fled to the fort just days before. Each of those women took up the whip and set another fifteen marks across Clatyon's back. People were cheering as though the whipping was a party, with General Wild smiling and clapping like he was watching one of them coon shows they love so much up North. That man led us into battle, and still we were nothing more than that to him."

The remembrance turned my husband's features nearly ugly. "Wild ordered the chaplain to preach a sermon on the whipping, and we all had to stand round and give praise while he blustered about how the righteous demanded blood."

"Hebrews 9:22," I said. *"And almost all things are by the law purged with blood; and without shedding of blood is no remission.* McNiven told me John Brown preached it over and over, when he was being held at Charlestown after Harper's Ferry."

Wilson didn't find much comfort in that. "Brown is dead. But there are plenty of negroes who are going to be living once this war is over. If all we have is bloodlust, what kind of life will freedom bring? So long as we want to hurt and harm even when there's no battle raging, how different are we from the overseers and slaveholders?"

I felt the weight of the water jug in my hands, the force of my foot ramming the Confederate's skull. The ease with which I picked up the gun, pulled the trigger, and shot him dead.

What would my husband think when he learned what I'd done? What would he make me think of myself?

Screams erupted outside the tent. A nurse rushed in, addressing me in a hushed, official tone. "Two of our scouts were ambushed an hour past. The surgeon is operating now. You'll have to go, so I can make up places for them."

Wilson began to protest, but I shook my head, glad enough to take my leave from our conversation.

George had settled Sophronia and Bet before a sputtering campfire, where they breakfasted on what rations of hardtack he managed to wrangle from his fellow soldiers. He offered me a tin plate, but I waved it away.

"What we do now?" Sophronia asked.

"The supply wagons come later today. They'll take Wilson and the rest of the wounded out of the field," George said. "They can bring you to Bermuda Hundred, and from there you'll go by boat out to Fort Monroe. Thousands of former slaves are living there, with ladies from up North come to teach them reading and writing. Including that Quakeress you were always so fond of, Mary."

"Zinnie Moore?"

"Yes indeed. She came down when we did, said she meant to do whatever she could to aid the freedmen. Though with her funny way of speaking, who knows how those poor negroes will sound when she's done with them."

I tried to smile at George's joke. But I was haunted by the words Zinnie had said to me the day I left the sewing circle. *Take care that neither a blow to thy body nor a mark on thy soul will be the consequence of whatever work thou chooses.* The patchwork of lamp-oil burns no longer pained my flesh. But I felt the fresh-made mark upon my soul keenly.

"You come, too?" Sophronia's face was pinched with worry.

I shook my head. "I have to get back to Richmond. It would be too much work for Hortense with both of us gone, and—"

Bet cut me off. "Perhaps you ought to go with Sophronia."

I stared at her, not believing she meant for me to give up our spying. "Like I said, there's work to be done in the Gray House. I best be back there."

Bet's eyes bore icy blue into mine. "Whatever work is to be done will be seen to one way or another. I think it best for you to go out to Fort Monroe."

I told myself she just wanted to believe it didn't matter whether I was in Richmond or no, because she never could bear to admit how much of the espionage was my doing. But when I looked down and saw the dance of bloodstains along the hem of my skirt, for once I wondered if maybe Bet was right.

The rain let up by mid-morning, and George some-how connived to move Wilson out of the hospital tent for a few hours. I was plenty apprehensive when I took my place beside where he sat wrapped in an army-issue blanket, his back propped up against the trunk of a maple tree. Much as I longed to be with my husband, I wasn't any too desirous of taking up the conversation we'd left off.

I waited until he was eating a bit of salt pork and cornmeal fry, then said, "Maybe I ought to stay and tend you while that wound is healing. After you're well, I can go out to Fort Monroe. Bet suggested I help with the teaching at the school there."

He set down his fork and looked at me hard. "When Bet means to get you into danger, you're glad enough to take up whatever she proposes. Lord knows, I've tried to make my peace with that. But since when do you let her talk you into something so fiddle-come-foolish as giving up important work? Don't you think what you've been doing means more to slaves' freedom than teaching a bunch of *ABC*s?"

I'd long grown leery of Bet drawing me into danger. But what I did just hours earlier proved I had my own vast well of danger, bubbling hot-headed and murderous, inside of me.

"What's the matter?" Wilson asked. "What's keeping you from going back to Richmond?"

I kept my gaze on those dull tines, unable to meet his eyes as I told him everything that passed with that Confederate. Once I related it all, I swallowed hard over the lump of shame in my throat and forced myself to look up, as I asked if he was angry.

"Of course I'm angry. Maniac like that, threatening my wife, Sophronia, even that Crazy Bet. What sort of a man wouldn't be angry to hear it, knowing he was nowhere near to protect you?"

"I mean, are you angry at me?"

Puzzlement sowed troughs along his brow. "Why would I be angry at you?"

"What you said before about bloodlust, and violence outside battle . . ." My voice trailed off.

"This wasn't the same as all that. That man meant to harm you."

I laced my fingers, clasping my palms tight together, wanting to feel myself solid, instead of feeling the cold, heavy memory of the jug I used to strike a man down. "Once I knocked him out, he didn't stand much chance of harming anyone. But I kept at him. I kicked him, and I shot him, because I wanted to. I liked it."

"You don't much look as though you like it now."

"Of course not. I'm sick with it. But when it was happening—"

"When it was happening wasn't the same as now. If something like that happens again, you'd be right to do as you did, protecting Sophronia and Bet and yourself that way. But I'm not much worried you're about to do so to just any white man you come across. Are you?"

"Wilson, I killed a man. Don't you know what that means?"

"I surely do." He set a hand over where the thin wool blanket covered the hole blazed by the metal ball that had traveled through his body. "I hope I've killed a man or two, and I won't be sorry to try again, once this leg is healed." I started to object, but he stopped me. "Don't go telling me it's not the same for you as for me, Contrary Mary. If the Confederates would rather die than see negroes free and safe, that choice rests on them, not us."

I ached to believe him. Still, I wasn't sure. "Mama said so many times that Jesus had a plan for me. I guess I wanted it to be true, wanted to know I was special. But Jesus couldn't have planned for me to do what I did. Maybe that means there's no plan after all." Maybe I wasn't so special. "I just don't see how you can love me, knowing what I've done."

My husband answered me like only he in all the world could. "Years back, there was some baggage I took North in a hurry. Wisp of a thing, no more than a girl. Young as she was, she'd killed her master. He'd got her with child then sold the baby off, kept coming at her. I don't know if she planned it or just did it without thinking, but by the time the Railroad people got to her, she was lying as still as the dead. Even as she lay there, I prayed she'd live and get North. I wanted to believe she could fall in love, make a family, in freedom.

Because if that could happen, it meant I wasn't a fool to hope in the face of slavery, even though bondage took so many that carrying a few here or there to freedom sometimes didn't seem to make much difference."

It was the first we ever spoke of that girl. Wilson never was much for talking about his Railroad work, knowing how many fugitives' freedom, how his own safety, too, depended on him holding such things secret. But my reticence wasn't quite like his. Speaking of that troubled child, what she'd been through, all her owner did to her—how could I talk of such horror, when I just wanted it to be over and done?

He took my hands into his. "For all I know, that girl never did say another word. But I hope she did. I hope someone loves her like I love you, and she can tell him what passed and have him soothe her, without her needing to carry it like a guilty secret in her heart."

I didn't hold from him what glimmer I had that his hope might have come true. "That girl spoke again, I know that much," I said. "She spoke to me."

I related how I helped carry her toward New York. "When McNiven told me it was David Bustill Bowser's cousin who fetched that girl out of harm's way, I never much thought I'd meet the man."

"Well, maybe that was part of Jesus's plan. Much as I care for you, I do like to believe perhaps He had a hand in bringing us together. But even if He didn't, I know I'll always love you. Just like I know the work you do in Richmond is important, even if He didn't plan for you to do it. Don't you know that yourself?"

I nodded, loving Wilson all the more for showing me it was true.

"Well then, forget about Bet and your mama and all the rest. What do you mean to do? Strongheaded as my wife is, I wager she must have some opinion of her own on the matter."

I thought of the tantrum Queen Varina would throw once she discovered another of her slaves was gone, how much harder I'd have to slave in the Gray House to make up the loss of Sophronia's labor. How sharp the hunger of the last few months had cut, how much sharper it would slice come winter.

I regarded my sweet, precious husband and tried to imagine leaving him to be nursed by strangers, when we both knew that many a convalescing soldier took a turn for the worst if camp fever hit. I thought of how I missed Zinnie Moore, how good it would be to work beside her again.

But then I thought about that girl we brought to freedom, me and Wilson working together before we even knew of each other. I thought about Dangerfield Newby and the sermon Wilson's cousin preached on him. And I thought about Timothy Smith of Augusta, Maine, and the CSS *Virginia,* and the Bread Riot. I thought about Early's raid, how together McNiven, Bet, and I might well have saved Lincoln from assassination, and the Union from dissolution.

All my life, the hardest choices I made were about leaving. Leaving Mama and Papa to go North. Leaving off with Theodore once I realized I couldn't be the docile wife he wanted. Leaving Zinnie Moore and the rest when I grew impatient with the Female Anti-Slavery Society. Leaving Philadelphia when I believed war was coming, and with it the only real hope for emancipation.

I looked into my husband's eyes, knowing the choice I had to make now was as hard as any of those. But it was different, too. This time I was choosing to stay.

"Husband, you better hurry up and get healed, so you and the rest of the USCT can march on into Richmond. Because there'll be a slave working up in the Gray House who's going to need some liberating, nasty a mistress as that Varina Davis is. In the meanwhile, that slave will do everything she can to help you and the whole Union army get there. And she'll have quite a welcome for you when you do."

Wilson smiled. "I suppose she will."

Twenty-seven

23 December 1864

My dearest one

How many times I have wrote those words! Now before you go thinking I been carrying on with other women remember the US Army is full up with men cant write for their selfs & USCT got more than its share. Many the hour I take up a pen for to write out the words of this fellow or that to send to wife mother or child who ever they got home can read or be read to. So when a certain Scotsman turned up here I see time come to write for myself. He says he might as well bring my letter risk of being caught no worse than risk of what my dear wife do to him if he comes back with no missive from me.

I love you & miss you so. The loving could make a man impashent with the missing but I figure come spring Federals will be in Richmond & youll be in my arms. The thought of it is enuff to keep me warm though the nights are mighty chilly. Leastwise the cold keeps them from marching us around overmuch. Even then I dont grouse like some of the men glad enuff to feel my leg grow strong again. Yes I am recovered from my trial & hope my wife is recovered from hers.

Our friend is making noises about he needs to leave before nightfall so I guess time to close this with a Merry Christmas & know you are in my thoughts even when no messenger can carry a note between us.

Ever your loving
Husband

McNiven brought me that letter on Christmas Eve, and I fell asleep that night hugging the pages as though they were part and parcel of my husband. When I climbed Church Hill the next morning, I found Bet more agitated, her mother more fragile, and the dinner even more paltry than all had been the Christmas before. But still I had all the yuletide joy I could hope for, savoring the anticipation of the fall of the Confederacy as surely as I ever did a slice of goose or a mouthful of plum pudding.

Jeff Davis was about as popular among the Confederates as Abraham Lincoln, by the time 1865 rolled in. So when a pair of senators came stomping into the Gray House one late February morning, I could see it was more than the chill winter air that had them red in the face. Queen Varina tried to shoo them off, saying her poor husband lay abed stricken with neuralgia.

"I suppose he can converse with us as easily in his dressing gown as in his frock coat," said Senator Hunter as he strode past her to make his way up the grand staircase. Hunter's stern visage graced the Confederate ten-dollar note, but nowadays the downward turn of his features pulled even more severe than in the bygone time when he sat for that portrait. Back then, ten Confederate dollars might have bought a barrel of flour. Of late it wasn't enough to buy a loaf of bread, nor this week even a single slice.

"Queen Varina gonna throw a fit they talk at her so," Hortense whispered as we watched the exchange from the adjacent corridor. "Only a fool stay down here where she like to find 'em, make trouble just 'cause them white mens come barking."

She yanked me along as she headed up the servants' stair. Not even making a pretense of cleaning once we reached Jeff Davis's office, we cupped our hands against the passage door to the Davises' bedchamber. Hortense's open curiosity didn't much surprise me. Queen Varina and her friends complained loudly to one another over how impudent their servants had grown. Why not Hortense along with the rest?

The first we made out was Senator Wigfall's Texas drawl. "That infernal Jew Benjamin is behind it, I suppose."

"Secretary Benjamin supports it," Davis replied. "But the idea originates with General Lee. He has advocated this course of action for some time, although until this winter I did not deem it necessary to pursue. Now, however—"

Hunter wouldn't suffer him to finish. "We cannot allow a Confederate president to take away the very thing at the heart of our Cause."

Davis answered like a hyena whooping at his pack. "Without this measure, the Federals will defeat us in a matter of weeks."

Confusion tugged at the corners of Hortense's mouth. I shrugged back my own puzzlement and leaned closer to the door.

"We have insisted they are kept in the condition that best suits their limited capacities. Now you would make them our equals, in the very instance when honor and courage matter most," Hunter said. "If they are truly what we claim, it will be their slaughter, and that of many of our sons as well. If they are not what we have said, then even if they triumph, Confederate society will be ruined."

"We need hundreds of thousand more soldiers, when there are barely ten thousand white men left to draft in the Confederacy." Davis's declaration wouldn't have been much news to anyone, North or South. But what he said next was the single most astounding thing I heard uttered in the Gray House. "We hold millions of slaves among us. We would be fools if we did not enlist them at this direst hour for our Cause."

"Where are my damn servants?"

Queen Varina's demand resounded up the curving stairwell, causing Hortense to mutter, "Just let 'em 'list up this darky. Give me one a them rifles, see what way I point."

But even Varina Davis's heaviest wrath couldn't overpoise the pleasure I took at Hunter and Wigfall's distress. I knew those men were right. The Confederate army's enlistment of negroes would sound the death knell of slavery even more loudly than Lincoln's Emancipation Proclamation had.

White ladies from the ci-devant wealthiest FFV families toiling all day as government clerks. Mansions along Church Hill turned to boardinghouses, their finest possessions carted off to auction. And now colored men might be armed to fight beside the very whites who owned them. Though the war might rage some weeks more, it seemed the so-called Southern way of life was already gone.

Even Queen Varina saw what it portended. All through the next month, whenever her husband left off his sickbed to return to his Customs House office, strange men came to call on her. They departed the Gray House hauling off furnishings, adornments, even whatever stores of food she'd hoarded down in the cellar. Anything too big for her to take when she left the capital was sold, never mind whether those things belonged to the Davises or not. So long as there was coin to be chaffered for, she bargained away what she could, keeping her dealings tidy secret from her husband.

For once, I hadn't much standing to fault her. Biding her time and hoodwinking Jeff Davis, she wasn't so different from me.

Neither Hortense nor I bothered to put on the fool come the first April, when we packed Queen Varina and her children's bags for their final departure from Richmond.

Mary El, wake up now, child.

Let me sleep, Mama, let me sleep.

We your parents, so you know you best listen. You got to wake up.

But, Papa, I've been working so hard, I need to rest. You were here, you saw me. Tell Mama.

Minerva, the child did work hard—

That work is near done and you know it, Lewis. But it's not supposed to end like this.

Near done, Mama, yes. Queen Varina's already gone. Rumors Jeff Davis is going soon, too. I did just like you always told me. But it was hard work, and I'm so tired. Why can't it end now?

Dammit, Mary El. You got to get out this minute.

I want to stay with you. If I just lie here a moment—

Wind is blowing from the South today.

Mr. Jones, is that you? The wind won't have to blow from the South anymore. Freedom's coming, along with the Union troops. Be here today maybe, or tomorrow.

She must wake up. Why won't she wake up?

Mama? You don't sound right.

'Tis the damn wind, blowing fierce, carrying the hellfire with it. We hae not much time afore we be as wasted as the lass.

Who's there? How'd you get in?

She is delirious. We cannot let her lie here any longer.

Someone's hand under my neck, a strange arm beneath my legs. They lift me out of bed. Carry me downstairs.

Let us rest here a bit. The air is not so foul, and 'tis a long way yet to carry her.

I cannot rest until she is safe. She did not give pause when it was my life threatened. I shall hardly do otherwise for her.

Explosions. Shouting. A door slammed open. Hands on me again, pulling. I ought to fight. Wilson said I should, if someone comes after me. But I'm so tired. So tired.

Something was being forced into my throat.

"Swallow it down. Thomas must stay here to tend to the slaves, and I cannot carry you alone."

I blinked open my eyes. In the fumy dark, I made out the slave pens at Omohundro's. Devil's Half-Acre had never been truer to its name, flames and smoke and screams.

"Miss Bet? Why'd you bring me here?" She didn't seem to hear me. I couldn't make the words come out right.

"Don't try to speak. You haven't any voice just now." She tipped the canteen she held, sending another metallic rush of water into my mouth. "Can you stand? Lay your arm across my shoulder, there. If I slip a hand around your waist, like so, can you walk? Lean against me, we must get you out of here."

Bet Van Lew never was much for show and ought. But walking arm in arm with a negro, right up Broad Street? Good thing it was so dark, and everyone rushing about like hell had broken loose. They didn't seem to notice her, or me.

The odor was so sharp, it stung me full awake.

"Aromatic spirits of ammonia may yet make it worse, if she inhaled as much smoke as you say."

"I cannot let her just lie there."

Slowly, as though prying open an oyster, I forced my eyelids apart. I lay in Bet's bed. The Van Lew women bent over me, their faces pinched with worry.

"Thank God you are all right," Bet said. "We feared perhaps—"

I tried to ask what had happened, but pain tore at my throat.

Bet laid a hand on my cheek, her touch more soothing than I expected. "You must not attempt to speak." She slipped away from the bedside to rummage in the secretary across the room, returning with a writing pen and a scrap of news-sheet.

Did my house burn? I wrote.

"Quite possibly. The Confederates incinerated the Richmond arsenal before fleeing, setting half the city on fire. Mother and I could see the conflagration from here. By the time Thomas and I reached your house, the air was teeming with soot." She closed her eyes a moment. "Truly, I thought we might lose you."

I took up the pen. *Thank you, Miss Bet. For saving my life.*

She frowned at the message. "So weighty a sentiment as that, at least you should state it properly." Claiming the pen, she set a stalwart slash across the word *Miss.* "Now that Davis and his traitorous ilk have left the city, you may address me as we wish." She smiled in triumph. "You ought to rest. If you need anything, ring for me."

She gestured at the nightstand, to the very bell her mother had used whenever she wanted to summon one of the Van Lew slaves to tend her.

Shouts came through the open window, waking me from a deep slumber. Not the fearful screams I heard earlier. These were shouts of joy. Singing and cheering.

I eased myself out of the bed, pulled Bet's dressing gown over my chemise, and made my way down the stairs and along the hall. I found Bet and her mother on the back veranda. To the west and south, flames and smoke engulfed the city. But closer than that was a spectacle even more amazing to see.

Lines of soldiers clad in Federal blue marched along Main Street. Even from atop Church Hill, we could make out the gallantry that victory marked on their faces. Faces in every hue of brown—an entire corps of the USCT, conquering Richmond at last.

"You should not be up and about," Bet said. "You have had a great strain, and without proper rest—"

I cut her off, my voice a scratchy croak. "My husband is down there. I mean to go to him."

She began scolding me about being so stubborn as to put myself at risk, until her mother interrupted. "I don't suppose Mary can have much faith in your making such declarations, given the way you have comported yourself."

I might have thought Bet was taking her usual umbrage at being lectured, when she answered, "Mary and I—and you, too, Mother—we have all three of us exhibited the true patriotism one—"

"Ought to show," I said.

Her mother laughed at the way I finished the sentence, and Bet gave a look of bear-in-the-honeypot satisfaction. Shooing us both back inside, Bet set all three of

648 • LOIS LEVEEN

us to searching through her wardrobe, and her mother's. As we sifted over their war-worn garments for whatever might fit me, the Van Lew women took to the task with the same concentration as Hattie and her sisters dressing me for my first ball. Weary though I was, my heart soared with more excitement than if I were donning the grandest of gowns, as I put on the misfit combination of borrowed blouse and skirts, settling a bonnet of at least fifteen years' vintage atop my plaits.

"Do take care," my former mistress said, when at last I was presentable enough to go about in public. "The Federal soldiers will have much to contend with, and not only from the blazes. You are welcome here as long as you care to remain, though I suppose we may not be the only household in Richmond that finds its colored members departed today."

I held her words dear as I made my way down to Main Street, just as Mama and I did so many Sundays of my childhood. Colored Richmond lined the road, singing every song of jubilation they knew and making up a whole new choir's worth once those were through. I witnessed all manner of hugging and kissing, laughing and weeping among the crowd. But the USCT kept right on marching, looking more eminent than any troops the city had yet seen.

Until that moment, I had not properly understood that my husband, who wasn't enslaved a day in his life, could never believe himself truly free until he started marching to another man's—a white man's—orders. It is said that war, with its majestic maiming and majestic killing, makes animals of men. But the colored men who donned uniforms and fought had carved their own humanity out of the great hulk of combat, seizing a freedom so just and right and full, no white person could have given it to them.

Now here in Richmond, that humanity shone before us. Born free or slave, raised South or North, these legions of colored soldiers emanated a new selfhood, chiseled on their features and meted by their gait. Praying that these precious men and we for whom they'd fought might preserve all the strength and grace of this newly won personhood once the war was done, I joined the throng following in the troops' wake.

We crossed Shockoe Creek and turned north, skirting the edge of the blaze to make our way to Capitol Square. Upon reaching the green, the corps fell into companies. Every negro in Richmond seemed to be searching for someone among the USCT. Knowing I hadn't much time to seek out Wilson before they'd all be set to firefighting detail, I bizz-buzzed my way from one group of soldiers to the next.

At last I spied a flag bearing the legend *Sic Semper Tyrannis* and David Bustill Bowser's martial scene. As I pushed my way toward the standard bearer, I heard a low whistle. A familiar voice asked, "Bowser, is that your wife dressed up so?"

I turned to find George Patterson laughing to Wilson. I fairly skipped to them, kissing my husband and embracing our friend.

Wilson shook his head at my hastily acquired apparel. "The way you enjoy carrying on with that Bet Van Lew, I suppose I should be glad not to find you in calico and buckskins."

I didn't bother to explain why I was dressed so. I didn't much feel like confirming what he must have suspected, that the raging fire had likely destroyed our home and his shop, along with the rest of Richmond's commercial district.

"We can't all be so dapper as yourself, dear husband, dressed up in that fine uniform. I admit, it does make a colored lady proud to look upon men so."

"Men? I thought my wife didn't have eyes for any man but me."

George cupped his hand from the peak of his kepi, warding off cinders that fell like glowing snowflakes. "We aren't any of us going to have eyes for much, if this wind keeps up."

But I just grinned at him. "George Patterson, you know what Hattie's father always said. When the wind blows from the South, nothing you say or do can stop it. Not even Bobby Lee's whole army."

Not so long as I did my part to set all the slaves free.

Fires were still smoldering by the time I reached the Gray House the next morning. The Federal pickets stationed around the perimeter of the property didn't think any more about letting a negro maid pass than the Confederates had. I wondered what these blue-clad soldiers would say if they knew how I aided their army all through the war.

I'd come to the Gray House from a nagging sense my work wasn't quite done. But as I made my way through the cellar and up to the first floor, I couldn't yet tell what impelled me here. The mansion felt as still as a sepulcher. Jeff Davis and his staff had fled the city hours before the evacuation fires were ignited. Hortense and the rest of the colored servants scattered just as quickly on the winds of freedom. Denuded of what valuables Queen Varina had sold off or taken with her, the empty chambers seemed to echo Confederate defeat.

Tucking my plaits behind my ear, I marched defi-antly up the curving center stair and into Jeff Davis's abandoned office. But disappointment swallowed my defiance, when I saw that the desk and table were cleared of papers.

A great hullabaloo started up outside. Hurrying to the receiving room window, I saw a massive crowd coming toward the house. Most of the throng were negroes, a procession of civilians following the USCT cavalry. Impeccable in their uniforms and mounted proudly atop fine horses, the colored troops set a high contrast to the ragged Confederates who filled Richmond's streets only forty-eight hours before.

The white soldiers standing guard outside came to attention as the cavalry halted, but when a tall white man in civilian clothes at the front of the crowd nodded at them and strode up the Gray House walk, they forgot their military posture and burst into applause.

Realizing who the man inspiring such devotion must be, I hastened down the stairs to open the front door. "Welcome, Mr. President."

Abraham Lincoln smiled, sweeping the tallest hat I've ever seen from his head. From afar, I was struck by his likeness to Jeff Davis, the high, prominent cheekbones that defined both men's faces. But up close I marked the difference, Mr. Lincoln taller and lankier, nowhere near as handsome but with a kindness in his gray eyes that the dyspeptic Jeff Davis never displayed.

"Who might you be?" he asked.

"One of the maids, Mr. President. The only one left in the house." I stepped aside, and he passed through the doorway, to the crowd's hurrahs.

"The place is mostly empty now, though some of the furniture is still here," I said as I led him and the young officer who accompanied him upstairs to Davis's office. "Perhaps you would care to sit in Jeff Davis's chair?"

"I believe I would, yes." Lincoln's eyes sparkled as he settled in behind the desk. Swiveling back and forth in the tufted seat, he seemed as enchanted as a child on Christmas morning, the fall of Richmond as great a gift to him as it was to all the former slaves who stood outside cheering.

The soldier ordered me to fetch something cool to drink. It took me some time of rummaging through the remants left in the china pantry before I could find even plain mugs to fill and take to them. The two men were deep in conversation when I returned, the president shaking his head and chuckling.

"There is only water to offer you," I said. "It's been some months since we've had tea or ale or even just lemons and sugar in the Gray House."

Lincoln took the mug I held out to him. "Water in the Gray House will taste sweeter to me than champagne in the White House ever has." As he swallowed the first sip, his Adam's apple bobbed up and down his long neck. "Now, if you can spare a moment for a stranger's curiosity, tell me, what was it like to work for Jefferson Davis?"

I didn't imagine he'd ever heard by name of Mary Bowser, nor Bet Van Lew nor Thomas McNiven. And with Richmond fallen and freedom ringing at last, I had no need for self-gratulatory vanity. But I spied with humble pride how my president smiled as I replied.

"I wasn't working for Jeff Davis. I worked for freedom, and for you, Mr. Lincoln."

Acknowledgments

I wish I were clever enough to craft these acknowledgments so they could be sung to the tune of "The Battle Hymn of the Republic," as I once vowed to do. But having benefited from the support of so many people and institutions, the closest I can come is *Glory, glory, hallelujah, my thanks go marching on* . . .

Michele Jaffe told me to write this book. She, Rosemary Weatherston, Nan Cohen, Leslie Bienen, Molly Gloss, Stephanie Von Hirschberg, and Willa Rabinovitch read initial versions of some or all of the chapters, exhibiting great patience for my early efforts and keen insights on what could be improved. Wonderful faculty at Harvard, USC, and UCLA—Werner Sollors, Joe Boone, Alice Gambrell, Tania Modleski, Val Smith, Richard Yarborough, and Martha Banta—taught me to take care as well as delight in my research, my writing, and my thinking about American literature and culture; although this is not the book either they or I thought they were training me to write, nevertheless it grew out of what I learned from them. David Garrett and Judy Stone kindly let me impose on their access to university collections. Ben Metcalf, having spent an awful lot of years ensconced first in Virginia and then in the heart of American letters, encouraged my audacity in declaring myself a novelist of Richmond—he has no idea how much his confidence in me made me believe I could really pull this off.

Portland, Oregon, provides many riches, chief among which are the greatest public library system in the United States and Powell's bookstore, invaluable resources for my research. (Vote for your library bonds and support your local bookstores, for what they give to the community is far greater than dollars.) I drew on many scholarly articles and books to bring accuracy to my telling of Mary Bowser's tale, and I salute all the researchers whose diligence enables us to understand the nuances of American history. A Ruby Fellowship and other faculty support from Reed College enabled me to travel to a number of historical sites, including the Gray House, now better known as the Museum of the Confederacy. My students at UCLA, Reed, and in the many Delve seminars that I have the great fortune to lead throughout Portland, have reminded me time and again of the power and pleasure that literature has for its readers. Paulann Petersen and Peter Sears offered models of grace and humor as well as lessons in precision and revision that brought touches of poetry to my prose. Ariel Gore was an exemplum of how to become a famous writer before either of us was anywhere near dead. Bruce, Audrey Jane, "Stinkin' Lincoln," and Isabelle "the Mug" frequently persuaded me to spend just a few more minutes, which somehow morphed into many long hours, writing and revising. Friends too numerous to mention put up with all manner of exuberance, churlishness, and absences, depending on precisely where I was in the process; I am grateful to them all, and especially to Amy Bokser and Brenda Pitts, whose e-mails sustain me when visits are too few and far between. And John Melville Bishop made me look good, even without any leopard print.

From our very first phone conversation, I knew I was exceedingly lucky to have my wonderful agent Laney Katz Becker. She pushed me to make the manuscript stronger and stronger still, and she shepherded me with wit and wisdom through every step of turning it into the book you (or your e-reader) now hold. Laney and her colleagues at Markson Thoma believed in my novel and gave their all to bring it to readers around the world. I am deeply grateful to work with Jennifer Brehl, Laurie Chittenden, and Emily Krump, three exceptional editors at William Morrow, as well as their wonderful colleagues, particularly Laurie Connors, Trish Daly, and Jean Marie Kelly. Suzie Doore "across the pond" at Hodder & Stoughton has also been an astute editor and astounding champion of this book.

As always, my deepest gratitude goes to my best reader, best ally, and best friend, Chuck Barnes, who fell in love with me in the twentieth century, puts up with me in the twenty-first century, and indulges the many hours I spend obsessing about the nineteenth century.

THE NEW LUXURY IN READING

We hope you enjoyed reading
our new, comfortable print size and found it
an experience you would like to repeat.

Well – you're in luck!

HarperLuxe offers the finest in fiction and
nonfiction books in this same larger print size and
paperback format. Light and easy to read, HarperLuxe
paperbacks are for book lovers who want to see
what they are reading without the strain.

For a full listing of titles and
new releases to come, please visit our website:

www.HarperLuxe.com